DANYELLE FERGUSON

Love
UNDER CONSTRUCTION

*Jump into Love,
Work Boots, Tool Belt & All!
♡ —D[signature]*

DANYELLE FERGUSON

Love UNDER CONSTRUCTION

Wonderstruck Books
Kansas City, KS

© 2016 Danyelle Ferguson

This is a work of fiction. The characters, names, places, incidents and dialogue are products of the author's imagination and are not to be construed as real.
No part of this book may be reproduced in any form whatsoever without prior written permission of the publisher except in the case of brief passages embodied in critical reviews and articles.

Published by Wonderstruck Books, Kansas City, KS
ISBN: 9780692442630
Cover design by Danyelle Ferguson
Cover design © 2016 by Danyelle Ferguson
Formatted by Heather Justesen

Dedication

To my mother, who taught me that women aren't just beautiful, but also capable, strong and amazing. Thank you for raising me to believe that I can conquer my fears, endure hard things, discover joy, and share love.

Charlee, the heroine from Love Under Construction, was inspired by my mother's compassion for others in need. No matter if it was a hungry teenager rummaging through our cabinets, giving away the family station wagon to a mother at a women's shelter, or comforting an abused animal, my mother gave whatever she could to help ease burdens and add a touch of joy to others' lives.

Chapter One

THE CLINK OF CHINA and chatter of women filled the room at City Hall where the Women in Business' monthly meeting was well under way. The typically boring room had been transformed. The plain brown tables and chairs for committee discussions were replaced with round tables covered with pretty white table clothes and seasonal centerpiece decorations. Elegant flower arrangements graced the podium as well as the sign-in table. Today's decor theme included glass bowls filled with pretty white and blue frosted balls. A few snowmen were positioned around the outside of the bowl, each holding a little banner with January written in a swirly font.

While most of the ladies appreciated the ambience, what really kept them coming back month after month was the best part —the food. If there was one good thing about the Women in Business group, they didn't scrimp on salads and dainty foods that barely made a dent in your stomach. Nope, they served good-sized portions and incredible desserts. After all, the group was all about making connections and serving the community—and what better way to do that than chatting over a delicious meal?

Charlee Jackson shifted out of the way so the servers could clear the table, all while following her friend Rachel's conversation as she gushed about her new fiancé.

"Graydon's the first guy I've met who's actually interested in conversation that isn't all about sports, which is shocking considering he was a hockey player," Rachel said, pushing her auburn hair back over her shoulder. The sparkle from the princess cut rock on her finger practically blinded anyone looking directly at it.

The only thing marring the picture of perfection was Rachel's bruised arm confined to a sling and her broken leg, which meant she was wheelchair bound for the next few weeks. Charlee admired Rachel's positive outlook, especially after being attacked at her last cake design competition.

"Are you sure he's not gay?" Charlee asked playfully.

Kristen, Rachel's business partner and best friend, leaned close and confessed in a whisper. "Oh my gosh. I've caught them making out more than once, and all I can say is steam, baby," she said, fanning herself.

Poor Rachel's face flushed pink as she nudged Kristen with her elbow. "TMI, Kristen."

Charlee laughed. "Have you set a wedding date yet?"

"We're looking for a date in May," Rachel said. "I know it's only a few months away, but I'm pretty old-fashioned and I told Graydon I wasn't moving in with him until after we say I do."

"Ooh, that reminds me," Kristen said, leaning in. "Charlee, mark your calendar for the first Saturday in March. I'm planning the bridal shower. We're having a traditional get together with the parents, grandparents, and everyone, then something a little more fun for the evening with the younger ladies."

Before Rachel could reply, Marla Belliston called the monthly meeting to order from her coveted spot at the podium. As usual, Marla was dressed in a perfectly buttoned up, classy suit with her dark hair pulled up in an elegant twist. Charlee fidgeted in her seat, tucked a few pale blonde strands of her short A-line bob behind her ear, then folded her jean-clad legs to hide her work boots under the table. Not everyone could afford the business suits Marla wore and, honestly, working at a desk as an accountant wasn't Charlee's idea of fun anyway. Restoring and renovating houses—now that was her idea of perfection. Taking the old, updating it while keeping the charm of the original structure—pure happiness.

Still, a girl occasionally envies the whole put together feminine look.

"Before we continue to our program on community literacy by our wonderful librarian, Eden Tate, there are a few announcements from our secretary, Victoria Lyons."

Ah yes, another well put-together woman, although not nearly as formal and uppity as Marla. Victoria was actually quite nice and relatable, which was good since she was a Realtor and worked with a variety of people. She often called Charlee when she had clients who needed help getting homes on the market or a buyer who wanted to consult on renovations before submitting an offer. Victoria was smart, savvy, and sassy—a combination that made her not just a good business contact, but a fun friend, too.

Victoria took her place at the podium, dressed in dark pants and a French blue button-down blouse. Trendy, but casual. Her deep red hair was pulled back in a sleek, low pony tail. "Ladies, it's time to begin preparations for our annual

Autism fundraiser. The committee bantered around several ideas. Generally, we do a charity concert, a dinner and auction, or a golf tournament."

Charlee yawned. It seemed like the same choices every year. They'd raise the money they set as a goal, which was great, but still, boring.

"This year though," Victoria paused, waiting for the chatty members to turn their attention to the impending announcement. "The committee has come up with a twist on the auction theme. Instead of having items and services donated, we are planning a bachelor's auction."

Charlee sat up a little straighter. Now this could be interesting. From the gasps and oohs in the room, the rest of the club was eager, too.

Victoria continued. "The committee is still working out the details, but the bachelor's auction will be six months from now, in June. We need suggestions and contact information for your favorite single men. There's a box at the back of the room with slips of paper and pens next to it or you can email me after today's meeting."

Several women turned and eyed the box. Charlee could just imagine the wheels turning in their heads, plotting how to get there first and who to nominate for the auction block. They may as well skip the next twenty-five minutes dedicated to community literacy because the women's attention definitely wasn't on anything other than their top ten local hot guys list.

Victoria ran through a few additional business items, which Charlee mostly tuned out while she enjoyed her cheesecake drizzled with fudge sauce.

"I have one last announcement. Crystal Creek City Council

has given approval to go ahead with a new shopping district. A private investor has purchased the homes along Taylor Avenue in Crystal Creek."

That was Charlee's grandmother's neighborhood. Or at least it was before Grandma passed away. Her house had sold at auction last year. Most of the other homes in that area had been sold as well. It was sad to see it go from the neighborhood of her youth, filled with laughter and fun, to what it was now—run down and mostly vacant. Even sadder still was the thought of everything being torn down to make a new shopping district. She set her cheesecake aside to pay better attention to Victoria.

"This new shopping district will be unique. The homes will remain intact, although they will be brought up to current code standards and also renovated inside for whichever businesses decide to relocate there. Not only will the neighborhood charm remain, but the investor's vision is for the shopping to be targeted to women and each store must be local and self-owned. No chains or franchises. The tentative name for the project is Indulgence Row. If you or someone you know might be interested in more information, please contact me. Thank you."

The other women may have been occupied with making a list of bachelors, but for the remainder of the meeting, all Charlee could think about was the Indulgence Row project.

She wondered who the investor was, because he certainly had great vision. The more she thought about the renovations and revitalizing the neighborhood, the more excited she became.

She wanted in.

She wanted to use her talents to bring her Grandmother's home—and all her former friends' homes around it—back to something filled with joy and people. The thought of people creating memories there again made her heart sing.

She *would* be a part of it.

After the meeting came the expected mad dash to the bachelor nomination box. But Charlee headed in the opposite direction toward Victoria, with Kristen wheeling Rachel close behind her. Eden Tate, the librarian who presented, also joined them at the table.

"Tell me more about Indulgence Row," Eden said, as she took the chair next to Victoria.

Charlee was glad to see Eden join them. She really liked the spunky woman, who was nothing like any of the other women who worked at the Crystal Creek library. Not that there was anything wrong with the sweet, gentle, and mostly gray-haired ladies, but Eden's spunky, modern and outgoing personality brought a whole new energy to the place.

Victoria talked a little more about the shopping district, feeling each of them out on their interest levels. "Each house will be renovated to fit the business that wants to occupy the space. Do you have someone in mind, Eden?"

"I'm actually quite interested," she replied.

"Oh!" Victoria said. "I didn't realize you were leaving the library."

"There have been so many programs I've wanted to start, but with budget restrictions and different point of views about future readers, it's been difficult to implement them. I've been considering opening a bookstore for a while. Something charming and cozy, where readers can talk books, plots and even debate which couples from series are better than others." Eden continued, her excitement and enthusiasm showing through the expressive ways she moved her arms and hands as she shared her vision. "There's so much I want to do, to inspire a love of reading, host book clubs, hold genre spotlight nights, and oh so much more. I've been squirreling away bits of money here and there over the years. Once you mentioned Indulgence Row, I knew it was perfect for my shop."

"Me, too," Rachel chimed in. "Kristen and I have already talked to you about needing a new space. Our teeny tiny shop hasn't been able to handle the influx of customers we've had since the cake challenge. I can just see the quaint sign hanging from the front of the house. Sweet Confections," she said, with her hands raised as if framing an imaginary sign.

"Sweet Confections at Indulgence Row," Charlee chimed in. "That could be part of the branding. Each shop has its name, but followed with 'at Indulgence Row'."

"I love it," replied Victoria, jotting notes in her notepad.

"I totally want in," Charlee said, leaning forward. "I want to get together to talk specifics and have Elliott Construction put together a bid."

Victoria put her arm around Eden. "You all have brightened up my day. I'll contact the investor, then set up a time to meet with each of you. This is going to be an amazing project."

It will indeed, Charlee thought. Now, she just needed to get her boss on board.

RATHER THAN RETURN to her job site at the Johnson's house, Charlee headed over to Elliott Construction's main office. All the way there, her feet tingled. Odd as it might sound, she knew better than to ignore her feet. The buzzing bee feeling was a sure sign that she was onto something great.

She had many wonderful memories of spending time with her grandparents when she was young. Then Pappy died and the only time she saw Grandma smile was when she was surrounded by her grandchildren. They gardened together, tending flower beds around the house and a veggie garden in the back yard. They baked cookies and Grandma taught her how to make homemade chicken noodle soup with delicious matzo balls. A craving came over Charlee to go home and make her favorite soup and continue reminiscing.

Instead, she got out of her truck and fought the bitter January wind to enter the office building. She would convince George Elliott that this project was perfect for them. Not only for the company, but for her first lead project.

She had been working for the company since she was sixteen years old. She started out in the offices until she proved to George that she was just as handy with a hammer as his son, Peter. Not only handy, but she had a great sense for space and design, and could envision in her head what needed to happen to achieve the finished product the client desired. After a two year leave to get a dual degree in carpentry and home remodeling and preservation, she resumed her work with Elliott Construction, where it all began.

In all these years, she had yet to be the crew lead for her own project.

But this one she would. She would make sure of it.

Charlee knocked on the wood door frame of George's office. He was seated at his desk, busy with a phone call, but waved her in. His salt and pepper head bent over a yellow legal pad as he scrawled notes across the page.

"That all sounds good, Randy. Let me know when the supplies are delivered. Thanks." George replaced the phone in the cradle and made a few notes before turning his attention to her. "What can I do for you, Charlee?"

"I just got back from the Women in Business meeting," she said, sitting down in the hard, cracked chair in front of his cluttered desk.

"Oh, right. That was today, wasn't it?" He pushed up the sleeves of his flannel shirt, then started sorting through the mail piled on his desk.

"Victoria Lyons announced a new shopping district." That got George's attention, his eyes finally meeting hers. "You know the area where my grandparents lived?"

He nodded in acknowledgement. "Sure, I used to go down there for card games with your grandfather."

"They plan to renovate those blocks of homes into a shopping district. Not new construction, but actually restoring the houses themselves and renovating them to fit the businesses that will be there."

His face brightened. "That sounds great. Thanks, Charlee. I'll have Peter talk to Victoria and get a bid in."

She shook her head and tried not to fidget. Would he go for her plan? "I already talked with her. George, I want to lead the project."

He sat back in his chair, steepled his hands in front of his chest and sighed. "Peter has more experience in this area. He's done city bids before, he knows the ins and outs—"

"Only because you haven't let me," she interrupted. "Peter may have more years with the company, but I have more education. You know I've helped Peter with building plans and offered a lot of good suggestions for better techniques and plan improvements. Things he didn't know about because he didn't go to college and take—"

George's fist came down hard on his desk. "This job isn't about a college degree and just because you have one, doesn't make you more qualified."

She should have known better than to bring up her education. It had been a constant sore point between them. Instead she changed her tactics and continued with a calm tone. "George, I really want to lead this. I'm connected to it. Please, I'm ready. You know I am."

There was a moment of silence before he replied. "Peter will lead the project. You can have your pick of crew to work on, but he will be in charge. Maybe next time." George returned to sorting his mail. When she didn't move to leave, he glanced up, "Aren't you supposed to be working on the Johnson's place?"

Instead, Charlee leaned forward. He was never going to change his attitude. It was time to make her stand. "You put me on the most expensive projects. Why is that?"

Startled, George returned his attention to her. His eyes narrowed, making the wrinkles around them bunch up like craggy rocks. When he remained silent, she forged ahead. "You know it's because I'm damn good. The best renovator you have on staff."

"Maybe," he replied curtly, trying his best to not give her

any extra ground to prove her point.

She shook her head. "There's no maybe about it. If you don't let me take the lead, then I'll give notice."

His eyes widened briefly, before narrowing into slits again. "You wouldn't."

Charlee simply crossed her arms and met his gaze, not wavering.

"You can sit there, stubborn, as long as you want. I'm not budging either." He folded his hands on the desk, his face a cool, calm facade. His famous poker face.

But this time, he wasn't going to win. She had been sitting in the proverbial back seat, waiting for him to wake up and smell the coffee. During her last semester of college, she was a lead contractor for the construction company she interned for. She had been willing to step back a few notches when she returned home, assuming George would eventually get over the fact that she was a woman working in a 'man's job'.

It had been six years of telling herself to be patient, but she was done. Her tingling feet told her that Indulgence Row wasn't just a project—it was *her* project.

Charlee uncrossed her legs and stood, not once breaking eye contact. "Then I guess it's settled. Consider this my notice. I'll finish the Johnson project, then clear out." She pivoted away and walked to the door.

George's chair scraped against the hardwood floors. His voice boomed through the room. "You will not! Charlee," he warned, his voice menacing. "Don't be a stubborn fool."

She turned the knob, then paused before opening it. "There's only one stubborn fool in this room." She opened the door, then stepped out, closing it behind her.

His voice boomed through the door. "Charlee, get the hell back in here!"

Instead, she walked past the wide-eyed receptionist and gawking co-workers who were finishing their lunch break. It wasn't unusual for their boss to yell, but Charlee ignoring the boss—that was definitely new.

Charlee pushed through the front door, out into the bright afternoon sun. She fisted her hand, hoping the bite of short nails into her palm would release the frustration crowding and bursting within. Hot dog! Did she just quit her job?

Breathe, girl, just breathe.

Grandma always said to never be afraid of change because it could lead to some of the best things in life.

I sure hope you're right, Grandma, cause I'm jumping in—work boots, tool belt, and all.

Chapter Two

PETER SLAMMED HIS TRUCK DOOR closed, then stalked up the dimly lit driveway leading to his parent's house. He heard about what happened with Charlee through the gossip mill that runs rampant at the construction sites. Even though the construction workers loved to blow up stories, generally the foundation of it was solid. After all, the majority of them were men, not women twisting words around in their retellings.

Men just weren't that creative.

He entered the kitchen where his parents were finishing dinner. "What the hell did you do?" Peter asked, looking directly at his father.

"Now that's no way to greet your mother," George replied, taking a bite of German chocolate cake.

Peter pulled off his baseball cap and ran his hand over his smooshed light brown hair before bending down to give his mother a kiss on the cheek. "Sorry, Mom."

She patted his face, then held out her hand.

Peter sighed, pulled out his wallet and handed her a one dollar bill. Dang it all. Ever since his mother started that stupid swear jar, his wallet had been getting lighter and her first jar had been joined by an entire jar collection. The only satisfaction he got was knowing that while he put in dollar bills, his dad was putting in fives.

Once the money was in her hand, Betty stood and smoothed out her sweater. The faded bluish-gray color matched her eyes, which Peter had been lucky enough to inherit. "I'll just put this in the swear jar." She paused, her pointer finger swinging back and forth between the two of them. "I'll be listening."

"Betty—" George started, but his wife cut him off by taking his partially eaten dessert away.

"You need to talk to your son," she said, then sashayed away to the other side of the room. As always, his mother was the ruler of the roost.

Peter dropped into a wooden kitchen chair. "What happened with Charlee?"

"Nothing that you should be this riled up about," his father replied, folding his arms.

"Darn it, Dad," he said quietly, in case his mother decided darn counted as a swear word. "Everyone is saying she quit. Caleb was at the office today and said you were yelling and she walked out on you."

George knotted his cloth napkin in his hand, then pushed it aside with a sigh. "Well, that's true," he admitted.

Peter slumped back into the chair while his father relayed the events from the afternoon.

"Why didn't you let her take the lead instead of making it such a big deal?" Peter asked, frustrated with his father's stubborn insistence that he be the one to do all the big stuff. All he really wanted to do was get out to a site and get his hands on the wood, nails, and enjoy the echoes of building. He hated the office paperwork side of the business.

"Because it's not a job for her."

Peter sighed. This again. "You need to come into the 21st century and realize women have just as much talent in the construction industry as men. Charlee has more vision, more motivation than half the men on your crews who just want to get the work done and cash their paycheck."

His father leaned forward. "Not at my company. It's not right. If she wants to play with tools, she should go get her teaching degree and teach shop."

Peter clenched his fists. "Like Kimber?"

"Don't bring your sister into this." Red splotches spread across his dad's face.

"Because it's okay for her to be an art teacher, but not to follow her dream to be an architect? She could have been a great asset to Elliott Construction, but you just can't push aside your stupid feelings about what kind of jobs females should and shouldn't have. Charlee is one of our best employees and she's going to become our competition instead."

His father sputtered and his mother appeared at his side, calm as could be with a cup of coffee which she slid in front of George.

"I'm sure your father can fix it, dear," she said, always trying to smooth things over between father and son.

"I'm not so sure this time," Peter replied. He said goodnight to his parents, then left, knowing where his next stop needed to be.

PETER KNOCKED ON THE DARK hardwood door to Charlee's townhouse. He hoped she was home, but more than that, in a state of mind to be willing to compromise. He looked at the deep scars that marred the old door. Their friendship was kind of like it, old but solid, despite the interesting challenges they'd each dealt with. He practically grew up at her house, being best buddies with her brother, Tyler. Of course, back then, Charlee and her sister, Julie, were just little girls in the background, but a friendship forged between them when she started working at Elliott Construction. He smiled, remembering the summer after he graduated from high school and started working full-time at Elliott Construction. His father lost a poker bet with her dad and had to let Charlee intern with them for the summer. Her spunky determination to show his father what was what and never backing down from their differing point of views made the summer bearable as all his other friends took off on trips and prepped for college.

The door swung open, bringing Peter's focus back to the purpose of his visit. Whatever smile had been on Charlee's face disappeared into a scowl.

"You're not here to try to change my mind, are you? Because you won't." She let the door swing open, a casual invitation to enter.

"Come on, Charlee. You know how Dad is." He followed her into the kitchen, where hot pizza sat on the counter. His stomach grumbled, a reminder that he'd skipped dinner to talk with his dad.

Charlee nodded to the food. "Help yourself." She opened the refrigerator door, then handed him a cold bottle of cream soda. They both sat at bar stools, grabbed the paper plates that came with the pizza delivery, and chewed in silence for a few minutes.

Peter looked around her apartment and realized Charlee lived more like a bachelor than she did an average woman. Her apartment was sparse—a couch, an entertainment center and average size TV. No dining room table, just some bar stools around the counter, and family photos on the walls. Her latest restoration project was in the center of it all. The one thing that truly said Charlee lived there.

"What's up with the cabinet?" He figured neutral ground was a good starting point.

"Don't you know the difference between a cabinet and a hutch?" She smirked and wiped away a smear of red sauce at the corner of her mouth.

He shrugged. "I guess not."

"I picked it up at a yard sale for $20."

"Seriously? How did you get such a good deal?"

She shrugged. "The owner was deaf. I used my rusty high school sign language skills to talk with him. He was happy to not have to use his son as an interpreter and gave me a good deal. Of course, it didn't hurt that it was his mother-in-law's and he just wanted it gone."

Peter laughed. "I've heard in-laws can have that effect. What have you done with it? The cabinet looks pretty great."

"It wasn't as beat up as other projects, just a lot of scratches, dents and a few deep gouges. Nothing some good wood polish couldn't fix."

"Where's this one going?" Peter knew Charlee searched yard sales for items to be fixed up and donated to a variety of charities. He sometimes wondered how much of her paycheck went to helping others.

"There's a family at the women's shelter who's ready to move out and set up their own home. The shelter has donors for the basics, but this was an item on the mom's furniture wish list."

"You're pretty amazing. You know that, right?" Peter didn't understand how his father couldn't see this side of her.

She just shrugged and slid a second slice of pizza out of the box. Hoping that her hunger was staved off, which might mean a better, more open mood, he jumped into his campaign. "Listen, I know Dad can be a pain in the ass, but I talked with him tonight. You can take the project lead. He just wants me to be involved."

"To hold my hand," she said. "No thanks. I don't need a babysitter."

He shook his head. "It'll be more like a partnership. He just wants us to work together." That much was true anyway. "We can't afford to lose you, Charlee."

She swallowed her bite and looked down at the remaining pizza in her hand. "Because I'm the best renovator you have on staff."

"You are," he agreed. When she looked up at him, her eyes just about slayed him. He knew, before she even opened her mouth. She'd already made her decision and there was no way he could convince her otherwise.

"I am the best, but the boss doesn't consider it enough to let me progress, to be a leader in the company. He likes my work, but there's no way in heck he's going to let a mere girl lead his men."

Peter softly swore under his breath. He paused, searching her face. "What are you going to do instead?"

"I'm going to do what I dreamed about—open my own renovation business and focus on restoring and rehabbing older homes."

Peter nodded. He knew she had been happy enough with Elliott Construction, but new and commercial construction weren't what filled her soul. Every time the company picked up a renovation job, Charlee glowed. And honestly, the only reason those jobs were even contracted was because Peter convinced his father they needed to keep her happy enough to stay. Renovations were her pride and joy, but blast it all, he wanted to yell and fight for her to reconsider.

Instead, he nodded and asked for more details. Her eyes shone with excitement as she talked about possible business names, logos she'd messed around with for the last few years, and her excitement about getting in on the Indulgence Row project.

"I have enough saved to buy some equipment, but not for the heavy stuff. I need to look into a bank loan for starting costs to pay my first crew, but I'm hoping by the end of the Indulgence Row project, I'll have the starter loan paid off."

He felt like a bobble head, nodding away as she chattered. Her hands flying this way and that, just like they always did when she was excited about something. He grabbed one hand, bringing it to a stop, then folded it between both of his. "You're going to be awesome, Charlee Jackson."

Her eyes got suspiciously shiny before she blinked to clear

them. "I haven't told my family yet. That will be interesting."

He reluctantly released her warm hand. "Oh, they'll be excited. Your dad will ask about all the financials and Tyler will want to know where your office is going to be so he can make sure it's in a low crime area of town."

Her laugh filled the room. "You're probably right. I already have an idea of where I'd like the office to be located, but—" she said before he could ask. "I'm not sharing until I get the okay."

"Fair enough. Well, I better head home." Peter slid off the stool and straightened. Charlee walked him to the door. Just before he opened it, he turned to face her. The smile on her face was infectious.

"Thanks for coming over, Peter. Be happy for me, okay?"

He nodded, then she leaned up on her tip toes and gave him a quick hug, her usual goodbye to friends. Peter left the building, shoved his hands in his pockets and walked the four blocks from Charlee's building to his own townhouse. The cold winter wind threatened to blow the ball cap off his head, but he shoved it down more securely. He hoped the walk would clear his head, help him find some good in the situation. Instead he unlocked his front door still in a funk.

He was greeted with his golden retriever's happy barks. He knelt to give Petunia a good rub down. Charlee had given the dog to him as a puppy as a birthday prank and had even prenamed her. Their friends thought it was a great joke. He could have changed the dog's name when he took her to be registered but had kept it instead. The smile on Charlee's face each time she saw Petunia was worth all the harassment he fielded from Tyler, Noah, and Cameron.

"Come on, girl," Peter said, pulling open the sliding doors leading to the small back yard. It wasn't much, but it was fenced in and big enough to throw a ball so Petunia could exercise on late nights like tonight. He was lucky to find this place on the outskirts of town before everything turned from pseudo city to open family homes with big yards. Plus, it was close to a great walking trail and dog park, too.

Petunia bounded across the yard, happy to be free from the house. He wondered if that was how Charlee felt—happy to be free to do what she wanted.

Everything was changing and Peter certainly didn't like it.

Chapter Three

WEDNESDAY MORNING, CHARLEE STOPPED in at Victoria's office, armed with mocha caramel lattes. LyonsReal Estate Offices were located near City Hall in an old building that had been updated. In fact, the office renovations were part of a project Charlee worked on when she returned to work at Elliott Construction after college. She checked out the wood molding and refurbished brick, happy to see that it continued to look great.

She passed through the main room to where the receptionist sat, guarding the set of Realtor offices behind her desk. "Is Victoria available?" she asked the college-aged girl who was more interested in the bodice ripper romance novel a mere six inches from her face.

"Ya-huh," the receptionist replied.

Charlee shifted from foot to foot. "Can I meet with her?"

"Yup." The receptionist swung her hand in the direction of Victoria's office, her gaze never leaving the pages she was enamored with.

Charlee shrugged, then crossed the room and knocked before nudging the office door open. She peaked her head inside. "Hey there. Do you have a few minutes to chat?"

Victoria put down her pen and whatever she had been reviewing and smiled. "Absolutely."

Charlee moved into the room and pushed the door closed with her foot. She handed one latte over and was happy to hear Victoria's sigh after her first sip. Charlee settled into the cushy chair across from the desk. "That's quite the secretary you have."

Victoria chuckled. "Heidi's my niece and an aspiring romance author."

"Really?" Charlee tentatively took her first sip of the delicious drink. She didn't depend on coffee to wake her up each morning, but she certainly enjoyed a cup every once in a while.

"You'd be surprised how much she marks up those books. Something about mapping out conflict, resolutions and beats. I don't understand it at all, but she claims all her reading is research. I thought those books were all about skipping to the good parts."

Charlee grinned. "You mean the hot kissing scenes?"

"Well, if you think those are the good parts . . . Sure." But Victoria's wink and grin showed that she agreed with Charlee's assessment. "Anyway, what can I help you with?"

"I'd like to talk more about the Indulgence Row project."

"Excellent! I'm excited to have a female on board for the construction side."

Charlee turned her latte in a circle in her hands. She met Victoria's whiskey brown eyes. "About that. Some things happened with Elliott Construction and, except for a project I'll have completed for them at the end of this week, I won't be working with them anymore."

Victoria tilted her head to the side. "What are your future plans?"

"I need to do a little research, but I plan to set up my own renovation company. No new construction or home additions, like I mostly did for Elliott Construction. Instead, I'll focus on home restorations and upgrades that keep with the structure's original integrity."

Victoria leaned back in her chair, continuing to sip the latte. "How long will take to get fully running?"

Charlee gulped. If she could land part of the Indulgence Row contract, it would put her business on solid starting ground. If she didn't, well, let's just say things would be rocky for a while.

"I estimate it will be about three weeks. I'll finish this project, then have two weeks to hire crews and set up terms with my subcontractors. But I need to be honest. I won't have all the heavy equipment and resources Elliott Construction does. It will take some time for me to build up to that point, but I have enough money for a solid start."

"Hmm . . ." Victoria set the latte down and folded her hands in her lap. "I assume you plan to work out of your home as the company starts up?"

"Actually, I was hoping to make a deal with your investor. If I'm chosen as one of your construction crews, I'd like to trade services for office space. My grandmother's house is located on Indulgence Row. I would love to use the upstairs portion as my office. I would be willing to discount my bid by either 10% or the first full year of rent, whichever the investor prefers, as well as provide all of my own space renovations."

"Well, I can't promise anything, but I'll discuss it with the investor. He's very open-minded right now. Of course, he prefers to have long term leases."

Charlee nodded, having already anticipated possible lease terms. "I'd be willing to negotiate those terms."

"Excellent! How about I get back to you by the end of the week?" Victoria rose from her seat.

"That sounds fantastic." Charlee stood and they shook hands. "Thanks, Victoria. I really want to be a part of this project. It means a lot to me, personally."

Victoria stopped her before she could turn to leave. "One last thing, are you okay working with Elliott Construction or will that create problems? We anticipate hiring two or three construction companies to work on various homes. We would like to avoid any contention between crews."

"There won't be any from my end. I know Peter plans to bid for the project and I don't anticipate any conflicts. He and I have already discussed it."

Victoria nodded, seeming satisfied with her answer. "We'll talk again soon."

Charlee left the office, waved to Heidi who was still absorbed in the romance novel, although she did notice the girl had multi-colored pens and was, indeed, marking passages in the book. She tossed her latte into a trash can before leaving the building, then slid her sunglasses into place while she walked to her truck.

The Johnson project would be wrapped up on Friday. They were absolutely thrilled with the renovation project, how the walls looked after they stripped off all the paint and wallpaper, ripped out the carpets down to the original hard wood floors, then sanded everything and stained it back to its original color and shine. It was coming along beautifully. All that was left was some final painting, then everything would be wrapped up. The Johnsons already asked about getting a bid for their next project, but Charlee referred them to George. No way was she going to be accused of stealing business. She was there representing Elliott Construction and she wouldn't say anything about her new company. At least, not until after her time with Elliott Construction was over.

Two more days. Then her new life would begin.

A new life she hadn't told her best friend about yet. Once in the warmth of her truck, Charlee pulled out her phone and sent a text to Mari.

Hey chick chick. I finally did it. My last day at EC is this Friday.

She couldn't remember if Mari was currently at her home in sunny L.A. or at one of her many other homes located around the world. It seemed lately like every other month Mari was off to either New York, Paris, or Milan.

The life of a model. Well, mostly retired model. She would be jealous if Mari wasn't her best friend. The world only thought Mari was beautiful and brave, especially since the death of her husband and son. She could only imagine the amount of pain and suffering she had experienced over the past three years.

Her phone vibrated.

Excellent! Does this mean I get to snag you away to do those remodels for me?

Charlee laughed. Mari had been nagging her for several months to do some remodeling, but in reality, Charlee knew she could hire someone local with just as much talent.

I thought you were going to check out the beach for some

hot construction guy to help you out? :P Actually, I'm starting my own business and bidding on a remodel project converting a set of older homes into a women's shopping district. I'm really excited about it.

With the talent of fast thumbs and a good network reception, the time between texts was short.

I'm excited for you. And hey, I'm totally saving these projects for you. Any excuse to lure my bestie away for work/girls vacation. Just let me know when and I'll fly you out.

When they wrapped up their conversation, Charlee started her truck and headed back to the Johnson's house. She couldn't help but feel like everything was brighter—the color of the sky, the fluffiness of the clouds, and a song she loved came on the radio. Heck, not even the wicked sharp Kansas City wind could dampen her mood.

Life was moving forward and she couldn't wait for the next step.

Chapter Four

CHARLEE CLAPPED HER HANDS to get the class's attention. A handful of women stopped chattering and turned to face her.

"Hello, everyone! I'm excited about tonight's class. As promised, we're going to make some child-sized benches for around the women's shelter. All the supplies were donated by local stores and are set out on the table along the side wall. Please take a supply list from the far end, then make your way through, picking up the items for your stations."

The chattering returned as the group formed a line to collect their supplies. A tap on her shoulder had Charlee turning around to find the head of the women's shelter, Anita, behind her. Next to her was a thin woman with long, dark brown hair falling across her face as she kept her gaze down, avoiding eye contact.

"Charlee, I'd like you to meet Naomi. I thought she'd enjoy your class."

Charlee nodded. She knew the code. Naomi was new and Anita brought her to class hoping to get Naomi out of her shell. The classes Charlee taught weren't just about do-it-yourself skills. The biggest benefit was giving the women the chance to rebuild their self-confidence by completing projects. "Welcome, Naomi. Have you used power tools before?"

"A little," she said softly, still avoiding eye contact.

"That's just fine. Tonight's project doesn't require any big tools. Just a drill, staple gun and glue gun. It's a great project to start with. If you need anything though, just ask me or Anita. We'll both be nearby."

Naomi nodded, then followed Anita to get her station set up.

Once everyone was settled, Charlee started the class. "Okay, ladies. The only prep work I did for you was spray painting the bench legs. I thought Anita would appreciate not getting light-headed from the fumes." Anita nodded and laughed along with the women. "Let's start with the big board. This is going to be the bench seat. We need to drill a hole to insert the threading nuts. The nuts will let us screw in the legs later."

More snickers came from the stations to Charlee's right. She smiled and shook her head. It never failed that whenever she talked about nuts and screws, Lucy and Carla thought it was funny. Lucy was barely nineteen years old and pregnant. She wanted a better life for her child than the one she had with her gang-member boyfriend. Charlee could understand a rebellious teen going for the raunchy, but Carla's teen years were a thing of the long past. The sixty-something woman had lived an entire lifetime filled with abuse. First with a domineering father, which she thought she could escape by marrying young, only to find out her husband wasn't any better. Somehow the woman found her inner-pluck in her early fifties and left to start a new, happier life. Now Carla was an active leader in the shelter's support group. Lucy and Carla were like two peas in a pod.

"Lucy and Carla, you need to get your minds out of the gutter." Charlee turned to the other side of the class. "Gail, what's something we should remember when using the drill?"

Gail's smile was contagious. "Know when to stop. It's not a good idea to drill all the way through to the work table."

"Exactly. You only need to drill a small hole to install the nut into the board. Like this." Charlee picked up the power tool, gave the throttle a couple short squeezes for effect, then demonstrated the next few steps. From there, the women got to work. The evening went smoothly as Charlee guided the class through hot gluing the padding to the bench, securing the decorative fabric with the staple gun, and finishing the project by screwing in the table legs. All in all, this was one of the shorter classes she'd done over the years, but she found it was good to mix easy projects with more in-depth ones so the women didn't get burned out or feel inadequate.

"Good job, ladies. Now you know how easy it is to make a padded bench. You can also use these methods to recover a used chair to fit your style. Let's stack the benches against the wall near the door, and then we can enjoy the snacks Anita brought. If anyone has suggestions for upcoming classes, come chat with me."

Gail was the first to find Charlee. "I have these super ugly dark dressers and I keep seeing these Pinterest posts about how to make them cute. Everything from spray paint to chalk paint, chevron stripes and fancy knobs, but I'm worried I'll just make the dresser look worse. Could you do a class on that?"

Charlee pulled out her cell phone and opened a text

document to take notes. "That would be a great class. We could talk about prepping the wood and what type of paints adhere the best. There's nothing worse than painting furniture and having the paint run or bead up because of the wood finish."

"Which is exactly what would happen to me," Lucy said, joining them with Carla at her side, their plates loaded up with brownies and chocolate chip cookies. Anita and Naomi joined the circle too. "I'm kind of wanting something similar, except my question is how to tell if a table that looks like wood is actually the kind that can be stained."

"I need some bedside tables that don't cost $80 each. Can you teach us how to make some?" Carla asked.

Charlee's thumbs moved fast as she made notes of their requests and ideas of things to research. "These are great ideas. I'll do some research and send Anita a schedule."

The ladies mingled and eventually gravitated back out to the shelter's living room while Charlee and Anita cleaned up.

"I heard there are some changes coming up in your life," Anita said when it was just the two of them.

Charlee shook her head. "Nothing stays a secret for long in Crystal Creek."

"Especially not when it involves juicy gossip about George Elliott."

Charlee ignored the bait to dish on what happened and just dived into her upcoming plans for Indulgence Row. "I'm also hoping to get some smaller side contracts I can work on solo to keep some cash in the company rather than most of it going out to payroll. Before any of that really goes into play, I need to finish my business paperwork and figure out a name."

"What have you come up with so far?" Anita asked, putting

the staples and staple guns into a bin.

"I thought about Creation House, but I think it sounds too new construction or architecturish. Then I considered Renew to go along with the idea of old and new. For a while, I was excited about Metamorphosis, but then thought too many people would spell it wrong or think it's a beauty makeover or something. I'm still brainstorming." Charlee put away the bins into the class cupboards.

"How about Transformations?" Anita suggested. "It plays off the old and new concept and describes the house after it's done. Going from old and worn to new and loved. Transformed."

Charlee tilted her head, thinking over the name, weighing it against what she wanted the company name to represent. "I really like it! Are you going to charge me a finder's fee if I use it?" She nudged Anita with her elbow.

"Just keep teaching these classes. You know, they're another transformation you provide, helping the women who attend your classes and their families. Thank you again for Patty's hutch. Your talents and friendship are what make the women enjoy the classes. Promise me you won't get too busy to do it."

Charlee took Anita's hand in hers. "I promise. You know I love being here."

Anita patted Charlee's hand, then let go. "And maybe after you get the kinks worked out of starting a new business, you can do a class on what you learned."

"I'd love to." Charlee followed Anita out of the room and said good night before leaving the shelter.

Transformations. She more than just liked the name. She

loved it.

She got into her truck, excited about researching projects for the shelter classes and moving forward with her new business.

Chapter Five

PETER PULLED HIS TRUCK UP to the curb behind Charlee's, which now had a logo for Transformations emblazoned across the back. It had been two weeks since she left Elliott Construction and she was plowing straight ahead with her plans. That was one thing he admired about Charlee. When she knew what she wanted, she didn't let anything hold her back.

He climbed out of the truck and made his way over to where she sat in the driver's seat, scrolling through a social media app on her cell phone. He tapped on her window, then laughed when she jerked and fumbled the phone.

She set the phone in her lap, then rolled down the window. "You tapped?"

He leaned his elbow on the door frame. "Am I interrupting something important? Someone update their latest wardrobe purchase? Or post embarrassing pictures their toddler will one day hate them for?"

"Like this one?" She grabbed her phone, refreshed the screen and pulled up a picture a mutual friend posted of her toddler. Apparently potty training was exhausting because not only was the little boy sitting on the toilet, but he was bent over, his head resting on his knees, fast asleep.

"Holy jumping jellybeans," Peter exclaimed, taking the phone from her.

Charlee snorted, then quickly covered her mouth and nose with her hand. "I haven't heard you say that since you and Tyler were teens."

He cringed, both from the jellybean slip and the photo on the screen. "There should be a rule book, do's and don'ts for mothers on social media." He handed the phone back, shaking his head, wondering where some people put their common sense and once again thankful he avoided the entrapment of social media. With everything that kept him busy at work, he didn't need yet another thing in his life to suck away the little precious time he had to himself. "I'm grateful social media wasn't around when I was growing up. Can you imagine what our mothers would have posted?"

"Have you seen what they post now?" Charlee swiped at her phone again.

"Now?" His voice cracked, cut short by fear. His mother was on social media? No. Way.

Charlee held up her phone, proudly displaying proof of his mother's misdeeds. A sepia picture complete with six-year-old chubby cheeks, a half toothless smile and an obnoxious striped shirt. The caption was even worse. *My little snuggle bug. #TBT*

"TBT?" he asked.

"Throwback Thursday. It's when you share photos from your past."

"And does my mom share TBT's of me often?" he asked, dreading the answer.

"Oh, you're her favorite child of all time. Snuggle bug." Charlee snickered, her eyes sparkling with delight.

He closed his eyes and thumped his head against the truck door. How many of his friends were connected with his mother? Even worse, how many of his crew and business contacts?

Charlee nudged his arm. "It's not all bad. You were a cute kid. I especially love the bath tub pictures."

Mortification complete. He needed to find a geek to hack his mother's computer and wipe her social media accounts. Quick.

"One of my favorite people to follow is Miss Marjorie. She used to live here near my Grandma." Charlee indicated the homes that would soon turn into Indulgence Row. "Miss Marjorie cracks me up. She's better than any local gossip column. Right now she's on a kick about Rachel and Graydon's engagement. She's posting all sorts of speculation about wedding dresses that would flatter Rachel's figure, what flowers would be right for a spring versus summer wedding and more. Just be glad you're not on her radar." Charlee patted his arm, then pushed it off the door frame. "Hey, Victoria and someone else just pulled up. We better get moving."

Good, he thought, opening her truck door and holding it while she slid out. He needed a change of topic, one that put him back on safe ground. Together they met Victoria and another man on the sidewalk. Victoria greeted them, then let them take the lead on introductions.

"Mark Bannerman," the newcomer said, going straight for Charlee.

Peter couldn't blame him. She was the cutest one there, no offense to Victoria or anything. Not that the forty-something guy had a chance, no matter how athletically fit he was. Or at least Peter didn't think Charlee went for older men.

"Bannerman Landscaping, right?" Charlee asked.

Mark tilted his head to the side, still grasping her hand. "That's right. Longtime family business. How did you know?"

"A former client uses you—Mr. & Mrs. Day on the north side of Crystal Creek. I adore their rose arbor and cobblestone walking path. I'm Charlee Jackson from Transformations."

Mark returned her smile. "I know they had some work done last fall, but I don't remember them mentioning a company called Transformations."

She slid a glance over toward Peter. "Well," she started, but Peter cut in.

"She used to work for us, but she decided to follow her love of renovation and start her own company. Peter Elliott, Elliott Construction," he said, extending his hand and breaking the drawn out handshake between Mark and Charlee.

"Awkward," Mark commented, after a very brief handshake.

"Not at all," Peter replied, adjusting his tool belt. "Charlee and I grew up together and we're both looking forward to working on Indulgence Row."

"Exactly," Victoria said. "Let's discuss the project, shall we?" She handed each of them packets with more details about the homes—year built, square footage, layouts, any known damage, pictures, and other basic information. Of the eight houses on the row, three of them were two stories, and one actually had a third story that was used for storage space. The other five houses were ranch styles. Some looked a bit square with a flat front façade while others had a little more charm. They all needed extensive landscape design, new sidewalks, and updated porches.

Victoria took charge and led them down the street. "A few more people have approached me about the project. A hair salon, a photography business, and an accessory shop. But today, our goal is to do a walkthrough of each home, consider retail space and look for the best possibilities for the bakery and bookstore."

Peter flipped through his packet. "Considering the square footage the bakery needs, there are only two logical spaces for it. The ranch-style #1462 or the two-story #1465. They both have slightly wider homes, but extend further into the back yard, giving enough space for the front of the shop, as well as the kitchen in the back."

Charlee turned to the houses he indicated and agreed. "Maybe we should start there and see where it leads."

"Sounds like a plan." Victoria led the group to the ranch-style home. "This house was a rental for twenty years but has been empty for the past year." She unlocked the door and gestured them inside.

Mark stood aside and allowed Charlee to go first. Peter followed from behind, feeling like a caboose. The interior was dim, lit just by the light streaming through the windows. Still, he noticed the cobwebs and layers of dust. Here and there were trails made by little scampering feet. Mice, of course.

"You might want to get some exterminators out here to take care of the bugs and rodents," Peter said. Victoria nodded and made notes in her leather-bound notepad.

"Mice don't bother you, do they, Charlee?"

Peter turned at Charlee's squeak and saw Mark with his hands on her waist.

"Sorry," Mark was apologizing. "I didn't mean to startle you."

Peter rolled his eyes. "Charlee's not going to run away like a little girl at the mere mention of rodents."

Charlee turned her head toward him, her face showing surprise as she stepped back, breaking contact with Mark. "No, I'm not," she replied, moving slightly closer to Victoria.

Peter was annoyed as the landscaper followed Charlee around, chatting with her while she inspected each room. Peter double checked some measurements, examined the flooring, and discussed possible renovation techniques with Charlee. Overall, it was a nice space and would be a good spot for a bakery.

After locking up, they crossed the street to the two-story. When they stepped into the deep entry, Charlee immediately went to the dark wood staircase set against the right wall.

"It's not often that you find homes with stairs on the side instead of the middle."

Victoria ran her finger along the dusty hand rail. "The wood is beautiful, but definitely needs some work."

Peter moved to Charlee's side to check out the staircase's stability. The supports looked good, although the railing was a bit wobbly. "Let's go upstairs first," he suggested.

This time, he made sure he was between her and Mark. Charlee noticed and gave him a brief smile over her shoulder.

There were a few additional stairs that needed attention, but overall, the staircase was in good shape. Not bad for being over sixty years old with little recent maintenance.

The upstairs had four small bedrooms compared to today's age of bigger is better. There was also a decent size bathroom in the back right corner. "If we knock out these walls, take out the carpet . . ." Peter knelt down, pulled out a carpenter knife and sliced through an edge of the carpet near the wall, then nodded. "You'll have some gorgeous hardwood floor. It needs to be sanded and polished, but I bet the entire upper level is the same."

"And the woodwork is beautiful up here. All the trim is the same dark hardwood," Charlee said. "We could salvage the upper trim and use it for wall ornamentation. The bathroom is expandable too, at least to a point of having a men's and women's separate bathroom space."

They continued through the upstairs, making notes about bearing walls and possibilities for layouts.

Back on the main level, they explored the typical rooms, formal dining room, living room, and a large kitchen and pantry area. With the extended space and staircase on the side, the downstairs actually had a better flow for the bakery.

"Imagine this," Charlee said, leading the group to the front entry. "You come in the doors and right here," she indicated a spot even with about the fourth step of the staircase. "We could put in a separation wall. Something solid on the bottom and with lots of glass, possibly stained, on the top to make it roomy. It would create separation from the two businesses with a set of doors here to lead into the bakery or the stairs leading to a top floor business."

"I like it," Victoria said, frantically scribbling down notes.

Peter joined in, motioning to show the renovations he envisioned. "On the bakery side, we can pull out these other walls here and here to open up the front space for display cases and tables for the customers. Then we can keep the natural wall here, but widen the doorway for double swinging doors to lead into the kitchen."

"We would need to upgrade the gas, electricity and water throughout the house, but especially back here," Charlee said, motioning towards the kitchen area. "The professional ovens, refrigerator cases, freezers, and appliances will need extra support both utility and flooring-wise. The bonus is how the addition of the servants' space and butler's pantry gives extra room to make the kitchen not just functional, but roomy, too. I can see it though."

Charlee turned to face him. Her face glowed, excitement shining from her eyes. He always knew he hit the jackpot when Charlee looked like that. "This is definitely the spot for the bakery," he told Victoria.

"What would you think about doing the bookstore upstairs?" Charlee asked him.

"Put both the two businesses that are ready to invest in the same location—definitely. Give the other businesses a chance to see how they can work with each other and keep construction mess at a minimum while you're showing the other houses," Peter replied.

"And there's nothing better than cookies and books!" Victoria scribbled more notes before she looked back up at them. "I'll make an appointment with Rachel, Kristen and Eden. I'll want you both here when they do the walk through, help them see what you envision and let them share their dream with you, too."

"Of course," Charlee said. "But—" her brow wrinkled. "Who is doing the project?" She glanced up at Peter, worry in her large light brown eyes.

"Why, both of you," Victoria said, still scribbling away.

"Peter will take the bakery and you can handle the bookstore, the stair case and entry way."

Peter held his breath. How would Charlee feel not getting the bakery? Or splitting the house with him? But instead of looking upset, her shoulders relaxed and she nodded, then changed the subject to the front porch renovations and landscaping. Mark joined the conversation and the group moved outside. Peter scowled when Mark put his hand on Charlee's back as they descended the steps. It might seem like a nice thing for a guy to do. Gentlemanly or some other mumbo jumbo girls like, but if he didn't stop the touchy-touchy thing, he might just have to break the guy's hand.

And that made him smile.

Chapter Six

THE FOLLOWING WEEK, CHARLEE and her crew began work on the book shop. Eden was delighted with the space and had several suggestions for how she wanted it set up, the layout and feel. Her vision fueled Charlee's desire to pull it all together and to see the space come alive.

The end goal: A modern yet comfortable bookshop with lots of warm colors—Eden was partial to a peanut butter brown paired with the natural dark chocolate brown of the original hard wood. The Reece's Peanut Butter Cup look, she called it. Charlee could see how the colors would appeal to both men and women.

First, they needed to start with tearing down most of the walls. A few bearing walls would remain, but the first part of a renovation like this involved a lot of destruction. Pulling everything apart saddened Charlee. It was the exact opposite of what she generally enjoyed doing, but the end goal of the community made up for it.

Today was all about dust masks, heavy gloves and sledgehammers.

She picked up a pile of debris and lugged it across the

room to the open window and tossed it out into the large construction grade dumpster below. As she went back to repeat the process, she looked across the room at her team. She had five employees now. Juan One and Juan Two, who incidentally were cousins who looked more like brothers with their bronzed skin and jet black hair. She grew up with both Juans and after reading Dr. Seuss's *The Cat in the Hat*, their friends adopted the new names for Juan One and Juan Two. Also on the team was the brunette pony tail swinging Sadie, who was a single mom in need of a part-time job during school hours that paid better than cleaning houses. Sadie insisted she knew how to work hard, having grown up on a farm. Charlee decided to give her the benefit of the doubt and agreed to a trial period of three weeks to see if it was a good fit for both of them. So far, Charlee was not only impressed, but grateful for the energetic vibe Sadie brought to the job.

The crew also included her longtime mentor, Bob, and his friend, Crank, a big muscle motorcycle dude who was passionate about art. Construction was his way of keeping food on the table. Both men were transplants from her crew at Elliott Construction. She'd asked them to stay in their former jobs, but they weren't keen on working with a new crew leader. As much as that cheered Charlee, she also feared George's wrath.

A fear which was apparently not unfounded.

As Charlee called subcontractors whom she'd developed relationships with over the years, only a few were willing to sign term contracts, which detailed fees and any discounts offered to Transformations. Nothing stated they were exclusive, but simply outlined their business agreements with each other. Some subcontractors, a few who truly surprised her, refused to set up terms, stating that they couldn't afford to have George go elsewhere.

She understood. She honestly did. Elliott Construction provided a lot of steady work, which translated into income. But still, she was disappointed and couldn't help but wonder if George contacted the businesses and asked them not to work with her.

Which made her a little angry. Well, more than a little. But, she reminded herself, she had no proof that was the situation. She needed to keep a calm head. Besides, she could make other contacts and fill those spots.

Seeing that Juan One, Bob, and Crank were smashing away, she went back to hauling debris with Sadie and Juan Two.

By the time lunch hit, they were about a quarter of the way done and ready for a break. Charlee released everyone for a 90-minute lunch. They needed to eat, rehydrate, and truly let their muscles relax before returning to work. She trailed behind her crew down the stairs, but before she got to the doors, someone called her name. She turned and found a very sweaty Peter crossing the room.

He tossed her a bottle of water. "How's it going upstairs? It sounds like a demolition party."

Charlee twisted the cap off and took several swallows before answering. When she looked back up, his eyes were on her throat. She reached up to feel if something was stuck to her skin. "Is something wrong?"

Peter blinked his eyes and returned his attention to her face. "No, you're just all dusty."

She shrugged and leaned back against the staircase. "All

part of the job. How are things going for you guys?"

"Good. We have most of the kitchen stuff pulled out. We had a late start, waiting for the power and gas people to be sure everything was disconnected before taking out the appliances. But things are moving along." Peter stepped, then turned and leaned on the staircase next to her. "Listen, Charlee, now that you're not working for Elliott Construction, there's something I wanted to talk to you about."

She looked up into his gray eyes, saw something serious glinting there. Something he was worried but excited about. She shifted towards him, then startled when the front door banged open.

"Well, let's see this project you got yourself into." George stumbled to a halt and looked between the pair.

Charlee wasn't sure what to say, but she straightened, waiting to see what he would do next.

Her former boss simply nodded. "Charlee."

"George, good to see you," she replied. Apparently that was all the greeting she was going to get because he just stood there, looking between them. "Listen, I have to get lunch before my crew gets back. I'll see you later, Peter."

Charlee walked past George and was well-mannered enough to wish him a good day. Her parents did teach her to respect her elders, after all. Before she closed the door, she heard the beginning of George's conversation with Peter. "What were you doing with her?"

All Charlee could do was shake her head. She hoped George wouldn't always hold a grudge. Maybe someday, they would be friends or at least friendlier. At the very least, she hoped Peter wouldn't let his father's anger change their relationship.

PETER SHOOK HIS HEAD. "Really, Dad. You could have been a little more polite."

George snorted. "To that little traitor? I certainly hope you aren't taking on this hole in the wall project just to be around her."

Peter ignored his father's attempt at poking around for information. "You know this project is good for Elliott Construction's community image. It shows that we aren't just about new construction but also care about making the older parts of the community a better place for the residents."

"Mmm hmm, that better be the reason because I'm not turning my company over to a traitor lover."

Peter just shook his head. It had been over a year since his father had the company transfer papers drawn up, but they'd sat in a file in his father's home office cabinet gathering dust while he continued to make it known that he didn't think Peter had what it took to take over his precious company. Peter wondered if he would ever live up to his father's expectations. George wanted a hard core desk jockey, someone who aspired to be a George, Junior. But that just wasn't Peter's thing. He wanted to be on the job with his crews, not stuck behind a desk running numbers and schmoozing clients. He wished his dad would let him figure out how to run the company his way, but that wasn't going to happen, no matter how much his mother hounded his father to retire and take her on a cruise.

Even if his dad did retire, Peter wondered if George would

be capable of staying away, rather than constantly meddling in the business.

Instead of letting it eat at him, Peter shoved it all aside and took his father through the site. He took notes of his father's many 'suggestions.' He'd consider them, but Peter knew as soon as his father was back at the office, he'd be caught up in paperwork and forget about anything he suggested for the actual job.

"Knock, knock," Victoria called as she appeared in the back kitchen doorway. "How's everything going?"

George straightened up, his scowl disappeared and he shook hands with Victoria. "Everything is just dandy," George said jovially, no trace of his earlier antagonism.

Peter shook his head as his father gave Victoria an abbreviated version of the tour Peter had just given. The way his dad was talking, you'd think he was the on-site crew leader. Victoria laughed at his dad's corny jokes. He'd give his dad credit for one thing—he definitely knew how to schmooze a client. Peter wasn't much of a salesman. He preferred the honest, straightforward approach, but each received good results.

"How are things coming with the signs, George?" Victoria asked, as they walked back to the front door.

"Good. In fact, they're supposed to arrive this afternoon. I'll make sure they get put up this evening."

"What signs?" Peter was confused. No one had mentioned anything to him about signs.

George waved his hand, as if brushing off Peter's question. "Victoria and I talked last week and I offered to have the project signs made, one for each end of the street."

A warning bell went off in Peter's head. What was his father doing talking to Victoria? Normally all the communication went through the project lead. That way everything was notated and nothing got overlooked.

Victoria raised her eyebrow. "I thought you knew, Peter."

George jumped in before Peter could say anything. "He's busy with the actual renovation details. This was something I could do from the office to contribute. You know, give back to the community and all."

Victoria nodded, then promised to follow up the next day.

Peter hoped his goodbye came across as normal, because all he really wanted to do was talk to his father to find out what was going on. As soon as Victoria was out of ear shot, he turned to face his father. "Want to tell me what's really going on?"

"Weren't you just lecturing me about being nice?" His father made a show of inspecting some work in the room.

Peter put his hands on his hips. "Nice to Charlee, yeah."

"Well, in a roundabout way, this should count, right? Her company's name is on the sign with the other contractors." George looked at his watch. "I have to go. This lunch break took longer than it was supposed to."

Peter didn't bother to mention that things would have gone more smoothly if it had been a scheduled meeting. Instead he said goodbye and watched his father head across the lawn to his Elliott Construction truck.

Something continued to nag him about the signs. If his dad really wanted to contribute, why didn't he just tell Peter to order them like he had a dozen other times. It wasn't the fact that Elliott Construction was doing the signs as much as the fact that his dad stepped in and had them done without any input from Peter or the other contractors. The thought that George's actions were less than stellar continued wouldn't go away, but Peter pushed it aside. Maybe his dad really was trying to do something proactively good and needed to be given the benefit of the doubt.

Later that evening, as Peter drove out of the Indulgence Row site, he stopped on the side of the road, the truck headlights illuminating the construction sign. It was even worse than he imagined. The large white sign announced that the new Indulgence Row shopping district was coming soon, then listed all the contractors working on the project. The problem was across the bottom the name Elliott Construction was bigger and bolder than any other business listed.

The other contractors were going to give him an earful tomorrow. Peter needed to think of something quick to show Elliott Construction was a team player. He pulled out his phone and hit the speed dial for his secretary, Jan.

"Hey, Jan, sorry to call after hours," he said when she answered. "I need some emergency help."

"Oh boy," Jan said, after listening to his explanation of the situation. "I have a pen and paper ready. Tell me what needs done."

"First, call a local donut shop and order enough donuts, bagels and coffee for all the crews at Indulgence Row, as well as have some delivered to Victoria's office. Then put in a call to the sign company to pull down the signs and have them fixed the right way."

"You know your dad is going to have a hissy fit when he realizes what you did."

"Well, when he shows up, you just redirect him to Victoria,

who will surely rip his head off for pulling a stunt like that."

Jan giggled. "Oh, I'll be sure to do that. I'll get right on this. Will you be avoiding the office tomorrow?"

"Most likely," he admitted.

"I'll send you an email with messages to return, and I'll just keep a running tally at the bottom for how many times your father stopped by or made Betty call to check if you were in."

"Have I told you lately how much I appreciate that you're my secretary?"

"I'm sure the gift card to Olive Garden you'll be getting me will show your appreciation just fine."

The not-so-subtle hint was noted for tomorrow's to-do list. "It sure will. Thanks, Jan, and good luck." Peter disconnected the call and sighed, reviewing the sign once again before pulling away.

So much for being nice.

Chapter Seven

IT WAS DUSK ON THURSDAY night when Charlee took the old silver key out of her dusty jeans pocket and inserted it into the lock. With a twist and some wiggling, she finally got the lock to give and stepped into her grandmother's house for the first time since it was sold at auction three years ago.

She flicked the light switch, but the power had not been turned on yet. Thankfully she'd thought to bring a flashlight along. She pushed the rubber button and the mediocre stream partially illuminated the entryway.

The house was dusty, but not nearly as bad as she expected. She closed the door behind her, then walked through the downstairs, trailing her hand along the wall, feeling the ridges of the textured wallpaper under the pads of her fingertips as she moved from room to room.

She remembered the living room's fireplace and how the flickering flames warmed her face and hands after building snow forts with Julie and Tyler in the back yard. The big window once framed the Christmas trees that they decorated with strings of popcorn, cranberries and funky salted dough ornaments. She always thought Grandma's tree was more fun than the fake one all decked out with twinkly lights, glass balls, and garland back at her house.

Charlee moved from the living room into the kitchen, taking in the faded blue Formica counters. Scents from pies and cinnamon sugar crust strips bombarded her from memories long past. So much living had happened in this bare house. She quickly moved from the kitchen to the stairway and up to her space. This was her reward for staying focused on the bookstore for the last four days.

The landing led to three bedrooms and a bathroom. To the right of the landing were two bedrooms, then the bathroom just off to the left with the master bedroom at the end of the hall.

She turned in that direction, once again trailing her hand along the wall as she so often did as a child. At the end, she grasped the cold door knob, twisted, then pushed it open to reveal the chilly bedroom.

The hardwood floors needed some elbow grease, but she'd make them shine and gleam again. They missed the warmth from her grandmother's homemade braided rugs created from scraps left over from quilts and other clothing projects. All the colors braided together created funky patterns she and Tyler once loved to use as roads and mountains for their Hot Wheels cars. Whatever happened to those braided rugs? Did her mother keep them? Were they sold at auction or, even worse, discarded into the trash?

She grimaced and hoped someone in the family kept them. Maybe she could get them back for her office space.

Because yes, this was going to be her private office. She couldn't stand to take a sledgehammer to these walls. This space would be perfect for her drafting table and creation space.

Charlee froze when a solid thump drifted up from below, followed by creaking noises.

Prickles shot up her arm as she realized she didn't lock the door.

She flicked off the flashlight, then tiptoed over to the door and tried to peer down the hall. Shadows swayed from side to side from the tree and street light outside the window at the end of the hallway, but there was definitely another creak.

Oh Crap. Crap-crap-crap.

She reached for her back pocket, fumbling for her cell phone. She needed to call Tyler. He would help. He worked for the police. Yes, she needed Tyler.

Her hands trembled and she pushed the wrong numbers, had to hit cancel and try again. Sweat beaded across her forehead, her breathing shaky.

Suddenly a light flashed into her eyes. "What's going on here?" A loud voice boomed, the door swinging wide open.

Charlee screamed and threw her phone straight into the light. She heard a thump and swearing, the light swung haphazardly. She took advantage and kicked out with her work boot in a swinging arc, hoping to catch the perp's legs and trip him up so she could escape. She connected hard, but lost her balance and stumbled backwards, losing her balance and landing hard on her butt. Her flashlight went rolling across the floor. Dang it, why didn't she think to hit him with that? She started to scramble after it.

"Son of a monkey's uncle! Charlee, is that you?"

She looked up. With the light no longer blinding her, she saw her brother dressed in uniform, bent over and clutching his knee. His dark brown hair was disheveled, his blue eyes narrowed as he peered at her sprawled on the floor.

"What mischief are you up to now?" he demanded.

"Nothing. I'm just checking out my business space. What are you doing here, scaring the living daylights out of me?" She sent him her best glare.

"Answering a breaking and entering phone call. Miss Marjorie was passing by and saw shadows. She thought some kids broke in and were up to no good. I'll be sure to tell her it was just my sister the troublemaker."

Charlee stuck her tongue out at him, then pushed up off the floor and rubbed her sore behind. "Just the info she needs for her next status update. Charlee Jackson busted for B&E by her officer brother."

Tyler smirked. "Are you hurt?"

"Yeah, I fell on my tush and it hurts like the dickens."

"Good," he responded, finally straightening.

"Hey!"

"Don't hey, me. What were you thinking, kicking me in the knee like that? And what did you hit me in the head with?" Through the bright light from his mega flashlight, she could see his glare. Yeah, her glare wasn't nearly as good as his. Ten years in the military could teach a man some pretty intimidating stare tactics.

"I was thinking of the defensive moves my older brother taught me in case an idiot ever tried something stupid." She folded her arms, letting him know just who she thought the idiot was.

He sighed, then pulled his radio off his belt and called in a code to the dispatcher, letting her know that back up wasn't needed after all.

Back up? Just what she needed, a bunch of flashing lights outside the house announcing their mishap.

Once his radio was back on the belt, Tyler returned his attention to her. "Better safe than sorry, right?"

She snorted. *Especially when the only person stalking you turns out to be your big brother.*

"Why are you in the dark, anyway?" he asked.

"The electricity has been out for a few years. They haven't turned it back on yet. I just wanted to do a walk through, see how things looked after all this time."

Another heavy sigh escaped. "It didn't occur to you that it would be better during daylight hours?"

She punched him in the arm. *Ouch.* She forgot how hard his muscles were. Better stick to using her work boots. "That's why I brought a flashlight." Speaking of, she walked over and picked it up.

"This is your new office, huh? Grandma would love it." He swung his light around the room. Its high voltage definitely lit it up better than her flashlight. He opened the closet door and peered inside.

"What are you doing, Tyler?" she asked.

"Checking out the space. Let's go explore." He grabbed her arm and off they went through the rest of the rooms. It was like an adult version of a nighttime hide and seek combined with flashlight tag. They explored, relived a few memories and swapped thoughts about taking out walls and setting up the office. It actually turned out to be a pretty good night.

Back downstairs, they closed the door and locked back up.

"When you come back, be sure to lock up behind you. Especially if you're alone. I know this was a safe neighborhood when we were kids, but it's been empty long enough to attract some vagrants and troublemakers. Which is exactly why Miss Marjorie called."

"Yes, sir," she saluted him.

He glared at her again. "And get the electricity turned on or don't bother coming at night. If I catch you here again, I'll tell Mom."

"Ooh, I can't believe you're pulling the mom card," she said. "What are we, teenagers?"

"You're right. If I find you here again without proper paperwork and functioning equipment, such as electricity, I'll fine you instead."

She narrowed her gaze, not appreciating his horrible sense of humor and wished she was big enough to really sock him one. "You're a pain in the butt, you know that right?"

He slung his arm around her, his grip tight. "Better that than finding you hurt . . . or worse."

Cold trickled through her. He never talked about his time overseas and the horrible stuff he saw in the line of duty, but her once easy, fun-loving brother came home from his overseas tour broken and solemn. When she agreed to his terms, his shoulders visibly relaxed.

Tyler walked her to the truck and made sure she was all set to go. "Are you coming to Freddy's tomorrow night? A couple of the guys are getting together after work."

Charlee put her key in the ignition, turned it, and the engine flared to life. "Probably. I'm sure some of the crew will want to celebrate completing our first week."

"Great. I'll see you then." He thumped the truck door before shifting away. "Be safe getting home."

She called good night and pulled away. As stupid and annoying as her older brother could be, she was grateful it was him that scared her and not the 'something worse' he warned about.

"THANKS, FREDDY," PETER SAID, signing his name across a red heart for the American Heart Association fundraiser Freddy's Sports Bar did every February. Pink hearts were one dollar and red hearts were five. Freddy did a good job guilting his customers into the red heart donations, plus it was a convenient way to decorate for the upcoming Valentine's holiday. Peter nodded at the bar owner, then took a long sip of cold beer, relishing the end of a hard work week. It was six-thirty and the hallelujah-for-the-weekend crew was straggling in. He left some cash on the bar, then nabbed a chair at the table where his friends Noah Anderson and Cameron Wilson were already harassing Tyler.

"Tell me again how you got the bruise," Peter said, settling into the chair and crossing his foot over his knee.

Noah and Cameron snickered, while Tyler scowled at them all, determined to sip his beer and ignore their pestering.

"I heard he knocked his head on a door frame early in the morning after a wild night with Mandy," Cameron confided. "Or maybe it was Candy. I can't keep track of Tyler's ladies these days."

"Nah, I heard he was reading a how-to manual on bedroom techniques and fell out of his chair when he realized he's been doing it wrong all this time," Noah joined in.

Peter smirked, watching Tyler's irritation grow as he remained silent, tapping two fingers on his knee.

"You know they're going to keep at it until you give in," Peter said.

Tyler just shrugged and Peter changed the subject, hoping to divert attention from his best friend for a few minutes at least. "How's the move going, Cameron?"

"It's okay. Anna's still pretty mad at me for making her leave New York to come to Hicksville." Cameron shrugged and picked at the label on the bottle in his hands. "She'll get over it eventually."

"Have you heard from her mom?" Peter asked, not sure he wanted to open that tender topic, but hey, if Cameron didn't talk to his friends, who would he have to spill his ugly guts to?

Cameron sighed. "Not since she left for Europe. No emails or calls since the divorce was finalized either. I figure she'll eventually show up and want to be Super Mom again, but until then, it's just me and Anna." He looked up at his friends. "And honestly, it's been a relief. It's good to be home. Eventually, Anna will see that it was the right decision, too."

"What's she into?" Noah asked.

"Up until now, it's been all dance, but I'm hoping she'll take a break and find some new interests. I want her to get into some summer camps and classes—tennis, swimming, whatever." Cameron grimaced. "Mom wants her to help out in the dance studio, but I said no."

Peter didn't know a lot about the situation, but when Cameron arrived in Kansas City with his daughter in tow a month ago, the girl was gaunt, exhausted, and furious. Apparently the gaunt and exhausted was from a mother who pushed her into constant dance, acting, and other performance classes and productions. The furious was all aimed at her father for taking her away. "What about a job?" he asked.

Cameron looked interested. "What could a twelve-year-old do, though?"

Peter shrugged. "My dog is bored out of her mind when I'm at work. She would love someone to come take her for walks or to the dog park. Think Anna might be interested?"

The first genuine smile since his return spread across Cameron's face. "She just might. She always wanted a dog, but we couldn't have one in the New York apartment. That and she was always gone. I'll ask her about it. Thanks."

Peter nodded. The conversation moved on to dating—and some razzing on Cameron putting his hat back into the dating pool. There were certainly some women in the area waiting for the chance to pounce.

Speaking of pouncing, Charlee finally arrived. She was at the bar, laughing with some of her crew. She must have gone home to change first because she was in clean jeans and a fitted navy top, rather than her usual muck jeans and t-shirt. She turned from the bar and spotted them. She waved, then said something to Juan Two and came over to join them. Tyler cursed under his breath and Peter slid him a 'what's up' glance.

"Hey there, big brother." She touched the bruise on his forehead and winced. "Dang, sorry about that."

"Whoa!" Noah jumped in. "You did that?"

Charlee looked amused. "Trying to keep our run in a secret?"

The poor guy looked defeated. "Not anymore, apparently."

Charlee laughed and told them about the previous night's

incident—from her fear that someone was breaking in, then beaning her brother in the head with the phone and even the part about falling on her butt after trying to kick him to the ground. The guys were busting a gut laughing and teasing Tyler, who was taking it surprisingly well.

"Must suck getting injured in the line of duty—by your sister, no less. Did you file a report in case you have any lingering injuries?" Noah teased.

"Hardy har har." Tyler rolled his eyes.

Noah grabbed Charlee's hand and kissed it. "I have to take you out to lunch and thank you for providing material to hold over Tyler's head for the next two or three years."

Charlee just laughed and patted his cheek. "Anything for you guys. Hey, I need to get back to my crew. It was fun to see you. Be nice to my brother!" She nudged Tyler's shoulder, which he returned in a gesture that everything was fine before she left their group.

"Dang, little Charlee is all grown up. How did I miss that?" Cameron asked, watching her walk back to the bar.

Tyler smacked him upside the head. "Keep your eyes off my sister's butt," he grumbled.

Peter couldn't agree more, although he had a hard time prying his eyes away.

"Hey, did you guys hear the update about Hope?" Noah asked.

Peter swiveled back to face his friends. Ah yes, Hope. They had dated in high school and were fairly serious. Or at least he was until Hope screwed things up their senior year. Funny how something that hurt so much then ended up being a blessing in disguise.

"She texted me last week," Peter said. "It's too bad things didn't work out for her and her husband."

"Texted, huh?" Cameron asked. "I wasn't under the impression you two kept in touch after she left town."

Peter shrugged. "We haven't, other than just a message here and there. I think she needed a friend to talk to."

"Or a rebound guy to fall back on," Tyler suggested.

"Dude, it's not like that. Not at all," Peter insisted.

Cameron looked down at his watch and pushed his bottle to the middle of the table. "I gotta go. I don't like to leave Anna for too long. Thanks for the beer, guys. It was good to catch up."

Peter gave Cameron a quick fist bump and reminded him about the dog walking job, then Cameron was out the door. Peter took the chance to return to the bar to order nachos and to get a few minutes to talk to Charlee without the guys goofing off.

He shoulder bumped her and squeezed in between her and Juan One. Or maybe it was Juan Two. He could never keep them straight, even in school. He motioned to Freddy and placed his order, then turned to Charlee.

The light reflected off her soft blonde hair, making it look almost golden. The edges of her eyes crinkled as she laughed at something Bob and Crank were disagreeing about.

"Hey, how are the office renovations coming?" Peter asked, prying her attention away from Bob's tall tale. She shifted and turned to give him her full attention. This close, Peter could see the dark brown line edging the clear light brown of her eyes. He swallowed past the lump in his throat.

"Well, I haven't started anything for the front room. I'll get to that. I want to get the master bedroom set up as a temporary office first."

Peter leaned his arm against the bar. "What can I help you with?"

"Are you sure you want to help the competition? Your Daddy might not like it. I'm betting he wasn't the one who sent the donuts and bagels this morning." Charlee said, turning the bottle of ginger ale around in her hand.

Even though Charlee was teasing, Peter could see that a little bit of it was sincere. "Don't worry about my dad. Just tell me how I can help."

Charlee leaned closer, looking around the bar suspiciously. He struggled to stay in place, not wanting to admit how much he liked having her this close. "What are you doing?"

She cupped her hand around one side of her mouth before whispering, "Checking for spies before relaying the secret code."

He laughed. It had been a long time since he and Tyler's detective days. Her eyes crinkled up in the corners when she laughed even back then.

"Well, if you're sure," she continued. "I do need help getting my desk and file cabinet upstairs. Are you available Tuesday after work?"

"That works for me." Peter nodded to Freddy when he returned with Peter's nachos. "I'll see you Tuesday then."

Charlee nodded and Peter returned to where Noah and Tyler were discussing the upcoming NBA playoffs. Peter joined in with his thoughts about which teams would make it to the finals. He glanced back up to the bar, just in time to see Charlee join the debate between Bob and Crank, motioning for the Juans to be part of the discussion as well.

Excitement twirled inside him. Charlee leaving Elliott Construction was beginning to take on a new light. Tuesday couldn't come fast enough.

Chapter Eight

THE FOLLOWING MONDAY, Charlee met with the Women in Business group again. January had slipped to February so quickly with all that happened since the last meeting. She couldn't believe that it was almost Valentine's Day. Charlee enjoyed her lunch and listened to Eden and Victoria talking about the book shop, swapping decorating and layout ideas.

"I saw this photo on Pinterest that I would love to incorporate into the entryway." Eden pulled a printed sheet of paper out of her purse and handed it to Victoria.

"This is fantastic! What a great idea for the transition to the book shop." Victoria passed it on to Charlee. "Can your crew do this?"

Charlee smiled when she saw the wooden staircase. The top of each step was polished wood, but the front side was painted to appear like a book spine. The classics like Jane Austen and Charles Dickens, mixed in with contemporaries like Kristan Higgins and Stephen King. "Let me take this with me. Crank is actually quite artistic and teaches classes at the community center. He would love this."

Victoria and Eden were delighted. Everything was coming together smoothly. Or at least as smoothly as any construction project does. There were the typical hiccups, but in general, everything was working out.

Eventually the topic changed to the upcoming bachelor's auction and the ladies speculated who would and wouldn't agree to participate.

"A few of the firefighters and guys from the police department have already agreed. They are even participating in a photo shoot to advertise the event," Victoria confided. She leaned forward. "And ladies, let me tell you, they have no qualms about unbuttoning their shirts or leaving them off all together."

Miss Marjorie, a retired member of Women in Business, waved herself with the monthly agenda. "Mercy me," she said, faintly. "Has anyone from the Mayor's office or City Council volunteered yet?"

Victoria's eyes narrowed. "Not yet, but I'm working on someone in particular. No worries there, I'll definitely have him signing the dotted line within the next week."

Charlee felt bad for whoever she was going after. He had no hope of escape.

"What about Peter Elliott?" Eden asked. "He's dang hot. I can just imagine him up on the stage, tool belt around his hips, holes in the knees of his jeans, tight white shirt hugging his muscular chest and those arms . . ." She sighed.

Charlee choked on her water. Holy bejeebers. Peter? "Um, you like Peter much?"

Eden shook her head and laughed. "Well, a girl can't help but notice when she walks through his construction site."

"No, you're right," Victoria said. "Not all the bachelors should be prominent men in the community. We need some sexy everyday guys, too. I love it."

Charlee's eyes widened. They were talking about Peter. Her Peter. Well, not actually hers. They were both single and he was a friend and yeah, any warm blooded female would find Peter attractive. Not that that meant she'd ever admit to the dreams she had about him wearing exactly what Eden had described—well, if she was honest, he was missing the t-shirt, but still. He was her brother's best friend. They grew up together. That was just, ew. She wasn't supposed to think of him that way. Looking down at her tomboyish body, she knew he didn't think of her that way either.

No guy did. Or at least, not for long.

"What do you think, Charlee?" Victoria asked.

She shrugged. "I don't know. He's actually kind of reserved. I'm not sure if he'd go for something like this."

"But you could ask him, right?" Eden said, leaning forward, eager.

"Why don't you ask him? I'm sure he'd rather hear the proposition from you." Eden was a walking fantasy. Confident, poised, straight midnight black hair that fell just past her shoulders, big gorgeous blue eyes, curves that could make a taxi driver squeal to a stop, and she even had a tattoo on her upper arm. No matter what she wore, men's gazes followed her until she was well past them.

Eden cocked her head to the side. "From what I've observed, I think he'd prefer it if the proposition came from you."

Charlee tilted her head, meeting Eden's sincere eyes. "What do you mean?"

Eden and Victoria exchanged looks. Victoria shrugged,

then was called to help with something up front. Eden scooted over into the chair Victoria left empty beside Charlee, leaned in close and lowered her voice.

"Have you and Peter ever dated?" she asked.

Charlee was startled. "N-no."

"Why not?" Eden propped her chin on her hand, as though her question was natural, no big deal.

Charlee opened and closed her mouth. Why not? Well, because . . . Because. "He's my brother's best friend. We grew up together." Yeah, that's why.

"So?"

Charlee's eyes widened. What did she mean, so?

"Haven't you ever noticed how he looks at you? How his eyes light up and his smile is more genuine when you walk in?"

Her mind swirled and she shook it to clear the jumbled thoughts. "He doesn't think of me like that. I'm just an annoying sister." Even as she said it, disappointment settled in. But why should she be disappointed? She'd always known Peter was her friend and that was all.

Victoria returned to the table, but before Eden moved, she took Charlee's hand. "I think you're wrong."

With those parting words, Eden scooted over and Victoria reclaimed her place. The rest of the meeting was a blur. Charlee couldn't concentrate on anything without her thoughts wandering to Peter, making her question their relationship and her feelings for him.

Wait a minute, her feelings? For Peter? She pushed the thought away.

How did everything become so complicated, so topsy-turvy, so unexpectedly?

TIME SEEMED TO CRAWL at a snail's pace the next day. By the time Tuesday night arrived, Charlee was a jumpy mess as she worked with Peter to move the file cabinet into her new office. After they got it situated, Peter looked at her oddly.

"Are you okay?" He pulled off his Royals ball cap and scratched his head.

"Sure, of course." She met his eyes, blushed, then turned to go back outside to get the desk. "Why?"

"You just seem nervous or something."

Yeah, he nailed that one. He followed her down the stairs. She could feel him behind her, knowing he was wondering what was going on in her head. She sighed. "I've just been thinking about some stuff that came up at the Women in Business meeting yesterday."

They arrived at the truck's tail gate, but before she could climb up, he stopped her.

"What's on your mind? Maybe I can help."

She froze. Oh boogers. Now what should she say? Hey, Peter, some of the girls think you have a crush on your best friend's sister. That wasn't going to work. Before she could think too much about it, words started tumbling out.

"Eden thinks you would make a good addition to the Bachelor's auction. Do the whole hot construction worker guy, ripped jeans, tool belt look." Peter's shocked expression kept her mouth moving. "Of course, I told them I wasn't sure you would be into it."

Peter shook his head. "Eden thinks I'm a hot construction guy?"

Of course. Eden. What guy could pass that up? "Yeah, perhaps you should talk to her about it."

Charlee climbed up into the truck. Peter joined her in the truck bed, helped shift the desk to the edge, then jumped down to lower it to the ground. Together, they maneuvered the desk into the house and started up the stairs. All the while, Charlee stole little peeks at Peter. She had been right all along. Eden and her stupid theories.

Peter surprised her by continuing the conversation. "Eden's a little intimidating, don't you think? I'm glad she didn't ask. I probably would have blanked and looked like an idiot."

Charlee just rolled her eyes. "You wouldn't want to look stupid in front of the hot chick."

Peter's eyebrows scrunched together. "Some of the guys think she's hot—and she is. She just isn't my type."

"What is your type?" She was surprised when his face flushed. "Sorry, that's none of my business." As much as she and Peter were longtime friends, their conversations normally centered around construction, sports, and Tyler. Relationships definitely weren't their norm.

They got the desk into the new office. As they set the desk into place, Peter broke the silence. "Have you been seeing anyone lately?"

Charlee looked up, met his blue-gray eyes, then quickly back down. "No, most guys aren't interested in girls like me." She moved around to the other side and knelt down to assemble the drawers, a good excuse to hide her embarrassment. She hoped Peter would get the hint and change the topic.

PETER PULLED OFF HIS baseball cap and tapped it against his leg, contemplating what Charlee just said and not sure he understood. "What do you mean, girls like you?" He stared at the top of her head, as she kept her head tucked down. He could tell she was avoiding him while she put the drawers into their respective spots.

"I just mean I'm not exactly the type guys take a second look at. You know, the curvy girls. They walk by and guys practically drool all over themselves to get another look from the backside, like Eden. Me, not so much, but I'm used to it. I'm just not the sexy type." She shrugged and moved on to another drawer.

He couldn't believe what she was saying. He set the cap aside and placed his hands on the desk. "Charlee?" He peered over the edge where she adjusted a wheel on the side of the drawer before sliding it in smoothly.

She glanced up, her light brown eyes framed by wispy blonde hair. "Yeah?"

"You are sexy," he said matter-of-factly.

She laughed. *Laughed!* He couldn't believe it.

"You're just saying that to make me feel better." She stood and patted his cheek.

What the heck? She laughed at him, then patted his cheek like a little boy. Looked like it was time to shake things up.

He caught her hand in his, raised it to his mouth. He kept his eyes focused on her, watching her eyes widen as he placed small kisses from her fingertips to the palm of her hand, where he gently sank his teeth into the flesh there. She gasped, her wide eyes darting from his to where he now laid a tender kiss on the spot he had nibbled. She didn't pull away, but her breathing had quickened, just as his blood was also rushing and his heart pounded against his chest.

"You are very sexy." His gruff voice emphasized each word as he slowly made his way around the desk, keeping his hand intertwined with hers. She followed his progress, turning to face him when he reached her side. He could see curiosity and a little bit of hesitation in her expression.

"Wh-what are you doing?" she asked.

She trembled as he placed his hands on her slender hips. "Showing you how I see you," he said, his thumb brushing just along the edge of her t-shirt. He brought up one hand, unable to resist the temptation of sinking his fingers into her soft hair, loving the feel of the strands gliding between his fingers. He tilted her head back, wanting her to see the truth as he spoke.

"You are amazing. Strong and kind. Smart, but not in a cocky way, in a quiet solid way. You consider everything, everyone. You give so much more than you ask. And when you make a decision, when you know you need to choose a fork in the road, you do it and move forward. No looking back." His lower hand slid around to her back, pulling her closer, their bodies just brushing against each other. "And yes, you are sexy, but all that other stuff, it makes you beautiful."

He stepped forward, backing her up until her knees met the edge of the desk. "Hold on," he whispered in her ear. He loved her little gasp when he lifted her onto the desk, her hands grabbing onto his shoulders, her legs tangling around his.

"Every day, I'd see you at work and wished—" He swallowed the lump in his throat. Could he say it? Admit his feelings to her? He sucked in a deep breath, then plunged ahead. "I wished that we could be more." He trailed off as his finger traced the outline of her lips.

"I-I didn't know." Her warm breath washed over his fingertips, making goosebumps break out over his arm.

"My father was very clear about his stance when it came to employees and relationships." She simply nodded, breaking the contact of his fingertips. He let his hand glide over her shoulder and down her arm, again intertwining their fingers together.

He desperately wanted to lean forward, to capture her mouth. Instead he lowered his head and kissed the base of her neck. Her quick intake of breath sent an electric thrill through him. She tilted her head to the side, allowing him better access to the curve of her neck. Then, with lips just barely touching her skin, he trailed soft kisses up, stopping only to rest his lips along the throbbing pulse just below her ear. Satisfaction welled up inside him, knowing Charlee was just as excited as he was. He tightened the grip where their hands were intertwined, ready to take the next step, to kiss Charlee for the very first time, hoping it would live up to how he imagined things could be between them.

"What the hell? Get your hands off my sister!"

Peter froze. Charlee went from soft and compliant to stiff as a 2x4.

Holy monkeys in alligator-infested waters.

"Charlee?" a high feminine voice squeaked.

"Mom?" Charlee's voice cracked over the word.

Hot diggity dog. There just weren't enough pseudo curse

words for this situation.

CHARLEE CLOSED HER EYES in mortification. "Could we get a few moments of privacy, please?"

"I don't think that's a—" Tyler started, then was cut off by a thump and a yelp, which Charlee assumed was her mother hitting him upside the head.

"We'll be just down the hall, dear," her mother replied. The office door closed with a soft click and their footsteps faded away.

Charlee loosened her grip on Peter.

Peter.

Wow. Just wow. Where had that come from? One minute they were talking and then...

Her hands fell to the cold surface of the desk. Peter stepped back, shoved his hands through his light brown hair, then into his front pockets. Her skin prickled as she remembered where those hands had just been and how they felt.

His gray eyes met hers. She sucked in her breath. His eyes were filled with uncertainty.

Did he regret kissing her? She was shocked by the hurt that clamped around her heart, squeezing it like a vise. She slid off the desk and let her work boots hit the floor with the loud thunk, breaking whatever thoughts were running through Peter's head.

"Charlee—" he began, but she cut him off.

"I know. You're sorry, it shouldn't have happened." She turned away, wanting to escape. She needed to put some space between them, but Peter caught her arm and pulled her around to face him again.

"I'm not sorry," he said, heat blazing from his eyes, soaking into her.

"You aren't?" she squeaked. Had she heard him right?

His grip on her arm gentled and he slid an arm around her waist and held her loosely against him. He lowered his forehead to rest against hers. "No. Are you?"

She shook her head from side to side. From this close, she could see tiny blue flecks mixed in the gray.

A small smile appeared, then he dropped a kiss on her nose and stepped back. "Then we'll continue this conversation later."

"Later." She grinned, wanting to go up on her toes and press her lips to his, but before she could, he stepped back.

"Later," he promised.

Anticipation thrummed through her. Then she frowned. "What are we going to do about Tyler?"

"Let's not push his buttons tonight. I'll talk with him after he has time to calm down." He tucked a short strand of hair behind her ear, tracing his fingers around the back, then down her throat.

Just that simple touch sent cascading tingles through her, making her shiver. She resisted the urge to let her eyes close, to prolong the moment. Not a good idea with an audience outside, waiting for them to emerge. "We better go."

He agreed, took her hand and kissed her fingers, then led her to the door.

When they emerged from her office, she found her mom and Tyler waiting at the other end of the hall. As they neared the stairs, Tyler's eyes widened in disbelief.

"What the—" he started, but was cut off by Mom.

"Language, Tyler," Mrs. Jackson warned.

Tyler simply narrowed his eyes into his wicked death glare.

"Mrs. Jackson," Peter nodded to her mother, studiously ignoring Tyler.

"It's good to see you, Peter. How's work going?" she asked, trying to be polite and keep the peace, too.

"It's going well, ma'am. Thank you."

"Peter, if I remember correctly, yesterday you were calling me Mom."

Peter smiled and Charlee was grateful to her mother for setting him at ease.

"Do you have plans for this evening?" Mrs. Jackson asked. "We popped in to steal Charlee away for a surprise celebration dinner. Perhaps you'd like to join us?"

Seriously, Charlee was going to give her a bear hug later.

"Thanks, but I have plans. I'll see you later?" He looked at Charlee. No one else. Just her.

"Absolutely," she replied.

Tyler growled—or at least that's what it sounded like as Peter thumped down the stairs and out the front door.

"Some best friend he is," Tyler grumbled.

"You know, son, I believe Peter wasn't the only one groping someone on that desk," Mom said. "Charlee's hands were plenty busy, too."

"Holy—" Tyler started, his eyes squeezed tight and his

hands rubbing his forehead as if wishing to erase the image from his mind.

"Language." Mom leveled her eyes at him. And man, she didn't need glare practice. She had the 'I'm the mom and you listen to me' look down pat. She smoothed her shirt over her hips, then turned towards the stairs. "Let's just be happy your sister is dating again. Now, let's drop the subject and go meet your father and Julie."

And with that, Charlee's happiness dropped like a deflated football crushed under a pile of 300-pound guys. She should have known better than to trust her mother's enthusiasm. Charlee certainly wasn't following the life plan her mother etched out for each of her daughters, but her beloved sister, Julie, did.

Julie was on the honor roll, Charlee was an average student. Julie was the prom queen, and the only dance Charlee attended was her senior prom after dire threats from her mother, who also bribed a friend's son from another school with spending money, a limo, and a tux if he agreed to be her escort. Julie chose an acceptable family-oriented college major and received a full-ride scholarship. Charlee ditched her parent's house as soon as she could and went to an out-of-state school specializing in construction and architecture. When Julie graduated, she received a beautiful leather briefcase and her mother cried. When Charlee graduated, she received a card and a gift card to her mother's favorite clothing store. And just her father came to the graduation because her mother was with Julie, waiting for her to go into labor with her first child. Even though the due date was three weeks away.

She clomped down the stairs behind her mother, once

more feeling like the tarnished child.

Settled into the passenger seat of her mother's car with her brother sulking in the back, Charlee shoved aside thoughts about her mother and the dreaded dinner ahead. Especially now that Tyler was in a funk. She couldn't count on him to make the family dinner bearable.

Instead, she bit her lip and thought about seeing Peter the next day. Would it be awkward? How should she act? How would Peter act? Her head began to ache with all the questions. But most of all, feared that if things didn't work out, she could lose his friendship forever. How many of her friends had tried similar relationships, only to end up hating each other in the end?

Was it too late to stop now? But oh, how she yearned to see what might happen next.

Chapter Nine

WEDNESDAY MORNING, PETER'S MIND was filled to overflowing as he drove to work. Charlee, Indulgence Row, and Elliott Construction were all crowded together, fighting for his attention. To be honest, Charlee was winning by a landslide. A silly smile spread over his face.

Last night was pretty amazing. He just wished they would have at least had time to talk. He didn't like that Charlee immediately jumped to the conclusion that he was playing with her. He definitely needed to get that straightened out. But the rest of it—wow.

Bleep. Bleep.

Peter was startled and glanced into his rear view mirror to see flashing lights. He immediately took his foot off the gas and looked down to see the speedometer was slightly five miles over the speed limit. A little fast for this neighborhood, but definitely not speeding excessively. Must be a newbie being hyper-vigilant about his job. He pulled over and parked along the curb, still a few blocks from Indulgence Row. He shifted in his seat and took out his wallet. He had just retrieved the insurance and registration from the glove compartment when the officer tapped at his window.

He turned and clicked the button for the window to roll down.

Officer Jackson stared down at him with a solemn expression. Or at least Peter assumed he was staring at him through those stupid mirrored sunglasses.

"What's up, Tyler?" Peter asked.

Tyler flipped open his thick black leather bound book. "License and registration, please."

Peter handed it over. "What's going on?"

"Sir, are you aware of how fast you were going?" Tyler asked while writing some info in the book.

"About five miles over. Ty, seriously? What's up?"

Tyler used his pointer finger to lower his sunglasses just enough to make eye contact over the rim. "Eight miles. Speeding through a residential area is dangerous. Especially on a school morning. I do believe you passed through a school zone, too. Which means the fine is doubled."

Peter wanted to swear, but he held it in. "Is this about me dating your sister?"

Tyler's face flushed red.

Not from embarrassment. I'm more likely making him mad, which might not be a good idea while he was armed, Peter thought, eyeing the gun strapped to his best friend's hip.

"Would you like me to write you up for arguing with an officer as well?"

"Not at all, sir," Peter said. *Butt munch.*

Tyler pushed the glasses back up the bridge of his nose and flipped the book closed. "I need to call this in, run your plates. I'll be back in a minute."

Peter just nodded and watched his friend through the side

mirror as he went back to the patrol car to finish things up. Peter propped his elbows on the steering wheel and scrubbed his face with his hands. What in tarnation? Did Tyler think this would prevent him from dating Charlee? All it really made him want to do was get out and kick Tyler's ass. But he couldn't do that—at least not while he was in uniform.

Officer Jackson returned, extending the documents he retrieved. "Your papers, sir. I recommend you get that taken care of right away."

Peter took the license and papers, with the ticket right on top.

$125. Doubled for a school zone. Quite a few choice words entered his mind about his so-called best friend.

"You have a nice day," Officer Jackson said, a slight smirk ticking at the side of his mouth.

"Sure, see you at poker tonight?" The only response he got was one raised eyebrow before his friend walked away. He shoved the ticket, insurance, and registration into the glove compartment. He'd take care of it later.

Before he could put the truck into gear and pull away, his cell phone rang with the special ringtone for his father's secretary. Business stuff.

"Good morning, Velma," he said, seeing Tyler's patrol car cruise pass him. He shook his head, wondering what other torture Tyler had in store for him.

"Peter, your dad wants you to come into the office today. There are some new project meetings he'd like you to sit in on."

Grr. "I'm almost to the Indulgence Row project. Literally a few blocks away. Let me stop in there, get things going, then I'll be in."

"Better be quick about it. The first meeting starts in forty-five minutes."

"Thanks, Velma. Tell him I'll be there as soon as possible."

Peter hung up. First Tyler and now his dad was pulling him away from where he needed to be this morning. If only his dad understood how much Peter hated these meetings. Going over costs, time frames, income projections, and other necessary but boring details. It made him want to hang himself by the mandatory neck tie his father made him wear to company meetings.

Peter parked, then grabbed his gear and headed into the Sweet Confections shop—or at least the site for the new Sweet Confections shop. His crew was already there, picking up from where they left off the day before. Peter talked to the guys, followed up with their different goals for the day, then headed back out. He was in and out without a glimpse of Charlee or her crew. He heard them upstairs and paused, tempted to head up to say hi, but he had already taken too long talking to his crew and knew he was going to be late getting to Elliott Construction. As much as he wanted to go up, he pushed through the front doors instead, ready to grit his teeth and make his way through a the meetings.

Those few meetings turned into an entire day behind a desk, on the phone, or hashing out contracts and proposals with his dad. In other words, his day was beastly.

On top of it all, it was raining when he got home. Not a light rain or even a medium rain, but a step out of your car and get drenched to the bone, monsoon style Midwest rain. He pulled his jacket over his head and sprinted from the truck to his front door, scrambling to unlock it while listening to Petunia bark on the other side. The key turned in the lock and he stumbled in, then slouched against the closed door, dripping in the entryway. Petunia thought it was great fun and started chasing her tail in circles, making him laugh for the first time that day. At least he had this gem to brighten his spirits. He scruffed her fur and played with her for a few minutes before heading into the kitchen.

"I'll let you out when the rain dies down. Give it about fifteen minutes, girl," he said, Petunia following him close behind.

There was a note on the refrigerator from Cameron's daughter, Anna. She had started coming to his house to walk Petunia after school. So far, she seemed to like it. Her note told him that there was a stack of wet towels on the bathroom floor from when they got back from their walk in the rain.

"Sounds like you already had a good time with Anna." Peter rubbed Petunia's head, then picked up the phone to order buffalo wings and bread sticks. It was his turn to host poker night. Cameron had texted and said he was coming, Noah was still in town and said he'd be there if he met his work deadline, but Tyler? Well, who knew if he would show or not.

Tyler surprised the crud out of him. Not only did he show up, but he came loaded with cash. Apparently he was planning to not only give Peter tickets, but to kick his ass at cards, too. Tyler was sulky, sipping on beer, eating more than his share of wings and bidding high. Combined together it made for a piss poor night. Cameron, good lawyer that he was, tried to divert the tenseness with conversation about Anna.

"Dude, the dog walking thing is backfiring on me. Now she's begging for a dog. On the other hand, at least she isn't bugging me about dance classes anymore."

"Hey, she's welcome to borrow Petunia anytime," Peter said.

"Yeah, be careful about that, Cam. He says that now, but he might renege later," Tyler said, drawing another card.

Peter ignored him. "Anna seems like a good kid. Give her some time, she'll come around."

"Yeah, at least you don't have to worry about Peter kissing her," Tyler said, slumping down into his seat.

Peter threw his cards down. "Seriously?"

"Kissing? Who was Peter kissing?" Noah leaned forward, ready for some juicy gossip.

Cameron gave Peter the stink eye, and Peter threw up his hands. "Not a kid! She's an adult and it didn't get all the way to kissing."

"Ooh, making out. Base count?" Noah egged the conversation on.

"No base count," Tyler said, his eyes scrunched into slits. He shoved the chair back and stood, then grabbed his coat and walked out. Noah called after him, but all he got was the crack of the door as it slammed shut.

"Dude," Cameron said, shaking his head. "What did you do to Tyler?"

"More like who," Noah said, waggling his eyebrows. "What girlfriend did you steal, bad boy?"

"No girlfriend and it's none of your business." Peter reached across the table and swiped all the cards into a pile, shuffling them.

Cameron reclined in his chair, crossing one leg over the other. "Holy hell. No way."

Peter concentrated on shuffling. No way was he adding

fuel to the fire.

"What?" Noah asked, anxious to be in on the secret. "Spill the beans, Petey." When Peter remained silent, Noah turned to Cameron who was shaking his head. "Let's go, lawyer boy. Use your reasoning to figure it out."

"Well, there are only two people I can think of that would push Tyler's buttons this bad." He held up a finger. "There's only one girlfriend Tyler ever really cared about and that's Mari. Since she's a gorgeous model, there's no way Peter landed her."

"Not only that," Noah said. "But we'd be searching for Peter's dead body rather than sitting here playing cards."

Peter shuddered. That was a truth he could agree with. He thanked the heavens that wasn't his fate.

"If it's not Mari . . ." Noah trailed off, his eyes going wide. "Dude."

Peter pushed back from the table, but Cameron hooked his foot around the leg of the chair, blocking his escape.

"The little sister," Cameron said, shaking his head in astonishment. "And from the blush spreading up your girly face, I guessed correctly."

Peter smacked Cameron across the back of the head. Then he pointed at Cameron, his finger going back and forth between the two. "Nothing is official yet. We haven't figured out if there is anything to be official about, so keep your pansy mouths shut."

"You, my friend, are still under examination," Cameron said in an authoritative lawyerly voice. "My first question is how exactly did Tyler find out?"

Noah bust out laughing when Peter sputtered and flushed

what he imagined was an even deeper shade of red. "None of your beeswax."

"Interesting." Cameron stroked his chin, like a detective.

"Just let it go," Peter said. "And keep your mouths shut."

"Man, this is even better than reality TV. I can't believe I have to leave for work tomorrow. I'm gonna miss the good stuff," Noah complained.

"No worries, my friend. I'll keep you updated via text," Cameron promised.

"You're both like gossipy old women. Now, are we going to play or call it a night?"

The guys put in their money and Peter dealt the cards. He looked at the empty chair, emotions warring inside him between wanting to kick Tyler's butt and wondering how long his best friend would hate him.

Chapter Ten

CHARLEE SLAMMED HER FRONT DOOR shut. It had been a frustrating few days filled with delayed permits, undelivered supplies, and impromptu visits from Miss Marjorie, Victoria, Rachel, and Eden. The ladies had well-meaning purposes for being there, but nevertheless were constantly mixing up schedules and making it impossible to find private time with Peter. The only time the two of them talked to each other was in someone else's company, with each meeting more awkward than the last. Other than a few sparse texts trying to find a time to meet up, their 'talk' still had yet to happen.

And to top it all off, it was Valentine's Day. The one day of the year devoted to love, or the potential blush of love in her case. Nothing ever seemed to work out in that area of her life.

A soda pop crackle and fizz sounded, signaling a text on her cell. Charlee pulled the phone out of her back pocket, disappointed to see Eden's picture on the screen.

Girl's night. Unvalentine's. 7 pm.

She chewed on her lip. Freddy's Unvalentine's Celebration was uber popular. Live bands and giveaways drew in both couples and singles from the area, but she generally skipped all the hoopla and stayed home. Would Peter be there? Tyler and the other guys generally went, trying to win tickets for the upcoming baseball season.

What the heck. Why not? Her fingers tapped out a reply.

I'll be there. See you soon.

Eden's response popped right back.

Awesome.

Charlee skipped the kitchen, planning to eat at Freddy's, and went straight to her bedroom. More specifically to her closet, where she found the typical t-shirts and work jeans. She had a few nicer outfits, but nothing really appropriate for a Valentine's get together.

She pulled her cell out and sent another message to Eden.

I don't know what to wear.

There was a short pause, then the soda pop crackle and fizz bubbled up from her phone.

Who is this and what have you done with Charlee?

She snorted.

Ha ha. So funny. Which do you think would be better: My Little Pony Apocalypse or the new Go Smurf Yourself t-shirt?

She didn't have to wait long for Eden's reply.

Makeover time! Enjoy a hot bubble bath, then leave the rest to me. See you at 6 pm.

Charlee set the phone on her bathroom counter, then started filling the deep soaker tub. She glanced at the phone, torn between wanting Peter to call and the thrilling anticipation of surprising him.

She just hoped he'd be at Freddy's tonight. And maybe, just maybe, Valentine's wouldn't suck for once.

She grabbed her phone and gave in to the impulse, except instead of texting Peter, she sent a message off to Mari wishing her a Happy Unvalentine's Day. By the time Charlee was sinking into the hot, bubbly water, Mari had responded.

Unvalentine's. I forgot about that quirky Crystal Creek tradition. Have any plans for tonight?

Charlee was careful to keep a good grip on the phone and leaned over the edge of the tub. *Meeting up with some of the girls at Freddy's. Maybe we'll score some good gift certificates. You?*

It's me, some yoga pants, and mastering the Downward Facing Dog.

Charlee almost dropped her phone to the floor as she laughed. Another message from Mari came up on her screen.

That sounded dirty, didn't it? Didn't mean it that way. Promise.

Charlee typed, deleted, and retyped her message because she kept spelling things wrong while she laughed. *You are a bad, bad girl. You totally need to be here. We'd have a blast together.*

Maybe next year. Have fun tonight. Remember, don't kiss any frogs. They generally don't turn into princes.

Charlee smiled, sent one last text, then set her phone aside to enjoy the remainder of her bath before the makeover torture began.

When Eden arrived, she had a duffel bag over her shoulder and a boat load of clothes on hangers draped over her arm.

"You weren't kidding when you said makeover, huh?" Charlee tried to laugh but fell short.

Eden grabbed her arm and dragged her back to the bedroom. "Charlee, you have a gorgeous body that you sadly cover up in grimy jeans and huge t-shirts. Tonight, you are going to knock every single guy off his bar stool."

This time Charlee truly laughed. "Have you had a few drinks already?"

Eden pulled out the vanity chair and shoved Charlee into it. "Relax and learn, my friend."

Charlee was amazed by all the pots and tubes of makeup, not to mention the hair products. Eden started on her hair first—adding mousse, then grabbing a flat brush and hair dryer. She was amazed by the magic she created with just those three things. Her hair—though still short and choppy—actually looked cute and flirty.

"How did you do that?" she asked, awed.

"My friend Taralyn is a hair stylist. She taught me all sorts of tricks when she was going through beauty school. It's a good thing I paid attention, too, because now she's married with a toddler and far too busy." Eden smiled. "I'll have to introduce you sometime. You'd really like her."

Charlee nodded, then winced when Eden broke out the makeup.

"Listen, I'm not going to clump up your face. I'm going to clean and moisturize, then add some light touches. I know you're not a big makeup fan and we don't want you going out looking like a clown. Trust me, though. Alright?"

She looked at Eden, with her perfect funky black hair and beautifully made up face. Charlee sighed and nodded. Then she closed her eyes while Eden worked her magic.

It was actually rather relaxing to let someone do her makeup. Eden chatted and told her what she was doing. Charlee listened with half an ear. She'd never used all this gunk before. If it turned out okay, maybe she'd ask Eden for some additional lessons on hair and makeup.

After what was only about ten minutes, Eden declared she was done. Charlee was surprised, but also disappointed. There must not have been much Eden could do to make her look good.

She opened her eyes and met her reflection. Wow! Was that really her? She raised her hand and lightly touched her cheek.

"The mineral powder foundation evens out your skin tone and takes away any shininess. You are a lucky duck and have a gorgeous even tone, flawless skin." She narrowed her eyes at Charlee. "Some of us would kill for that, you know."

Huh. Imagine that. Another female actually envious of something she had.

"Aside from that, I only used a touch of this sheer blush to give your cheek bones some sparkle, added black mascara, a little neutral eye shadow—again, for some sparkle, then this sheer lipstick. It's a natural pink color and adds just enough kiss-ability to your lips. Plus it's a fourteen-hour lipstick, which means no worries about it coming off. Unless you do some major making out."

Charlee flushed. Making out with a certain someone was on the top of her hope-to-do-tonight list.

"Hmm, you won't need any blush if you keep that up." Eden winked. "Now, let's go check out your closet."

Charlee groaned.

"Where do you keep your jeans?" Eden rubbed her hands together, ready for the next part of the makeover.

Charlee motioned to her dresser and Eden dug through it. "What are you looking for?"

"I saw you a few months ago with a pair of clingy dark

jeans, but all I can find in here are work jeans."

"Yeah, those don't actually fit me." Charlee stopped when she saw Eden's surprised look.

"They fit perfectly!"

Charlee squirmed. "They were too tight."

Eden narrowed her eyes at her again. "Too tight where?"

"Across my butt and, well, everywhere." She couldn't have a perfect body like Eden, who was now rolling her eyes.

"Charlee, they're stretch jeans. They're supposed to be tight. They loosen up as you wear them, but the molded-to-your-body effect is great on the testosterone."

"Oh . . ." Charlee went to a box of clothes she kept under her bed that she only took out when her mother nagged her enough. She pulled out the jeans in question and slipped them on. They did indeed fit like a glove. "You don't think it makes me look too much like a boy? I have no butt."

"You have an excellent butt and those jeans hug it just right."

She turned and for once actually admired her butt in the mirror, wondering if Peter would like the backside view. She flushed again.

"Curiouser and curiouser," Eden murmured from behind her.

Charlee simply met her gaze in the mirror and smiled. "How about a top? I can't walk into Freddy's like this.

"At least not without starting a riot. That bra, though." Eden looked at it with disapproval. "Don't you have anything sexier?"

Charlee looked down at her simple nude bra. "Ah, no. This is as sexy as I get."

Eden's smile was wicked in a somewhat good, but slightly terrifying way. "I see a shopping trip in our future, my friend."

Charlee grinned, too, while Eden sorted through the pile of clothes she brought with her. She found what she wanted, then tossed a tank top and short sleeved shirt at her. "Layer the tank under the top, then we'll talk accessories."

The tank top was a medium turquoise color and had a round neckline. She pulled it over her head, then topped it off with the deep V dark charcoal gray top. The material wasn't like a t-shirt though. It was light and airy, similar to the tank top under it. With the material hugging her torso, she actually looked like she had curves for a change. Not super curves and not the sexy curves like Eden, but still. She looked like she actually had boobs—and they looked pretty good, too.

"They'll look even better with the right bra," Eden said, reading her mind.

"Shopping trip," Charlee said and Eden's face split in a happy grin. There may have even been an exchange of giggles, but she wouldn't admit to it in public.

"Accessories!" Eden brought out a bag filled with jewelry. "Now, the secret of accessories is that they accent and draw attention to details. A few bangles for your wrist." She clamped some gold bracelets around Charlee's wrist. They made a pretty clinking noise when she moved. "Every time you lift a glass, men will look from the bracelet, up your arm and into your eyes. Where they might see a glimpse of these." She handed her some sparkly studs, which Charlee put on. "And last, a little bling for your lovely neck."

Eden draped a necklace around her and secured it. Charlee reached up and fingered the strands of gold which held a sparkly circle pendant nestled at the base of her throat. It was simple, but like Eden said, it added just a touch of bling.

"Some sandals, my dear." Eden pulled out a pair of black, closed toe sandals with a slightly raised heel in the back. Charlee slid her feet in and looked at the full-length mirror in her room. Amazing. Such simple things, but such a big impact.

"Perfect," Eden declared. "You're going to knock some poor guy off his feet tonight."

Charlee knew exactly who she hoped that someone would be.

Chapter Eleven

CHARLEE FOLLOWED EDEN down a few steps and into the bar where the Unvalentine's celebration was going strong. Of course, men took notice of Eden. Who wouldn't with her dramatic look? Charlee envied Eden's style, especially her hair in a twisted messy knot, the back cascading down just past her shoulders.

But for the first time, the guys' gazes slid from Eden to her and stayed there.

Dang! Did that ever feel good.

As they worked their way through the long balloon streamers to where Victoria and Rachel waited, Charlee looked through the crowd, but didn't see Peter. Disappointment fell heavy on her, but Eden nudged her arm.

"Don't worry about it. He'll probably be here later."

Charlee looked up in surprise. "Wh-who?"

Eden rolled her eyes. "You know exactly who. Don't sweat it. Just have fun. Hey, hey, look who's free from the cast!"

They reached the table and greeted Victoria and Rachel with hugs and compliments on being able to see Rachel's toes again. A waitress arrived for their drink orders, but before Charlee could order, Eden asked for two strawberry daiquiris.

"You know, I can order for myself," she grumped.

Rachel leaned over, her auburn hair swinging to the side. "Oh no. Unvalentine's Day tradition. Daiq's to kick off, then no beer. Only the good stuff."

Charlee hoped the 'good stuff' included soda because she wasn't a big drinker. The daiquiris arrived and Victoria raised her glass. "To being single, smart, and sexy women."

The ladies smiled, toasted, and sipped their drinks.

"So, who's looking good tonight, ladies?" Victoria asked, scanning the dance floor.

Rachel's face flushed deep pink. "Well, I know who looks good to me."

Everyone's attention turned to the bar, where Graydon was chatting with Tyler and some of the guys. His tall, muscular frame made him hard to miss. She often wondered what it had been like to go from a sports celebrity to retired at such a young age. There was just so much time spread out before him.

He looked up and did the manly nod thing towards the ladies at their table. Charlee turned her attention to Rachel and the sparkle in her eyes as she gazed back at her man.

"Graydon is here? Not exactly our normal Unvalentine's Day tradition, but I guess we'll let it pass." Eden picked up Rachel's left hand, admiring the ring's glimmer.

"Well, there's only one man I want to dance with, especially now that I actually can dance. Besides, tradition or not, I couldn't celebrate tonight without my sweetheart."

Charlee took another sip of her drink to keep an internal sigh from escaping. Her friends' relationship statuses had never bothered her before. So why did it make her feel, well, extremely single, now? And yes, a little bit lonely, too.

"Excuse me, ladies." Matthew Craig sidled up between Eden and Victoria. Victoria scooted to the edge of her chair, putting more distance between the Crystal Creek City Councilman. Matthew greeted each of them, then turned to Victoria. "I heard you left a message for me at the office."

"Yes," she replied, her face passive and her tone disinterested. "Generally a message that comes through an office implies the request of a reply during business hours, Mr. Craig."

Matthew sighed. "Always so formal. Don't you ever loosen up, Tori?"

Victoria shrunk back, eyes wide and blinking, but she quickly pulled herself together. A saucy grin graced her red lips. She leaned forward and trailed her red-tipped pointer finger down the front of Matthew's shirt, coming to a stop at center of his chest. "So you prefer things, shall we say, friendlier?"

Charlee felt like she was sitting at a tennis match, watching Rachel and Eden's heads bop back and forth between the two, knowing that her own head was doing the same thing. What in the world was going on? First Victoria was like ice and now she's all honey and sweet?

"I like friendly, too, Mr. Craig. In fact, the Women in Business group is all about strengthening our friendship with organizations in the community. Which is why I contacted you." Victoria moved her hand away from Matthew's chest and rested it against his forearm. Then she twisted in just the right way to display her cleavage to a better advantage. At least to Matthew's viewing advantage. "You see, Mr. Craig, we are holding a special auction for the local Autism society, to benefit all those sweet kids and their families. We would love to have you participate."

Matthew's Adam's apple bobbed up and down as he swallowed before answering. "I'm happy to help however I can."

"Perfect." Victoria returning to a more business-like pose, her hand dropping to her lap. "My secretary will call yours to set up a fashion consult and the photo shoot."

Now it was Matthew's turn to blink. "Photo shoot?"

Victoria nodded, innocently—but the curved smile on her lips reminded Charlee more of the cat who got all the cream. "For the bachelor's auction, of course. You will fetch quite a bundle for the society."

Matthew's face flushed. "Tori—"

Victoria's eyes narrowed once again. "We can talk more during business hours, Mr. Craig," she said firmly, then smiled. "Have your secretary call mine." With that, she turned back to her girlfriends, giving Matthew a cold shoulder as she started a new conversation before he stomped off.

"What in the world was that?" Charlee exclaimed. Before she got the answer she craved, they were once again interrupted.

"Charlee, it's wonderful to see you again."

She turned in her seat to find Mark, all decked out in cowboy dress attire for the evening. Dang it all. Just when the evening was getting interesting. "Mark, it's nice to see you outside of Indulgence Row. How's the landscaping going?"

"Great, but no business talk tonight. Would you like to dance?" He extended his hand in an invitation.

Charlee looked at her table companions. Eden gave a slight nod, so she took his hand and accepted.

Out on the dance floor, Mark proved that he actually had good rhythm. He soon had her laughing and twirling around to a thumping country song. When the song ended, Juan Two from her crew asked for the next dance, which ended up being a throwback Bruce Springsteen song. Oh, the memories it evoked. And from there, the evening just got better. Line dances with her girlfriends, a second strawberry daiquiri, and more men asking for her, yes, tomboy Charlee, to dance and flirt. It was incredibly fun and dang it all if she didn't feel desirable.

After yet another song ended, Charlee declined another dance invitation from Mark and made her way to the bar for something non-alcoholic and a snack too.

"Having fun, Charlee?"

She turned to find Peter at her side, a bottle of beer dangling from his fingers. "Peter! When did you get here?" She beamed at him, but he seemed to just scowl. "What's wrong?" She placed her hand on his arm.

"I don't think I've ever seen you out on the dance floor quite so much before," he said, sounding like a petulant teenager.

She giggled. "I'm just having fun with the girls."

"Looked more like you were enjoying the men to me," he replied, leaning closer. "Getting all dressed up, flirting. Looking for a better offer?"

Now it was her turn to scowl. Frustrating, irritating men! "Maybe I decided to test your theory out."

"My theory?" He arched his brow quizzically.

She stepped a little closer, raising wide, innocent eyes up to meet his frustrated ones. "That men find me attractive. Sexy even." She had the pleasure of seeing his eyebrows smash down. The bartender had perfect timing, sliding her cream soda across the bar. "Well, I should get back to my friends. Later, Peter."

She patted his cheek and sauntered away. Irritating idiot, she fumed. She took a few deep sips of her drink, then rejoined her girlfriends on the dance floor.

WHAT IN HADES was she up to, Peter wondered as he watched Charlee walk away, swinging her sweet behind. He took a gulp of his beer.

"Screwing things up already, Elliott?" Tyler jostled him, almost pushing him off the bar stool.

"Dammit, Jackson. Don't mess with me right now." Peter elbowed Tyler so he wasn't crowding his space. He was still ticked about the $125 that went out of his bank account to cover the speeding ticket.

Tyler regarded him steadily, then blew out a breath. "I may not like the idea of my best friend and sister together, but I'm glad she's choosing a good guy for a change." He nodded out at the dance floor. "What's going on?"

Peter leveled a glare at Tyler, before nodding. That was probably the only apology he was going to get. "Dang if I know. I showed up and she was out there, dancing away. And the guys are flocking to her like bugs to a zap light."

Tyler chuckled. "Dude. You're jealous."

Peter did not appreciate his best friend's assessment, even if it was true.

He took another drink, mulling over what to do next. This week had not gone well. Between work and his dad constantly hounding him, keeping him working on bids, contracts, and other pain-in-the-butt paperwork until late each evening, he never got to talk to Charlee. He wanted to take her out for their first official date tonight. Treat her to something romantic and memorable.

There was nothing romantic about how the night was turning out.

"You know, if it was me and that was my woman out there, I sure as heck wouldn't be sitting here watching other men put their hands on her." Tyler shot him one last glance before turning back to the bar.

Peter looked back out to where Charlee was indeed getting pawed, not that she seemed to mind. Then the guy's hand slid down over her behind.

Well, that was enough.

He set his bottle on the bar with a decisive clink, then strode out onto the dance floor. Just in time to nudge the other guy away from Charlee with a brief, "Excuse me."

"Hey," the guy started to say, but backed off when Peter leveled a stare at him. The poor fellow scrambled away, just as a slow dance came on. Peter pulled Charlee in close until their bodies barely brushed against each other in the gentle sway of the song.

"What was that all about?" Charlee asked, her hands resting on his upper arms.

"I don't like anyone messing with what's mine," he said, knowing he sounded like an idiotic caveman.

"Yours, huh?" Charlee quirked her eyebrow.

What did she think was so funny? He expected her to be ticked off. Instead, she slid her hands from his upper arms to clasp behind his neck and pull his head down close until her lips were just a breath's beat from his ear.

"And why exactly do you think I'm yours?" she asked, tilting her head to the side.

"Well," he stammered. "I know we haven't had a chance to talk more, but I thought it was pretty clear the other night about how I feel and stuff."

Her eyes sparkled and teased. "Exactly how do you feel, Mr. Elliott?"

He sighed. He needed more time and somewhere a heck of a lot quieter than a bar room dance floor packed to the brim to talk through it. "Can we talk somewhere private, where it's just you and me?"

She nodded her agreement. "Are you done being an idiot?"

His hands gripped her hips. "Charlee, I have a feeling I'll always be an idiot where you're concerned."

She softly smiled. "I kind of like that."

Quiet settled around them as they swayed together. He wanted to slide his hands around her waist, but he wasn't sure if he could control them. Better to stay where they were on her hips, his thumb just brushing her waist.

"You look really pretty tonight," he said softly.

She lowered her head, not meeting his eyes. "Eden gave me a makeover."

He put his finger under her chin, bringing her head back up

to see his sincerity. "It's not the makeover. You're more confident, your eyes sparkle." He shrugged. "You're just you, but in 'come get me' mode."

She tilted her head to the side, as if weighing his comment. "Maybe," she replied. "Or maybe it's the tight jeans."

It was his turn to laugh. He had to admit he rather liked the jeans.

All too soon, the song was over. Before he could suggest grabbing a bite to eat, Mark was back, urging Charlee to dance. She shook her head no, saying she needed a break.

"Come on, Charlee," Mark grabbed her hand. "You promised me another dance."

Peter removed his hand from around her waist. "She said she needed a break. Why don't you ask again later?"

Mark moved in closer, the stench of a few too many beers on his breath. "Don't think that just because you decided to get your behind off the bar stool means you get to call the shots."

"Hey, there aren't any freaking dance cards here. She said no, so back off," Peter hunched his shoulders. Tyler came up beside him and rested his hand on Peter's shoulder.

"Boys, settle down." Tyler said in a good-natured tone with an underlying firmness. "You're causing a scene in front of the ladies."

Peter looked over at Charlee, whose eyes were wide. He started to apologize, then Charlee cried out and his face exploded in pain. He stumbled backwards, knocking into the people dancing behind him before regaining his footing. He looked up to see Tyler holding back Mark. Everything else faded away, except for Mark's octopus arms, grabbing at air while Charlee scrambled out of his reach.

Then Peter charged forward, his shoulder plowing into

octo-jerk's soft stomach and tackled him to the ground. They grappled and rolled. He got one good punch in before hands hauled them apart, shoving them to opposite sides of the room.

"Cool it! Peter!" Tyler gave him a sharp smack on the cheek, drawing Peter's attention from Mark to him. "Knock it off or I'll put you in a jail cell until you calm down. Is that what you want?"

Peter drew in some ragged breaths and shook his head. "He wouldn't stop badgering Charlee."

"I know," Tyler's voice was grim. "Are you in control now or do I need to find a babysitter to watch you?"

Peter reached up to his jaw and winced in pain. "No, I'm fine."

Tyler gave him a serious once over, making sure he was indeed good, then nodded. "Wait here while I take care of the rest of this." He turned and marched over to where Mark was whining and pitching a fit about being attacked.

"You okay?" Charlee asked, drawing his attention to his other side.

Her face was creased with worry. He hated that he put it there. "I'm sorry. That was stupid."

Her hand cupped his jaw where it throbbed and was already swelling. "You need to get some ice on that," she said. Rachel, Victoria and Eden joined her, each babbling about what happened.

The combination of women's chatter and the punch made his head ache. Yeah, he needed to get home, down some pain meds and grab a bag of peas for his face.

Tyler returned, standing next to his sister, his hands on his hips and a frown on his face. "Let's go, Elliott. I'll give you a ride home."

"I can drive myself," he replied.

"Did you have more than one beer tonight?" Tyler demanded. "Cause if you did and you got in a bar fight, then I'd say that could be thought of as overindulging, inhibiting your ability to think clearly."

Aw, nuts. He nodded for Tyler to lead the way. "Sorry," he muttered again to Charlee.

She stood on her tip-toes and surprised him by placing a light kiss on his cheek, then ushering him out to follow her brother.

This was not how he envisioned the night ending. He climbed into Tyler's truck and slammed the door shut. A couple other guys escorted Mark out of the bar and into another vehicle, presumably to get him safely home as well. At least he knew Charlee would be safe with her girlfriends.

He groaned and leaned his head back against the seat. All of his hopes for the night went up in smoke.

Tyler pulled out of the parking lot. A few blocks down the road, he reached over and thumped Peter on the chest. "Thanks for looking out for my sister."

Peter rubbed the sore spot on his chest. "You're welcome." He glanced over at Tyler, who had a wicked grin on his face. "What's so funny?"

"Never thought I'd see 'Peter the Good Guy', the one my mom is always telling me I need to be more like, in a bar room brawl. I can't wait to tell her about it."

Peter's lips curled up a bit, too. "She'll just say it's your bad influence."

"Probably, but it'll be worth it to see the look on her face."

And just like that, Peter knew everything was good with his best friend. Maybe the night wasn't a complete loss after all.

Chapter Twelve

CHARLEE GRIPPED PETER'S TRUCK KEYS in her hand, staring at the closed door before her. Peter's door. All she had to do was knock. Just reach out her hand and tap three times. How could such a simple thing be so difficult?

Instead she straightened her brown polo, pulled on the sleeves of her winter coat and wiped her hands over the thighs of her just-washed jeans. Having only one pair of girly jeans proved problematic this morning when she decided to call her brother to get Peter's truck. So she threw the jeans into the washer for a quick cycle to get rid of the smoky bar room smell. She definitely needed to take Eden up on her offer of a shopping trip. And before that, to make a list of the various types of clothes she should buy.

She also needed to stop procrastinating. She took a deep breath and knocked. Petunia's deep barks carried through the door, then a few thumps and Peter's murmured voice calming the dog before opening the door.

Peter stood before her in a casual t-shirt and jeans with bare feet. Why she noticed his feet and surprisingly hairy toes, she had no clue. When she glanced back up and met his eyes, she saw a brilliant burst of blues and yellows across his cheek. Her hand itched to reach up and gently pass her fingers over the injury, but uncertainty held her back. Instead she shifted her weight to the other foot. "Hey," she said.

"Charlee, come in out of the cold."

He stepped back and she edged past him. "So, um, I went with Tyler to pick up your truck." She dangled the keys from her finger, expecting him to take them. Instead he pushed the door closed, then stepped closer while she automatically stepped away until the door was at her back. Peter tugged on the edges of her coat, making the space around them feel more intimate. Her eyes widened as he tipped her head back.

His voice was deep and smooth when he spoke. "We didn't get to talk last night."

"Nope," she squeaked, then cleared her throat. She clutched the keys in one hand, while the other pressed flat against the door behind her, hoping it would keep her grounded. "No, we didn't."

He ran his thumb over her cheek, the light friction from calluses sending a shiver of delight down her neck. Then he reached into her coat pocket, took out her cell phone and turned off the ringer before returning it. "I'm not taking any chances," he said. "No interruptions."

"No interruptions," she agreed, her heart pounded against her chest, much like a plank of wood must feel as nails were hammered into it.

Bam, bam, bam!

This was it. No backing out. She and Peter. Her brother's best friend. The guy she'd known for just about forever. They were going to have a DTR. Define the relationship talk. Do people still call it a DTR or was that just high school? Holy magnolias. She was so nervous, she almost wished she could ask for a time out to go puke, then get back to the conversation.

But no. She was in. All in.

Right?

And really. He could talk now. Cause she was just standing here, her hand against the door, grounding her to reality, trying not to puke. Just waiting for him to start.

Instead, he smiled. "You don't have to hold your breath, Charlee. I'm not going to punish you. Unless, of course, you like to be punished." He winked.

Winked! Then she just about swallowed her tongue, because, oh-my-gosh, what if Peter was into that stuff? She dropped the truck keys.

"Charlee! I was just kidding!" He brushed the hair back from her forehead, then down to tuck strands behind her ear. "It's just me. Relax. More importantly, breathe. I don't want to have to call 911 because you passed out."

She sucked in a deep breath, then another.

Peter leaned back a little. "Do you always get like this when a guy tries to tell you he likes you?"

Her breathing hitched. He leaned in, his forehead rested against hers. "Breathe with me. Deep breath in, then let it out."

She did, her eyes on his. From this close, his eyes looked mostly crossed and she couldn't help but giggle.

"You're cute." He dropped a kiss on the tip of her nose. "Think you can handle a little more truth?" She nodded and he continued. "I've liked you for a while, ever since you returned from college."

This time it was her turn to confess. She reached up and

placed her fingertip over his lips. "Really? I mean, you're Tyler's best friend and I'm like an annoying sister, right?" She shrugged, her hand moved to his shoulder. "I've had moments when I thought about it, but you were totally out of my reach. So I pushed any feelings other than friendship aside."

"And now?" he prompted.

She felt warmth infuse her cheeks and desperately wanted to look down, but braved it out, keeping steady contact with his blue-gray eyes. "I like you, too."

Four simple words, but she wished for a whole pile of blankets to duck her head under and hide.

His eyebrow lifted. "A little or a lot?"

"A lot," she squeaked.

"Like, a lot, a lot or a lot, a lot, a lot?" he teased.

A laugh bubbled from deep inside and she whacked his shoulder. "You are such a dork!" He lightly tickled her sides while she squirmed and giggled. When they calmed and he held her in a loose hug, she chewed on her lip. "Do you think it will be weird? You know, with us having known each other for most of our lives?"

Peter rubbed his hands down her back, coming to rest in a secure, comforting hold. "I think it will be perfect."

She tilted her head back, releasing the poor lip she had gnawed on. "Really?"

In answer, he lowered his head until his lips met hers. At first it was just a light pass, brushing against each other, but then he deepened the kiss, capturing her lips with more meaning. Her hands met at the back of his head, sinking deep into his light brown hair, lost in the feelings and wonder of Peter. As the kiss gentled to light brushing strokes again, his fingertips caressed her cheek until he tucked her head to his shoulder as he held her in his arms. He broke the silence with just one word that made her heart warm.

"Perfect."

IT HAD BEEN A GLORIOUS DAY—spent completely together. They took Petunia to the dog park. Charlee's toes froze in her girly shoes, but it was worth it to see Petunia knock Peter on his butt while playing tug of war with a rope. Peter landing in a big, cold puddle made it all the more hilarious. When they returned to his apartment, he quickly showered while Charlee ordered pizza, which landed them in this moment. All snuggled up on the couch, each with a plate piled high with slices of extra cheesy gooeyness.

"So, how is this going to work?" Charlee asked.

"Well," Peter said, holding up a slice of pizza. "First you take a bite, then chew, chew, chew—"

Charlee thumped him with a couch pillow. "Not that. I meant us. This," she said, waving her hand between the two of them, indicating their relationship.

"I vote for dating. And kissing. Lots of kissing. And more pizza," Peter said, giving her a wink before taking another bite.

She rolled her eyes. Did boys ever actually grow into men? Or did men just get good at hiding their little boy side in public? After a moment of silence, because really, she didn't need to respond to his answer, Peter set the pizza aside and got serious.

"What are you worried about?" he asked, taking her hand

in his and playing with her fingers.

Where to start? There seemed to be a million what if's tumbling around in her head. Maybe the best place to begin would be the people closest to them. "Let's start with my brother. You guys are best friends."

Peter nodded. "Yes, we are, and he and I will figure it out."

What a frustrating response. Seriously? Charlee just wanted to shake them both. "Why are guys like that? Shouldn't he be happy about a good guy dating his sister?"

Peter shrugged. "It's complicated. Guy's just don't talk about all that emotional stuff, at least not to each other. Not sincere stuff, like you and your friends. We razz on each other and talk smack. Sometimes it involves the women we date. Adding a friend's sister into the mix, well, it's just not cool. It's messes up the code."

"There's a code?" She was intrigued by this new insight into a guy's world.

"To not take women seriously." He held up his hand, stopping her rebuttal about that comment. "Not that we don't take women or relationships seriously, but that as friends, as buddies, we let it all roll. If we break up with someone, we joke about asking her out or that she was too hot for him anyway. Just stupid stuff, right?"

"Sounds pretty pathetic to me." She couldn't believe her brother and his friends were such idiots. Didn't they ever take a psychology class? Or simply remember home economics from high school? Their home economics teacher didn't pair them up into marriages with babies, jobs and finances to juggle simply for her amusement.

Peter just shrugged again. "It's guy language. We don't get

offended, we laugh it off and move on. Adding someone important into the mix, like you, complicates things."

Charlee nodded, trying to understand their system of friendship. "Because talking smack about Tyler's sister and how she's too hot wouldn't make Tyler very happy, huh?"

"Or me," Peter said, pulling her in for a quick kiss before letting her settle back onto the couch again.

"Okay, I get it, but you do think Tyler is going to come around, right?"

"See this," Peter said, pointing to his bruised face. "Taking a punch for you put him well on the way to being okay with us."

Charlee snorted. Of course, a punch in the face would make a bigger impact than a conversation with a sibling or friend. In some ways, men were still a bunch of cave-dwelling dweebs.

"What else?" Peter asked.

Charlee grabbed a throw pillow and pulled it onto her lap, squeezing it to her middle before asking her next question. "Okay, how about work and your dad who hates my guts?"

Peter looked down, took a deep breath and released it before meeting her eyes again. "As far as my dad goes, he'll have to figure out how to accept us. I can date anyone I want and I choose you." He squeezed her hand for emphasis. "On the work front, I'm still trying to figure that one out. I don't think Elliott Construction is going to be doing very many renovations after the Indulgence Row project, so maybe there isn't much conflict there. Any thoughts?"

Her fingers twisted the soft corner of the pillow around and around, making it tight, then releasing it to unspiral back to its normal shape. "I honestly hope things can get smoothed out with your dad. I would hate to pull you apart from your parents."

Peter placed his hand over hers where she was twisting the pillow corner. "Even if that were to happen, it wouldn't be because of you. It would be his stubborn pride."

"Still . . ." Charlee paused, not sure how to continue, to express the knot of worry tucked inside that she'll be the root of ruining the relationship with his parents. She sucked her lower lip in and sunk her teeth into it.

Peter placed his finger over her mouth, gently nudging her lip out. "There isn't anything you can do to change how my dad chooses to behave. It's going to okay. How about we figure out our working relationship instead?"

She still felt like he wasn't considering the full impact their relationship could have, but decided to go with his suggestion to move on. "Well, I think you're a little optimistic on the work front. There are going to be times when we bid on the same projects. Your dad has a lot of connections in the community. It's impossible for us to not cross paths."

"But he doesn't have a master renovator anymore," Peter countered. "That was where you made Elliott Construction shine. I think there will be a mix of customers who return to Elliott Construction for bids, but I anticipate a good number of past clients deciding to go directly to you for renovations."

Charlee winced. Taking business from EC was just going to fuel George's anger, especially if he thinks Peter gave her any leads. There was really only one solution she thought would work. "It might be best not to talk about work at all."

Peter laughed. "Construction is a big part of our day. We need to be able to talk about it together."

"Okay, I get that. How about if we agree not to talk about

potential projects we're bidding on? That way no one can accuse us of stealing bids or having inside information."

"That sounds fair. Should we shake on it?" Peter extended his hand.

When she took his hand, he pulled her in for another kiss, this one a little longer than the last one. She brought her hand up, rubbing her fingertips over his five o'clock shadow. The rough stubs of his beard combined with the deepening of the kiss sent a cascade of tingles through her. She was reluctant when he pulled back, not ready for their contact to end. She blinked and focused on Peter again.

"Anything else?" he asked, waggling his eyebrows.

"Well..." Charlee said, hesitating.

"Woman, you're killing me!" Peter put his hand over his heart and collapsed into the back of the couch.

Heat rushed through her face. She actually didn't want to bring up the next topic, but figured if they were talking, they may as well get it all out there. Peter must have sensed the change in her thoughts because he sat up and stopped goofing around. "Ahem, yeah," she began, trying to get up the courage to blurt out her admission. "I've never really been good at relationships. I mean, other than short kind-of boyfriends in college, things usually didn't go past the second or third date. So, yeah, I guess I'm trying to say I'm not good at this whole boyfriend/girlfriend thing."

"Hmm..." Peter said, stroking this chin with his hand like a detective. "I'm thinking what you need are some lessons. Relationship lessons." Charlee whacked him with the couch pillow again. Peter laughed and grabbed the pillow, tugging it out of her hands. "No, seriously, I think it will be fun. We can call them 'How to remodel a friendship into a romantic relationship.'"

"Don't you think I should get those kinds of lessons from experts, like a couple whose been married for twenty or more years?"

His hands came around her waist and pulled her a little closer. "Nah. Their tips worked for them, but we need to figure out our own secrets for success. Let's start with lesson number one right now. We'll call it the pizza lesson."

She shook her head. This had to be the craziest thing she ever heard. "What does pizza have to do with dating?"

"In friendship mode, pizza was all about brainstorming our next steps for a project or hanging out with friends." His hand moved up and he stroked her cheek with the back of his knuckles, ending by brushing the edge of her lower lip. "In relationship mode, it means ordering pizza with no onions and bringing breath mints for kissing."

She smiled. "Dang it, I forgot the breath mints. Guess that means no more kissing."

Peter tugged on her hand. "But you ordered cheese pizza, so I think we'll be okay."

She couldn't help but laugh as Peter pulled her closer until she was sitting across his lap. His hands slipped into her hair, cradling her head, then he lowered his head until their lips met and clung. Her hands moved up over his strong arms, feeling his muscles bunch and move as their kiss deepened, each touch like sparks showering down from a hot metal power tool.

She needed to rethink these relationship lessons. They might not be so bad after all.

Chapter Thirteen

I KISSED A FROG and he just might be a prince.

Charlee squirmed into a cozy spot on her bed, then stared at the message she typed for Mari. She bit her lip, then tapped the send button. She turned the screen off and set the phone face down on her bed, thinking about the past few days. Life had been normal—work, grocery shopping, sharing meals together, and working on projects in the evening, or just chilling in front of the TV. Nothing special, yet it was.

Peter had been there for all of it. His presence made it all new, even fun. Especially in the grocery store aisles. That man knew more commercial jingles and taglines than anyone she'd ever met. She couldn't help but smile as she thought about him acting out and singing the Double Mint gum commercials.

He was proving to be into the whole relationship analogy thing, too. Earlier that evening as they pushed a cart through the store, he talked about how relationships were like grocery shopping.

"You shop around for the best price, brand, flavor, and texture," he said. "It's all about trying different things until you find what you prefer the most. In relationship mode, you've dated, met people and discovered personalities or traits you liked or didn't like, which has narrowed down the guys you would date in the future."

Her heart thumped against her chest as she remembered his next words.

"When you finally meet the right guy, you'll keep him around forever."

Charlee laid absolutely still, just as they had frozen in the aisle, their gazes locked, taking in his words. She didn't know what he was thinking, but she certainly had been wondering where their relationship fit into his shopping analogy. Were they on the same wave length? Or did they view it differently?

Peter broke the moment by snatching up a candy bar and softly singing, "Sometimes you feel like a nut. Sometimes you don't."

She smiled, remembering how his goofiness had lightened the mood.

But still, she wondered what he had been thinking during that one brief moment...

Pop, crackle and fizz. The phone signaled a return message from Mari. *Ew. Frogs have warts! =)*

I'll take my chances, Charlee messaged back.

The replies came fast now. *Sounds like we need a girls' weekend to catch up on your love life.*

For sure. When things slow down. Maybe we can meet halfway in Colorado?

Pop, crackle and fizz. *Or I could fly you out to California. Or New York. Do you have your passport? There's great shopping in Paris!*

Charlee smiled as she typed her message. *No on the passport. Maybe to the others. BTW—I'm a big girl. I can buy my own plane tickets.*

Pop, crackle and fizz. *Sweetie, I'm not talking commercial. Believe me, my plane is much, much better.*

"Of course it was," she muttered and rolled her eyes, then composed her next message. *Okay, chick. Gotta get to sleep. Some of us need to work in the morning. Don't let the bed bugs bite. (Are there bed bugs in the pile of money you sleep on?)*

Pop, crackle and fizz. *Har har. :P   'Nite. Talk to you soon. Xoxo PS—who the heck doesn't have a passport? Get with it, woman!*

Charlee smiled before setting her phone to silent for the evening and putting it on her night stand. It was times like this she missed being a teenager and having sleepovers, talking all night long with Mari. Of course, Mari's life had been much more interesting. She actually had boyfriends to talk about, while Charlee just talked about college, architecture, and the new tools she saw at the hardware store. They were total opposites, but it worked for them. Best friends forever. At one time, she thought they might be sisters-in-law, but after high school, Mari went to California for a chance to model and Tyler enlisted in the military.

Life sure had a way of constantly changing, more often not the way you wanted. But a certain someone had her hoping that was all changing now. Her eyes fluttered closed with thoughts of Peter.

PETER GULPED DOWN SOME lukewarm coffee and noted the

time. 7:30 A.M. and he'd already been at work for an hour. He flipped over another page of the bid he was reviewing and sighed. If he could just get through this pile of paperwork, then maybe he could run out to the Indulgence Row site after lunch. Lately, he'd been leaving work with Charlee at the end of the day rather than going back to the office to put in a few more hours. Spending time with Charlee was much more rewarding than crunching numbers and fine-tuning contracts and bids. Hence the mountain of paperwork that had accumulated. His secretary, Jan, called him the night before with a warning that his father would soon notice Peter's lack of presence in the office, especially if the bids weren't filed on time.

He punched a column of numbers into his calculator, then scribbled some notes in the margin of the page for adjustments to make. He was slowly, but surely, making progress.

"It's about time you came into the office," George said, as he entered the office. He let out a grunt as he collapsed into the chair across from Peter's desk.

"Yep, trying to get this paperwork done," Peter said, only sparing a short glance at his father. Maybe if his dad saw he was busy, he would go instead of launching into a lecture.

No such luck.

"You know, if you want to take over Elliott Construction one day, then you need to show you're responsible. Not just this come into the office whenever you want junk."

Peter set his pen down and pushed aside the contract. "I am here every day. Maybe not during the hours you'd like, but I come into the office each and every day."

His father humphed again. He shook his head, as if disappointed by his son's response. Peter was sure his father would continue the often heard lecture, but surprised him by changing the subject. "I have a client dinner with the Sorenson family this Friday. Clear your schedule and be there."

Peter stifled his frustration. Dinners with long-term clients every six months was a company tradition. The husbands and wives attended together. The women gossiped while the men talked politics and business. While Peter knew the dinners were important, he also knew it didn't just come up on the schedule. It had been planned for weeks with no indication his father expected Peter to attend.

The dinner gave him an idea.

"That's a great idea, Dad. I'll be there."

George looked taken aback, but then nodded, happy with his son's compliance. He smiled and shoved himself up out of the chair. "Good, good. Friday, 8 P.M., at Brisket and Noodles. I'll call and have the reservation number changed."

As his dad turned and sauntered toward the door, Peter added. "Be sure to make that change for two."

George slowly turned to face him. "Two?"

Peter shrugged nonchalantly. "Of course. It's a couples dinner."

His father crossed his arms over his chest. "Mind telling me who the lucky girl is?"

He should play it safe and bring his sister or a casual friend. At the same time, if he really wanted to pursue a relationship with Charlee, then his father needed to deal with it now. Not later. And being with Charlee definitely trumped avoiding his father's wrath.

"Ms. Jackson."

George's eyes bulged and the vein just above his father's

eye throbbed. "Ms. Jackson's first name better not be Charlee," he said in a controlled, even voice.

"Charlee is my girlfriend," Peter stated simply.

And then all H-E-double hockey sticks broke loose.

"What in tarnation are you thinking? Did you sustain a head injury I wasn't informed about?" George paced back and forth across the room. "Do you not understand the consequences of dating someone like her?"

Peter kept his voice calm and even. "You mean someone smart, funny, and beautiful?"

His pacing stopped abruptly and George spun to face his son. "The competition!"

"Oh," Peter said. "You mean the woman who became our competition because the boss she worked for previously didn't appreciate her skills and value?"

George sputtered and shook his fisted hand with his finger pointing at Peter. "Don't you dare—"

Peter held up his hand, cutting his father off. "What do you think she's going to do, Dad? Steal our clients? Make our company go bankrupt? Haven't you figured out yet that she isn't even interested in our construction market? She doesn't want to do new construction, just renovations."

"She's taking work from us right now," George insisted.

Peter snorted. "On a project you never would have considered if Charlee hadn't brought it to your attention. The only reason you went after Indulgence Row was to be a thorn in her side. The only person trying to hurt someone else's business is you."

George's eyes were hard as they stared Peter down. "Don't even think about showing up to dinner with that traitor."

Peter shook his head. Maybe his father thought it was in defeat, but it was pity Peter felt for him. "I won't. This time, at least," he added before his father thought he won. "But don't bother changing your reservation either. I'm willing to give you time to come to grips with our relationship, but don't expect me to leave my girlfriend at home just because you're afraid of her."

"You need to have more loyalty to your family and the legacy you're going to inherit. Find someone else to date."

"As long as Charlee will have me, I consider myself a lucky man."

Peter could have sworn a growl came from deep within his father before he turned and stormed out of the office. He sucked in a deep breath, then let it out. He looked at the clock again. Had fifteen minutes really been all that passed? He didn't regret the things he said to his father. It was true, George needed to accept his relationship with Charlee, because Peter sure hoped she would be around for a long, long time to come.

He looked at the paperwork he still needed to get to. Instead of sludging along, he gathered it together and shoved it all into his briefcase. He couldn't work near his father right now. He needed some space. A corner booth at the local coffee shop sounded like the perfect respite. As an added bonus, he could grab some lunch to go to share with Charlee.

Chapter Fourteen

CHARLEE MASSAGED HER TEMPLE, hoping to ease the throbbing pain behind her eyes. She was grateful it was the end of this superbly awful work day. If only she could get the echo of the pounding hammers out of her head. She reviewed the task list on her phone. She had anticipated the list being shorter by the end of the business day. Instead, it was much, much longer. Delays in deliveries meant work didn't get done, resulting in needing to reschedule multiple inspections, which meant even more delays.

"Anything else you need from us before we head out, boss lady?" Juan One asked. Juan Two was with him, finishing off the last of his water bottle before pitching it into the recycling box along the wall.

"If you could haul the tools down to my truck and lock them in the storage box, I'd appreciate it. You guys doing anything fun tonight?"

"It's Aunt Paola's birthday," Juan Two replied with a big smile as he rubbed his stomach. "Big ol' family dinner, lots of teasing the gossipy women and playing with the kids. Want to join us?"

Having attended other family functions with the Juans, Charlee knew how fun and rambunctious the events could be. They were definitely a family she admired, but she had other plans for the night.

"Thanks, but I have some paperwork to get done. Give Paola a big hug from me though."

"Will do," Juan Two said, then gathered some more tools and followed his cousin out to the truck.

Charlee sat on a five-gallon bucket and switched her phone screen away from the ominous task list to her phone log. Several calls were listed on the log—mostly about the delayed deliveries and reworking schedules. A missed call from Anita—probably about the women's shelter class on Saturday. She'd call her back tomorrow morning. She scrolled a little more and saw a missed call from the Wheeler's.

Walter and Jenny were a sweet southern couple who purchased an older historic farmhouse in need of a lot of TLC. They weren't interested in ripping out and making the interior an updated version of a newly built house. Instead, they wanted to restore as much as possible to the original style while tastefully adding modern conveniences. Charlee had previously renovated one of their bathrooms and a sitting room.

Her thumb hovered over Jenny's name, debating if she should return their call or not. She originally did work through Elliott Construction. But at the same time, if they didn't know she wasn't working for EC, then she should let them know they needed to contact George for a bid. Not that she wanted to do any favors for George, but she also didn't want to fuel the angst if he blamed her for leading customers away. She tilted her head from side to side, stretching her neck. No matter what she chose to do, she could see George twisting it around, if he wanted. She looked back down at Jenny's name. She really did like the couple. If they don't answer, she could just leave a quick message to contact Elliott Construction directly.

She tapped the number and lifted the phone to her ear.

After a few rings, Jenny answered, excited and chattering away. "Charlee, hello! So glad you called back. We finally have enough money saved up to redo the kitchen. I'm so excited! I just know it's going to look amazing when you're finished with it. When can we get started?"

"That's why I was calling. I no longer work for Elliott Construction. If you have a pen handy, I can give you Peter's number to get a bid," Charlee said, figuring she may as well refer the Wheeler's to someone she trusted.

"Oh, sweetie, we already know you started your own business. Why, we saw Mr. Elliott just the other day and told him how excited we were to start our next renovation project. We were absolutely astounded when he said you no longer worked for him. But you know Walter, he did some research and discovered you started your own business and landed a contract with that new ladies' shopping center. Why, I told Walter, that girl's got gumption and an overflowin' bucket full of talent. We couldn't be more proud of you, sweetie. So, when can we get started?"

"I really should refer you back to Elliott Construction since they were the original company you worked with."

"Pish posh, that's just nonsense. George knows full well that we want you specifically. If he has something to say about it, he can just pay us a visit and I'll drown him in my sweet tea until he comes around to my point of view."

Charlee couldn't help but laugh. She could absolutely picture Jenny sitting at her front porch with a glass of sweet tea, batting her eyelashes. Her southern charm maneuvered even the most stubborn people to see things her way and give in. "If you really want me—"

"Oh, we do, sweetie. No one else is touching my home without your supervision."

"Well, my team is small right now and our schedule is pretty full over at Indulgence Row, but if you're willing to stretch the time frame out, I could work on the project a few evenings each week and the weekends. It means there will be more mess to live with until it's completed though, which isn't exactly ideal."

"I'm sure we can work everything out. Besides, it gives me the perfect excuse to get Walter out of the house for some weekend excursions."

Charlee did a quick mental run down of her calendar. "How about we meet Saturday to review the work you'd like done, then I can get a bid and time line together for you."

"Perfect," Jenny said. "Does ten o'clock work for you?"

"I'm teaching a class that morning. Would two o'clock in the afternoon work?"

"That's just fine. We'll see you then," Jenny said.

After wrapping up the conversation, Charlee put the appointment into her calendar. Her mind whirled with ideas. There would be parts of the project that she'd definitely need an extra set of hands, but if she could do most of it herself, it could be a great influx of cash for Transformations. She could definitely use a little more wiggle room with the business finances.

The idea of committing herself to working in the evenings and weekends didn't excite her. Especially the thought of losing time with Peter. She gnawed on her lower lip, worried how Peter would take the news. Starting a new business meant making sacrifices, and unfortunately, that meant a lot of her time right now. Success often came with difficult choices, but it was worth it in the end. She just hoped the end included a thriving business and a growing relationship with Peter.

Footsteps thumped up the stairs towards the book shop. Charlee slipped her phone into her back pocket just before Peter appeared at the top of the stairs. Even in faded jeans and a dusty work shirt, the man looked delicious. She smiled, thinking how nice it was to be able to have thoughts like that now without feeling weird about Peter being her brother's friend.

"Hey, I just wrapped up downstairs and saw your truck was still here. What's up?"

"Just finishing my to-do list for tomorrow. Are we still on for dinner?"

He pulled her up from where she sat. "Yep. How about we meet at my house?"

Charlee agreed, then gathered her binders and plans before they both left, all the while wondering how to bring up the Wheeler's project.

CHARLEE FOLLOWED PETER into his apartment, greeting Petunia as she jumped back and forth between the two of them.

"Can you let her into the backyard while I figure out dinner?" Peter asked.

"If that means I don't have to cook, you're on. Come on, Petunia," Charlee said, moving past Peter towards the sliding glass doors.

Peter snagged the back of her shirt before she could escape and pulled her into a kiss.

She playfully nipped his lower lip, then wrapped her arms around his neck and deepened the playful kiss. His hands caressed her waist, making her feel feminine and beautiful. She loved how everything felt when she was with Peter.

"Mmm . . . I was thinking about that all day long," Peter said when he broke the kiss.

"Me, too," she murmured, then tucked her head into his shoulder and breathed in his scent—a mixture of sweat, wood dust and the cologne he used when he shaved that morning. Some girls might think it was gross, but to her, it was perfection. She gave him a quick kiss on the side of his neck, then eased out of his arms. "Come on, Petunia," she said. "Let's get you outside before he changes his mind about cooking."

She heard Peter laugh as she slid open the back door and followed the dog into the yard. She checked the water dish and threw Petunia's favorite ball for a few minutes before the neighbor's dog was let out. The two dogs barked at each other, then started their nightly game of running up and down the length of their connected fences, playing together. Charlee waved to the neighbor before going back inside to join Peter.

Packages of Ramen and a bowl of cut up leftover chicken were on the counter beside the stove where Peter was busy chopping carrots and broccoli. "Is there anything I can do to help?" she asked, going to the sink to wash her hands.

"Nope, I'm just about done with the prep. Dinner should be ready in a few minutes, if you'd like to get the table set."

"What *are* you making," she asked, moving through the kitchen to gather the bowls, utensils and glasses.

He shrugged. "I just grabbed some stuff from the fridge to make a quick soup."

She sidled up to Peter to give him a kiss on the cheek. "A man who cooks. Now that's sexy."

Peter kept chopping as he replied smoothly, "A wench to do my bidding. Now that's sexy."

"Hey!" Charlee objected.

Peter paused to give her a loud smacking kiss on the lips. "Get back to work, wench."

"You know you're going to pay for that later, right?"

He winked. "I'm looking forward to it."

Charlee shook her head. "You wish." She made her way to the kitchen table. Her phone cracked, fizzed and popped from her back pocket. She set the stuff down, then pulled her phone out. After swiping and turning on the screen, a photo text from her sister, Julie, popped up.

Look who lost his first tooth! Writing a letter to the tooth fairy now!

Attached was a picture of her four-year-old nephew, Brian, with a big cheesy grin where, yes indeed, there was a tooth missing right in the middle on the bottom row.

Charlee groaned. Not because of her nephew's news, but because Julie had sent the photo on a group text and she knew what was coming next—a slew of messages from a bunch of people who haven't figured out to send their replies without hitting Reply All. As her phone started a constant vibrating and pinging frenzy, she tried to send a note to her sister. After all, her nephew deserved a cute response from his aunt, but every time she tried to type, another message came through, popping up over her keyboard.

Congrats, Brian! This from her mother.

So proud of my amazing grandson! Watch for something in the mail from Grammy and Pop Pop. From Julie's mother-in-law.

Not to be out done by the competition, her mother responded. *Mimi is going to talk to tooth fairy and make sure she brings him a special treat!*

And the conversations evolved from there with even more messages from friends and relatives, eventually going from talk about the tooth fairy to planning a play date the next day at the park, as well as an invitation from Mimi to take Julie and the kids out for lunch. She wondered if they ever thought to invite her to their mother-daughter dates? It kind of sucked being the silent bystander to their mother-daughter duo awesomeness. Charlee persevered and finally got her note sent, then silenced the phone. It should be safe to look at again in a few hours. She quickly set the table, let Petunia back in, then scooped some dry dog food into the dog's dish.

"Good timing. Dinner is served," Peter said, setting a hot pad and pot of soup on the table. He ladled the concoction into bowls while Charlee filled the glasses with ice water before joining him at the table. She eyed the Ramen noodles, chopped chicken, and steamed veggies combination as she twirled some noodles around her fork. The combination was nothing like the normal quick cup of noodles she opted for on nights she was too exhausted to cook.

She jabbed the fork into a chunk of broccoli, then watched Peter shove a forkful of soup in his mouth before grabbing for the glass of water. She laughed and blew on the food to cool it off before braving her first taste. The noodles weren't mushy and the veggies weren't undercooked. She was impressed. The art of cooking didn't make it into her gene pool. She wasn't ashamed to admit she relied on well-written recipes. She just wasn't the kind of person who opened the fridge, checked the cupboards and figured out how to combine stuff together to make something that was actually palatable. Interesting to learn that was one of Peter's talents.

"Did your mom teach you to cook like this?" she asked, motioning to her soup before dipping her fork in for more.

"Actually, my dad did."

"Really? Huh, I wouldn't have guessed that."

Peter paused before taking another bite. "You know, my dad's not all bad. He actually has some good qualities."

Charlee looked up at him in surprise. "I know he does. I have some fond memories of learning to work on construction sites with him. I remember how fun it was to conquer each of the challenges he set up for me that first summer we worked together. I know he was testing me, showing me how difficult the construction business could be, but the harder I worked, the more I loved the job." She smiled, remembering the handshake George gave her when she picked up her first paycheck. It was one of the few times he had complimented her, telling her that he wasn't just giving her money for her time, that she had worked hard and earned it. She reached across the table and put her hand over his. "I'm sorry things have been so negative and frustrating between your dad and I."

Peter's eyes shifted to the side, avoiding contact with her.

"Hey," she said. "What are you thinking about?"

Peter sucked in a deep breath, then let it out in a big whoosh. "Dad and I had a disagreement." He picked up his fork and stabbed at the noodles in his bowl before shoving a huge bite in his mouth.

"About?" she asked, trying to lead him into talking about whatever was bothering him.

He took his time chewing before swallowing and continuing the conversation. "He asked me to attend a client dinner this Friday."

"That's good, isn't it? Maybe he's getting closer to deciding to actually retire."

Peter shook his head. "The dinner has been on the company calendar for at least a month, probably more. It's frustrating that he thinks I'll drop whatever plans I might have and show up."

"Are you sure that's what he was doing? Maybe he hoped you would volunteer to come on your own and since you didn't, he asked you to join them."

"It doesn't matter. I already told him no."

"Well, I think you should call him back and say you changed your mind."

Peter shook his head again. "I told him I wouldn't go unless my date attended, too."

Charlee froze. That wasn't good. Not one itty bitty bit. "And your date is who exactly?" The exasperated look on Peter's face confirmed her suspicions.

"You, of course," he exclaimed.

Now it was Charlee's turn to shake her head. She pushed her bowl aside, not hungry with all the twisty knots developing in her stomach. "I'm sure that didn't go over well."

He snorted, then jabbed the fork into the soup. "That's an understatement."

She folded her arms in front of her and rested them on the table as she leaned forward. "Why did you even do it? You know I wouldn't have gone."

Peter straightened. "Why not? You're my girlfriend. I should be able to invite you wherever I go."

"We've already talked about this, Peter. We agreed not to talk about potential client bids or to interfere with each other's business."

Now Peter folded his arms across his chest. "It's unrealistic to think we'll be able to keep things that way. Especially the longer our relationship continues. What about when I'm running Elliott Construction one day. Will you still refuse to go to client dinners?"

"Timing is important," Charlee pointed out. "Right now, your dad isn't my biggest fan. He needs time to let me prove that my business really is separate from his. Having me at a dinner where he'll certainly be talking business with a client isn't a good idea. We just need to be sensitive to your dad's point of view, too. Does that make sense?"

Peter's hands fell to his lap and he tipped his head up to look at the ceiling for a moment before meeting her eyes again. "It does. I guess Dad and I are pushing each other's buttons right now."

"Promise me you'll think about calling him back and going

to the dinner. It would be a good gesture towards mending things."

He nodded and pushed her soup bowl back in front of her. "I will, now let's finish eating."

Charlee twirled some noodles around her fork. If she was going to bring up the extra work projects, now would probably be the best time. "Speaking of work," she said, continuing the conversation. "I've had some calls for smaller renovation jobs. I'm thinking about taking on a few, then invest the proceeds into Transformations."

"Every little bit counts. Who are you planning to pull off the bookshop crew?"

"I'm going to leave the crew there. I think it would be most cost effective if I do the majority of the work. The client I talked with today was agreeable to letting me work evenings and weekends."

Peter's expression went blank. "Which means no time for us."

"Not much, no," she admitted with disappointment.

Peter drummed his fingers on the table top.

"It's not for forever, but I can't say it would be just one job either. I think it's the best thing for Transformations right now though."

The drumming continued. Charlee wasn't sure what else to say. She felt the need to give excuses, but why should she have to get approval from Peter to do what was best for her business? It was her job to make sure it stayed afloat and had money in the bank to pay not just her bills, but her employees' bills, too. She strengthened her resolve to tell him just that when the drumming stopped.

"I'm not thrilled about it, but I understand where you're

coming from. Could we at least plan one night or few hours on the weekend to go on a date each week?"

"Absolutely," Charlee replied, relieved he didn't get upset.

Peter smiled. "Then we'll figure the rest out." He picked up his fork and speared a potato, lifting it up for her to see. "Now it's time for another relationship lesson."

Charlee laughed, relieved to have the stressful conversation over and see Peter back as his normal self. "And just what does a potato have to do with it?"

Peter lifted his eyebrows up and down in quick succession, making her laugh. "Let's start at the beginning."

"With friendship," Charlee said, resting her chin on her hand, ready to discover how Peter's mind put potatoes, friendship and romance together.

"Friendship is like French fries. They come in all sorts of shapes and sizes, but making fries all comes down to potatoes fried in oil."

"So friendship comes in all different forms, but they're all fried in oil?" Maybe she was getting the hang of this analogy thing. Or not, as Peter went on to correct her.

"No, a friendship forms because you have something in common."

"Like oil," she said, blinking her eyes like an innocent learning from a great teacher.

Peter tapped her nose and moved on. "But relationships are more like mashed potatoes."

"Mmm . . . I like mashed potatoes. Especially with gravy and corn and turkey—"

"Shush, silly girl. No mocking The Relationship Master."

A delighted laugh bubbled up out of her. "The Relationship

Master?"

"Our Relationship Master." Peter pressed his palms together and bowed his head in a Japanese greeting before continuing the conversation. "Mashed potatoes. They're still potatoes, but it's all about the little things—which spices you add, how much butter and milk, how you whip it."

"You're saying what, exactly?" Curious how he would wrap it all together.

"Meaning that even though we may not have a lot of time to spend together, we can still do little things to brighten each other's day. The little things make a big difference in how the grand scheme of the day—or relationship—turns out."

Charlee considered what he'd said and pulled out a few nuggets of wisdom. She pressed her palms together and bowed to Peter. With her head bowed, she peeked up at him and winked. "Not bad, Relationship Master. Not bad at all."

Chapter Fifteen

THE WHEELER'S OLD FARMHOUSE sat on its original thirty acres of pastures and fields, now all rented out to locals who kept their family farming traditions rolling forward, generation after generation. With the cold end of February season, the fields lay dormant. Charlee looked forward to the warmer spring weather. She loved seeing the deep brown earth churned up in rows in the rural areas of Crystal Creek. She closed her truck door and headed across the gravel driveway to the front porch. The grass was turning green, but the plants were confused with all the back and forth weather that was so common in this area. For a few days it would be warm and beautiful like late spring, but then the weather would turn to freezing rain. Some of the daffodils and tulips even pushed up through the ground searching for sunshine, only to be frozen soon after blooming.

She skipped up the steps, then paused to unbutton her coat. Thankfully, today was one of the warmer sunny days. Charlee used the knocker on the front door, then turned to look over the Wheeler's front yard. Walter and Jenny spent a lot of time planting flower beds and making their yard charming and welcoming. The flowers that were brave enough to sprout looked cheery in the sunshine. The funky wind chimes made of old pots, pans, and metal cooking spoons clunked here and there as the wind blew, then died down before it came back to gently push at the chimes again.

Charlee turned to greet Jenny as the front door opened.

"Dear sweet Charlee," Jenny exclaimed in her southern twang before gathering her into a squishy hug.

One thing Charlee learned from observing Jenny over the last few years was how you could tell a Southern woman's affections for another just by how she greeted people. General acquaintances received a loose hug and pat on the back. Businessmen were the recipients of a very lady-like handshake accompanied by a sweet smile and batting eyelashes. The ladies on the community committee you couldn't stand received an air kiss that, while looking all nice on the outside, you just knew the hugger was wishing for a can of Lysol to disinfect the area before putting her lips anywhere near it.

But family and dear friends were greeted with deep squishy hugs and rocked from side to side until they were sufficiently off balance.

When she was finally released, Charlee tried to lock her knees to stop the swaying while Jenny patted her cheeks.

"I can't tell you how happy I am to see you, darlin'. Now, let's get into that kitchen so you can work your magic."

Charlee smiled as she followed her client through the front entry. In true Jenny fashion, she was in comfy blue jeans and a solid short-sleeved shirt topped by a bright long-sleeved button-up shirt. Today's shirt was pink with little blue birds embroidered on it. Her long brown hair was pulled up in a ponytail because, as Jenny said during their previous project together, pulling her hair up hid some of the gray that was a little more generous in its appearance than she preferred. And that was just Jenny Wheeler in a tidbit.

In true old farmhouse style, the kitchen took up the entire back half of the home. After all, it's where the women did all their work back in the day, as well as educated their children and tended the little ones. Charlee stood in the center of the room and took it all in. The old, dinged up counters along the outer wall enveloped a tiny sink and old oven. The counters ended at the corner. A set of narrow cabinets lined the wall above the counters. Charlee knew from touring the house previously that the basement was set up with cold storage and gobs of shelving for canned foods. In the middle of the outer wall was a door leading to the back yard. On the other side of the door were two big clunky sinks—one for washing produce, the other for rinsing and packaging meats. Or at least they once were. She doubted Jenny actually used them. Then there was the funky black wood-burning stove along the short wall to the left, as well as a small set of windows. The opposite short wall was the same, minus the stove.

Charlee did a rough sketch of the original kitchen and set up on her yellow legal pad. "Tell me what you're hoping for, then we can talk ideas."

Jenny's hands went wild, gesturing here and there while she shared her hopes for the space. "Well, first of all, I would just love a dishwasher. It may be just Walter and I, but when our kids and grandkids come, why that sink and counter just overflow with plates, cups, silverware, and what not. It's such an eyesore and an absolute disaster when it comes to clean up."

Charlee grimaced. "I can only imagine. Your poor hands."

Jenny displayed her hands, turning them this way and that. "Sweetie, these hands are pruney enough as it is! They certainly don't need water wrinkles to boot!"

Charlee tried to hide her smile. She hoped she'd have Jenny's sense of humor when she was a grandma one day.

"I would also just love a dining room. I'm gettin' awful tired of having everything all in this one big room. It would be wonderful to leave the mess in the kitchen and enjoy dinner together in a nice clean room." Jenny continued while Charlee scribbled furiously on her notepad. "More storage space would be heavenly. And of course, the wood will need some love and we truly want to keep the original farmhouse charm as much as possible." Jenny sighed and her shoulders drooped as she looked around the room. "I just don't see how any of that can work though."

Charlee patted the sweet Southerner's shoulders. "That's why you have me. I can see it all and it's beautiful."

Jenny's eyes glistened and she clasped her hands in front of her. "Show me."

And Charlee did. First, she gestured to the wood stove and utility sinks. "Are you attached to any of this?"

Jenny wrinkled her nose. "We don't touch that old stove. I will admit it's charming though. We only rarely use the utility sinks."

"I suggest we take it all out. We can keep the stove to use as decor, but if you aren't using it to heat your home, it's just taking up space where it is." Charlee walked about 14 feet from the wall and spread her arms wide. "This area could become your dining room. Imagine a wide archway about here," she said, making general motions to show the area. "It will be open, but hide those dirty dinner pans in the sink. We could update the window, something wider to add more natural light and will be better for your utilities."

"Ooh . . ." Jenny cooed, as she followed Charlee to the next point.

"Now, if we take out these sinks, we could take advantage of the existing water lines, add in some plumbing and make a downstairs powder room."

Jenny gasped. "That would be fabulous! I didn't even think about a bathroom. It would be a joy to not to have to run upstairs or send guests into our messy upstairs bathroom."

Charlee nodded, happy that Jenny was seeing the possibilities. "You could add some cute decor on the outside walls or even add hooks for coats and a storage bench to sit and take off shoes, then store the shoes inside the bench."

"That would be mighty handy with all the grandkids' stuff."

That was one of the things Charlee loved. A good renovator didn't just update things, but also took into consideration the home owner's lifestyle and anticipated their needs.

"Speaking of grandkids, I bet they fight about getting out the door first."

Jenny chuckled and nodded her head. "They certainly do. It's a stampede for who gets to the door first."

"My nieces and nephews are the same way. How would you feel about taking out this door and installing glass French doors?"

Jenny ran her hand over the old wood door. "I'd hate to see it go. I fell in love with those funky old doors when we walked through the house for the first time."

"I absolutely understand. However, I was thinking we could simply move it to be the new powder room door. Plus, the double doors will let in a lot of natural light and open up the feel of the room, but also give you a broad view of the backyard while the kids play."

Jenny's eyes brightened. "Okay, you've got me on board."

"Great, let's move into the kitchen." Charlee stood in the middle of what would be the new kitchen space. "I'm assuming you'd like to replace the kitchen counters." At Jenny's nod, she asked, "Is there a material you've settled on?"

Jenny wrinkled her pert little nose. "This is where Walter and I disagree. He wants marble, but I just hate the cold, hard feel on my arms. I don't think it's inviting. But I'm not a fan of Formica either. Do you have any suggestions?"

"Marble is very popular, but I wanted to suggest something different. I'm not sure if you'll like it and it's definitely something you'll want to talk over with Walter."

"I'm open to suggestions. So far your ideas have been pretty spot on."

"I've seen a few designs lately of counters made out of thick solid wood, like the butcher chopping blocks you see in stores. Normally I wouldn't consider that look for a new house, but with your farmhouse, it would be charming. There are pros and cons, like any material. In this case, it's softer than marble, but the counter versions are harder and coated to be more scratch resistant than what you're used to with a wooden chopping block. I would definitely recommend still using some type of cutting board and not the counter itself to preserve the look. We can also order it to either match or be a complementary color to the house's original wood work. I brought some brochures for you both to look through. There's a sticky note inside with the name and address of a Kansas City showroom where you can see the counters first hand."

"I like the concept, but you're right. Walter and I will want to spend some more time researching it."

"Good. Your counters are very important to pulling together the look and feel you want for the kitchen. Now that we've talked about materials, let's talk about design. I envision replacing the base of all the counters. We'll preserve the original doors, sand them down, and restain them. By replacing the base, we'll be able to give the counters a firm foundation, one that will be able to hold the weight of the new material you choose. I think the counters will still start here," she said, gesturing to the original counter. "Then go down to this corner, turn and come three-quarters of the way down this wall. We can talk options for cabinets versus drawers on the base, but it will give you a lot more storage space." She turned back towards the original counters. "We'll keep the sink in the same place, but it will become your deep utility sink, perfect for pots and pans. To the right, a new stove top and oven. Would you prefer to keep the original cabinets or replace them with a unit that can wrap around and follow the new counters?"

"Oh, I don't want to block this wall," Jenny said, moving to the shorter wall. "I'd like to have the window updated, but I'd want to keep this space to display my knick-knacks."

"I like that idea. Then we could sand and stain the original cabinets."

"Um, where will the dishwasher be?" Jenny asked, looking concerned.

"You're standing on it." Charlee chuckled when Jenny looked down. She pulled Jenny a few steps back. "This kitchen is huge and has a lot of empty space. Let's use it to add a big island here. On the side by the sink, there will be a dishwasher, as well as a shallow double sink with a disposal and a hidden trash and recycling door. Scrape, rinse, and load. Makes for much easier clean up after family dinners."

Jenny placed her hand over her chest. "You just stole my heart, Charlee dear."

"Well, that's not all. The island can be wide enough to include a sitting area. Imagine three or four bar stools where you can grab a quick bite to eat or have visitors sit to chat while you whip up a sweet treat." Charlee could have sworn Jenny's eyes did a little swoon.

"That would be absolutely delightful!"

"Of course, there's the woodwork and trim to be sanded and stained and painting the walls whatever colors you choose."

"I already settled on a cheery light yellow for the kitchen." Jenny put her finger to her chin, considering the would-be dining room space. "Perhaps something between a light to mid-tone blue color..."

"There's plenty of time to figure that out," Charlee said. "Is there anything you'd like to change or add?"

"Everything sounds perfect. I just wonder if it will fit our budget."

"You know my process," Charlee said. "I'll work up the bid, separating out the different projects as well as adding what order it would be optimal to do them in. Then you and Walter can look it over and decide what works best for you. Even if you do part now and save for the rest, you'll have a vision for what's coming."

Jenny clapped her hands in excitement. "I just knew you were the person for this job. I can't believe that silly Elliott Construction let you go. It's too bad, really. I know we aren't the only ones who decided to look elsewhere when they found out you were gone."

"Really?" Charlee wasn't exactly surprised, but if there were more, she had not heard from them. "Do you know which other companies the clients are using?"

"Well, sweetie, I know the Gentry family was looking into Taylor Design. They were concerned with your business being so small and wanting their work to get done quickly."

"I can understand that. Taylor Design is a good choice for them then."

Jenny cocked her head. "You're not upset about losing their business?"

Charlee shrugged. "I would love to work with them again, but you know the only way I was able to commit to doing your project was for me to work on it after hours. I knew it would be difficult for the first year trying to figure out the balance between growth, income and expenses. I'm trying to be conservative. I really appreciate that you and Walter are willing to be flexible."

"Like I said, sweetie, I knew you were the only person for the job."

Charlee smiled as she gathered all of her notes and documents. Clients who had such faith in her talents warmed her heart and reconfirmed that she did the right thing starting her own business. "Thank you, Jenny."

"Now, you just figure out everything and let me know what the damage is going to be," Jenny said, following Charlee out to the front porch.

"Absolutely. I should have the bid to you in about a week." Charlee was enveloped in another squishy hug before leaving. Back in her truck, she jotted down a few additional notes, then turned on her favorite radio station. The weather outside may be cold, but inside, she was a bundle of enthusiasm ready to dive into her new project.

Chapter Sixteen

CHARLEE'S FINGERS CRAMPED as she gripped her cell phone and focused on the conversation with her plumbing contractor. All the clichés about Mondays being the worst day of the week were certainly on par with how this conversation was going. "Frank, I understand the schedule is messed up from the delivery delays, but this sort of thing happens all the time."

"And I'm telling you, Charlee, that my crews are booked solid for the next week."

"Every single one? How is that possible? You know I can't move forward with the bathrooms until the plumbing is in place. We have a signed agreement for this project, but if you can't get out here to do it, then I'm going to have to ask you to cancel the contract."

"I think you know the other local subcontractors are going to be busy, too," he replied, just as frustrated as she was.

He was right. Many of her subcontractors were flaking on her, saying they couldn't risk their business with Elliott Construction or suddenly getting so busy they can't deliver on their work. Was George really that determined to put her out of business that he would put that much money and resources into making it almost impossible for her subcontractors to follow through? Victoria already expressed worry about the delays and even hinted that they may bring in another renovation company to work on the upcoming projects because the bookstore was taking much longer than expected. "Then I guess I need to look for someone who isn't local."

Frank paused on the other end of the line. "That might be the best route to go," he admitted.

Charlee was crushed. She'd worked with Frank for the last two years. He was the first subcontractor to agree to work with Transformations. Having him jump ship made her feel like a failure. She swallowed past the hard lump in her throat and did her best to make her voice sound as normal as possible. "Thanks, Frank. I hope when things calm down, we'll be able to work together again. Good luck on your projects."

She ended the conversation, then clenched her fist and fought the sting of tears. But what was the point? Why fight it when it was so much easier to give in to a good cry? Her head dropped into her hands.

Why was George so utterly bent on making her life miserable? Was it truly just the fact that she quit her job and started her own business? Or was it because of her relationship with Peter? If this continued, she just didn't know if she could handle the constant conflict. Which made her wonder if she and Peter should be dating. Maybe it would be better if they went separate ways.

No, she shook her head. She couldn't let such a miserly old man be the reason for giving up on anything—her work or her happiness. She swiped at her cheeks, then grabbed a few tissues to dry her face. Her desk was a disaster with paperwork for Indulgence Row, the bid she was working on for the

Wheeler's and a do to-list which included figuring out the upcoming pay roll.

But at that moment, she needed to take a break. She grabbed her cell phone and truck keys. She had some supplies to deliver to Anita at the women's shelter. Twenty minutes later, Charlee was sitting across from Anita at the shelter's kitchen table, sipping soda and venting about the day's stress. The newbie from her last class, Naomi, had just come in and started making lunch for herself and her preschooler. She was dressed in simple jeans and a plain gray t-shirt that did nothing for her pale complexion, but Naomi managed to make it look put together with her hair in a twisted bun and simple hoop earrings.

"Can things get any worse?" Anita asked, trying to sympathize with her friend, but Charlee just laughed.

"You don't want to know."

Anita picked up her drink. "Do tell."

"Are you sure you want more?" At her friend's nod, she continued with some of what Charlee considered the funnier aspects of being a new business owner. "You know the new computers I got for the office? Well, let's just say that the software is a lot different than when I last used it back in college. I set up some bill pay stuff, but I didn't set up the auto pay right. So I missed my cell phone payment and got a honking huge late fee. Plus, all the employer taxes and stuff makes my head spin. It takes me all day to figure payroll out for just one crew."

Anita winked. "If you had a hammer, I'm sure you could probably fix it."

"You joke, but I assure you, there were times I definitely

wanted to take my hammer to the computer. Stupid technology stuff. It's just going to get worse though as the business grows and I hire more crews." Charlee shook her head and lifted her soda for another drink.

"It sounds like you need an office manager," Naomi said.

Charlee turned towards Naomi, who twisted the lid back onto the peanut butter and jam containers before putting them away. "How would that help? It seems like it would be yet another person to pay."

Naomi rested her hip against the counter and folder her arms across her chest. "If you hire the right person, an office manager can take care of payroll, schedules, and technology stuff, which would free up your time. You could be on-site more, which would allow you to eventually hire people with less experience at a lower wage, then give them hands-on training to produce the quality of work you expect. An office manager can be an invaluable asset to a small company. One that new business owners often overlook."

"I like your perspective. I'm just not sure if now is the right time. Shouldn't I wait until my business is bigger to do that?"

Naomi shrugged. "It depends on how you value your time. Like you said, it takes you all day to put together payroll for just one crew. A good office manager would be able to do it in just a few hours. How many evenings are you spending in your office doing paperwork instead of at home?"

"Hmm, good point," Charlee said, thinking over Naomi's suggestions.

A little girl with pigtails ran into the room. "Is lunch ready now, Mommy?"

Naomi twisted a pigtail around her finger, before letting

the silky hair slip free and smiled. "It sure is. Peanut butter and strawberry jam."

The little girl clapped her hands, took the plate her mother offered her and scampered over to the end of the kitchen table. Naomi placed a cup of milk beside her daughter's place, then sat next to her.

"How are you today, Elise?" Anita asked.

"Today in preschool, we're going to talk about the letter S and we're going to make super silly snakes and then I'm going to scare Landon with my snake when I get home," Elise replied before taking a big bite of her sandwich.

Charlee tried not to laugh. She remembered pulling similar pranks on Tyler, although he often got her back with an even more inventive prank.

"That sounds like fun," Anita responded, hiding her own smirk. "I bet we could think of something to make for dinner that starts with the letter S, too."

Elise's eyebrows scrunched together and she took another bite of her sandwich. After a moment, she blurted out, "Strawberry shortcake!"

"No, silly girl. We don't eat that for dinner," Naomi chided her daughter. "What else starts with the letter S?"

Elise looked around the group and pointed to Charlee. "Who are you?"

"Elise, that wasn't polite. Sorry," Naomi said to Charlee.

"No worries. My name is Charlee. I'm Anita's friend."

"Charlee is a boy's name. Are you a boy?" Elise's nose was once again scrunched up as she considered Charlee's name and short hair.

"Elise!" Naomi exclaimed, her cheeks flaring pink.

Charlee simply laughed. "Nope, I'm a girl. I bet most of the girls at your school have long hair, huh?" Elise just nodded. "I used to have long hair. All the way down to my tush."

"Wow! What happened to it?"

"Well, I probably shouldn't tell you this, but . . ." She leaned closer to Elise and lowered her voice. "My mom used to put me in girly pageants. You know, the ones with all the poufy dresses and pretty curled hair and stuff?"

Elise was so excited, she squished her sandwich between her fingers where she held it. "Ooh, I love dresses!"

"Guess what?" Charlee scrunched up her nose like Elise had earlier. "I don't. So you know what I did?" Elise's eyes were wide as she shook her head. "I got out my mom's sewing scissors and I cut off all my hair."

Naomi's gasp was just as striking as Anita's hoot of laughter. "I can just see you doing that," Anita said.

Little Elise's eyes went wide. "What did your mom do?"

"Well, first she took me to get my hair fixed. When the stylist saw my hair, she asked me what happened. By then, I knew I wasn't just in trouble, but I was in super big trouble, so I tried to find a way out of it. I told the lady that I was jumping on the trampoline and my hair fell out."

"You didn't!" Elise exclaimed.

"I did. But of course, she didn't believe me. So I told her that there were magic scissors at my house and while I was watching my favorite TV show, they just magically flew up and gave me a haircut. For some reason, she still didn't believe me. The only way she could fix my hair was by cutting it really short, just like my brother's hair." By this time, Naomi and Anita were red in the face from laughing.

Elise's solemn expression stood out in stark comparison.

"What did your daddy do?"

Naomi's laughter died and she again smoothed her daughter's hair. Elise's big brown eyes stared up at Charlee. Her heart broke seeing the depth of worry in eyes that were way too young.

"You know what my daddy did? He laughed. He even got out our ruler and measured to see who had longer hair—me or my brother."

Elise's eyes relaxed, even brightened a little. "Who won?"

"Well, my dad said I had longer hair, but he winked at me when he said it. I always thought he fibbed so my brother wouldn't have a fit about having longer hair than a girl."

"Cause a boy with longer hair than a girl would be silly." Elise shoved the last bite of her sandwich in her mouth, then mumbled to her mom. "Can I go finish getting ready for school now?"

"Finish your milk first, then you can go brush your teeth. We'll leave in about fifteen minutes." Elise quickly did as she was asked, then said a quick goodbye before running out of the room.

"She's sweet," Charlee told Naomi when she stood to take her daughter's plate to the sink. Naomi nodded her thanks as she pulled out the dish soap and cleaned up the plate and cup.

"I was thinking about what you said before, about the office manager," Charlee continued. "I think you're right. The business would run smoother if I could focus on what I'm good at and had someone else to do the same in the office."

"I'm glad I could help," Naomi said, drying her hands, then hanging up the dish towel.

"You don't by any chance have a background in office

management, do you?"

Naomi looked up surprised. "In business, yes. Not necessarily as an office manager."

"What kind of business?" Charlee asked, trying to get Naomi to open up a little bit. Instead, her questioning seemed to upset Naomi.

"Listen," Naomi said. "I didn't say anything to try to get a job offer. I don't need a pity job."

"Whoa," Charlee said, putting her hands up and glancing over to Anita, who looked ready to jump in. "I wasn't handing out any pity. I wouldn't want someone to treat me that way either. I just thought you had a keen insight on running a business and wanted to continue the discussion. Find out what your background was and see if I could pick your brain a little more."

Naomi's shoulders relaxed. "I'm sorry. Work was always a point of contention between my husband and I." She looked down briefly before making eye contact again. "I actually have a business degree and a double minor in accounting and marketing from a business school in Chicago."

"Wow. That's pretty impressive." Charlee didn't know why she was surprised. She knew the women who came through the shelter's doors were from all walks of life.

"I did pretty well." She paused, then amended her statement. "Actually, I did really great. I worked for a kitchen supply company. By the time we decided to have children, I had worked my way up to a mid-level executive job."

"It sounds like you enjoyed what you did." And that was the moment Charlee saw Naomi's first real smile.

"I'm an organization junkie and spreadsheet geek. I would

be given projects that were falling apart and within a few weeks, I'd have it all back on track. I loved my work. It was sad to leave, but I agreed with Richard. It was important for a mom to be home with her kids. It was tough to go to just one income, but we made it work. It was actually pretty great, until he lost his job. By then, the market had changed and he struggled to find another position with the same pay. We came here because I was offered a job. That's when things changed." She shook her head and looked away. "Our divorce will be finalized next week."

"I'm sorry. I wasn't trying to pry."

Naomi shrugged. "I know. Anyway, we're here now and I actually am looking for a new job. I can give you references, but they probably won't be very good. I called in sick often so they wouldn't see the bruises, but I figure you understand that with doing work here at the shelter and all. If you do decide to hire an office manager, I would like to apply. I'm excellent at what I do. I just need someone to give me the chance to prove it again."

Charlee nodded. "It would be part-time to start, see how much work there actually is and how we work together."

"That actually would be great. Then I can be here in the mornings with Elise and come in while she's at preschool."

"You could even bring her to the office. It used to be my grandmother's house. We can set up an activity area for her to color and play. It would be nice to hear laughter in the house again. Why don't we both think about it tonight and we can talk some more tomorrow?"

Elise ran in, a pink My Little Pony backpack in tow. "Let's go, Mom!"

Naomi nodded, then stepped across the room to shake Charlee's hand. "Until tomorrow then."

After they left, Anita turned to Charlee. "You're a good woman, Charlie Brown."

Charlee laughed at the Peanuts reference. "I get where she's at. I mean, not the abuse part, but the part where I knew I was stuck and needed to jump into a big, scary change. Transformations was what I needed. I think that just maybe, it might be what we both need." She lifted her soda can and swiped at the water that gathered on the table with a napkin. "Well, friend, I better get back and check on the crew."

Anita stood and walked Charlee to the front door. "So, in the next class we're painting furniture?"

"Right. And after that, the hardware store is donating supplies to teach the women to build bedside tables. Don't forget to talk to Gail about me picking up her dresser for next week's project."

"Will do." Anita squeezed Charlee's hand. "Thanks for being you."

Back in her truck, Charlee scrolled through the text messages she missed. She found one from Eden. She tapped on the message, expecting either a question about the bookshop or something about Rachel's bridal shower that weekend.

Just stopped by for an update. Guess who's back in town? Hope. And she's here hanging all over Peter's every word (as well as anything else she can manage to touch.) Get your butt over here.

Chapter Seventeen

CHARLEE PUSHED THE SPEED LIMIT as much as she could without getting pulled over as she drove across town. Since Tyler joined the local police department, she had only been pulled over once. After the chastisement she received from Tyler after the fact, she vowed never to be pulled over again. When she arrived at the Indulgence Row house, she found Eden leaning against the porch railing and tapping her foot. As soon as Eden saw her pull in, she darted from the porch over to meet Charlee on the sidewalk.

"What took you so long?" Eden grabbed Charlee's arm and pulled her towards the front door. "I told Peter I was waiting for you to show up and do a walk through."

"Why did you do that?" Charlee asked.

"Duh," Eden said, rolling her eyes. "To keep an eye on what was going on."

"I'm sure it can't be that bad," Charlee said, slowing her step. Did she really want to go in there and essentially spy on Peter? Shouldn't she trust him to not do something stupid? Just because the only other girlfriend he was ever serious about was back in town didn't mean he was going to jump ship and dump her. They were together now and solid. Right?

Eden elbowed Charlee hard in the ribs. "You came running as soon as you got my text, didn't you?"

"Okay, you have a point," Charlee said, as Eden dragged her up the porch steps and did an awkward shuffle so that Eden was between her and the doors, giving Charlee a direct view over Eden's shoulder into the foyer.

"Do you understand why I texted you now?" Eden shoved her hands in the pockets of her jacket.

Charlee certainly did. Peter stood with his arms crossed in the foyer with Hope at his side. The woman looked just like her high school cheerleader days, as her tight-fitting jeans and sparkly top attested. She even still had her trademark ponytail with the poof thing on top of her head. The thing Charlee honed in on though, was the way Hope kept reaching up and touching Peter's arm every few sentences. Charlee gasped when Peter looked up and saw her spying on him.

"Busted," Eden said in a low sing-song voice.

From the way Peter took a few steps back from Hope, Charlee surmised that he felt the same way. There was no use putting it off. She pushed the door open, leaving Eden hang back by the door and focused on the two people before her.

Peter coughed into his fist. "Hope, you remember Charlee Jackson, right?"

Hope's smiley face stayed frozen in place when Peter put his arm around Charlee's waist, but Charlee saw the change in her eyes as they flitted from Peter then back to her.

Yep, that's right, chick. He's mine. Hands off, Charlee thought when their eyes connected.

"I can't say that I do. Were you a few years ahead of us?" Hope's voice dripped with honey, but her eyes were laced with poison.

Fat chance on playing the age card, Charlee thought. "Three years behind actually. I'm Tyler Jackson's sister."

Hope took the hand Charlee extended to her in a loose, girly handshake that looked more like someone should kiss her hand before letting go.

"Oh, I remember you," she said. "You were that sweet little kid who followed Peter around with googley eyes. Quite the little tomboy with a school girl crush, if I remember right. I thought it was just the cutest thing, although Peter didn't always agree."

Charlee didn't dare look to see how Peter reacted to this revelation, just feeling him stiffen was like seeing the wince on his face. Before she could respond, Hope looked at the leather and gem encrusted watch on her wrist. "Oh dear, I have to go. It was wonderful to meet up with you Peter." Hope put both her hands on his chest and leaned forward to place a kiss on his cheek. "You have my number. See you soon." She shot a quick glance at Charlee. "It was nice to meet you, Carly."

Charlee didn't even bother correcting the obvious misuse of her name. Besides, she preferred having Hope gone. Unfortunately, the flame of anger didn't accompany her departure. She turned to face Peter.

"It's not what you think," he said immediately. "She just moved back to town and is looking up some old friends."

Charlee's eyebrow arched. "Really? How many others has she reconnected with?"

A flush spread across his face.

She shook her head. "I don't need this, Peter. You're either in or you're out." She put her hand up and cut him off when he tried to interrupt. "Don't give me the you're-my-girl line right now. It just makes me even more upset."

Silence settled between them as Charlee put her hands on her hips and looked at the ground while she took a deep breath. "I don't think we should talk about this right now. We'll just say something to make things worse. I need to give Eden an update on the shop." She still couldn't meet his eyes, not wanting to see what was there as she turned away.

His hand slipped around her upper arm, stopping her, but she kept her back to him. "I'm honestly not interested in Hope."

She wanted to believe him. Wanted to so much, she had to clench her hands into fists to keep from turning around and throwing her arms around him. But she had trusted guys in the past, only to find out they were less than honest. She turned her head towards him. "Are you planning to see her again?"

"She was my friend for a long time. Do you want me to just avoid her?"

His irritation was clear through the tone of his voice. Charlee shook her head. Couldn't he see her point of view of the situation? "She was your girlfriend, Peter. There's a big difference between girlfriend and just a friend."

"It was high school. Be reasonable."

And that irritated her all the more. "Are you going to see her?" she asked again. A lot rested on his answer. Was he going to open himself up to Hope's flirting on the pretense of friendship or would he choose to stay focused on their relationship?

There was a slight pause. "She needs her friends right now. She just went through an awful divorce."

Charlee simply nodded and turned her focus back on Eden who continued to wait near the stairs. "I need to get back to my client."

Peter released her arm and she walked away, with each step wondering if this was the beginning of the end. Would their relationship end after just a few weeks because a prettier face appeared? If so, Peter would join the ranks of all the other guys she'd tried dating, and that was depressing. She motioned for Eden to follow her up the stairs to where the crew was working on the book shop.

"What happened?" Eden asked when they reached the top.

"You wanted an update, right?" Charlee turned to go through the doorway leading into what was slowing morphing into the Bibliophile book shop.

"Hey, wait a minute," Eden said, nabbing the side of Charlee's tee and tugging her to a stop. "Do you want to talk?"

Charlee sucked in a deep breath. She wanted to unleash some of anger that was making her skin itch. Just lash out, fast and hot, to someone. Instead she exhaled and pushed it all down, hopefully deep enough that she could keep her calm until she was alone later. She shook her head. "Let's talk about the shop."

She led Eden into the main room where the crew was hard at work measuring, cutting and hammering wood down one wall. "Unfortunately, I don't have great news right now. The crew is working on the built-in shelves, but the holdup is the plumber for the bathrooms. I had to part ways with the guy I had lined up. It will take me a few days, maybe a week, to find a replacement."

Charlee hoped that was true, because if she didn't come up with someone quick, then she was going to lose the ability to bid on the remaining Indulgence Row projects.

Eden must have been in a sympathetic mood because she just nodded instead of freaking out about yet another delay. "The shelves are looking great," she said, focusing on the positive.

"While you're here, why don't you talk with Crank about the shelving colors and designs you want painted in different sections," Charlee suggested.

"That's a great idea. Thanks for all your hard work and hey, call me, if you need to talk." Eden squeezed Charlee's hand before heading over to where Crank was cutting wood.

Charlee took the opportunity to go through the plans, checking the work against the specifications. She trusted Bob and knew he was as much of a perfectionist as she was, but she just needed to see that something was going right. Especially when she felt like everything was unraveling.

"How's it going, boss lady?" Bob peered at the plans in front of her as he used a scrap towel to wipe off wood dust stuck to his hands.

"It's a good-bad diagnosis. At least this room is progressing."

Bob nodded towards the hall where the bathrooms were. "What's going on over there? They didn't show up."

Charlee sighed. "Looks like things aren't going to work out with Frank."

"George strikes again?" Bob asked, crossing his arms. At her nod, he swore under his breath. "I don't know what's gotten into that man. I can honestly say I'm glad I don't work for him anymore. If I did, I'd have to quit and you can bet I would have made a big stink and taken as many of the other men with me as I could."

"Because that would have made everything so much better," she replied, rolling her eyes.

"Would've made me feel better. Listen, I have some plumbing friends in Missouri, over near Chillicothe. It's a bit of a drive, but it's just far enough away I might be able to get a good crew over here without any fear of George interfering."

Charlee thought it over. She had honestly gone through all of her Kansas City contacts as it was. She would need to do a lot of research before trying to hire another crew. Then again, Bob had been in the business for a long time and had a lot more connections than she did. "If you're willing to vouch for their work, then do it."

"You got it, boss lady. I'll get to work on it now." Bob pulled out his cell phone and headed off towards the bathrooms where he could review the work that needed to be done with whoever he was contacting.

Charlee set the plans aside and checked the time. It was almost time to call it a day. At least on this project. She needed to walk Eden out before heading back to the office to work on the Wheeler's bid and the stack of problems waiting there.

This had to be the worst Monday ever. If only she could be like Garfield and pig out on some lasagna, then fall into bed in a comatose bliss, oblivious to the remainder of the day. Instead, she pulled up her big girl panties and prepared to make progress on her overwhelming to-do list.

Chapter Eighteen

THE BLARE OF THE ALARM jolted Charlee awake. She fumbled, smacked her nightstand and sent her phone flying onto the bedroom carpet, but she found the snooze button. Once the annoying thing was off, she covered her head with her pillow for ten more minutes of sleep. Just ten minutes. That's all she needed...

A minute later, she knew it just wasn't going to happen. She kicked the mattress, shoving the sheets off and fought back the hot prickles in her eyes. It had been a long, frustrating night at the office, fighting with computer software and trying to avoid thinking about Peter. Although the latter ended up being wasted energy. The only good thing that came from the very long night was that by midnight, she was certain hiring Naomi to manage the office was the right move.

She sat up, swung her legs over the side of the bed and flicked off the alarm before pulling on a pair of thick socks and wrapping up in a warm robe. Winter in Crystal Creek was fickle, but one constant was the cold mornings that made her want to be snuggled in all things fleecy. She shuffled down the hall and into the kitchen. She bypassed the orange juice and grabbed the kettle from the base of the mini-coffee maker. Today was one of the rare mornings she needed the black sludge to kick start the day. If she added enough sugar and milk, it didn't taste too bad. What body wouldn't jump start after an infusion of sugar and caffeine?

Once she was ensconced at the end of her couch, she set the coffee aside and pulled out a pen and paper. Even with some java, her brain was going to be tired and slushy today. She jotted down several to-do items, starting with hiring Naomi. She contemplated her list as she sipped the sugary concoction. She needed to talk to Peter today. She was honestly surprised he didn't call her last night. She moved the mug to her left hand and picked up the pen, then paused. Clicking and unclicking. It felt weird, making a to-do list item about their relationship. Wasn't that rather unromantic? Like maybe she was forcing something?

She set the pen down and tried not to chew on her bottom lip. Instead she took another sip of coffee while an inside tug of war ensued. To call Peter or not? Maybe she should wait to see how long it took him to contact her. After all, he's the one who wanted to keep in touch with Hope. And why didn't he call her last night? It was very unlike him. She lost the war with the lip chewing as all sorts of scenarios about how Peter could have spent the previous night tumbled through her head. Every last one involved Hope.

Dang it all. She hated feeling like the mixed up, confused, overanalyzing everything girlfriend. She was happy when she finally left the awfulness of college social life and could spend her time consumed in the world of construction. The last few years had been filled with security. She knew her goals and was happy with her place in life. Sure, it was lonely sometimes, but it was a thousand times better than this angst-ridden, twisty knot in the pit of her stomach.

She gulped down the remainder of the coffee, then ripped off the top sheet of her notepad. She needed consistency and the comfort of her to-do list. The other stuff, well, that would have to wait until later.

She picked up her cell, dialed the shelter, and asked for Naomi.

"Hello?" Naomi's voice was timid, as if she wasn't sure she wanted to talk to the person on the other end.

"Hi, Naomi, this is Charlee Jackson. How are you?"

"Oh, hello!" In just those two words, Charlee could hear the relief Naomi must have felt. She went from sounding unsure to the confident woman Charlee talked to yesterday. "I'm doing good, and you?"

"Honestly, I'm a little sleep deprived. I was up late last night fighting with some stupid software stuff and didn't make much progress on the things I actually needed to get done. Which is why I'm calling you. Are you still interested in being my office manager? Before you answer, please know I'm really, really hoping you'll say yes."

A soft laugh came through the line. "Ever since we talked yesterday, I've been itching to get my hands on your office and fix it."

"I am so happy to hear you say that! Any chance you can come to the office today while Elise is at school? We could start the payroll paperwork and I can fill you in on what I do, what I need help with, and you can tell me what I'm missing."

"That sounds great. I drop Elise off about 12:30. Her

preschool isn't far from your office so I should get there just a little after that."

"Perfect. See you then," Charlee said, before ending the call. She checked the time. It was almost nine. Bob and the crew would be getting to Indulgence Row and setting up for the day's work. She texted Bob that she would be there soon, then quickly got ready and headed out the door.

She pushed through the doors to the Sweet Confections/Bibliophile foyer and immediately headed up the stairs, purposefully not scanning the foyer for a glimpse of Peter. She needed to stay focused.

The hum of saws was soothing. Crank and Sadie were working together on measurements, cutting, and placement for the shelves. About half of the custom bookshelves were installed. If everything went well, the final units would be built today and ready to stain a few days after that.

"Morning, boss lady," Bob said, handing her a fruit smoothie.

"Thanks," Charlee said, taking a sip and enjoying the burst of strawberry and banana. "Since when did you know I prefer fruit smoothies?"

Bob shrugged. "Can't take the credit. Peter dropped it off."

"Oh." She set the smoothie aside, the tanginess overridden by the need to push anything Peter-esque aside.

"Not that it's any of my business—" Bob stopped short when she raised her eyebrow. "Well, I'm just gonna say it anyway."

Charlee sucked in a deep breath, preparing for Bob to tell her to get her crud together and fix things with Peter.

"I was at Freddy's last night."

Charlee's brow crinkled in confusion. He was going to tell her a bar story?

"So were Peter and Hope."

Her lips formed an 'oh', but she didn't think the word actually came out. She grabbed the plans and spread them across the table. "Yeah, I saw her yesterday. I guess she just went through a bad divorce and came back to Crystal Creek for a little support."

Bob snorted. "That wasn't a broken up woman looking for friendship last night." Charlee looked up and met his concerned and wise eyes. "That was a woman looking to relive her glory days."

Charlee nodded. It was what she already surmised. Hope wanted Peter. The question was whether Peter wanted Hope back in his life. "And did Peter seem interested?"

The pause while Bob scratched his balding head, then crossed his arms just about killed her. "I can't say for sure. He didn't encourage or discourage her. They hung out, talked a lot. She did a lot of posturing and flirting. Don't know if he went for it though."

She tried to swallow past the thick lump that formed in her throat and quickly nodded to cover it up. "Okay. Thanks." She leaned over the table and smoothed out the plans again, intending to change the subject, but Bob put his hand over hers, stilling the nervous gesture.

"Just one more thing. I like Peter."

She nodded. Here it came. Suck it up. Make it work. Don't be the fool who loses the guy. All the stuff her mother told her every time things went south with a boyfriend.

"But," Bob said, raising his finger to make a point, "no

cheater is worth having in your life. If he thinks that hussy is a better choice, then you cut him free and don't look back. You deserve better."

She gasped, her eyes darting up to meet his. Words she never heard from her mother. Yet she knew he meant them. This time she couldn't get past the lump and a sob escaped before she sucked it all back in. She straightened and shook her head, wiping away the few tears that escaped. She cleared her throat, then met his gaze again and nodded.

He returned the gesture. "Good, now let's talk about the plumbing." He pulled out some paperwork and notes, shuffling things around, she suspected to give her time to compose herself and shift back into work mode. "I talked to the Thompson crew over in Chillicothe. I've known Ned for almost thirty years. He took over the business from his dad and his sons work in the company too. Good small business with quality work and fair prices. Ned said he'd be willing to send a crew out to do the work tomorrow and have them stay until everything was done and inspected for the amount you have budgeted."

Charlee looked at the numbers and considered the proposition. "And if I agree, what would they like in return?" A business wasn't going to send out a crew to do work that would flush even or barely make a profit without asking for something in return.

"If you like their work, he'd like you to use them for any plumbing or other contract items they can handle for the remainder of the Indulgence Row projects you contract. He's willing to negotiate pricing at that point. On the negative side, they would be about 10 to 15% more expensive than a local crew. On the plus side, they won't flake out on us and can meet their deadlines."

She considered how to work the additional fees into future proposals. It could work, and at the rate contractors were dropping out, this might be the best option overall. "Let's do it. Get them on the phone and tell them I'll fax over the contract paperwork this afternoon."

"Thought you couldn't figure out the fax machine?" Bob teased.

Charlee smiled, probably for the first time that morning. "My new office manager will take care of it."

"Office manager, huh? Fancy schmancy," Bob said, elbowing her arm.

"More like a lifesaving necessity. Her name's Naomi. You'll like her."

"Looking forward to meeting her. What's next, boss lady?"

Charlee pushed her to-do list into her pocket and grabbed her tool belt. "Some real work. Let's get dirty," she said with a wink, enjoying Bob's deep laugh as they joined the crew.

All the other junk crowding her mind melted away as they cut, sanded, hammered and assembled the shelving units. The sweatshirt was discarded as the work warmed her up. It felt good to not be behind a desk, but to be using her muscles, and yes, sweating. The smell of the sawdust, the jabs and chuckles as they teased each other soothed Charlee. Sadie shared some of the crock pot recipes her kids preferred instead of a tired mom telling them to eat PB&J sandwiches. Crank told them about the sculpting class he was taking this semester, and that next semester he was teaching an oil painting class at the community college. And Bob talked about the countdown to fishing season and reserving a cabin at his favorite lake.

All of it together filled Charlee's soul. They were an odd bunch, but she couldn't imagine sharing the journey with anyone else, and this afternoon, she was adding another to their crew.

Charlee met up with Naomi a few blocks down at the Transformations office. She was thankful her office was close, but couldn't help but wonder what might happen if she lost the Indulgence Row contracts. She'd be devastated if she had to give up her Grandma's house.

Naomi was all bundled up in a thick winter coat, huddled by the front door. Charlee called a greeting as she jogged the last few steps over to meet her. They exchanged greetings while Charlee got the door unlocked and they were safely enveloped in the warmth of the house.

Naomi jerked in a body wracking shiver. "Man, I love how much milder Kansas City winters are compared to Chicago, but seriously, I hate anything under 65 degrees."

"I understand. I've lived here all my life and every winter I dream of traveling somewhere warm with a nice, sandy beach."

"You're talking my love language," Naomi replied as they went upstairs.

"Well, this is it," Charlee said, motioning down the halls to the bedrooms and two bathrooms. "Renovations for the office space probably won't happen until we have a downstairs renter. I'm planning to put it off as long as I can to get some income in the business first."

"That sounds reasonable, but if you're planning to meet clients here, you might want to consider working on it in stages. Especially if part of the plan is to create a reception area for the office manager."

"That's a good point," Charlee acknowledged. "We'll have to talk more about that after we finish up the bookstore and get more bids lined up. But for now, the office is in the master bedroom. It isn't fancy," Charlee said, leading her into what was once her grandparents' bedroom.

"It just needs to be efficient for now. Fancy comes later."

Charlee waved to the far wall where a filing cabinet and table with printer and fax machine were set up. "You're welcome to change the filing system to whatever you think is most efficient. Just be sure to let me know how things are organized."

Naomi simply nodded, pulled off her winter coat and draped it over the chair in front of the desk. Her simple black slacks and charcoal gray sweater were professional and classy without being too dressy for a construction office.

Charlee grabbed an extra chair and they both sat down at the computer. "Let's get a profile set up for you." She had looked up instructions about how to set up a profile with a separate password, but apparently it was for a different version than the operating system she currently had.

"Do you mind if I help?"

Charlee scooted back. "If you know what you're doing, go for it."

Within a few clicks, Naomi had the profile set up and ready to go. She chose a password they would both remember. "After all, you should have access to the accounting programs."

Charlee navigated on the Internet to the employee forms and left Naomi to fill them out while she pulled together some files from the cabinets to train Naomi how to research and create bids. They spent the next few hours going over the list of stores and contractors Charlee used, how to find the discounts they offered, their websites and contact info, and everything else that went into putting together a bid.

"Once you have a bid compiled, you can email it to me to be reviewed and approved. I'll walk you through the first couple of bid submissions. I have an account on the city development website. All their bids are uploaded directly to specific projects."

Naomi pulled up the website, pinned it to her navigation bar, then Charlee walked her through how to find projects and the submission links and directions. Naomi asked questions and made notes on a little notepad she brought with her.

"Most of the other projects I bid on are either for individuals or businesses and are simply an email to the homeowner or project manager. I'm going to need to set up another cell phone account for the office so we can direct inquiries to you. When you're not in the office, the calls can forward to my cell." Charlee took a moment to jot the note down.

"We might also want to consider starting a shared calendar and to-do list that can be installed on the phones," Naomi suggested.

"That might be wise. I've already had a few panic moments when I couldn't find a list or note with information I needed. Here, let me show you a subcontractor agreement and the info that needs filled out." Charlee pulled up a file for the new plumbing subcontractors. She verbally gave Naomi the info and let her fill out the file, save and print it. Then they faxed it over to Thompson Plumbing.

Once that was completed, she pulled out the file for the Bailey project. "I have two projects I'm currently doing research for. One for the Bailey Office of Realtors and another for an expansion and remodel at Peterson's Pet Store. They're both due next week on Friday. Here's my run down and notes for the work, the supplies list, estimated hours, and subcontractors we'll need." Charlee glanced up at the time on the computer. It was already 2:30. "How about we wrap up for today so you can get your daughter? Tomorrow I'll help you with rounding up information for the bids."

Naomi gasped. "That went by so fast." She followed up with a smile. "I'm really looking forward to working with you, Charlee."

"I think we're going to make a good team." They gathered their things and walked out together. Naomi went one way to get her daughter and Charlee took the opportunity to call Bob for an update on the bookshop.

CHARLEE WENT TO HER cell phone provider's kiosk at the mall and signed a contract for another phone. It was a huge two hour time suck. It always seemed like getting a phone shouldn't take much time, but it took forever. It was dusk when she finally emerged from the mall. She did another follow up with Bob, who told her his friend in Chillicothe received the contractor agreement forms, signed them and faxed them back.

When she hung up, she scrolled through her messages while her truck warmed up. There was a text from Peter, asking how her day was going. She thought about messaging him back, but decided to take him a peace offering instead. He usually took Petunia to the dog park before it closed. She quickly drove over to Sweet Confections for something yummy to share.

When she pushed through the bakery doors, a little bell chimed and Rachel came out from the back. "Charlee! It's wonderful to see you," the sweet redhead said, as she crossed the room and enveloped her in a hug. "What can I get for my friend, Queen of the Power Tools?" she asked, pulling away and scooting around to the other side of the bakery display cases.

It only took a few minutes of being in Rachel's presence and you just couldn't help but smile. "I wanted to get a treat for Peter."

"Well, I know he loves the Peanut Butter Cup Explosion cupcakes, I have a few of those left."

"Perfect. One for each of us, please." Rachel boxed the treats up and met Charlee at the register where she rang her up at a significant discount. "Rachel, you've got to stop doing that."

"Hey, after that horrific break-in and all the work you did to fix the gashes in the walls and repainting, you deserve a little love."

Charlee shook her head. "You would have done the same for me."

"Except those walls would not have turned out nearly as nice."

Charlee laughed. "But the cookies you bring for the people doing the work would be a lifesaver."

"Tell you what, you enjoy the discount. When we move, I'll

charge you full price again."

"Deal. Are you taking the display cases with you to the new location?"

Rachel cringed. "I really want to, especially after we paid extra on top of what insurance covered for these new ones, but the new space is bigger. Kristen's been researching display options and put out some feelers to see if anyone is interested in buying these."

"I'll put a note up on some of the construction boards I'm on too. Contractors are often looking for good deals for their clients."

Rachel clapped her hands together. "That would be fabulous, Charlee. You're amazing."

"No problem. I better get over to the dog park to meet up with Peter."

"Tell him I said hello. Not that he hasn't seen plenty of me and Kristen. It's hard to stay away from the new Sweet Confections shop."

"I absolutely understand. It's an exciting time. Is your project still on track?"

"Peter says they're even running ahead of schedule. Upgrading the kitchen utilities has taken a lot of time, but everything has gone so smoothly."

Charlee forced a smile. *Of course it has. George hasn't been sabotaging* them. "That's fantastic. I'll see you at your shower on Saturday."

Back in her truck yet again, she shoved the annoyed feelings down and took a deep breath. She needed to be calm when she met up with Peter. It wouldn't do any good if she was irritated before they even got to talk.

It was short drive to the off-leash dog park. Charlee

grabbed the cupcakes and headed across the parking lot. She saw Petunia and Anna playing in the field. She didn't think about Cameron's daughter being there. Oh well, she could just give Anna her cupcake. She didn't need the extra calories anyway. She let herself through the gate and stopped to search for Peter. He wasn't out with Petunia, but he must be nearby.

Then she spotted him, coming out of the dog shelter house where owners could fill up dog water dishes. She called out his name and waved. He turned towards her, surprise crossing his features, then he jogged over to meet her, a big smile on his face.

"I wasn't expecting you." He took her free hand and played with her fingers.

"I thought I would bring a peace offering," she said, holding up the Sweet Confections bag. "Peanut Butter Cup Explosion cupcakes. Rachel said they're your favorite."

"They are, but seeing you is a hundred times better."

His smile made her heart skip a beat. "Well, that's good because I wasn't expecting Anna to be here, so you might have to share one with me."

He lifted her hand and kissed her palm. "I'd gladly share anything with you."

See, Charlee, peace offerings were good. Now they just needed to get Anna home so they could actually talk. A shadow joined theirs and Charlee looked over, expecting to see Anna and Petunia. She jerked in surprise to find Hope hovering just behind Peter with a stupid yippy dog running circles around her ankles. She pulled her hand back. "Hope."

Peter stepped beside Charlee and wrapped his arm around her waist. "Hope decided to get a dog today. I was just showing her where the water and dog treat vending machine is."

Hope scooped up her dog, scratching the scrawny Chihuahua behind the ears while it squirmed and wriggled. "I thought I'd bring Bling Bling to play, but the dogs here are so much bigger. There really should be a sectioned off part for the more delicate dogs to play. Isn't that right, Bling Bling?" Something in the woman's babyish voice got the yippy dog to stop squirming, but then it started to lick Hope's face. *Oh, ew! Did she just let the dog lick the inside of her mouth?* Charlee swallowed down some rising bile.

Yeah, there was no way she'd be eating those cupcakes now.

She tried to smile, but her lips mostly just wobbled. It was hard to put on a happy face when your stomach wanted to spew. Bling Bling was now licking the inside of Hope's ear. She reached up and squeezed Peter's hand at her waist. "Um, we should probably get going. I'll just go get Anna."

"Oh, sure," Peter replied.

Charlee quickly moved away. She had to escape before she gagged all over Hope's shoes. She crossed the field, happy when Anna and Petunia joined her. She scratched the lab's floppy ears while she panted in delight.

"I don't like that woman," Anna blurted out, dragging her feet as they headed back to Peter and Hope.

Charlee glanced sideways, taking in Anna's hard expression. "What makes you say that?"

Anna's hands came together and she twisted her fingers this way and that, staying silent. Charlee had given up on a response when Anna said in a soft voice, "She's like my mom, always looking for something better, something perfect."

Love Under Construction

Charlee put a gentle hand on Anna's shoulder, remembering what Tyler told her about how hard Anna's mother pushed her to be the perfect size, the best dancer, the best everything until the poor girl was twisted in knots, eventually the stress making her so sick her body stopped functioning the way it was supposed to. That's what changed Cameron's life from a busy big-city married lawyer to a divorced small-town family lawyer with full custody of his daughter.

"Peter's your boyfriend, right?" Anna's big brown eyes were filled with concern.

"Yes, he is," Charlee said.

Anna sighed in relief. "That's good."

Charlee hoped Anna was right. She didn't want to see their relationship turn sour.

Petunia ran ahead and Peter hooked her leash on, ready to leave the park. "Let's go, ladies."

Charlee said good night to Hope and followed Anna out of the park. She tried not to analyze the disappointed expression on Hope's face.

"How about I take Anna home, then meet you back at your place?" Peter asked, walking her to her truck while Anna climbed into his truck and got Petunia situated.

She agreed and handed him the Sweet Confections bag. "Here, give one to Anna and you can have the other one. I'll order some Mexican delivery when I get home."

He gave her a quick kiss on the cheek, opened her truck door, then once she was inside, he jogged over to his truck. Across the parking lot, she spotted Hope getting into her sporty little car. Bling Bling jumped and darted all over the back seat, only pausing to lick the back window and the leather seats. Charlee pulled out of the parking lot and flicked on the radio, hoping something good would come on to distract her from the revolting images from the dog park. The station was featuring throwback hits. Charlee sang along with Tina Turner and pondered the lyrics, wondering where love fit into the triangle of Hope, Peter, and herself.

Chapter Nineteen

PETER ARRIVED AT CHARLEE'S townhouse just as the delivery guy pulled up to the curb. He paid for the meal, then knocked on Charlee's door.

"Well hello, delivery man," Charlee said, all teasing and smiles when she answered the door.

She had changed her clothes. Yeah, guys aren't supposed to notice things like that, but that's just garbage. What man doesn't notice when his woman dresses up for him? She ditched the work clothes and had on a simple black button-up shirt, kind of like a man's shirt with the sleeves rolled up to her elbows, and those clingy jeans that emphasized her amazing butt—not that he could do much appreciating from this angle. Great balls of fire, he loved her sassy smile. He tipped his ball cap and played along. "Ma'am, I've got six tacos and a couple burritos. That'll be thirty dollars."

She put her hand to her chest and widened her eyes. "That's outrageous!"

He leaned in just enough to go from guy at the door to a little more intimate. "But it includes the tip." He stepped inside, slid the sack of food onto the entry way table, topped it with his ball cap, then pushed the door closed with his foot. His hands found her hips and he stepped in closer, his body almost brushing hers. "I missed you."

Her beautiful eyes softened. "I missed you, too."

He slowly lowered his head, all the while keeping eye contact, ready to back off if she decided she wasn't ready to make up. When she didn't pull away, he touched his lips to hers. They met and clung, a small kiss here, another there. One hand cupped the back of her head as he deepened the kiss just a little, still holding back. He wished he could pour all of his feelings out just like this, but she wanted words and he wasn't good with them. He got all twisted up with stupid guy emotions tangled in there. If only she understood that his kisses reflected how much he cared for her.

Loved her.

She put her hand on his chest and eased back, breaking the contact. "We should, um . . ." She glanced away from him to the entryway table. "We should eat before the food gets cold."

Cool air rushed between them as she grabbed the sack and set it on the bar counter. He took a deep breath and exhaled. Patience, man. Patience.

So he sat and they ate and talked about mundane things. Anna taking care of Petunia, how their projects were going, that she hired an office manager.

"What made you decide to go that route?" He genuinely wanted to know more about what went into this big decision.

"I'm just not cut out for office work. I decided hiring someone to take care of the majority of it so I can manage my crews and projects was a better use of my time. Not to mention, hopefully less frustrating."

He nodded, processing the idea. "I like it. I sure wish I could pass off the bulk of my paperwork."

"I'm sure it's more difficult with a bigger company. I'm grateful Transformations is just a small business."

He processed that, trying to imagine Elliott Construction back in its startup days. "Don't you want to get bigger though?"

She tilted her head to the side, her short blonde hair swinging away from her chin. "Honestly? I don't think so. I want to leave my touch on every Transformations project. From the initial meeting with my clients to working on the projects, giving feedback to my crews, helping them see my vision. I want Transformations to be personal." She sighed, then took another bite of the burrito in her hand.

"Your eyebrows are doing that scrunchy thing. What's wrong?"

"I just realized I've been so wrapped up with delays and issues with contractors that I haven't been able to give Eden that personal touch I want my clients to experience. I did in the beginning, but once the project started, everything has been in constant chaos."

And of course, that chaos was because of his father's meddling. "I'm sorry," he said, the words feeling inadequate.

She simply shrugged and grabbed a burrito. "It is what it is."

He couldn't imagine she actually felt that way, all nonchalant about it. From her time at Elliott Construction, he knew how frustrated she became when things didn't go right. It made him wonder how much she was hiding from him.

The pause in their conversation stretched until it started to get uncomfortable. That was new for them. He guessed someone needed to bring up the topic neither of them wanted to discuss.

He scooted away from the bar, went to the fridge, and grabbed two fresh bottles of cream soda. He popped the caps, then offered one to Charlee. "Are we going to talk about it?"

She briefly glanced up at him as he settled back into his bar stool. "You mean her?"

"You know," he said. "Hope isn't so bad."

Charlee snorted. "Says the ex-boyfriend."

He put his hands up. "I really don't want to fight. Can we please just talk?"

She shifted her shoulders around, trying to relax. "Want to tell me about last night?"

"I was irritated after our conversation and went to Freddy's. I assume you're bringing it up because you heard Hope was there, too."

She nodded, concentrating on peeling the label off the soda bottle rather than looking at him.

"She called, I was already there and thought it would be a good place to meet. Public, nothing to hide."

"And?" she asked, leaving the question open ended.

"We just talked, mostly about high school, where our friends are now, that kind of stuff. She mentioned how quiet things are at the house she's renting and I suggested she try getting a dog."

"Looks like she took your advice." She paused, as if waiting for more, but he didn't know what. "Anything else?"

"That about sums it up." Now he knew he was in trouble. The look on her face went from calm to irritated.

"I heard she was being all flirty."

He shrugged. "She was just being Hope."

"Because she can't help but flirt with you." Charlee rolled

her eyes.

"No, because Hope shows off for everyone. She's a charismatic person, it just comes off as flirting." He hated feeling like he needed to defend Hope, but at the same time, it was the truth. Hope was like that with everyone, not just him.

"I saw how she kept touching you yesterday. Believe me, she wasn't just being charismatic. Obviously it was concerning enough for Eden to call me."

"Is that what this is about? What Eden and your other friends have to say?" He shoved his hand through his hair. "What about what I say, Charlee? Maybe you need to think about who you trust more, the gossip mill or me."

"That's not fair—"

"Or are you jealous because she's completely different than you?"

Charlee stilled. "You mean because she's gorgeous?"

He sucked in a deep breath. "I didn't mean it that way. I meant the way she interacts with others."

Her eyes narrowed into teeny little slits. This was not at all going the way he hoped. Of course, he knew it wouldn't. A miracle allowing them to get through this conversation without fighting would have been nice, but here they were, caught between her hurt feelings and misconceptions and his inept ability to verbalize the things in his head.

Because really, Hope was just Hope. She was his past, but Charlee was his now, and hopefully his future. Maybe that's what Charlee needed to hear. He sucked in a deep breath, trying to find the courage to say the words tumbling in his head or to at least blurt them out and hope they came out right.

Then Charlee dropped her head into her hands. "You know

what? I think we just need to take a break."

Screech!

Whoa. Wait. A break?

As in break up?

All the words Peter meant to say flew from his mind. Charlee kept talking, but it was hard to concentrate on her words.

"Peter? Are you listening?"

Her light brown eyes were moist and so very sad. Somehow he put that sad there and it clawed at his gut. Would this be the last thing he remembered about her? This couldn't be their last moment as Peter and Charlee.

"I just can't handle all this drama," Charlee said, rambling like she was prone to when upset. "I'm starting the renovation at the Wheeler's house, training Naomi, and putting in bids for the Bailey and Peterson projects. Everything is utter chaos right now and maybe I'm just not seeing things clearly, or maybe you're right and I just don't trust you like I should."

He wished he could take those words back right now so they couldn't be used against him. He reached across the table and cradled her cheek in his hand, his thumb brushing away a tear. Desperate to make everything slow down, to not rush to an end neither of them wanted. Or at least he hoped she didn't want it.

"Shh," he tried to calm her. "Please, Charlee, trust me when I say that Hope is nothing more than a friend. Please. We don't need to talk about her, we can set it aside." Her eyelashes fluttered against the side of his hand as anxiousness built up, making him want to give her anything she wanted. Just so long as it wasn't a goodbye. "If you need some space, I can do that. I just want to get back to me and you. Before all the crazy stuff interfered."

She choked on a soft laugh. "It's been crazy since the very beginning when I left Elliott Construction."

"Maybe we thrive on crazy," he replied, trying to lighten the severity of the moment.

She shook her head, making his hand drop away from her face. "Everything is piling on top of each other and I need to sort it out. There isn't much I can do to figure out Hope, but I can work on Transformations, figure out how to get it on the right track."

There wasn't anything he could do except nod in agreement. Afraid that if he pushed too hard, he would lose it all. Instead he retreated, but he also needed some reassurance. "Can we at least plan some time for us? Maybe Thursday evening?"

Charlee winced. "My evenings are going to be full with the Wheeler's project."

"How about next week? Could you squeeze out a few hours, maybe late afternoon from four to six-thirty?" Relief flooded through him when she nodded.

"I probably could towards the end of the week."

"Thursday?" Yeah, he was pushing a little, but he needed something concrete to look forward to.

"That should work," she agreed.

He searched her eyes. It was hard to tell what she was thinking, how she was feeling. She was trying too hard to keep her face impassive. Then she looked down to her hands, turned the cream soda bottle around in circles. His stomach flipped and flopped, knowing it was his cue to go.

"I'll let you get some sleep. Let's at least text, okay?" He got up from the table and shoved the ball cap back on his head.

"Of course," she replied, kind of automatically.

She followed him to the door, but before she could open it, he pulled her into a hug. Her head lay on his chest, his head tucked against the top of hers and he just held her for a moment.

"Good luck with Naomi and your projects," he said when he stepped back.

"Thanks."

It was the last thing she said before she closed the door behind him. The word repeated over and over in his head as he drove the few short blocks to his townhouse. As he thanked Anna for walking Petunia, then filled the dog's food and water dishes.

Thanks.

Not *I'll see you tomorrow.*

Not even *I'll text you.*

Definitely not *I love you.*

Just *thanks.*

It felt like the loneliest word in the world.

Chapter Twenty

VIBRATIONS FROM THE ELECTRIC sander rippled up her arm as Charlee worked on the Wheeler's original cabinets. They chose a pretty white oak for their counters, but had not decided if they wanted to stain or paint the original cabinets. Either way, the cabinets needed to be cleaned and lightly sanded. Thankfully, the Wheeler's decided to go away for the weekend so she wouldn't get in their way for this part of the job.

Yesterday, Bob helped her remove all the cabinet doors and unmount the cabinet base from the wall. This way Charlee could see which shelves needed repairs and have easy access to them. Plus, sanding from a sitting position was much easier than standing on a step ladder.

Charlee was looking forward to seeing the kitchen come together. Jenny and Walter decided to do the project in stages. Partially so it was easier on their budget, but also so they weren't in a constant construction zone. First up was getting the kitchen whipped into shape. Measurements were taken for the bottom cabinets, new counter tops, as well as the island. Naomi worked on putting together the specs for the order today, so all Charlee needed to do was review them tomorrow morning. Not how she wanted to spend her Saturday, but work was work and keeping the project moving along was important. Her goal for the weekend was to get the cabinets sanded, repaired, cleaned and remounted. That way Jenny could continue using them while they waited for the bottom cabinets and island supplies to arrive.

Get your phone ... Cause someone called. Get your—

Charlee grabbed her phone and answered the call before the Minions could continue their crazy ring tone.

"Charlee, where are you?" Her mother sounded peeved.

Charlee quickly did a mental run down. It was Friday night. Not their normal once-a-month family dinner night, that was next week. "Um, I'm at work. Is something wrong?"

Her mother harrumphed. "What's wrong, Charlee, is that you are supposed to be here for your nephew's birthday. We've been waiting and waiting for you and now dinner is getting cold. Hurry up and put away whatever you're playing with. How long will it take you to get here? I'll see if I can keep dinner warm long enough."

And once again, she was the bad daughter. "I'm sorry, Mom, but I can't come."

"What do you mean you can't come? We planned this, it should be on your calendar."

"Actually, you planned the party. If it was on my calendar, I would have let you know I wasn't going to be able to make it. I can't just drop work. I have deadlines to meet."

Her mother sputtered on the other end of the line. She never did like when Charlee pushed back, upsetting her plans. "Talk to the birthday boy, and be nice."

Before Charlee could offer to call him the next day, her nephew was on the phone. "Hewo?"

"Hey, Brian, how's your birthday going?"

"It's tomowow, Aunt Chawlee. Not today. But Gwanma thinks it's today," he giggled.

"I bet she made all your favorite things for dinner," she said, knowing her mother's tradition for birthday meals.

"And a chocolate cake!"

They talked for a few minutes about what he hoped to get for his birthday—the big number five. He told her about the Star Wars cupcakes he took to preschool that day and the super hero crown he got to wear during class.

"Oh, Gwanma said dinner is ready. Gotta go, Aunt Chawlee."

"Happy birthday! Love you," she said, just before she heard the phone drop, then get fumbled and picked back up.

"I can't believe you ditched me," Tyler whispered. "Get your butt over here."

Well at least this was something she could smile about. She doubted she'd ever grow out of the satisfaction of torturing her brother. "No can do, bro. Got to work, so suck it up."

"Where are you? Are you at Grandma's house?"

She just loved the desperation in his voice. Sadly, she wasn't close enough for him to join her. "No, I'm at the Wheeler's farmhouse, getting their cabinets done."

"Awesome. I'll see you as soon as I can escape."

"Tyler—" But it was too late. The line was dead.

Charlee just shook her head. There was no way her brother was going to escape their mother's clutches. Not during a birthday dinner.

This was just another example of why her mother thought she was a failure in the daughter department. She sucked at remembering birthdays. Even though Tyler told her she needed to put them in her phone's calendar, she just kept forgetting. She added getting a birthday gift for her nephew to her to-do list before getting back to work on the cabinet base.

A half hour later, someone knocked on the back door, startling Charlee.

"Hey, open up. It's me," her brother called from the other side.

Charlee crossed over to the door and let Tyler in. Bitter cold wind rushed in and she pulled the door shut as soon as he crossed the threshold. "Brr, it's cold out there tonight," she said, rubbing her hands up and down her arms. "How did you get out of dinner so fast?"

"I had a buddy from the station call to say they needed me. Plus, I got the little dude an awesome Lego set which means I scored extra food to take with me to the station." He held up a plastic bag. "Roast beef, mashed potatoes and green beans. I left before they did the singing and cake stuff."

Charlee just shook her head. "How is it that you're Mom's favorite? Doesn't she realize how devious you are?"

"Nope and she never will. Now eat up while I work." He handed the food off to her and she gave him instructions. Tyler grabbed a chair and settled in to continue what she had been working on.

"What's up with missing the dinner?" Tyler asked, running the sander along the wood grain, sand dust covering the bottom of his jeans.

"I must have missed a text or voicemail about it. I honestly don't remember getting the update." Charlee pulled out a fork and took her first bite of dinner, realizing she had been so focused on work, she had ignored her stomach's need for food. *Mmm.* One good thing about Mom, she really could cook. Her roast beef was tender and her mashed potatoes were the absolute best.

"Well, Mom was not happy." Tyler glanced up at her. "But then again, when is she ever happy at a family dinner, right?"

Charlee just nodded, nothing more needed to be said about their perfectionist mother who found fault in everything except her oldest daughter and grandchildren. Maybe if Charlee got married and popped out a few kids her mom would like her better. It was more likely that her mom would feel the need to fix Charlee as a mom, too. When her stomach was full, she grabbed a few cabinet doors, some sandpaper and got back to work.

"Okay, tell me the truth," Tyler said. "Did you really not know or were you just trying to get back at me for pulling your boyfriend over?"

"Would I be that cruel?" She winked at him.

Tyler did a one shoulder shrug thing. "Yeah, well, I'm over it, you know. I'm on board with you and Peter dating."

Charlee continued to sand, letting silence fall between them. Because of course, once things were on the rocks her brother would come around. Sometimes fate just sucked.

Tyler's sanding motion stopped abruptly. "Alright, what's up? Trouble in paradise already?"

Charlee wasn't in the mood to talk about Peter, especially with her brother. They were best friends which made it oh so awkward. Then again, maybe Tyler would have better insight on the whole Hope thing. "Have you seen Hope since she's been back?"

"Oh yeah," he said, returning to the task at hand.

"And," Charlee prodded.

Tyler shrugged. "She asked me out. When I said no, she asked if I'd be interested in some fun, no strings attached. When I told her no, she went off in a huff to find some other sucker to lure into her web."

Charlee blinked, taking all that in. Hope propositioned her brother. Whoa. Getting back to the info she wanted, she followed up with the question that had been on her mind. "As in Peter?"

Tyler snorted. "As in some stupid guy at the bar. Peter's not dumb enough to get involved with her again, especially after the way she treated him before we graduated."

"What happened?" Charlee knew they broke up, but not the specifics of it.

Tyler paused for a second. "It was a long time ago, so don't read a lot into it." She nodded, then he went on with the story. "It was senior year, right? You probably remember Dad always hounding me about where I was going, who I was with, and all that."

"Yeah, trying to keep you from doing stupid senior pranks," she said.

"And stuff," he continued. "There were lots of parties that year. Some of the rich kids were hosting parties two and three times a month, and suddenly, everyone was invited. No more division of the cool kids and the geeks. Everyone was hanging out together. It made for some interesting parties. The closer we got to the end of the school year, the more outrageous the parties became and the stupider some of the seniors got, taking risks they shouldn't have."

"Like what?" By the time she hit her senior year, her parents wouldn't let her go to any parties unless one of them supervised, which meant she was invited to precisely two parties, both of which were hosted by Mari.

"Like drinking, some drugs, and a lot of sex."

"Doesn't that happen every year though?" Other than some really good teenagers who had their heads on straight as far as morals and looking ahead to the future and herself being exiled from guest lists because of her parents, what Tyler described seemed to be what happened her senior year too.

He set the sanding tools down and stretched briefly before returning to work. "Yeah, the department cracks down on it a lot more. It's why I like working with the youth programs, trying to keep the kids from doing stupid stuff, but that year was different. There were a lot of pranks and dares. Hope loved to double dog and triple dog dare other seniors. She also got a real thrill out of being dared herself. The crazier the better."

While that didn't surprise Charlee, she knew there had to be something bad coming up. She chewed on her lip, wondering what Hope did and how it involved Peter.

"Skip forward to the beginning of April. Peter was out of town with his family for spring break, but Hope was stuck at home. Some seniors got together for a weekend party. There were a bunch of drinking games and a lot of dares. The smaller group egged each other on and did some really crazy stuff. Hope and a few other girls were dared to do a strip tease. One of the guys got out his parent's video recorder and taped the whole thing. The dancing, stripping, lap dances, and things went further."

Charlee felt like she was going to be sick. She couldn't

imagine being a part of something like that, even now as an adult.

"Peter found out a few weeks later at another party when a bunch of guys were playing the video in someone's bedroom. Let's just say it ended up smashed to bits and the ensuing fight between him and the guys who were watching the tape, then later with Hope, was pretty epic."

"How did all that happen and I never heard about it?"

"The power of fear. The parents of the girls on the tape found out and threatened to sue every single person at the party if they didn't keep their mouths shut and forget it ever existed. Some of the rich girls' parents made a few college contributions. I'm sure that helped keep it under wraps."

She just couldn't believe it. It was insanity. Sure, it happened now with cell phones, the internet and the ease of posting photos and videos online. But back in her high school days? Compared to the cell phone technology of today, it was like the dark ages. It was all land lines. Heck, she purchased her first digital camera while she was in college. Her first cell phone came after that and was provided by Elliott Construction.

The thought of Peter discovering the video . . . She just couldn't even imagine how that ripped him up. "How could Peter possibly be friends with Hope after all that?"

"A lot can be forgiven with the right amount of time. Besides, we all did stupid things our senior year."

"What did you do?" she asked, needing to change the subject.

Tyler kept his head down, focused on the cabinet door. "Besides propose to my girlfriend, then run off to the army when she rejected me?"

A sharp pang shot through Charlee. Once Tyler left, he refused to speak about Mari ever again. "I thought you wanted to go into the Army. Did you really go just because of Mari?"

He shrugged again, but this time his demeanor was solemn. "I thought she was it, ya know? I had all these plans. Guess I was wrong though." He gruffly cleared his throat, then changed the subject. "So what's the deal with you and Peter?"

She sucked in a deep breath, then let it out. "I'm afraid he's going to choose Hope over me."

Did she really just admit her deepest fear to her brother? That she would once again be inadequate at holding onto a man she cared about, and she definitely cared more for Peter than she ever cared about the guys from her past. Not that there were a lot of them. But Peter, he was important. What if he rejected her like Mari rejected Tyler? It ended up being the right choice for them, right? At least it had been for Mari. It broke her brother in a lot of different ways.

Would she end up like him? Broken and unable to move on? Doomed to never open her heart again for fear that it would be torn to shreds and never recover?

She looked at her brother, saw him quietly watching her, like he knew what she was thinking.

He tapped his chest with two fingers before returning to the sanding.

She got the warning, loud and clear.

Be careful or she'd end up just like him.

Chapter Twenty-One

CHARLEE HUFFED AS SHE DRAGGED Eden up the front porch steps of Graydon Green's house where Rachel's bridal shower was being hosted.

"Wait," Eden protested. "Just give me a few more minutes to check out the fountain."

"You've already circled around it three times. You can see it again after the shower." Charlee pushed the doorbell button, hoping to get Eden inside before she escaped into the front yard again. As soon as they pulled up to the house, Eden went nuts over the Charlie Brown hockey fountain. Apparently she was a big Charles M. Shultz fan and had every Peanuts comic book and video made.

Eden's bright eyes turned to Charlee. "Did you know Shultz owned a skating rink? He loved figure skating and hockey. That's why there are so many ice skating scenes in the plots of his comics."

Charlee rolled her eyes. This chick obviously had it bad, although it shouldn't surprise her. Eden was addicted to books after all. "Are you like this only for Schultz or are you a crazy fan girl for other authors, too?"

Eden turned very serious eyes on Charlee. "I can't divulge that information."

Charlee just laughed and was grateful Kristen opened the front door, allowing her to usher her friend safely inside.

"Charlee! Eden! I'm so glad you could make it." Kristen gave them quick hugs before releasing them.

"You look fabulous," Eden said, referring to Kristen's cute baby bump. "How are you feeling?"

"I've finally hit the good part of the pregnancy. I've seen way too much of my toilet bowl the past few months," she said, scrunching up her nose. The doorbell rang again. Before answering it, she motioned off to the left of the spacious foyer. "Why don't you head into the living room and say hello to Rachel?"

Charlee and Eden went through the archway leading into the living room, then paused just inside, overwhelmed by the abundance of decorations. Tissue paper fans, tassel garlands, paper flowers in vases, white vellum bags with battery-operated candles that showed off the heart designs, a white bridal shower banner with a boatload of glitter all over it and more.

"It's like the decorations aisle at Hobby Lobby threw up in here," Eden whispered.

Charlee tried to hold back a laugh, but ended up letting out a very unladylike snort instead. "Uh huh," she agreed.

Victoria sidled up to them, her gorgeous red hair pulled up in a twist gave an elegant flair to her simple jeans and emerald green cable knit sweater. "Blink, ladies. It grows on you after a few minutes."

"This isn't like Kristen at all," Charlee commented, focusing on Victoria rather than the distracting decorations.

"I believe the only thing Kristen planned was the guest list and invites," Victoria said. "The rest is actually part of a very smart compromise. Rachel wanted a sweet and simple wedding, but with her being the only daughter, her mother wanted to go all out. So they made a deal. Rachel gets the wedding she wants and Mom got to do anything she wanted for the bridal shower."

"Very smart, indeed," Eden agreed.

Victoria placed her hand on Eden's arm. "You'll have to ask her, but I think Rachel told me she got the idea from a book Graydon gave her mom when they got engaged. Something about a wedding survival guide for mothers and daughters."

"Ooh, that would be a great addition to stock in the store. Thanks for the tip." Eden pulled out her phone to make a quick note, then placed it back into her purse. "Well, the line is just going to get bigger to see the VIP. Let's get these gifts on the table and say hello to the bride."

Once the gifts were safely deposited on the designated table, they waited in the bridal greeting line. When they reached the front, Rachel pulled them both into a hug.

"Save me," Rachel covertly whispered.

Charlee chuckled. Rachel never did like being the center of attention. She could just imagine how smothered she must be feeling. "It's only two hours. You can do it."

"If anyone starts talking about the wedding night, please, please, please change the subject," Rachel pleaded.

"I promise," Eden said. "Even if I have to throw myself to the ground and fake a seizure."

Their friend smiled. "I might hope someone brings

something up just to see that. Now, go eat. The sooner everyone has food, the sooner we can get on with the party."

They gave her another hug, then went through the buffet line and settled onto a very comfy overstuffed leather couch. Charlee had a chance to see who the guests were. The usual suspects were there of course—the mothers of the bride and groom, the grandmothers and what looked like some aunts and nieces. She also recognized Faith and Eva who were married to Rachel's brothers. She met them during the clean up when Sweet Confections was vandalized. Some employees from Sweet Confections were chatting together near the gift table. Charlee was happy to see several friends from the Women in Business group, including Miss Marjorie, Adelyn from the city manager offices, and Eden's hair stylist, Taralyn.

Eden nudged Charlee. "Look who just walked in."

Charlee twisted around, then quickly turned forward again. Kristen had just greeted Betty, Peter's mom. She hadn't expected to see her here. Didn't even know she was friends with Rachel. Oh my.

"By the expression on your face, I can't tell if this is a good or bad development," Eden said, stealing a strawberry from Charlee's plate.

"I'm not sure. I mean, I assume Peter told her we were dating. His dad knows, so his mom should, too, right?"

Eden waggled her eyebrows. "We'll find out soon enough."

What? Charlee looked up. She'd been spotted and Betty was making a bee line right to where she sat.

"Charlee, dear," Betty said, putting her arms out for a hug.

She stood to greet her boyfriend's mom and ex-boss's wife, still not sure what to expect. Was a hug a good sign or was it a chance to get her close enough to issue dire threats to stay away from her husband and son?

"Mrs. Elliott," she began. "I didn't expect to see you today. How do you know Rachel?"

Betty pulled her in for a squishy hug before releasing her abruptly. "I'm on a church committee with her mother, Natalie. Rachel has helped us with many desserts for our church socials. It's just delightful to see you. How's everything going?"

Charlee's eyes widened as Betty pulled them both down to sit on the couch, sandwiching Charlee between Eden and Peter's mom.

"Um, everything is going well," Charlee said, trying not to go into specifics. Who knew what Betty's reaction to business talk would be? And if Betty was oblivious to the stuff going on between her and George, she didn't want to bring it up. It would be nice if one of Peter's parents liked her. She felt like she was tiptoeing through a mine field, hoping she wouldn't say something that would blow up and cause a scene.

"I have to say, it's been wonderful seeing my son so happy. He was just over at the house this morning, telling me about a surprise date he's planning."

That was an insightful tidbit. Not the part about the date, but knowing Peter actually talked to his mom about their relationship and that she perceived Peter to be happy.

"It's been fun to watch Charlee get all dopey eyed around Peter," Eden said, leaning forward to catch Betty's attention.

Charlee turned to her friend, surprised by her comment. She was even more surprised when Betty matched Eden's pose and continued to discuss their relationship. As if she wasn't sitting right in the middle of the two! Gah!

"I've known since Charlee returned from college that Peter was sweet on her. I was at the house the day she came by to talk to George about coming back to work at Elliott Construction. The look on Peter's face when he realized little Charlee was all grown up and an attractive woman to boot." Betty shook her head back and forth. "Well, that was priceless. I've wondered ever since if he was going to do anything about it," she revealed.

"I know exactly what you mean," Eden followed up. "When I moved to Crystal Creek to start my job at the library, I was intrigued by Peter. But it only took one time of seeing them in the same room together to know where his interests lay—and it definitely wasn't with me."

Betty reached across Charlee and patted Eden's hand. "Don't worry, dear, your very own knight in shining armor will come soon enough."

Holy hot dog on a stick. What in the world was Eden talking about? What she said couldn't be true. Eden had been in Crystal Creek for almost two years. Had she really been blind about Peter's feelings for her that long?

Charlee didn't think she could take much more. Thankfully, Natalie clapped her hands and announced it was time for the first bridal shower game which luckily involved everyone getting up and moving around to interview each other about Rachel and Graydon. After taking some paper and a pen from a basket, Charlee escaped to ask Rachel's sisters-in-law questions.

"Time for gifts," Natalie announced after the interviews were complete. With all the shifting around, Rachel found a seat between Chloe—who turned out to be Graydon's cousin—and Rachel's sister Faith. "After each gift is opened, the guest who brought it will share a story or fact about Rachel and Graydon."

After her mother's announcement, Rachel eyed the towering pile of gifts.

Charlee could just imagine Rachel calculating the amount of stories that could be told, which would likely take much longer than the end time printed on the shower's invite.

"Okay," Rachel said, rubbing her hands together. "Let's do this."

The guests laughed as Kristen lined up with a few gift bags in her hands. She handed Rachel a pretty black matte bag with a glittery diamond ring embellished on the front. Rachel read the card and announced the gift was from her friend, Piper. She pulled out the hot pink tissue paper, then gasped as she revealed a beautiful white ceramic frame with a swirly scroll design.

"Oh, it's perfect for our wedding photo," Rachel said, running her fingers over the design.

"Story time," Natalie reminded them.

"Let's start out with something easy," Piper said. "Rachel and Graydon are getting married on Saturday, May 4th. Rachel wanted to get married in the spring, but let Graydon choose the date."

"I think a May wedding is perfect, although Graydon wanted a short engagement, so I was surprised he didn't choose sometime in April," Rachel added.

"Seriously?" Chloe spoke up. "It's totally obvious, don't ya think?" When Rachel looked at her quizzically, Chloe stood and waved her arms around in some kind of fighter reenactment, ending in a familiar pose. "May the fourth be with you," she said in a deep voice, then straightened into a typical teenager stance with one hand on her hip. "It's, like, the awesomest wedding date ever."

Rachel's face slowly flushed red and her eyes looked like they were going to pop right out of her head.

"That sounds just like a typical man," Graydon's snobby Aunt Sarah said.

Natalie rushed in to soothe her daughter. "Just think of it this way, sweetie. He'll never forget your anniversary."

Rachel looked up at her mom. "But Star Wars? As in Yoda and that guy who wears all black?"

"Well, at least he rated your wedding as important as his love for The Force," Rachel's sister-in-law, Faith, said. "Wait a minute, that sounded much better in my head than when I actually said it. Sorry."

Rachel's eyes narrowed. "I'm going to kill him."

"Ooh, use a light saber and he'll totally die happy," Chloe said gleefully. The teenager's contributions weren't helping, so she whipped out her cell phone. "So, like, maybe I'll text Gray-Gray and let him know of his eminent demise?"

"You do that. Pass me the next gift," Rachel told Kristen, ready to move on from the topic. Although Charlee was sure it was filed away for discussion at a later point.

The remainder of the bridal shower was pretty typical with lots of funny stories, a few racy suggestions for the wedding night—which Eden and Charlee deflected to the best of their abilities. And best of all, it ended with a Sweet Confections lemon poppy seed cake filled with a light lemon Bavarian cream filling and finished with a French buttercream. It was truly a slice of heaven on a plate.

After goodbyes and giving Eden time to circle the fountain a few more times, they were back in Charlee's car, driving to the Kansas City Plaza for the Girls Night Out portion of the bridal shower.

Charlee tapped her fingers on the steering wheel, contemplating how to bring up some of the questions she had. She decided to just blurt it out and see where the conversation led. "You know earlier when you were talking to Peter's mom? You totally made up the story about Peter and me, right?"

Eden shifted in her seat to better face Charlee. "You know, I always wondered how in the world you didn't see it, when it was so clear to the rest of us."

"Define 'the rest of us'."

Eden shrugged. "Me, Victoria and a few other friends."

"Then why was Tyler oblivious?" Charlee asked.

Eden quirked an eyebrow. "Hello? Guy with testosterone overload. He's not paying attention to who likes who, unless it has to do with one of his buddies being humiliated and the ability to rub it in."

"Okay, that I can see. I just . . ." Charlee paused, concentrating on the road while she chewed her lip. "How did I not see that Peter was interested in me?"

"Sweetie, you were so focused on your job and earning George's trust, there wasn't much else you paid attention to."

Charlee's shoulders slumped. Even though she knew Eden was right, it made her sad to think of what all she missed during those years. Was that why none of her other relationships worked out? Maybe it wasn't her boyish body type, but because she didn't pay enough attention to the guy and their relationship. If she hadn't been so focused on proving herself at work, where would she and Peter be now? Would they have dated? Without the complications of leaving Elliott Construction and Hope returning, perhaps things would have gone smoother. Maybe they would have even gotten married by now.

The possibilities and what if's made her mind spin.

Eden placed her hand on Charlee's arm. "I've been a bridesmaid many times over, keeping a smile plastered on my face while college friends said I do. During a pitiful slump, I discovered some wise advice. Each woman has different experiences that mold her, hopefully change her into a better, more mature person with a deeper sense of who she is inside. Then one day, those qualities she's developed will attract a man's attention who will love her for the person she is, then they can share forever together. I've found it goes the other direction, too." Eden paused briefly, letting Charlee sort that out before continuing. "So you see, even if Peter is the one and he's known it for a while, you had some growing to do to become the person who was ready to love him."

"That's pretty profound. Who told you that?" Charlee asked, impressed by her friend's guidance.

Eden simply shrugged. "I'm a book addict. I spent some time thinking about all my favorite romance novels—what was realistic, what wasn't. Obviously the constant mind-blowing sex isn't, but the characters' flaws, how they grew because of their challenges and how the love story was related to that growth, well, that's one hundred percent life right there."

"Let me get this straight. What you're saying is your advice is based on fiction?" Charlee asked, questioning her friend's assessment.

"All fiction is based on truth," Eden said matter-of-factly. "Even futuristic space novels have characters with real emotions, reactions, and consequences. The world they live in may be made up, but the heart of who they are is based on truth."

Charlee let it all soak in. She turned the concept around a few times.

Well, dang. Eden was absolutely right.

Chapter Twenty-Two

PETER CHECKED OFF ANOTHER ITEM on the to-do list his secretary taped to his desk. Yes, she actually taped it—and not the easy-to-remove clear stuff either. It was an embarrassing heavy-duty duct tape with pink and purple hearts all over it. One of the guys added it to the Secretary's Day gift basket they gave Jan last year. At least she was putting it to good use, although he'd prefer it wasn't on his desk. Why couldn't she use it to make one of those weird purse things like his niece did?

The good thing was there were only two more items to finish up before he could head out the door and get ready for his date with Charlee. It had been a long week since that night at her house when she asked for a break. Other than dropping off smoothies and short conversations at Indulgence Row, he had stepped back to give her the time she requested. But man, it was killer. Now all he wanted was to wrap everything up and get to the picking-her-up part of the day. He did a lot of research, planning their date and the few hours they had together. He hoped all that time over thinking the date would pay off.

There was a knock at his door and he called for whoever it

was to enter.

"Hey, son, how are you?" his dad asked, settling into the chair on the other side of Peter's desk.

"Almost all caught up," Peter replied. "What can I do for you?"

"I just wanted to follow up on the bids that are due tomorrow."

Ah, the Bailey and Peterson projects. Peter knew the only reason his father wanted to bid on them was because they were projects Transformations would go after. A fact Peter had not confirmed for his father, but the old man knew how to find out details like that without his son's help. "Are you sure you want to move forward with those projects? There are others we could be bidding on that would use more of our crews."

"Don't worry about the crews. I have plenty of work planned for them. Can I review the bids?"

"Of course, you're the boss." Peter turned to his computer and pulled up the files for both projects, sending the final bids to the printer. His dad got up and pulled them off as they came out, reading through the stats, nodding and murmuring to himself. Once he had the last sheet, he returned to his seat.

"These look great. Let's go ahead and get them signed and stapled."

Peter tilted his head. "Are you in a hurry? They're not due until tomorrow."

"Better to get them in than to miss the deadline. Besides, we're both here to sign the forms."

Peter pulled out a pen and signed both sets of bids before handing the pen over to his father, who quickly scribbled his signature as well. Then George tapped the papers on the desk, evening them out again.

"I heard you're leaving early today. I can take care of getting these delivered," George offered.

Peter shrugged, not surprised by his father's micromanaging ways. "That's fine. Is there anything else you need me to do?" he inquired, hoping to steer his father away from asking why he was leaving early. He didn't want to fight about Charlee. Not today.

"Actually, there is. I'd like you to set up the next monthly client dinner. We're finishing up the mall parking garage. It would be a good time to take the Westhoff's out for dinner, as a thank you for choosing us. Plus, I heard they're getting ready to start taking bids for the stage three mall expansion."

Peter jotted down some notes. Thankfully, he rather liked the Westhoff sons who ran the retail side of the family empire. "Got it," he said. "I assume you and Mom will be joining us."

"I think I might let you take this one solo. See how you do."

Peter's head jerked up. "Really?"

"I figured I may as well see what I still need to teach you before I retire," George said gruffly, looking over at the wall of photos, avoiding Peter. "Just don't screw up." He pushed himself out of the chair, the bids in one hand.

"I won't," Peter replied, as his father nodded before leaving the room.

It was an odd conversation, one that left Peter wondering if his father was actually going to retire sooner rather than later. The old man had been talking about it for years, although most of the time it seemed to be more to appease his mother than any intentions of actually following through. George was tightfisted with the reins of the company. Letting go was not something he would willingly do.

Not that Peter minded. He dreaded the day he'd end up in charge, knowing it would be the last day he'd get to pick up a hammer and work on-site. On the other hand, it would also be the end of the tug of war between how his father ran Elliott Construction and how his father thought Peter should run the company. It was all a jumbled mixed up mess.

His father's retirement was a day he didn't want to arrive any earlier than needed.

"WHERE ARE WE GOING?" Charlee asked, peering out the truck's window.

Peter smiled as he turned onto a gravel road. They were about twenty minutes south of Crystal Creek, out on the country border.

Charlee turned to face him. "You know, my parents taught me not to go parking on dates. Do I need to call my father to come pick me up?"

"No, ma'am." He winked, enjoying the light banter.

"Seriously, where are we headed?"

"Patience, my dear. Our destination is just around the bend."

He loved the way she leaned forward, trying to get a glimpse of what was ahead. That was his girl, not a patient bone in her body. As they rounded the curve, a row of cement block storage sheds came into view with a big auction sign out front.

Charlee clapped her hands. "I love storage shed auctions. I

usually scan the ads for notices. This one wasn't on my radar. How did you find it?"

Peter parked at the end of the line of about a dozen other trucks. "This auction is by invitation only. You had to know the right people." He loved the confused expression on her face before he got out of the truck. She got out, too, before he could make it around to open her door. "Didn't your parents teach you to let your date open the doors for you?"

She just grinned up at him. "Sorry, I was too excited. So," she said, looping her arm through his. "Who do you know that I don't?"

"Well, it's not a matter of someone you don't know, as much as someone you didn't ask." He pulled a signed piece of paper from his back pocket and presented it to the lady at the check-in desk. Charlee peered over his shoulder catch a glimpse of the insignia at the top of the paper, then stifled a giggle.

The registration lady handed Peter his auction number and smiled. "Thank you for supporting Miss Daisy's Tumbling School."

Peter nodded. "I'm looking forward to the fundraiser. My niece loves Miss Daisy's classes."

The sweet lady beamed and wished them happy bidding.

"Your niece provided us with the hot date, huh?" Charlee bumped her hip against his before stealing the auction guidebook from his hand.

"What can I say, an uncle's got to keep his niece happy. Besides, it's critical she learns how to do the perfect cartwheel." Charlee's resulting laugh lightened his heart. *So far, so good.* "Daisy's husband runs a salvage business. Some items he sells in his shop, others he puts in these storage sheds to be auctioned off for the tumbling school fundraiser. The school limits the number of participants and they have to be invited by the tumblers to register. I actually had this planned for a while, knowing how you like to find fun things for the women's shelter. I'm glad you were able to come."

"Me, too," Charlee said, stretching up on tiptoe to give him a kiss on the cheek.

The best reward ever. "So what's in the guidebook? Anything good?" he asked.

They picked up a few water bottles, then found seats in a section where folding chairs were set up, and reviewed the storage shed content descriptions. Some had industrial equipment for restaurants. Another had fencing supplies and power tools.

She pointed to the list. "This looks perfect for the women's shelter." The one Charlee was most interested in was unit four. There were a variety of bed frames, random household furniture, lamps, and desks.

He leaned in close and said in a soft voice, "Then let's be sure we win it."

She linked her arm through his, shifting in her seat to be closer to him, warding off the afternoon chill. They still had about fifteen minutes before the auction began.

"How's everything going with Naomi?" That should be a safe enough subject, he thought.

Charlee's expression brightened. "That woman is amazing! It's only been a week, but already she has the office organized, she's become a bid researcher queen, and she even started a Transformations calendar all the employees can sync up to on their phones. Seriously, this calendar is amazing. It has different colors for each project, deadlines, and even the crew members' birthdays. There's a private section of the calendar that only she and I can see with office related stuff the others don't need access to."

"Sounds like it's a good fit for you."

Charlee nodded. "I really debated. I had doubts and was just crossing my fingers, hoping I had made the right investment choice. I have absolutely no reservations about it anymore. Naomi is a business genius. She's even putting together marketing plans for a company website and social media pages. Plus, she pitched some fun cross-promotional contests and giveaways with our subcontractors, vendors and clients. She has all this energy, and thankfully, it's contagious. Everyone on the crew loves her. I just wish I could clone about ten more of her."

"Elliott Construction is still in the dark ages when it comes to a web presence. Dad never really saw the potential behind it since Elliott Construction already had established contacts. I think Naomi has the right idea for Transformations, setting you apart from others, putting your talents in front of potential clients through the digital and social aspect of online marketing. Very modern and it has the potential to create a lot of buzz."

"The best part has been all the stress Naomi has taken off my shoulders. I didn't realize how thin I had stretched myself, how close to the breaking point I was, until I was able to hand it over and step away."

Peter dropped a kiss on the top of her head. "Sounds like I need to send Naomi a big box of chocolates."

A soft laugh floated up to him. "She certainly wouldn't say no to chocolate." Charlee straightened, moving away from him. "It looks like they're getting ready to start."

The rumble of the first storage shed's door opening alerted the other bidders to begin gathering. Peter and Charlee followed the small crowd, listened to the auctioneer go over the rules for bidding, when the sheds needed to be cleared out, how to arrange for delivery if needed and payments at the registration table. Unlike other auctions where people bid on specific items, storage shed auctions were a luck-of-the-draw event. There was a general list of items in each unit, but bidders didn't get to review the actual stock in advance. Whoever won hoped what they paid was low enough to turn a profit.

Peter had attended this particular auction last year and knew Miss Daisy's husband didn't fill the units with junk. There may be a few items that needed some repairs, but most of the stock was in decent condition. Definitely the kind of stuff Charlee liked to renovate in her classes.

The bidding began on the first unit. The auctioneer was hilarious, referring to bidders by clothing or other things that made them stand out, rather than by their actual bidder number. It was all part of what made the fundraiser much more interesting than a regular run-of-the-mill auction.

Peter paid attention to who was interested in what, noting a few potential competitors for unit four. When unit three's stock of restaurant equipment was completed with the highest winning bid so far, Peter took Charlee's hand and they moved to unit four. The doors were unlocked, then rolled up to reveal a menagerie of all things wooden and home furniture worthy.

Love Under Construction

The way things were stacked made it difficult to see what all was actually in the shed, but it looked promising.

"Now starting the auction for unit four. As stated before, please refer to the program for a general description of the unit's contents. Who would like to start the bid with $50? $50 to Mr. Green shirt."

"$60!" Came a call from the back.

"$60 to Mr. Cowboy Hat."

The bidding continued, up through $125. Charlee started to get anxious.

"Just wait," he said. "Be patient. It's going to slow down and we'll see who the serious bidders are."

Once the bids hit $175, they trickled down to two bidders. The man with the cowboy hat and an older gentleman in a plaid green shirt. When the bid hit $190, the plaid green shirt bidder gave up. There was a pause.

"$190 is our current bid. Do I hear $200?"

There was a pause, then Peter nudged Charlee. He could tell she was wavering. The bidding was higher than she expected. Generally, he saw her pick up a piece here and there, but never a big load like this all at once. "I'll split the cost with you. It's going to fill your classes with projects for the next year."

"Going once," the auctioneer called.

"$225," Charlee called out.

"Ooh, the pretty little blonde down front has joined the bidding." The auctioneer tipped his own cowboy hat in her direction.

The man in the black cowboy hat wasn't happy that the pretty little blonde just upped the bid significantly. "$230," he called back, challenging her.

"I have $230. Would you like to bid $240, pretty little lady?"

Charlee turned to face the man with the black hat. "$250."

Just seeing her stand her ground, not wavering, must have been enough because the Mr. Cowboy Hat backed down. "It's all yours," he said. Then he and the rest of the crowd laughed as Charlee did a happy dance.

"You haven't won yet," Peter reminded her, smiling at her enthusiasm.

"The final bid for unit four is $250. Any other bids? Going once? Twice? Sold to the pretty little blonde up front. Enjoy, sweetie." The auctioneer winked at her before moving on to unit number five. Mr. Cowboy Hat nodded to them both as he moved on to the next unit.

"We got it!" Charlee exclaimed, throwing her arms around his waist and squeezing tight. "Let's go pay for it. Oh man, how are we going to get it all back to Crystal Creek?"

He smiled at her enthusiasm, especially having her wrapped up close to him in the hug. "I planned ahead and reserved a trailer. I know how much women like to go shopping."

She smacked his arm, then pulled him towards the registration table where they split the cost of the unit. After some help from the volunteers, the trailer was hooked up to Peter's truck and pulled up in front of unit four.

Charlee was in hyper mode, noting the various items and how she could use them for her classes. She was particularly excited about three sets of bedside tables.

"I know ladies who need some of these. I'm going to make

this our next project!"

There were a few items that required more fixing up. One headboard had some wood rot and they pitched it into the on-site dumpster.

"It's too bad these legs are bent. It would make a fun homework spot for someone's kids," Charlee said, examining an old-style school desk. Peter remembered sitting at a similar desk when he was in elementary school. A metal base with a wood top the kids would scrape their names into. There was even an old clump of gum stuck inside the side shelf where books and pencil boxes were stored.

"I bet I could straighten them out. I have a bunch of metal shop tools back at my place. How about I see if I can get it back into shape?"

They loaded it and the remaining items that were keepers into the trailer, then closed and locked the back gate. They chatted with Miss Daisy and her husband for a few minutes before heading out.

Peter checked the time on the truck's clock. It was just before six in the evening. "That took a little longer than I expected. How about we get some food to go, then I'll drop you off at the Wheeler's. I can grab some guys and get everything unloaded into your storage shed, then come back to pick you up."

"Are you sure? I won't be done until around ten."

"Absolutely. There's an old-fashioned diner near here that got great reviews. Want to stop there?"

Charlee agreed. The Sock Hop Diner was a tiny building, reminiscent of the 50's with its glowing neon lights, red vinyl booths, and black and white checkered flooring. The best thing about it was the old fashioned soda and ice cream bar. They ordered bacon cheeseburgers and chocolate malts, then got back on the road.

"This is amazing," Charlee said before sucking more malt through the straw. "My grandma used to take our family out for meals like this, but that restaurant closed a long time ago."

"I'm glad it popped up on Google. For such a little place, it sure had a lot of great reviews. I never would have stopped otherwise."

When they reached the Wheeler's, Charlee unwound the storage shed key from her key chain and reminded him what number it was. Then she unbuckled, leaned over, took his face in her hands and surprised him by not just putting her lips to his, but by teasing him with nibbles before deepening the kiss. Peter sunk his fingers into her hair as they fed hot kisses to each other, making him wish they were anywhere other than parked in front of her client's house. He groaned when Charlee slowed down the action and eased back.

"I had a great time today. Thank you, Peter." Then she shifted away and was out the door, running across the lawn, up the front porch steps and into the house, while he sat there grinning like an idiot.

It took a few phone calls, but he wrangled Noah, Cameron and Tyler into helping him unload everything except the old school desk. He put up with their moaning and whining, then treated them to a beer at Freddy's.

Hope was there, but he just nodded and stuck with the guys. Besides, she seemed to be doing just fine with the guy she was talking to at the bar. If there was one thing he learned this week, it was that he couldn't let the past get in the way of his future with Charlee.

He kept his limit to one beer, then switched to soda, which meant all the more razzing from the guys, but he didn't care. He kept an eye on the time and once it hit nine-thirty, he was out the door and heading to the Wheeler's. To Charlee.

Jenny Wheeler invited him in and showed off her kitchen in progress. He complimented the new cabinets, the island base that was installed, everything just waiting for the new counter tops, sinks, disposal and dishwasher.

He watched Charlee as she talked Jenny and Walter through the upcoming weekend. He loved the animated way she moved her hands, how she pointed out different things to Jenny, then finishing up with a hug—initiated by Jenny, who was over-the-moon excited.

The rest was a blur. He listened to Charlee's excitement as he drove, as she talked through some ideas with him and followed up on the unloading of the auction items. It seemed much too soon when he pulled up to the curb in front of her home.

He walked her to the front door. She wrapped her arms around him and just laid her head against his chest.

"Today was wonderful."

He rubbed his hands up and down her back, giving her a light massage. "You're welcome. I've really missed us."

There, he got it out and didn't sound like a wuss.

She lifted her head and their eyes met. "Would you feel brave enough to come to a family dinner with me tomorrow night?"

Something bright and happy grew in his chest. Dinner, not as her brother's friend, but with Charlee. Together. "I think I can handle it."

She flashed him a mischievous smile. She unlocked her front door, then grabbed his sleeve and tugged him inside before pushing the door closed with her foot. "I don't think I'm quite ready to say good night."

He mimicked her earlier action and tugged her in close, one hand skimming down over her hip, then around to her behind that he loved so much. The other hand sank into her hair and tilted her head up as he dropped a kiss to her forehead, then the tip of her nose. Her soft laugh was cut off when their lips joined together, melting her smile into his.

Chapter Twenty-Three

FRIDAY MORNING, CHARLEE SAT in her office, reviewing the final bids for the Peterson and Bailey projects. Both were small office renovation jobs, but would add a considerable amount of cash into Transformations' bank account. She triple checked the quotes Naomi prepared, then emailed them off to their respective offices. She made a note on her calendar for Naomi to follow up at the end of the following week. It usually took about that long for companies to go through their bids, then select who they want to work with.

She moved on to some bookkeeping items. It was pay day, a happy day for her crews, but one with mixed emotions for the employer. All the local, state, and federal taxes made her head swim. Just another reason on top of the million others for why she was incredibly grateful for her office manager. Now all she needed to do was muddle through reviewing Naomi's work. She definitely looked forward to the day she could take Naomi's advice and hire a bookkeeper as well.

A ding sounded from her laptop, notifying her of an incoming message. She switched from the accounting software over to her email. It was from the Bailey project. Probably just a confirmation that they received her bid. She clicked to open the letter, which started off with a confirmation, but ended with a note that they chose another construction company. They invited her to submit a bid again in the future.

Wow. That was fast. They must have a decisive manager. She shrugged and mentally recalculated upcoming income possibilities. Between Indulgence Row, the few smaller projects she was taking on in the evenings and the Peterson project, she should be fine for a while.

About an hour later, her eyes were going dry but she was almost done with payroll when another incoming message alert sounded. She switched over to find an email from the Peterson project. The hair on the back of her arms stood up. She hesitated, then clicked on the email link. They also chose another construction company. What were the chances two companies would make decisions that quickly? Especially when bids were supposed to be open until noon and it was barely three in the afternoon now.

She wrote a reply email, thanking the manager for meeting with her and reviewing her bid. Then she asked which company they chose for their project. She chewed on her bottom lip and clicked send.

The next ten minutes dragged by, as Charlee refreshed her email, hoping and dreading the reply. It appeared in her inbox. She didn't even have to open it as the answer displayed in the preview bar.

Elliott Construction.

She pulled out her cell phone and looked up the phone number for Mark Bailey, who she met with to go over their needs for the bid. The phone rang a few times, then Mark picked up.

"Bailey Associates, this is Mark."

"Hi, Mark, Charlee Jackson here. I just wanted to call to say thank you for reviewing my bid."

There was a brief pause before Mark replied. "Of course, Charlee. You're welcome."

There was another pause and Charlee got a bad feeling. "So hey, which company did you choose to do the work?"

"Well, I believe it was Elliott Construction."

"Elliott, really? Peter will do a great job for you," she said, trying to sound upbeat.

"Actually, we met with George yesterday afternoon when he came in. Kind of old fashioned, but he wanted to hand deliver the bid."

Yesterday. "Can I ask when you signed with him?"

There was another brief pause. Too many pauses in this conversation. "Um, well, he made us a good deal, Charlee. I'm sorry."

That answered her question. They didn't even review her bid. Elliott Construction stole both bids out from under her and any other companies sending in bids.

"I see. Well, you can't pass up a good deal. Thanks again, Mark." She disconnected the call. Her knuckles turned white as she gripped the cell phone. She closed her eyes and resisted the urge to hurl it at the wall. Instead she dialed a number she knew by heart.

"George Elliott," came the gruff voice on the other end.

"How dare you?" she seethed.

"Who is this?"

"You know who it is. You knew who it was from caller ID before you even answered the phone. What right do you have to undercut and make deals before bidding was even closed?"

"Ah, Charlee, my dear, if you want to play the game, then you need to do it well. Put on your big boy pants." His deep, annoying chuckle came over the line. "I guess that analogy doesn't work quite so well for you, does it?"

Anger choked up her throat. She was so furious, she couldn't even speak to the devilish pain in the ass.

"Now," his tone smoothed out. "I understand you and Peter are dating. Maybe this would be a good time to give up this business nonsense and come back to work here."

Of course he wants me back, Charlee thought. *But only because he's losing business. Not because he values me, my talent or my goals.* "I am where I belong," she replied firmly. "I will never come back to Elliott Construction. Does Peter know what you did?"

"Who do you think worked up the bids?" George asked, taunting her.

Charlee froze. It couldn't be true. Peter wouldn't do that. He respected her work, her desire to own her own company. She shook her head. No, George is just messing with her, making her doubt her hopes, her feelings.

"I don't believe you," she said, although her voice didn't come across as convincing as she would have liked.

"Well, while you were otherwise occupied yesterday afternoon, I secured both the Peterson and the Bailey projects. How was your date, by the way? Did you enjoy the auctions?" George's deep-gut hacking laugh reverberated through the phone line. "Perhaps you need to learn to be more mindful of your competition."

Charlee disconnected the call and dropped her phone to

the desk. No. No, it couldn't be true. She put her head in her hands and pulled hard on the roots of her hair, trying to make sense of the crazy turn her life just took.

AT THE END OF THE work day, the crew came through the office for their paychecks. Charlee tried to cheer up and go along with the Juans' playful banter, but she just couldn't get into it. Crank and Sadie both asked if she was okay, but she just passed her bad mood off to a long week. Eventually they left to head home to their families and both Juans left for a night out.

Now if she could just get rid of Bob. She loved the guy, but really, her brain was fried from analyzing the conversation with George.

"So what's really going on?" Bob asked, settling into the old folding chair across from her desk.

Charlee played with a paper clip, not sure if she should tell him what happened or not. Then again, he had worked for George far longer than she had and might have a good perspective. She looked up, met his sympathetic brown eyes. "Do you think Elliott Construction would stoop to sabotaging Transformations?"

Bob's eyebrows drew together and he sat back in his seat, bringing a hand up to rub the side of his scruffy day-old beard. He spent a minute thinking it over before dropping his hand in his lap. "Well, it depends on who you're referring to at Elliott. We already know George can be ruthless. We've lost several subcontractors and vendors because of him. But Peter, he's more like his mom, which is one of the reasons the old man won't let go of the business."

Charlee tapped the paper clip on the desk top. Bob hadn't said anything she didn't already know. And really, she didn't care about George as much as she was worried about Peter's role in all of this.

"Talk to Peter," Bob said, drawing her attention back up to him. "He's your friend. He'll tell you the truth."

"That's what I'm afraid of," Charlee mumbled, then she thanked Bob for staying and being part of her crew. They both went downstairs and Charlee locked up the house. She looked at her watch. She was going to be late for dinner with Peter and the whole family.

Could she keep up a happy, nice façade until she and Peter left? She just wasn't sure, but she would try for the sake of not ruining her mother's night.

KEEPING UP THE CHARADE was harder than she thought it would be, starting with her arrival when Peter greeted her and leaned in for a kiss. She quickly turned her head, causing his lips to land on her cheek instead, then moved away to say hello to her annoyingly perfect sister Julie, her perfect banker husband, and their two perfect children. Little Brian was talking up a storm about his 100th day of preschool, while three-year-old Brooke latched onto Charlee's leg to compete for equal attention time. Charlee ignored Peter's confused looks and dived in to entertain the children while her mother brought out dinner. Peter tried to get her attention, but she just smiled and made excuses while she settled Brooke into her booster seat and helped prepare the kids' plates. The most distracting moment though was when he placed his hand on her leg, just above her knee and squeezed. She froze with a forkful of mashed potatoes halfway to her mouth, her wide eyes darting up to meet his very confused expression.

She just didn't how much longer she could keep up the charade. When her father asked about the business, she replied it was fine. When he asked for more details, she changed the subject to Tyler and the happenings around town. Of course, she was forgotten as soon as Julie announced she was expecting baby number three, which led to an absolutely diverting conversation about baby names. Julie was thinking Brody for a boy or Brandy for a girl.

Peter leaned over and whispered into her ear. "What is it with all the matchy-matchy names?"

She knew he was trying to make her laugh or at least talk with him, but she just shrugged and threw out the name Brianna into the mix. Peter was clearly unhappy, but she hoped he'd play along until they left. But she was wrong.

As soon as dinner finished, her mother started clearing away the dishes to bring out dessert. Charlee stood up to help, but Peter took her arm and excused them for a few minutes before dragging her into the living room.

"What's going on?" Peter asked, turning her to face him rather than the curious onlookers from the dining room table.

"Peter, please," she kept her voice low, avoiding looking at him. "Let's talk later."

He put his finger under her chin, forcing her to make eye

contact. Hurt and confusion shone in his gray eyes. He slowly shook his head. "I can't go back in there with you acting like this."

"Like what?" she challenged.

"Like you would rather fawn all over the sister you can't stand than be by my side for a few minutes." His voice softened, his eyes pleading. "Charlee, please, what's wrong?"

She clenched her hands, her fingernails biting into her palms, debating, debating, debating. She started this jumping in tool belt and all, so she may as well keep plowing ahead. "Tell me about the Peterson and Bailey bids."

Peter's eyes widened and his hand dropped from her face. He shoved both hands into his pockets, a sign that he was either nervous or guilty.

"Did you prepare the bids?" she asked.

His head jerked up and down in the affirmative, his lips closing into a hard line.

Her mouth dried and her tongue darted out to moisten her lips. "When?"

Peter hesitated, then looked down. "I finalized them Thursday morning."

"Then?" she prompted.

His shoulders slumped, still avoiding looking at her. "Then Dad wanted them."

"Did you know he was going to take them in Thursday afternoon?" She held her breath, waiting for his answer. Please say no. Please say no. She kept hold of that one frayed string of hope. She could mend it. He just had to say no.

He deflected the question. "We decided not to talk business, not to let it be a part of our relationship."

"Did you know?" she asked again, this time her voice even and clear.

"We said—" he started.

"Did you know?" she shouted, breaking past the constraints of privacy. Who cared who heard, she needed to get through to him. She needed the answer. She shoved at his chest, pushing an unsuspecting Peter back a step. "Did you know he was taking it in? That he was going to push them to sign early? To cut me out? Did you know?"

"Yes!" Peter blurted out, exasperated.

It was like a torrential storm broke. Charlee blindly shoved Peter, while he stood there, solid and still, and took it. "You jerk! You butt-faced toad. You played me."

Peter took a few steps back. "I didn't know he was going to lower the bid and get them to sign. There's more—"

"No! I don't want to hear any more. Just get out!" Charlee pushed him towards the front door.

Peter grabbed her wrists and pulled her close, trying to calm her. "Charlee, please. Let's talk about this."

She looked into his gray eyes, all of her hurt, frustration and anger were reflected back at her. How could she have trusted him? How could he have done this—to her, to them? "Get. Out." She bit out the words, hard, low and final.

"Charlotte Elizabeth!"

Peter released her wrists and she stumbled away, then she turned to see her mother, father, and the rest of her family crushed together in the entry way.

"Charlee, stop this," her mother said, rushing forward.

Charlee wanted nothing more than to have her mother's arms wrapped around her. She stepped forward to meet her, but instead, her mother took Peter's arm.

"Peter is a longtime friend of this family. This isn't your house, it's ours, and Peter is welcome anytime he wants," she said.

Charlee felt like her whole world stopped spinning. Her mother was taking Peter's side? Her own mother? She looked from her to Peter's stunned expression, then back to her mother, still holding his arm.

"He sabotaged me and you're taking his side? What about me? I'm your *daughter*," she cried.

Her mother seemed to falter, but recovered quickly. "I think you both need to talk and work things out."

Charlee laughed. First just a short bark, but then it started pouring out. She pressed her hands to her chest, as if that would push it back down, but she couldn't make it stop. Peter took a step toward her, but Charlee backed up, putting her hands out to ward him off as her laughing fit abruptly stopped. "Well, I learned something very important today, didn't I?" she said, her voice cold and hard, just like how she felt inside. "You can't trust anyone—not even the people you love."

She made a wide berth around Peter and her mother as she walked past them, then out the door. She heard her mother call her name, but it was too late. She wanted nothing to do with them. She pulled her keys out of her pocket, got into the truck and turned it on. Someone pounded on the passenger door. She looked up to see her brother.

"Unlock the door, Charlee. Let me in," Tyler demanded.

She just looked away and backed out of the driveway. She was vaguely aware of her brother swearing then running for his truck. But she didn't care.

Didn't care. Didn't care.
And she didn't think she ever would again.

Chapter Twenty-Four

CHARLEE DIDN'T REMEMBER the drive to her house, parking, or getting inside. Yet here she was, standing in front of the refrigerator. Why was she in front of the fridge? Why did she come here instead of going to bed? She couldn't think. Couldn't remember.

Didn't want to remember.

Then her brother was beside her, swearing at her for running away, for driving when she was upset and didn't she know better...

But it was like a radio playing in the background and all she could do was stand there, looking at the fridge, trying to remember what she wanted from inside.

She winced in pain when Tyler grabbed her arms and gave her a good shake. "Charlee! Dammit, talk to me."

She finally looked up. His face was stark, filled with anguish. Because of her. She just ruined his relationship with his best friend, walked out on her family and yet here he was. In her kitchen.

Her knees buckled and Tyler caught her, held her in a bear hug as she heaved huge body-wracking sobs. The kind that should make the earth quake and even the sturdiest of buildings to crumble. If only the tears could extinguish the fire as she felt her dreams, her wishes burned to a crisp.

Later, when dusk settled over the living room, Charlee blinked her irritated eyes, grateful for her brother, who still sat with her on the couch, letting her head rest on his shoulder.

"Sorry for ruining your shirt," she said, quietly. She was sure it was covered with lots of disgusting snot and slobber. At least she wasn't wearing mascara.

"Yeah, well, I needed a new one anyway," he said.

"Thanks," she said. He patted her back in response, then continued the soothing up and down motion. She remembered having nightmares when she was around ten years old and a teenaged Tyler rubbing her back to help her calm down and fall back asleep. Although he warned her if she ever told anyone about it, he'd never do it again. The memory made her smile.

"So, it was that bad, huh?" he asked.

She paused, reviewing the day in her head. "It sucked."

"Yep," he agreed.

They sat in silence, letting the minutes pass by. Charlee wished the minutes would turn into hours so the day could be over. But no, the seconds still ticked by on her grandmother's clock.

"Maybe you should go away, take a break from everyone and get some perspective," Tyler suggested.

She pushed up into a sitting position, his hand fell to his lap. "It sounds nice, but I can't leave Transformations. It would be irresponsible." She shook her head, wishing she could just get in her truck and drive away.

"You have Bob. He has more experience than you and

would keep the crew on track with Naomi's help. It's not like you're leaving forever, just a few days."

A few days wouldn't be so bad. And today is Friday, so really she had the weekend, maybe part of next week.

But she had work to do for the Wheeler's.

Sweet Jenny would probably let her reschedule.

And Bob would do a good job.

She chewed on her lower lip, thinking over Tyler's advice.

"Don't think about it so hard. Just do it," he urged.

Her lip popped out from between her teeth and she made her decision. She pulled herself up from the couch and left Tyler with instructions to raid her fridge for a drink, while she went into her bedroom, pulled out a large sports duffel bag and started packing. She called Bob and Naomi, told them she was going out of town for an emergency and asked if they could handle things next week. They were surprised, but willing to step in. Then she called Jenny, who said they were fine with Bob coming over to do the installations.

Now she just had to figure out where to go. What to do.

Or who to call, she thought as inspiration struck. She quietly closed her bedroom door, then went into the bathroom and closed the door there, too.

She scrolled through her phone contacts to Mari's name and clicked the call link. When Mari answered the phone with an excited greeting, tears threatened to choke her throat once more. She swallowed through the thickness.

"Mari? I need help." She didn't go into details, just that she needed to leave and asked if she was ready for the renovation to be done.

"Of course! Listen, you just get to the airport. I'll take care of the rest."

Charlee's shoulders slumped with relief. She packed a few final items, then grabbed her bag.

"What did you decide?" Tyler asked when she emerged.

"I made some calls and pulled a few things together." She couldn't tell him where she was going. Not just because it was Mari, but because she didn't want him to give in and tell anyone else where she was headed. "Do me a favor, don't call unless it's an emergency." Alarm flared in Tyler's eyes. "I'll text you to let you know I'm okay, but I need some distance."

"I didn't mean from me," he countered.

She hugged her overprotective brother. "Let me get my head back on straight. It's going to be okay."

Or at least she hoped so.

WHEN CHARLEE ARRIVED at the airport, she followed directions from Mari's text message to Hangar 7. She parked her truck in the private lot, grabbed the duffle bag and made her way through the VIP section of the airport until she reached the correct location.

She discovered a hunky guy in coveralls doing a final check on a private plane. He turned to her and flashed a bright white smile. "Can I help you?"

"Yes, I'm Charlee Jackson."

Hunky Guy extended his hand. "Yes, Ms. Jackson. Mrs. Diaz told us to expect you. Please go ahead and board. We'll be leaving shortly."

Charlee nodded and thanked him, then went around to the other side of the plane. She gripped the bitter cold railing and climbed the steps leading into the plane.

"Hello," a young preppy flight attendant greeted her. "My name is Kara. It's wonderful to have you with us today. I'm just finishing a few preparations, then I'll be right with you. If you'd like you may explore the plane before we take off. It's just us flying today, so you can choose any seat you prefer."

Charlee's head spun as the sugary sweet Kara made her way to the back of the plane. Following Kara's advice, she stepped into the main cabin which was light with smooth cream walls and accented with gorgeous dark wood trim. The seats looked more like cushy recliners. Charlee set her bag down. So this is how the rich lived.

"You need to stow that, you know."

Charlee gasped and turned to find Mari, or at least her smiling image on a screen mounted to the wall behind her.

"I can't believe this," Charlee said as she sank into the soft leather seat, laughed and even wiped away a few tears.

"The wonders of technology and businessmen who insist on making the most of every minute they have. So, have you met Garrett yet?"

Charlee tilted her head, "Who?"

"The pilot. Tall, good looking..."

Kara stopped beside Charlee and winked. "He greeted you when you arrived."

"Oh, Hunky Guy," Charlee said, blushing a bit. She glanced up at Kara who pressed a hand to her chest and laughed.

"No worries, I can keep a secret." Kara winked, then handed her a cream soda and a small bottle of Dramamine.

"I filled Kara in on your favorite drink and sad tendency towards motion sickness. Please don't puke on my plane," Mari said.

A smile tugged at Charlee's mouth. "I'll do my best." She popped open the bottle of soda then downed one tablet. With a direct flight to California, one should be enough to keep her stomach calm without making her overly drowsy.

"Hello again," Hunky Guy, er, Garrett greeted her. He ditched the coveralls to reveal dark navy slacks and a white dress shirt with all the fancy bars, pins and other stuff that decorates a seasoned pilot's shirt. He introduced himself and shook Charlee's hand. "I'll be getting you safely to California to meet with Mrs. Diaz. Ma'am," he said, nodding to the screen. Mari simply nodded back. "I'll let you get prepped for take-off. Please let Kara know if you need anything."

"That's my signal to sign off. No Wi-Fi during take-off." Mari paused. "Whatever is going on, just put it aside for a few hours, okay? You'll be here soon enough, then we can talk. So snooze or watch a movie. I'm going to head to the store to stock the fridge. If there's anything in particular you want, text me."

"Thanks, Mari," Charlee said, fighting back the sting of tears before their connection ended. She buckled up as Kara went through the safety protocols and stocked her up with a blanket, pillow, magazines and a selection of movies she could start with just the click of the remote control built into the seat.

As they took off, she looked down at sparkle of lights that lit up the Kansas City skyline, then the various suburbs until she could identify Crystal Creek. From up there, everything looked idyllic, but her heart ached for all she was leaving behind. She closed her eyes, thinking perhaps she'd fall into the oblivion of sleep. Instead the scene at her mother's house replayed over and over, making her question all the what-if's.

What if she had acted differently?

What if she insisted Peter wait to talk?

What if they would have left to talk somewhere else?

What if, what if, what if . . .

She sat up and clicked on the TV. She couldn't handle the torture. Instead she decided to take Mari's advice and got lost in the latest Disney cartoon. Two movies later, the plane touched down in a small airport outside of L.A. Clouds, or most likely smog, blocked the stars, making the night feel even darker, closer. Metal posts along the tarmac broke the darkness with brief circles of light that faded into darkness before the plane entered another. After what felt like the longest parking job ever, they stopped in front of another hangar and Garrett's voice came over the intercom.

"Please give us a few moments to get the door opened and the stairway in place. We'll deliver your bag to Mrs. Diaz's car."

Charlee's palms were moist as she rubbed her thumb into the opposite hand's palm.

Her best friend was just outside that door, a few steps away.

Then Kara motioned for her and Charlee unbuckled and was out of her seat, through the door, and rushing down the steps. Mari was right there, waiting for her in jeans, a navy terry cloth hoodie and her signature long, curly black hair falling over her shoulders and down her back. Charlee's arms went around Mari and she felt her friend pull her in. Not for a quick so-glad-you're-here hug, but for a firm I've-got-you-now hug.

Charlee sank into the embrace and soaked in the moment. It took several deep breaths to settle her emotions before pulling back.

Mari touched Charlee's short wispy hair. "I like it," she said. Then her expression turned serious. "As much as texting and phone calls are great, three years is way too long between visits."

"I agree. I've missed you," Charlee said. The last time they were face-to-face was during the funeral for Mari's husband and tiny son.

"We can talk more later," she murmured, then her smile turned mischievous. She threaded her arm through Charlee's and pulled her towards a black BMW with heavily tinted windows. "So, I rented a truck. I haven't driven one since my summers as a teenager working on a farm, but seriously, this thing is huge! I was afraid I'd squish all the little cars on the freeway like bugs so I left it back at the house. I figure tonight we'll talk, maybe get some sleep, then tomorrow we can hit Home Depot for whatever supplies you need."

An airport employee opened the passenger side door for Charlee while Kara stowed the duffel bag in the trunk. Mari skirted around to her side of the car and Garrett opened the door. She paused when Garrett's hand covered hers. Charlee wished for super power hearing, wondering just what Hunky Guy was saying to Mari. Maybe she was finally dating again.

Mari ignored Charlee's gaze as she slid into the driver's seat. Garrett closed the door, then she started the car and drove away. They remained quiet as they navigated through a tangle of roads before getting on a highway heading towards Palos Verdes.

"So," Charlee began. "Hunky Guy, huh?"

Mari gripped the steering wheel hard. "One thing you'll learn this weekend is that everyone thinks they're friends with celebrities. Do you know what he said? Believe me, it wasn't scintillating. He expressed his condolences. Again." She slid a frustrated glance over at Charlee. "It's been three years of condolences. Sometimes I just want to shove them down their throats."

Charlee shifted in her seat. "What you're telling me is that there won't be any fascinating sex stories of the rich and famous to look forward to? I'm immensely disappointed."

Mari threw her head back, her dark curls tumbling over her shoulders and laughed. "So irreverent. So totally my best friend." She reached over and squeezed Charlee's hand briefly. "Now, tell me why you're in California. I know it isn't to redo my bathroom, no matter how desperately it needs you."

Charlee sighed and looked out at the ocean of cars. So much of California was asphalt, cement, and more cars than she ever imagined being in one place. She wondered if the stretch of coastline and ocean made up for the claustrophobic urban wasteland.

"Is it Peter?" Mari asked.

Charlee tilted her head until it rested against the cool glass. "It's over." Saying it out loud for the first time tore open her wounded heart a little more.

"Are you sure?" Mari asked. "Sometimes what we think is our breaking point is actually workable and can make a relationship stronger for having gone through it."

"I just don't know." Charlee mulled over what Mari said as they exited the freeway. They drove in a comfortable silence through another tangle of streets, leading up higher and higher until Mari buzzed her way into a gated community situated along the cliffs. They pulled into a white brick-lined circular driveway, leading around a beautiful lighted fountain with water bubbling up from the center then stopped at the front entrance. The house took her breath away with its gorgeous white Italian renaissance style, arched windows, and curved balconies on the upper levels. She stayed here during the funeral, but forgot how elegant the mini-mansion was. If you could call 10,000 square feet a mini-mansion. To her, it was ginormous.

Mari exited the car, then leaned back in to tease Charlee. "Wishing you could click your heels and go back home?"

The force of all she had escaped from rushed in, but Charlee pushed it back and concentrated on the curve of the balconies and the swishy sound of the ocean coming through her open window. "The land of Oz can wait. Let's see that bathroom you claim needs my masterful renovation skills."

"One thing at a time, sister." Mari grabbed the duffel bag from the trunk, coming around to meet Charlee. "Tonight is all about gossip and fruity drinks. Tomorrow, we'll put those mad hammer skills of yours to good use."

Chapter Twenty-Five

PETER KNOCKED ON THE hard door. "Come on, Charlee. Open up. I know you're in there." He knocked again, only stopping when he heard the click of the bolt unlatching. He'd been aimlessly driving around, circling Kansas City, trying to make sense of what happened at dinner. He was prepared to launch into a speech about why she needed to give him one more chance, to listen to the whole story, not just the tongue-tied jumbled mess that came out at her parents' house.

Rather than Charlee, he came face to face with her brother. From the stonewall expression on his face, Peter knew Tyler wasn't just mad, he was furious.

Tyler's words came out quiet and controlled. "She's not here."

The door was almost closed before Peter jammed his hand against it. "When will she be back?"

His best friend's glare cut through Peter from the slit between the door and the jam. "All I know is she made a phone call, packed her bag, and left. She didn't look like she planned to hurry back."

Peter's heart felt like it skidded to a stop.

She left.

Gone.

He blinked. She couldn't be gone forever. It wasn't logical. She had to be back Monday for work. He'd talk to her then.

Tyler just shook his head. "She put Bob in charge. She's not coming back until she's ready."

The door swung open and the air whooshed out of Peter's lungs as Tyler shoved him. Peter stumbled backwards, barely avoiding tripping and falling on his backside.

"What were you thinking?" Tyler ranted. "You should have been the best friend you're supposed to be and left my sister alone. Now you've put a huge rift in my family and my sister is gone." Tyler fisted his hands, the muscles bunched and rippled up his arms and Peter braced himself for the punch that was surely coming.

Instead Tyler growled in frustration and stalked back into Charlee's townhouse.

"I love her," Peter said just before Tyler closed the door.

Tyler's hard eyes bored into Peter. "You should have manned up and done something then because right now, she wants nothing to do with you."

The door closed with a quiet but decisive click. Peter reached forward and gripped the door jam, gasping as he lost his breath.

She left. Even when she returned, she would still be out of his reach.

Gone.

Possibly forever.

Pain pierced his very core. Fiery and hot, like the time he shot the nail gun into his hand, only a thousand times worse. Is this how it felt to have your heart shattered?

The pain twisted and transformed from misery to a glimmering hard anger. Peter shoved away from the door and stalked to his truck. His jaws clenched tight during the short drive to his father's house.

The man who destroyed everything.

The tires squealed when he pulled to a stop, but he didn't care. He slammed the truck door, stalked up the drive, and through the front door. He found his mother in the kitchen.

"Where is he?" He turned and made his way toward the living room.

"Peter, what's wrong? What happened?" Betty trailed after him, frantically asking questions.

Finding the living room empty, Peter turned to her. "Is he in the office?"

Without waiting for an answer, he brushed past her, down the hall to the back of the house where part of the garage had been turned into an office space for his father when the kids were young. Said he needed his space from the noise and racket. Well, he was going to get all the space he wanted. Peter shoved the door open and found his father sitting at his desk.

"You bastard," he said, heading straight for the desk. His father's head jerked up, surprise flickered across his face, but Peter didn't care. He wouldn't allow himself to care.

"Peter!" Betty exclaimed behind him.

He thunked his hands down on the desk and leaned towards his father. "What the hell were you thinking?"

George stood up, his chair falling behind him, the initial surprise gone. "Don't you talk to me like that." He punctuated his words by poking his finger into Peter's chest.

Peter shoved his father's hand aside and straightened,

ready for battle. "Don't tell me how to talk to a cheater." He spit out the last word with disdain.

"Stop it, both of you." His mother put her hand on George's arm, but he shrugged it off.

"You better be careful," George's low voice warned.

Peter choked on a harsh laugh. "Of the truth? You cheated Charlee and every other contractor out of those projects. How did you get them to close the bidding early? What did you promise them in return? I hope it was good, because you destroyed everything." George's face turned a deep red. Perhaps Peter should have been alarmed, but he chose to ignore it. "You couldn't leave things alone. No. You had to get revenge on the woman I love."

George sputtered. "Revenge! She was the one challenging me. Who does she think she is, walking out on me, on my company?" George pounded his fist against his chest. "I started her career. I can damn well end it. And you . . ." George's laugh was bitter. "All you did was chase her around like a puppy obsessed with a chew toy. What you need is a fresh kick in the pants to stay away from her and focus on what's important—Elliott Construction."

Peter went to the filing cabinets that lined the wall. He pulled open the internal business drawer, found the file he wanted and pulled it out. He slapped it on the desk in front of his father. In a flat voice, he said just two words. "Sign it."

George's face paled.

Betty took George's arm and tried to break in again. "George? Peter, what's going on?"

Peter glanced at his mom, then shook his head. The innocent bystander stuck in the middle of a war. He opened the folder and removed the contract that had been sitting in the file for over a year, waiting for his father to turn the company over to his son. Peter plucked a pen out of its container and set it on top of the paperwork.

"It's your choice. Either sign these contracts by Monday morning or I'm done." He lifted his finger before his father could speak. "And make no mistake, there is absolutely nothing you could do to entice me to work with you for even a single day. We are done."

He locked eyes with his father, neither of them speaking. Then Peter turned and left the house he grew up in. Left the father he let meddle in his life for too long.

But no more. Peter would choose his own future from now on.

GEORGE TWITCHED AS THE door slammed shut behind his son. The ungrateful whelp. Betty tugged on his arm, averting his attention from Peter to her.

"What just happened, George?" Her voice shook and a glistening of tears shone in her eyes.

He had to look away. Damn, but he didn't like to upset her. He steeled himself up. "I did my job, keeping Elliott Construction productive."

"Is what Peter said true? Did you get the project managers to close the bidding early?"

He turned back to his desk. "They still accepted bids until the original closing time."

"But they already committed to you, didn't they?" When he didn't reply, he felt Betty come up behind him. "Have you lost your mind? This isn't like you, breaking rules and hurting other people. And Peter leaving the company—"

George turned to face her and cut off the direction of the conversation. "I don't need the boy to run my company."

She shook her head, her expression tight with concern. "How are you going to keep that up? You're not a young man anymore. You don't have the stamina like the men on your crews."

Stunned, George stepped back. Was she calling him old? "Are you saying I've gone soft?"

She patted his arm, as if he were some pathetic little kid. "Well, you have been sitting behind a desk for the last ten years."

George sputtered. He was so mad, he couldn't form coherent words. How dare she treat him like a child and talk about him like some washed up had-been.

Betty grasped his arm. "You have to stop this struggle between you and Peter.

He shrugged off her hold. "He's my son. I don't need you to tell me what to do."

His wife stepped back and squared her shoulders. "Well, apparently you do," she said, her tone firm and scalding. "You already drove away our daughter, crushing her dreams. The only time she comes home is for an afternoon visit during the holidays and she can barely tolerate that." When George tried to walk away, she blocked him. "When Kimber left, you said she wouldn't last a year before she'd be back, needing our help. I stood by you because I was raised to believe that's what a good wife did, even though I knew you were wrong. She's carved out her own successful life and we're barely a speck in it."

He tried to interrupt, but his Betty shushed him and continued her rant. "And what about us? Did you even think this through? How are you ever going to retire if there's no one to take over the business? Are you planning to live forever or are you going to sell to one of the corporations who've been hounding you?"

"It would be a cold day in you-know-where before I let those empty, soulless—"

"Then you'd better wake up and smell the coffee because that's exactly where this is heading if Peter leaves." Betty paused and took a deep breath. Her eyes were moist, but determined. "You've been promising to retire for a year now. You either need to act like someone ready to schedule his last day of work or tell me to my face, right now, that all those promises were just a bunch of horse manure."

George flinched. The silence in the room was louder than the stern lecture his wife delivered. But still, she stood there, unblinking and unapologetic, waiting for his response.

When he didn't say anything, she shook her head. "I won't let you destroy this family, George. You either need to choose us or Elliott Construction. The question is are you man enough to follow your wife's plan for a change or will you put your head in the sand and lose us all?"

The door quietly clicked shut behind his wife. George stumbled to his desk and sank into the chair. The dreaded contract sat before him. It marked the end of his career, his leadership, his time at the company he started and worked day and night to build. All to pass on to his son, the ungrateful whelp who didn't want to take his place behind the desk.

He shoved the contract off his desk, letting the papers scatter across the hard floor. His head dropped to his hands. He had to choose. His family—most of whom were well on their way to hating him—or the business he dedicated his life to making thrive.

Which one was he willing to lose?

Chapter Twenty-Six

CHARLEE STRETCHED, LOVING the squishy comfort of Mari's guest bed. She glanced over at the clock. It was only five in the morning in California, but back in Kansas City, it was already seven. She changed into a pair of yoga pants and a Transformations t-shirt, then padded down the hallway to the staircase.

Apparently Mari had been doing a lot more remodeling in the mini-mansion than she let on during their long-distance conversations. All the ornate and flashy stuff had been stripped away, leaving a soft, neutral look in its place. Instead of glaring white and hard marbles, the walls were cream, thick carpeting on the stairs in a soft gray color and lots of rugs on the new wood floors.

As she padded down the plush stairs, the smell of coffee wafted to her. She wondered if it was an automatic coffee maker or if Mari was actually awake this early. When she stepped into the kitchen, she discovered Mari was not only awake, but she also had company.

A hunky guy in jeans and a fitted navy shirt leaned against the counter, his arms folded in just the right way that showed off his very nice torso. His bright blue eyes clashed with short black hair. To top it all off, he even had that barely-there super sexy scruff along his jaw. Charlee resisted the urge to smooth her shirt or check her messy morning hair.

First hunky pilot and now hunky kitchen guy. Did California grow any other kind of man?

"Good morning," Mari said, all cheerful and disgusting. For goodness sake, it was five in the morning and the woman looked freshly showered, dressed and all around put together.

"Morning," Charlee replied, moving around the island to the coffee pot because she needed something to do with her hands while Mr. Hunky Guy 2 gave her the once over. She assumed the empty mug on the counter was for her and filled it with the fragrant black liquid.

"Charlee, this is Blake. He's my handyman."

She quirked her eyebrow, just so Mari could see, before turning to the man in question. "Nice to meet you, Blake."

He lifted his own mug of coffee and took a swig before lowering it and gracing her with a mmm-hmm.

"Oh, don't mind him," Mari said. "He's cranky because I wouldn't let him touch the master suite."

Huh. Handyman was denied access. "Well, the client is always right."

Blake just quirked an eyebrow. "We'll see."

He speaks! In a nice deep voice, too. "Did you work on the other renovations?"

He did a funky shrug-nod combo and drank more black sludge. A man of few words, she thought as she turned the hot mug around, using it as a hand warmer.

"Here, take this," Mari said, removing the coffee and replacing it with a mug of creamy hot cocoa. Mmm. Her friend knew her so well. "So, where do we start?" Mari asked.

"We?" Charlee took in the two early morning peeps.

"We're your crew. Put us to work," Mari said.

Charlee simply laughed. "No offense, Blake, but Mari, seriously. You want to help?"

Her friend's bottom lip stuck out in a pout. "Hey, I can swing a hammer just as well as you."

Charlee placed a hand on her friend's shoulder. "Yeah, but do you know what to swing it at?"

Blake barked out a laugh, then quickly went back to brooding and looking into the black depths of his coffee.

Well, if this was her lot, then she may as well roll with it. "Let's get upstairs and see what we have to work with."

For the first time that morning, Blake smiled. The man actually had nice teeth, too.

Standing in the master bedroom, looking into the master bath, she knew exactly why he was smiling. He was looking forward to her eminent demise.

"Holy wow." The only words she could get out as she stepped into the horrificness that lay before her.

White marble tubs, sinks, tiles were in competition with all the gold fixtures, gold leaf decor, and everything gold trimmed. Including an overabundance of mirrors. Every angle she turned, her reflection glared back at her. Even from the ceiling! It was the most uncomfortable, gaudiest room she had ever seen.

She turned around to face the master bedroom, just to escape the mirrors. Not that the view was much better. It definitely had its own level of crazy ornateness going on, but at least it wasn't lined with mirrors everywhere.

"So, Mari, what's your vision for this area?" Charlee asked, noticing that Mari had stayed near the doorway of the suite and had her arms folded, as if hugging herself. She crossed the room to be near her friend and laid a comforting hand on her friend's arm.

Mari squeezed her hand, then sighed. "I haven't been in this suite since everyone left after the funeral."

Charlee looked around the room with new eyes and noticed the absence of anything personal. There were no family pictures, no mementos that made it Mari's. It was just a room.

"Just fix it. I trust you," Mari said.

Well, that was a big order.

Blake glared at her, so she squinted her eyes and glared right back. She almost broke when she saw the corner of his mouth twitch, but she stood her ground. If he wanted to test her, he was going to find out she was a straight-A student. "Well, first things first. Rip it all out."

His jaw dropped.

"I assume you have crews you can call on? And salvage contacts?" She paused while he nodded and pulled a little notebook out from the back pocket of his jeans. "Get them here. I want both rooms gutted by the end of the business day. And I'm talking about five in the evening, not midnight. So make sure you get the right people who know how to take a room apart without damaging the goods. Do you know a good plumber?"

He gave her a brusque nod, but his expression held more respect than taunting. "I can do anything you need for plumbing or electrical."

"Perfect. Mari, call your decorator and tell her to be here at noon." Mari had her phone out and was frantically typing notes, more at ease now that the attention wasn't focused on her, but on action she could actually take. "Blake, I also need your best contacts for flooring and bathroom supplies. Get them here at eight with a full listing of what they have in stock. I'm not waiting for stuff to get ordered in. And tell them to have pictures too. If they don't have it, get someone else here who does. We're working on a deadline, so let's get moving, people."

She headed out of the room and down to the kitchen with Blake and Mari following close behind. She grabbed her sneakers from where they sat beside the back door.

"Where are you going?" Mari asked.

"To the beach. I'll be back in an hour with a plan. Make sure you stay on task and get everything lined up."

Charlee grabbed her phone, left the house and jogged down the steep sandy wooden steps that led to a private beach. She turned in slow circles, taking in the ocean, the sound of the waves breaking against the shore, the color and texture of the sand as it gave way beneath the soles of her shoes. Tall beach grasses grew in clumps along the beach's border.

She turned and looked back at Mari's house, sprawling along the ridge. Further down the beach off each side of her home were more mini-mansion beach houses, each with its own distinctive style.

What made Mari choose this particular house? She wondered if Mari and her husband chose the home together or if one pushed for it more than another. The renovations and decor changes reflected either a preference for a more modern style or that Mari was changing. Evolving.

Of the two, Charlee would lay odds it was the latter. After all that Mari had endured, how could she not change? She was definitely softer spoken than when she was at the height of her career, wrapped up in all the glitz and glamour. Of all the cities in the world Mari could live, she chose here. Why?

Charlee turned to take in everything surrounding the house. She found a patch of sand that looked dry enough for sitting, then pulled up an app on her phone and started sketching and jotting ideas for the bathroom and bedroom. Not so much the bedroom as the bathroom though. As long as the decorator was on board with Charlee's vision and could carry through with the flow from the master bath, then she'd leave the majority of that in his or her hands.

That bathroom was the real challenge and the real reason Mari wanted her to come to California. She could have had any contractor change things, but there was something she needed from Charlee.

She sketched, jotted, researched pictures from the internet and made more notes. By the end of the hour, she had a plan, one that she hoped was what Mari needed in this new phase of her life.

When she pushed open the door to the kitchen, she found Blake on the phone with a laptop open in front of him, giving directions and setting appointments.

"The decorator will be here at noon. She was a tad grumpy about being woken up so early, but she knows it will be worth her while," Mari said, rubbing her fingers together to indicate money. Then she went back to stirring whatever was in the bowl. "I'm baking muffins for the guys upstairs."

"They're here already? Who's supervising them?" Charlee turned, ready to dart up the stairs.

Thump, thump. Blake smacked the counter with his hand,

drawing her attention to him. He held his pointer finger up in a 'wait a minute' signal and finished his call. "They're removing the furniture from the bedroom. I trust them to do that much."

She let a small smirk show her chagrin. "Oh, well, you're right. I would have done the same. Sorry about that."

Blake gave a brief jerk of his head to acknowledge her apology. "I have three crews coming in. One to gut each room and another to haul stuff out. Salvage guys are coming to bid on items at one. Flooring will be here at eight, bathroom supplies at nine. They're scrambling to get pics loaded of their newer inventory."

Charlee checked the time. She had just enough time to shower and change into some work clothes. "Call flooring back and tell them to come at nine. It would be better to do the walk through with everyone so we're all on the same page. I'm going to run upstairs and get changed."

"And eat," Mari reminded her. "These muffins will be done about then."

She agreed then rushed upstairs, past guys moving the dismantled bed into another room where other furniture was already stacked. They were making good progress.

Other than the short time Charlee spent getting ready, the rest of the morning was a flood of working with people. By eight, Blake was supervising the crews as they carefully began dismantling the bathroom. She watched the crew for a while, but Blake had everything in hand. He was as much of a hawk as she was when it came to doing work right the first time.

Paul from the flooring company arrived early, giving Charlee time to look through his stock samples, pulling out a few possibilities to look at in the room. She already had colors in mind for the walls and tiles. Once Jim from the bathroom supply company arrived, she retrieved Mari from the kitchen and they all went up to the master suite.

"Wow," Mari said, eyes wide when she saw the disaster the suite had become.

"It's all a part of the process," Blake reminded her, joining them. "Guys, why don't you take a thirty-minute break?"

"Be sure to get some muffins in the kitchen, too," Mari said as the men filed out.

Charlee pulled out her cell phone. "Let me walk you through what I'm thinking, then we can talk specifics. Here in the bedroom, it's mostly going to be new flooring, paint, and an updated look as far as furniture and other stuff goes. Pretty minimal work on the renovation side."

She led the group into the bathroom. The flooring had been mostly ripped out and Charlee could see where they were prepping to pull out the vanities and sinks. Charlee led the group to the middle of the room.

"Okay, here's what I'm envisioning. The bedroom will be in tones of a bluish-gray. It's neutral but adds a peaceful color to the room. Creamy white trim, not the stark stuff. Here are a few samples for the flooring. I'm thinking the black walnut, unless you prefer one of the others, Mari."

Mari waved away the samples. "I told you, I brought you here to do this. I want to help, but you need to pull it all together."

"Okay, we're going with the black walnut," Charlee decided while Paul jotted down some notes. "The wood flooring will flow from the bedroom into the bathroom. The only tile will be around the edges of the wet areas. I'll want to look through your tile stock to coordinate the two."

She turned to the side of the room where the white marble and gold-laden tub still resided. "We'll knock out this wall and put in mid-to-ceiling windows. This room is way too confining. It needs some air. With the gorgeous beach behind you, we can put in some privacy windows that allow you to see out, but others can't see in. That coupled with blinds or gauzy drapes will help you feel comfortable soaking in the tub."

She motioned to the current tub. "All of this is going bye-bye. We'll build up to a relaxing bathing area, starting about here." She picked a spot a few feet before the existing bath area. "One, two, three steps up to the platform level where the tub will be. Something cozy enough for two, but not overwhelming for just one, and of course, with fabulous jets. I'm thinking a mini-bar area here with easy access to a mini-fridge for cold beverages. On the other side, we'll put a wall unit TV tucked inside its own cabinet with remote controlled doors so you can watch your favorite show or hide the ugly TV away when you want to just relax."

"I love it," Mari exclaimed.

"The tub area will be all stone tile, heated of course, and textured to be nonslip. From here, we'll move to built-in cabinets and a double vanity, new mirrors. Lots of creamy white from the bedroom trim. The walls will carry through the bluish-gray, but the color will be on the top third of the room with the cream bringing lightness into the room. The combination of new windows and paint will brighten the room. Let's get rid of the glass shower and build a walk-in with stone tile. While we're ripping everything up, we'll install some inline water heating for continuous running hot water for everything in the bathroom. I'll work with the decorator on the other details for the bath area. The master closet is also being ripped out. No more gold and glass in there either. We'll go with a midtone neutral gray with cream cabinets and shelves. I'll leave that more up to the decorator though. Any thoughts, Mari?"

"What metal will the fixtures be?"

Charlee laughed. "First, let me look at the sink and tub styles. I have a couple style ideas I'm looking for. How do you feel about the bronze or brushed nickel though?"

Mari sighed with relief. "Either of those are fine."

Paul, Jim, and Blake asked additional questions to clarify ideas and took measurements. Then Blake stayed behind when his crews returned while the rest of the group went to the kitchen to pour over samples and stock photos. The tub, sinks, and tiles were chosen and prices were negotiated.

"Here's the deal, guys, I like you both, but I'm a Kansas girl. Maybe you do things different in California, but see those prices, they're a good 60% more than the retail cost back home," Charlee said, pushing each bid back to its respective owners.

"We're willing to work with you. How about this?" Jim scribbled a number, the slid the paper back.

Charlee crossed it out and put down what she felt was more reasonable. "This is still above the prices back home, but more at the price I'm willing to pay."

Jim sputtered. "I don't know if I can do that."

Charlee titled her head, keeping steady eye contact. "Do you own the store? I do believe I specifically asked to work directly with the owner."

"Well, yes—"

"Then you can make it happen or I can go with another vendor." Charlee sat back in her chair. "Plus, you'd get a quote for your website and marketing materials from my client."

Paul, having observed the exchange, wrote down a quote, gave it to Charlee, who nodded and signed the dotted line. Jim grudgingly followed suit.

"Thank you, Paul and Jim," she said, following them to the door and shaking their hands. "I'll be ready for your deliveries tomorrow morning at eight am sharp."

After the door closed, Charlee watched to be sure they both were in their cars and driving away before doing a little happy dance right there in the foyer.

"I already got a text from Paul. Seems you're quite the wheeler and dealer."

Charlee spun around. Blake stood at the bottom of the stairs with his arms folded, shaking his head.

"A girl's got to do what a girl's got to do to keep the men in this business honest," she replied.

Hi mouth lifted into a smirk. "Let's see if you can work some of that magic with the decorator. When she's in the room, there's only one opinion that matters and it's not yours."

"Yes, that woman scares me," Mari said, joining them from the kitchen.

"Then why do you work with her?" Charlee just didn't understand why you would work with someone you didn't like.

"Because she's the best," Mari said, as if there weren't any question about it.

"Does best mean most expensive? Because best in my book means the person who values your opinion more than their own," Charlee replied.

Mari shrugged. "Maybe best means something else in California."

Meaning it had more to do with dropping names than it did on the quality of the experience. If so, then why did Mari bring her all the way to California?

Chapter Twenty-Seven

THE EVENING BREEZE RUFFLED Charlee's short hair as her feet sank into the cool, wet sand. Waves crashed up onto the shore, the bubbly foam tingling as it poured over her feet and past her before receding into the ocean depths. Her face turned up to catch the diminishing rays of the sun, her shoulders relaxed as she soaked in the comfort the beach provided.

Her first full day in California was proving to be very therapeutic. Well, not all of it. She could skip the traffic and all the people jammed into this idyllic spot, but the start of the renovations was a good venting activity for her emotions. Once all the wheeling and dealing was done, including a tug-of-war battle with the decorator, Charlee pitched in with Blake's crews to clear out the last of the bathroom stuff. The salvage people came, gave Mari a big check for the stuff they hauled off and the rest went into the dumpster. It was hard work, but satisfying.

Plus this stretch of private beach was like a little slice of heaven. Talk about the benefits of a home owners' association. The community pool was the Pacific Ocean.

A smile spread across her face. This was a far cry from

their teen days when Mari dragged Charlee along to shop the mall clearance racks. *Speaking of Mari*, Charlee thought as her friend appeared at her side.

"You wimped out on me," Mari said, breathing heavy from her run.

"Nah, I just couldn't ruin the scenery by rushing past it."

Mari chuckled and grabbed the water bottle from the sack Charlee had slung over her shoulder. Even though her long, curly, black hair was tied back in a ponytail, the wind picked it up and pushed it this way and that while she gulped down half the bottle. Finally satisfied, she twisted the cap back in place, then bent into a stretch.

"Running clears my head," Mari said. She paused, glancing up. "It helps me escape the shadows and cobwebs."

Charlee put her hand on Mari's shoulder, hoping to comfort her. "Trying to out-run the grief?"

"More like the devil," Mari muttered, shook her head, then straightened with a bright smile. "Ignore me. I just need to focus on the blessings."

Together they turned and walked along the beach, back towards Mari's beach house.

"You've done so much," Charlee said. "Modeling, traveling the world, and experiencing so many things. All I've done is go to college and return to Crystal Creek."

Mari stooped to pick up a smooth rock, rubbing it between her fingers. "The first tour around the globe was a façade. Everyone was wrapped up in their image, including me. The places the models and I went were all about how they appealed to consumers." Mari slipped the rock into her pocket. "The second tour was to search for peace, for who I am."

"What do you mean?" Charlee wanted to know more about the new Mari she was discovering.

"I dived into massage training, yoga, essential oil studies, meditation, and even Zumba trying to escape Luis' and Xavier's deaths. It sucked trying to find the meaning behind it all and to keep moving forward."

Charlee wrapped her arm around Mari. "I am so sorry. I just thought, well . . ." She looked away, not sure how to put into words how inadequate she felt at helping Mari with something so tragic, something she had absolutely no experience dealing with.

"That the rich don't have feelings. That they don't grieve like normal people," Mari said in an even tone.

Charlee looked at her in surprise, shocked by her assumption.

"My parents preached the 'you have a responsibility to your fans to be strong, to be a good example,'" she said, using her fingers to put air quotes around the words. "Which really meant that I needed to hide everything inside."

Charlee jerked back, shaking her head. "That's not at all what I was going to say. I didn't know what to say or do. Now I look back and feel like that absolute worst friend ever. I can't even imagine what these past three years have been like."

At the funeral, Mari held it together, only letting Charlee see her tears in the privacy of her home. She should have been more proactive about making Mari talk to her. She added Mari's name to the ever-growing list of people she let down.

"Enduring hard things is worth it." Mari bumped her shoulder against Charlee's. "I learned a lot. The most important being that the only way I could find peace was to be true to the real me. I still haven't figured out what all that entails, but I'm working on it."

"The real me. I wonder who that is?" Charlee muttered.

Mari arched her eyebrow, her signature pose. "Sometimes you need a little perspective from someone on the outside who isn't wrapped up in all the emotions."

Charlee couldn't help but laugh. "Go for it. Hit me with some life-altering perspective."

Mari turned at the base of the wooden steps leading up to the house, bringing them both to a stop. Her gaze searched Charlee's before beginning. "You're insecure."

"What?" Charlee choked out. Working around men made her the least insecure person she knew. Didn't she see how she just commanded a whole slew of men and whipped them into doing exactly what she wanted?

"It's true," Mari said. "You don't see your own value. It's like your renovation projects. You take something that others don't see any value in, sand it down, shine it up, give it the love it needs, then show others the potential they missed." Mari placed her hand on Charlee's shoulder, giving it a gentle squeeze. "You need to let others see your potential, too. You took the first step in your career, leaving your safety net and starting Transformations, but in your personal life, you're leagues behind."

Charlee's mind spun with her friend's revelation. Was Mari right? Part of her hoped she wasn't, but a niggling something inside said the things she heard were true. "Anything else you want to add while I'm mulling all this over?"

Mari lowered her head, making her dark pony tail fall over her shoulder. She stayed like that for just a moment, tapping her toes against the edge of the step.

"Just say it." Charlee braced herself for more advice.

Mari stopped the tapping and looked back up, her eyes soft with compassion. "You are amazing, Charlee, truly. You're generous, sweet, and always giving to people in need, but for some reason, you compare yourself to others and find yourself lacking. You're unique and incredible. You just need to be brave enough to believe you're worth loving, that someone can see the real you and want to stick around." Mari placed a hand on Charlee's shoulder and gave it a gentle squeeze. "I've been thinking about everything you told me about you and Peter. Is it possible that you're looking for a reason to walk away so that you're not the one left behind?"

Charlee's eyes stung as she looked up to the house looming at the top of the stairs. Whoever said that truth can set you free needed to be shot, because right now, all it did was hurt. She clenched her eyes closed, wishing she could unhear it all, remain oblivious to the new perspective bouncing around in her head.

"Now that I've dropped that bomb . . . How long are you planning to stay?" Mari asked hesitantly.

Charlee looked over at her friend. "However long it takes. I have a lot to think about, to process. You're not getting rid of me that easily."

A smile tilted up at the corner of Mari's mouth. "I'm glad."

Charlee grabbed the back of Mari's shirt when she started up the stairs. "Hang on a second. It's my turn."

Mari slowly turned back to face her. "Me?" she squeaked.

Charlee folded her arms, standing firm on what she felt needed to be said. "You need to go home."

Mari tilted her head and grinned. "To which one? New York, Paris, Milan. You might want to be more specific."

Charlee shook her head and motioned to the stark house looming at the top of the stairs. "Those are all houses, filled with designer stuff. No, you need to go back to your roots, where you're loved."

Mari's laugh has harsh. "Not everyone loves me in Crystal Creek. In fact, I can think of a few who quite detest me."

"Well, they'll just have to get over it." Charlee fell quiet, letting her words sink in.

Mari reached up and twisted strands of her long hair around her fingers in a nervous gesture. "What would I do? I can't just go back and hang out."

"You should open a shop and do something with all the stuff you've learned over the past few years. Become Crystal Creek's modern hippie chick."

Mari's eyes widened. "That's an intriguing idea."

"Good. You ponder that for the next few days while I figure out all this value and self-worth stuff."

"Deal," Mari said, sticking out her hand and shaking on it. A familiar devilish gleam came into her eyes. "First one to the top gets dibs on the strawberry shortcake."

Charlee yelped, then chased after Mari who had a head start up the staircase. They both had a lot to work out, but thankfully they had each other to bounce ideas and thoughts around. Charlee was once again grateful for her best friend, and some yummy strawberry shortcake, too.

Chapter Twenty-Eight

THE ELLIOTT CONSTRUCTION OFFICES were unusually quiet that morning. His dad's secretary, Velma, redirected calls and Jan was busy rescheduling the appointments for the week while George, Betty and Peter met with their longtime family and business lawyer. It had already been a long morning, reviewing documents and paperwork, getting passwords for computers and various software. Now they were down to the last few minutes of the meeting.

"Everything is in order," Ezra said from behind his father's desk, peering over his glasses at the group assembled in the semicircle of chairs before him.

Ezra's pale, pale blue eyes always weirded Peter out when he was younger. To be honest, they still gave him the willies, Peter thought as he suppressed a shiver.

The lawyer slid a set of paperwork over to George. "This defines the retirement package we discussed. You just need to sign next to the x's highlighted in yellow."

His father took the pen in his hand and when he hesitated, Betty took his free hand in hers and gave it a good squeeze. George didn't let his eyes wander from the papers in front of him.

Peter closed his eyes. From the beginning of the meeting, his father only looked at Ezra or the desk to review paperwork. Never once had his father looked in his direction. Finally Peter heard the scratch of pen on paper and the whisper of paper against wood as Ezra pulled the signed documents back, then tap, tap as he shuffled them so the edges lined up and placed them in the correct folder.

"This is the last set of paperwork, officially transferring the ownership of Elliott Construction from George Elliott to Peter Elliott. George, you need to sign the yellow highlighted areas, here, here, and here. The orange highlighted lines are for Peter's signature."

Peter watched as his father gripped the pen, then put the tip to the paper. His hand shook as he signed, flipped a page, signed, flipped a few more pages, then added the final signature. He dropped the pen, letting it hit the wood desk with a loud click, bounce, click.

Ezra slid the paperwork and another pen across the desk. Peter picked up the simple pen. With a few strokes, this pen would mark the end of their tug of war. There would be no hesitation on his part. Peter quickly and decisively signed all the designated lines, then handed the paperwork back to Ezra. He once again did the tap, tap routine and placed it into a file folder.

"That's everything. Congratulations on your retirement, George." They shook hands, then Ezra turned to him. "Congratulations and good luck, Peter. I'll get these filed today. Please call if you need anything."

"Absolutely," Peter replied as they shook hands. Ezra

placed the folders in his briefcase, then exited the office.

Leaving just the three of them in the room.

Both he and his mom looked at his father, who simply sat in the chair with his fingers lightly resting on the desk. His gaze shifted to the boxes of framed pictures, certificates and other mementos. He stood, picked up the stack, then headed for the door.

"Dad, let me help you." Peter stepped forward, but stopped when his father looked at him for the first time that morning.

His eyes were empty and his expression hard. He simply shook his head and put his hand on the doorknob. "Don't screw it up," he reminded Peter one last time, then turned the knob and left the room.

Peter and his mom watched as George walked past Velma who was quietly crying, past the employee lounge which was blissfully empty, and out the front door.

George Elliott had left the building.

Peter shook his head, then pinched the bridge of his nose, fighting back the sharp sting in his eyes. It shouldn't have happened this way. The stubborn old fool.

"Now, don't you go feeling bad about your father. He needed that kick in the pants, Peter, and you know it." Betty wrapped her arms around her son and patted his back. "Congratulations, Peter."

He returned the embrace. "What if I screw it all up?" he whispered.

"You won't." She stepped back, placed her hand on the side of his face. "You'll do a great job. Step up, put your own stamp on Elliott Construction. Really own it. Just remember if you're doing what you love and have people you trust to back you up, then everything will turn out just fine. In fact, even better than you expected." She patted his cheek. "Well, I let your father sulk long enough. I better get out there. By the way, if you need us, we'll be gone for the next two weeks. Your father has no idea, but I plan to jump in and start showing him how great retirement can be—beginning with a trip to Europe. It would be nice if there was a party with his business contacts and construction crews when he got back."

"I'll take care of it," Peter promised, then watched his mother say goodbye to the secretary before going through the front door to join her husband. Peter turned and looked at the bare office waiting for him. He tried to think of what he could do to make it his, to do like his mom said and put his own stamp on the company. His mind spun, but then it slowed and came to a stop.

He knew just what he needed to do next.

"LOOK WHO'S ALL DRESSED UP with nowhere to go?" Cameron said, taunting Peter about his black slacks, dress shirt, and tie.

Peter ignored him and clunked the six pack of Mountain Dew throwback bottles on Cameron's desk.

"It's a little early in the day for drinking, don't you think?" Cameron winked, then grabbed a bottle and popped it open. "What favor are you bribing me for this time?"

Peter grabbed his own bottle, popped the cap off, then sat across from Cameron. He hoped Cam was up for what he was about to ask. "I want you to come run Elliott Construction."

Mountain Dew spewed out of his friend's mouth and all over the desk.

"Well, that was unnecessary," Peter said, wiping some of the spit off his dress shirt.

"Holy son of a monkey's uncle." Cameron wiped his face with the edge of his sleeve, then pinched the edges of his eyes. "I think it even came out of my eyes." He blinked a few times, then focused in on him. "Now, what in Hades are you talking about?"

Peter tugged at the rolled up sleeves of his dress shirt. "Just came from meeting with Ezra. It's official."

"Whoa," Cameron lounged back into the office chair, letting the news sink in. "And you want me to do what exactly?"

"Run the company."

Cameron's laugh was full and hearty. "I don't know anything about construction, dude. Don't you remember in Cub Scouts when my bird house fell apart and you fixed it before the troop leader found out?"

"That's the beauty of it," Peter said, leaning forward, his elbows on his knees. "I'll take care of the construction, the building specs and everything related to the actual design part of the company. You would be over the contracts, employees and all the business stuff I can't stand."

He steepled his fingers, tapping them against his chin. "Let's see if I've got this straight. You want me to leave this quaint family law practice to come play CEO at Elliott Construction so you can play with hammers and nails."

Peter crossed an ankle over his knee and tapped the bottom of the soda bottle against his knee. "That about sums it up. You interested?"

Cameron closed his eyes, still tapping his fingers against his chin. Peter remained silent, letting his friend think through the proposition, the possibilities. Just the thought of putting together a team with various strengths to run the company sent a jolt of excitement through Peter. No more trying to juggle it all and feeling like he was dying inside.

Cameron's hands fell to his lap and his eyes were clear. "I'm intrigued and very interested."

"Then let's talk details," Peter said, jumping into what needed to happen next.

"Slow down, buddy. The next thing you need to do is talk to Ezra, go over the initial proposition, responsibilities and salary, then set up a meeting with all three of us to negotiate."

Peter lifted his bottle of Dew in salute. "See? You're already keeping me in line. I'll call Ezra and get the ball rolling. Thanks, Cam."

They clinked their bottles together. "I haven't accepted yet."

Peter tipped his head in acknowledgment. "But I'm confident you will."

Cameron simply stood and clasped hands with Peter in a firm handshake. "Mark this day on your calendar, Peter Elliott. It may well be the one and only time you hear me say you're right."

Chapter Twenty-Nine

CHARLEE SWEPT THE DEBRIS from the wood flooring, doing one final walk through of the master suite.

It had been a whirlwind weekend. She thought Saturday was insane getting everything ripped out and prepped for the renovation. She was impressed they even got the wall cut and new windows installed. The light flowing in was already an improvement to the room.

It didn't stop there though. The project ran twenty-four hours with new crews to keep things fresh and moving forward. Saturday night, the painters took care of the entire master suite. Sunday Blake's crews installed wood flooring, the TV area, tub, shower and vanity, as well as finished the stone tile work.

Today had been the easiest of them all. Completing the master closet and working with the decorator to get all the furniture and finishing touches in place.

There was no more work to be done.

The space was exactly how Charlee envisioned, bringing in the wood and stone for natural elements, the calming bluish-gray to give it a neutral but beachy feel. The decorator brought in sand and sea shells from Mari's beach for small touches in bowls here and there. The new furniture was simple and light. The bedding a textured cream with pops of yellow, orange, and gray pillows. Everything felt comfortable and peaceful. No pretenses.

Like the person Mari was growing into.

She had a lot of growing to do, too. Charlee had been thinking about the conversation on the beach with Mari. Analyzing her self-esteem, her fears, and how they affected the choices she made. She even started a list.

On the pro side, she wrote down areas of her life where she felt valued and happy. Volunteering at the women's shelter was high on the list. Her love of renovation was another. On the relationship side, she listed Mari, Edien, and her brother Tyler. She wanted to put Peter there, too, but held back adding him to a category.

On the con side, she listed things that brought her angst and tied her up in knots. She was surprised that most of them had to do with relationships. The constant feeling that she could never measure up to her mother's expectations. Of not being the all-amazing daughter, wife and mother her sister Julie was. Fear of rejection triggered her need to be blasé, like how she just went with the flow at family dinners and didn't actively engage. Or to overanalyze and not trust what others said, like when Peter insisted he only had friendship in mind when it came to Hope.

Admitting her strengths and flaws were the first step to become the woman she hoped to be and towards what she hoped would be a better future. She just needed to figure out the next steps. She'd have to ask Mari if there were some books she recommended.

"Looks good," Blake said, pulling her out of her thoughts as he joined her in the master bathroom. They had grown to respect each other during the past three days. Sure, they butted heads a few times, but nothing they weren't able to talk through and figure out. It felt good to work with someone new.

"It wouldn't have happened without you and your crews. You have a good group of men," she said, dumping the dust pan of dirt into the last worksite trash bag and tying the top of the bag into a knot.

Blake ran his hand over the stone work around the tub area, looking out over the ocean. "She was right to wait. You have a talent for seeing more than just what a customer says they want."

Other than when they had their head-butting bouts, that was the most he said to her in one breath all weekend.

He turned to face her, crossing his arms. "Have you considered moving your business to California? You could make a big name for your company here."

She blinked. Wow. She didn't see that coming. She fumbled for words, not sure what to say.

Blake simply held his hand up, halting whatever she might have said. "Mari said things in Kansas City weren't in the best of places for you right now. Perhaps you might consider your options. If there's nothing keeping you there, know that there are opportunities here."

Charlee swallowed. He had a point. She wasn't sure how she would feel when she returned home. There was a lot of figure out between Peter and her family. She pushed it all aside, because she was good at that. Tomorrow. She would think about it all then. She extended her hand to Blake. "I promise to think about it."

He shook her hand briefly, then gruffly changed the subject. "Now that the project is complete, it's time to celebrate. Come to dinner, both you and Mari."

"Oh, well," Charlee said, hedging. "I don't know what our plans are."

"I've already talked with her. There is a great seafood place you need to experience before heading back to landlocked Kansas. No arguments. I'll see you both in an hour."

Blake nodded before sauntering out of the room, leaving Charlee's mind spinning between both proposals.

AN HOUR LATER, CHARLEE was freshened up and glad she could put the new skills Eden taught her to good use. The Catch of the Day was California casual, meaning the guys showed up in whatever while the women tried to pull off the casual glamorous look, even though every female there knew just how much primping it required. Only the men were clueless.

Blake was right about one thing though—the food was amazing. They shared a sumptuous seafood platter, pulling off chunks of crab, lobster, shrimp, calamari, and breaded cod. Everything was served with fresh sautéed veggies and side sauces.

What surprised her most was how the customers at The Catch of the Day were the equivalent of Freddy's back home. Blake's crews were there with their wives and girlfriends. The single guys moseyed around, flirting with the single chicks. A live band played covers of popular songs while customers crowded onto the makeshift dance floor near the veranda, overlooking the beach. Lantern lights were draped around the restaurant, leading out to the veranda. It was quaint and cozy, all wrapped up together.

Jared from the crew stopped by the table and held out his hand. "Let's go, pretty little boss."

Charlee looked between him and the dance floor, where couples were swinging, twirling, and definitely way past her dance abilities. She shook her head. "I can't do that."

Jared's grin widened. "Sure you can. Just follow me."

"Go, Charlee," Mari encouraged, giving her a little push towards Jared.

"We'll follow you," Blake said, challenging Mari to dance as well.

The four of them joined the dancers. It took a few twists and turns, but Charlee caught onto Jared's leading style. He was right, all she needed to do was follow him. The group stayed out on the dance floor for several more songs, switching partners each time. Charlee finally begged for a break, thanked Jared, and found her way back to the table, where she gulped down a glass of water.

"California isn't so bad, is it?" Blake asked, joining her.

"If you just got rid of about three-quarters of the people, it would be paradise," she replied, smiling to show she was teasing.

"Nothing is perfect," he said, tapping his fingers on the table to the beat of the music. "This was my new start, you know."

She turned her attention from Mari twirling around on the

dance floor to Blake's bright blue eyes. "Why California?"

The corner of Blake's mouth turned down. "It put about a thousand miles between me and a bad divorce."

Charlee tilted her head to the side, considering the distance and if it could be a cure. "Did it help?"

"In some ways, yes." His fingers stopped tapping, his thumb rubbing the empty spot on his left ring finger. "Not seeing someone each day doesn't mean they don't continue to haunt you in your sleep though. Sometimes that's worse." His bright blue eyes caught hers, reflecting an empty pain inside. "When you go back, be sure you know how things really stand before you make a decision. If you find yourself needing a new start, just know there's a place for you here."

Charlee took Blake's advice to heart, vowing to herself to make her next choices carefully.

TUESDAY MORNING BROUGHT CHARLEE full circle. The wind whipped at her short hair, making it all haphazard and crazy.

Mari unwound a beautiful dark gray silk scarf from around her neck and covered Charlee's head with it. "I wish you could stay," she said, tying the scarf off with a pretty flare around Charlee's neck.

"You could come with me," Charlee suggested.

Mari's laugh came out choked. "I'm not that brave."

"Well, get brave." Charlee put her hands on Mari's shoulders. "I love my brother, but seriously, you're my best friend. Promise me you'll think about opening the store we talked about."

"What if you end up coming to California?" Mari asked, hopeful.

She shook her head. "Believe me, it was on my mind all night. I need to find my own brave and I don't think California is it."

A sigh escaped Mari's lips. "I'm not gonna lie, I was really hoping you'd relocate."

"It was immensely tempting. If I find out I made the wrong choice, it's my backup plan."

Garrett, aka Mr. Hunky Pilot, approached them with a greeting. "We're ready whenever you are, ma'am," he said, nodding to them both before returning to the plane. Kara was also joining them again, but this time she waited at the base of the steps for Charlee to board.

"Hug me quick," Mari said, pulling Charlee in for a tight hug. "Thank you for being my friend. I know we rarely see each other, but you're my anchor."

Hot tears pricked the back of Charlee's eyelids. "Love you, girly girl."

"Love you, Char-Char," Mari responded, following up with a choked laugh about their teenage nicknames. She pulled back, tugging at her loose cardigan sleeves. "Let me know when you're home."

"Will do. Next trip you're coming to Kansas City."

Mari simply nodded, then Charlee turned and boarded the private plane. Kara followed her on board, then handed her a bottle of cream soda and Dramamine. A repeat of her previous flight, only this time she was returning home.

California gave her a chance to breathe, to gain a new point of view. Now it was time to return, reevaluate and move forward. Only there was a great big fork in the road and both paths were like blank blueprints. She wished for a flashlight powerful enough to allow her to see part way down each road. At least then she'd have a glimpse of what she was getting herself into rather than forcing herself to step onto a dark path and hope for the best.

Chapter Thirty

"BOSS LADY IS BACK," Crank yelled up the Bibliophile stairway before he grabbed her up in a big hug. "It's good to have you back. No offense, Bob's nice and all, but he isn't nearly as good to look at as you are."

Charlee laughed, found her feet again and greeted the rest of her crew who had stomped down the stairs. It had been a long afternoon of flying, but she was glad she decided to stop in to see everyone rather than wait until tomorrow. "The entry looks amazing, you guys!"

In the time she was gone, the stairs leading from the main entry up to the bookstore had been refinished with each step to look like book ends with a mix of book spines from classics and modern best-sellers. "You totally outdid yourself, Crank. I bet Eden absolutely loved it."

"She just about fainted," Sadie confirmed. "Wait until you see upstairs."

They all tromped up the stairs together to show off the bookstore. The Thompson crew from Chillicothe completed the plumbing and bathrooms in a speedy manner, just like they promised, all with the quality Bob vouched for.

"The inspectors will be here Thursday," Bob followed up.

"They tried to put it off for another week, but Naomi sweet talked them."

She surveyed the store. The bookshelves were installed. There were just a few things that needed to be finished up in the cafe area, then it was just clean up. Plenty of time for that tomorrow.

"I should go on vacation more often. Things seem to actually work when I'm not here." She shook her head when the crew protested. "Seriously, you guys are amazing. Why don't you take off? Get an extra hour for yourself as a thank you."

The Juans were excited about the prospect of getting off early. Crank and Sadie also said their goodbyes before heading out for the day.

Bob was the only one who stayed behind. Charlee was sure he hoped for an update. "How are things with the Wheeler's?" she asked instead.

"Good. We got everything installed. Just waiting for the counters to come in later this week." Bob leaned against the wall, waiting for more. Before he could ask, there were feet pounding up the stairs.

Everything inside her tingled, not in a happy way, but in a scared not-ready-to-face-Peter way. She should have waited to catch up with the crew until tomorrow. She wanted to close her eyes, to not see Peter's head pop around the corner. The steps made it to the landing. In the next few seconds, he'd be in the room. Was she ready?

"Hey, you're back!" Tyler said, charging into the room and sweeping her into a big hug.

The breath she didn't realize she'd been holding gushed

out in a big whoosh. She couldn't move as Tyler squished her in a straight-jacket hug with her arms pinned to her sides. When he finally released her, she smacked his upper arm. "You big oaf," she said.

But it didn't wipe the smile from his face. "Yeah, I missed your ugly face, too."

Bob coughed into his hand, drawing their attention before rolling his eyes. "I'll just let you two enjoy your little family reunion. Tomorrow, Charlee?"

"Yes, sir. Update first thing in the morning."

Bob simply nodded before taking his leave.

"Not to break the festive mood, but we have a lot to talk about. Want to go to grab a drink?" Tyler asked.

She hesitated. "I'm not sure I want to go to Freddy's just yet."

"If you're worried about running into Peter, you don't need to. He's too busy running Elliott Construction."

Charlee double blinked, certain she had not heard correctly. "I'm sorry, say that again."

The celebratory expression slid off Tyler's face. "Lots of things changed while you were gone."

"Then I guess we better have that drink," she said, apprehensive about what the changes included.

At Freddy's, Charlee grabbed a back booth while Tyler put in an order for food and grabbed drinks before joining her. He handed her a bottle of cream soda before settling into his chair.

"George retired?" Charlee jumped right into the conversation. Her mind had run a million miles a minute all the way to Freddy's, filled with who, how, when, and what if's.

"Yep," Tyler said, taking a swig from his bottle. "I heard it from Cameron. Seems Peter gave George an ultimatum."

"Holy hot dog." She twisted the cap off the bottle and took the first sip. She couldn't imagine what that must have been like for Peter. "How's George taking it?"

"From what I hear Betty is taking it just fine. She has them on a cruise."

Charlee was still floored that George wasn't behind his desk at EC. "Can you imagine George on a cruise? I don't think he's ever taken more than a long weekend vacation."

"I can't imagine he'd be lounging in the sun, but I've heard the all-you-can-eat buffets are pretty good."

"So, Peter's running EC." Charlee mulled that over.

"Well, kind of. I heard they're in the process of negotiating Cameron becoming the CEO. Peter will still be the owner but Cam will run all the day-to-day business stuff."

Like how she hired Naomi. She wondered if that's what gave Peter the idea. "That was a smart move."

The waitress brought out a couple of burgers and onion rings. Tyler dug into his food while Charlee picked at the onion rings.

"How is Peter doing?" she ventured to ask.

Tyler shrugged. "We haven't talked since that night."

"You know, just because Peter and I aren't talking doesn't mean you need to avoid him, too. He is your best friend."

His eyebrows lowered into a scowl. "Not right now, he isn't."

Charlee just shook her head. There was no use talking to him about it, not when he had walls built up.

"He came looking for you, that night after you left," Tyler admitted.

She gulped. "And?" Another shrug. The man frustrated her

to no end. How did he end up being her brother? She kicked out and was satisfied when her foot connected with his shin.

"Geez, I buy you dinner and you abuse me. This is why sisters are annoying."

She rolled her eyes. "And?"

"He asked for you, I told him you were gone. Didn't know when you were coming back."

"That's it?" she asked, highly doubting Tyler's version of the story was accurate.

"Pretty much."

Which meant there was more, but since it wasn't related to her directly, he wasn't going to share the details. "Has he asked about me since?"

"Do I look like your dating service? I just said I haven't talked to him." His lips flattened into a tight, hard line.

She threw an onion ring at him. "You said that *before* you mentioned that he came by. Who knows what other details you're leaving out? Has he texted? Called?"

Tyler just grimaced. "Sorry."

"No, it's fine. Thanks for telling me." She grabbed her burger and took a big bite, even though eating was the last thing she wanted to do.

Tyler finished off his burger, then pushed his plate aside for the waitress. "Listen, we need to talk."

She quirked her eyebrow. Wasn't that what they had just been doing?

"About Mom," he added.

Well, dang. Now she really didn't want to eat. She set aside the burger and washed the food down with some soda. Angst curled up and swirled in the pit of her stomach.

"Okay," she said, letting him lead the conversation. She

wasn't about to jump into it.

"She's kind of a mess," he said.

"Only kind of?" She raised her eyebrow again.

"Just listen, okay? Julie and Dad really laid into her about what happened that night. In fact, Julie isn't letting her see the grandkids until Mom fixes things with you."

"Really?" Charlee was surprised. Why would Julie do that for her? She annoyed Julie as much as her perfect sister annoyed her.

"Mom keeps texting and calling, asking when you'll be back. I'm giving you fair warning because she's going to track you down."

"Anything to get off grandkid suspension, right?" Charlee rolled her eyes, trying to make light of the situation, then catching herself from falling into the same old habits she wanted to change.

Only this time, Tyler didn't laugh with her. "I don't think it's that. I think she's actually been thinking about what kind of mom she's been to each of us. Just don't bite her head off right away. Let her talk first and actually listen."

"Then I can bite her head off?"

He nodded. "If necessary."

Well, she could live with that. She still wasn't looking forward to the confrontation but at least she was forewarned. Hopefully it would give her a chance to prepare and try to be in a better frame of mind whenever the discussion with her mother did occur. "Anything else, oh wise one?"

"Yeah." He crossed his arms and narrowed his eyes, examining her. "Where were you?"

Now that one was harder to go into. Better to tell a broad

version of the truth. "I had an out-of-state client who was waiting for me to have time to do a bathroom remodel. I called him and made arrangements to do it."

"And the remodel was where?"

"On the west coast."

"Really?" Now it was his turn to be surprised. "I didn't realize you knew people out that way."

"Brother, you would be surprised how many people are vying for my skills. In fact, they proposed I move my business and work for the richie rich crowd."

Tyler went still, assessing what she said.

"You know I'm not going, right?" she asked. "It was flattering to get the offer, as well as good to get away so things could settle."

He just nodded, but continued to look spooked. Tyler never liked changes, not since he returned from his military stint overseas. It took a little more cajoling before he moved on and loosened up again. They wrapped up their meal, then Tyler accompanied her to where she parked.

"You know," he said, opening the truck door for her. "Fresh starts aren't all what they're cracked up to be."

She thought of him leaving, the years he was gone, then returning home injured. A changed man. She supposed Tyler's decision to leave was part of wanting a fresh start. She wondered what his and Mari's lives would be like if they had chosen a path together instead of breaking apart.

Right now, her path seemed to be breaking away from Peter's. She wondered what a future down that path would be like. Lonely? Maybe a surprise love? More likely it would include sharing her townhouse with eight cats.

Love Under Construction

BOB HAD THE CREW hard at work when Charlee arrived Wednesday morning. The café and checkout nook were positioned and in the process of being assembled.

"After all the delays and hassles, it seems unreal that we're so close to being finished," she commented to Bob.

"How do you feel about that?" He watched her from the corner of his eyes.

"Are you trying to play shrink, Bob? I don't think it's your forte. Just sayin'."

Bob turned his focus to Crank and Sadie working together. "Well, this old man is just trying to see if his friend needs to talk."

Charlee was quiet for a minute. Mari said perspective was important, and hers proved invaluable, but Mari didn't know Peter, didn't know the two of them together. Not like Bob knew them.

"Remember I asked you about George and the bids," she began. Bob just nodded, so she continued. "He squeezed us out of both jobs before the bidding was closed. Peter and I got into a fight about it, at my parents' house of all places. Everything just kind of imploded. I was mad, Peter was defensive, and Mom got in the middle."

"She usually does," Bob commented.

"She sided with Peter." This earned a sharp look from Bob. "And I melted down." Talking about that night made the feelings leak through the walls she built. She had to work hard and fast to dam it all back up.

"Well, that puts the past four days into perspective."

Charlee rocked back on her heels, nervous energy flowing through her. "Tyler suggested getting out of town, taking a break."

"How far out of town did you go?" he asked.

"California."

Bob nodded again. "Went to see Mari."

She snapped her head around to see him standing there, all nonchalant. "How—"

"I've known you since you were a teenager begging George for an internship. Just because she and your brother went separate ways doesn't mean diddly squat when it comes to girls and their best friend. I've got daughters. I know how it is."

"Tyler doesn't know or at least I don't think he does." She scrunched her eyebrows together, thinking. Was that why he was so quiet when she said she went to the West Coast? Did he know who she really went to see?

Bob folded his arms and shook his head. "He's pretty much shut out anything outside the borders of Crystal Creek. Some men do that to cope after coming home from a war. It's a way for them to compartmentalize—there and here, then and now."

What Bob said made sense, but didn't make Charlee feel any better about the challenges her brother faced.

"You going back?" he asked.

"I got an offer to relocate," she said, feeling out what Bob had to say about that.

"They'd be fools not to after seeing your work." He left it at that, not saying anything more. Their quiet was filled with the sounds of hammers and Sadie cussing out Crank for crowding her space and making her hit her thumb with the hammer.

"So, no advice?" she prodded.

Bob hung his head and closed his eyes. "Just one thing for you to think about." He lifted his head and looked at her, serious, solemn. "Whatever happened between you and Peter was so strong it made you run, but it also made Peter stand up for himself. It takes some mighty powerful emotions to push two people to do such drastic things."

It felt like a heavy weight settled onto her chest. He was right. She needed to sort through everything she kept walled up. She just didn't know how to examine it a little piece at a time without the whole dam breaking loose and flooding her again.

"Hello, everyone!"

Charlee shifted and saw Victoria coming through the store doorway. She squeezed Bob's arm and he tipped his head ever so slightly, acknowledging her thank you.

"Good morning, Victoria," Charlee said, turning her attention to the real estate agent. "Here to see the final results?"

Victoria pushed her long, red hair over her shoulders and scanned the space. To anyone else, it seemed as though she briefly looked things over, but Charlee saw the specific spots Victoria's eyes went to, examined, then moved on to the next spot as she processed the work versus what the Indulgence Row client requested. Finally, her eyes rested on Charlee. "Eden will be thrilled when she does the final walk through."

Charlee felt a burst of pride. "She's meeting with us for the last of the inspections tomorrow. The rest of the work will be up to her."

"I imagine filling the shelves will be her favorite part. Do you have a few minutes to talk?"

"Of course. Here or at the office?" Charlee said, moving away from Bob and the crew. They settled on a spot towards the back of the room, grabbing a few folding chairs.

Victoria pulled out some documents and a map of the Indulgence Row project. "I know this project has been rocky, but I assume you've found solutions to the kinks you ran into?"

"Everything is resolved and I'm working with new subcontractors who won't be swayed by competitors."

Victoria nodded. "I sincerely hope that with the changes at Elliott Construction everything will run much smoother from now on."

"Me, too," Charlee said, sharing a reserved smile with her friend.

"Great, then let's get down to business. The Indulgence Row investor has decided to grant you one more project. If you can prove to be able to meet the deadlines on time, without the drama you encountered this time around, then you'll be in on the remainder of the Indulgence Row businesses."

Charlee gulped. They needed to prove themselves yet again. All because of one man's vendetta. She took a deep breath and reminded herself that was the past. She needed to forget about the yesterdays and concentrate on the todays and tomorrows. "That's fair."

"I wouldn't be offering this to you if the investor and I weren't absolutely positive you can deliver. It's more of a formality."

Well, that made her feel a hundred times better in a sort of twisted up kind of way. "So, what's the next project?"

"The ranch house next door needs to be converted into two

spaces. One a salon, the other a photography studio. Here are the plans for the house. It's one of the smaller ranches in the development, but it does have a full basement. Ideally, the basement will be divided in a way that each client can have private access for storage."

Charlee studied the plans, moving her finger along the lines. "I have a few ideas on how that could work out. Am I doing the salon or the studio?"

"Transformations is doing it all."

Charlee's head snapped up. "All? The entire house?"

"It's all yours." Victoria winked and stood. "I'll send the clients' information to Naomi to set up appointments for walkthroughs."

Charlee scrambled to her feet. "I—I," she stumbled over her words. She stuck out her hand. "Thank you."

Victoria ignored the hand and pulled her into a warm hug instead. "You deserve it. I look forward to seeing another Charlee Jackson transformation come together."

Victoria barely left the shop when the crew descended.

"What's the prognosis?" Bob asked.

"We got our first complete house." That was all she got out before Crank grabbed her up and the crew whooped and hollered. From the corner of her eye, she saw Peter in the doorway, but Crank was twirling her around. When she looked back again, he had disappeared.

CHARLEE WALKED DOWN THE dark sidewalk towards her

townhouse, lugging a few bags of groceries. Home sweet home wasn't so sweet when your brother took it upon himself to eat all your food so nothing went to waste. He claimed he was doing her a favor, not knowing how long she'd be gone.

Growing closer to her home, she rummaged in her purse for keys, when she spied something sitting in front of her door. What in the world? She hurried forward, then stopped abruptly.

It was the desk.

The old school desk from the day Peter took her to the auction. What was it doing here? She looked over her shoulder, but there was no sign of Peter. She maneuvered around it, unlocked the door then quickly put her bags on the kitchen counter before returning outside. She picked it up and hauled it into her living room. She ran her hand over the rough top, stopping at the edge of the envelope with her name scrawled in Peter's handwriting across the front. She carefully peeled it off, then pulled the back flap out of the envelope. Peter never did like the taste of stamps and envelopes. The thought made her smile just a little. She pulled out a sheet of paper and unfolded it to find one simple phrase.

Forgive me.

The words on the page blurred. Was it Peter who needed forgiveness? Or her?

Or maybe they both did.

She swiped at the wetness on her cheeks, then made her way back into the kitchen, setting the note on the counter. She busied herself with putting away groceries, then making a chicken salad sandwich, which she ate automatically, barely tasting it while she examined the old desk.

Peter did a good job getting the kinks and bends out of the metal. The desk itself needed to be cleaned up, sanded down, and refinished. She went into auto mode as she changed out of her work clothes, shoved them in the overflowing pile in the hamper, then put on a pair of yoga pants and a comfy t-shirt that had seen better days. She returned to the living room and cracked open the windows before selecting supplies from shelves lining the walls of her work space. Once she had everything organized, she flipped the desk upside down and unscrewed the metal base from the wood top. She donned a dust mask and gloves, grabbed some steel wool and began the process of scrubbing down the metal base.

From this close, she could feel the little indentations where Peter worked to fix the dents. She felt a slight burn in her arms as she worked on the rusty base, rotating it from one side to the next, rubbing the steel wool over it again and again. The rust gradually disappeared, leaving the good metal behind.

The process cleared her head enough to mull over the situation between her and Peter. There was so much rust filling the space between them. Anger, misunderstandings, frustration. Even if they talked things through, could they salvage their relationship? It wasn't a matter of just getting rid of the rust and repainting, like the desk. The dents in their relationship couldn't be smoothed out and forgotten. Scars would remain as a reminder of everything that happened. Even though George was no longer there to create strife in their businesses, he was still Peter's father. Could she handle being in a relationship that had even more drama than her own family, especially when the sole root of the contention would be her?

Charlee moved from the metal base to the wood top of the desk, pulling out a fresh batch of steel wool and a variety of sandpapers. Her arms, wrists and hands ached as she worked that part of the desk, cleaning away grime, sanding away names written in marker to last forever on the desk.

Jenny + Jason '84.

Go Eagles!

Mrs. H's English class sucks.

How easily it all disappeared with the right tools. When the wood was thoroughly sanded, she pulled out a fan to clear away the dust in the air. She filled a bucket with warm water and some cleaning solution before returning to her work station. She soaked a rag, then began cleaning everything she had worked on, following up with drying it all with a chamois cloth.

She stepped back, reviewing the results. It was a start. She made a list of items to pick up the following day at the hardware store. She didn't write it down, but she tasked herself to find an opportunity to talk with Peter. If she was staying in Crystal Creek, she needed to smooth out some of their dents so they could at least continue to work together.

Then she'd see what happened from there.

Chapter Thirty-One

"JUST SIGN HERE and here and we're done," said Mr. Dunkle, the final inspector of the morning.

Charlee added her signature to the spots indicated, then suppressed a squeal when he ripped off the copies and handed them to her.

"Have a nice day," he said, gathering his bag before leaving.

"You, too," Charlee said, playing it cool with Eden by her side. Once Mr. Dunkle left the room, both of them turned to each other and let out the happy shrieks they had held in. Charlee laughed as Eden shook her hips and turned in circles, doing her own version of the happy, happy dance.

"It's all mine," Eden said, running her ring-laden hands over the checkout counter, then turning, eyes closed, her long, black hair falling straight down her back and taking a deep breath. "Can't you just imagine the intoxicating smell of paper and ink, ready to fill your mind with a whole new world, a new adventure?"

Utter happiness filled Charlee, reflecting Eden's light and radiance. "It's going to be amazing, Eden. When do your deliveries start?"

"The sign people are coming tomorrow for the vinyl on the door and entry. I think the outdoor signs for Sweet Confections and Bibliophile will be installed next week. This afternoon I'll make calls to schedule the deliveries for the furniture, books, bags, trinkets, decor, and the café. The baked goods are the easiest part since Sweet Confections will be supplying them fresh each day. I'm just handling the drinks." Eden barely took a breath as she continued to babble about her shop, her excitement contagious. "Thankfully I should have a little time to spare before the grand opening of both shops in a few weeks. It's coming up so fast. I can't imagine how Rachel and Kristen are doing all this on top of planning Rachel's wedding and Kristen expecting a baby. They are the epitome of Wonder Women."

"No argument on that front." Charlee was sure Todd and Graydon were just as busy as the ladies, who were lucky to have such supportive men in their lives. "Well, I'll be here," she said, turning the conversation back to the grand opening. "Victoria wants all of us here for the ribbon-cutting ceremony. Be sure to let me know if there's anything else I can help you with. Now, let's go to lunch to celebrate, my treat."

The two women went downstairs. In the entry way, Charlee glanced into Sweet Confections. Peter had finished his part there while she was in California and now Rachel, Graydon, Todd and Kristen were there with a crew, directing traffic and setting up the shop. Charlee still felt bad that Eden was behind schedule, but thankfully, they were able to make everything come together in time for the grand opening.

Lunch with Eden was filled with more talk about the bookstore. She was grateful to concentrate on her friend's excitement.

"What are your plans for rest of the day?" Eden asked, moving the subject to Charlee.

"Just back to the office to brainstorm with Naomi for the next Indulgence Row project. Then I'll pop over to the Wheeler's to see the new counters before the crew wraps everything up."

"I have to say, Naomi is pretty awesome," Eden said, then took a bite of her salad. "She's a hive of knowledge. I've been picking her brain about some stuff for Bibliophile. The woman is a genius."

Charlee pointed her fork at Eden. "She's my genius. No stealing her away."

Eden snorted. "As if Naomi would even consider it."

Charlee was glad to hear that because she felt the same about all her employees.

"So..." Eden trailed off.

Oh no. Charlee could see it coming.

"What's happening with Peter?"

There it was. The thing she didn't want to talk about. She just shrugged, hoping Eden would drop the subject.

"You know, I've been keeping tabs on Hope," Eden said, leaning slightly forward and lowering her voice. "She's not chasing Peter anymore," Eden confided when Charlee didn't respond. "She's actually dating Kason Kippling."

Charlee's eyes went wide. "The guy who owns the electronics store?"

"Well, Kason, Jr. and it's pretty hot and heavy too."

That made more sense. Kason, Sr. was older than her father. Not that Kason, Jr. was young. He was probably about ten years older than Charlee. "Huh," she said, wondering if she had interpreted everything all wrong when it came to Hope.

"Just thought you might want to know." Eden finished her drink and thankfully changed the subject for the remainder of the lunch.

THE REMAINDER OF THE AFTERNOON moved fast. Naomi was ready to get right to work when Charlee arrived. They reviewed the house plans while Naomi made notes for the new set of renovation plans. Together they talked timelines, bids for materials and subcontractors, and scheduling appointments to meet with the clients. Charlee appreciated Naomi's no-nonsense and thorough approach to everything she did. She kept Transformations running much more smoothly than Charlee was able to.

After Naomi left to pick up her daughter from school, Charlee checked in with the crew at the Wheeler's house. Jenny was superbly happy with the kitchen and was itching to get to the next phase of the renovation.

"I know exactly how we're using our tax return next year," Jenny said. "I'm impressed you were able to finish the kitchen so quickly and your crew was just fabulous. Especially Sadie. That girl is just as sassy as can be around the men. She certainly holds her own, doesn't she?"

Charlee definitely agreed. It helped that the guys were all good men who didn't have any qualms about working with—or for—a woman. With the Wheeler project wrapped up, Charlee made her way to the hardware store to purchase spray paint for the desk.

The bell tinkled as she pushed through the double glass doors. She nodded to Sylvester who was checking out another customer at the register. She quickly made her way down the main aisle towards the back of the store where the paint was located. If she could get in and out fast, then she'd have time hit a drive-through to grab dinner before heading home to work on the desk. She was thinking through her evening when someone walked out from another aisle and they ran smack dab into each other, knocking her off balance. Something metal clanged to the floor, while a pair of strong hands grabbed onto her upper arms to keep her from falling over.

"I'm so sorry. I was hurrying and didn't see you," Charlee said, regaining her footing and stepped back to meet her helper's startled expression. "Peter!"

She felt like a guppy, her mouth opening and closing, not sure what to say. Her mind was a scrambled mess as Peter crouched down and picked up the items he dropped.

He jostled the metal door hinges between his hands as he stood before her. "Some doors at the office need repairs."

She shifted her weight from foot to foot, trying to find a position that conveyed she was comfortable, but it seemed impossible. "Tyler told me the news about Elliott Construction. How's the transition going?"

"Good, good." He nodded, his eyes flitting from her to the front of the store.

She shifted to see what caught Peter's attention and saw Sylvester leaning against the back counter, his arms crossed, brazenly watching their encounter. She turned back to Peter, ignoring the unwanted attention. "How does Cameron like the switch from law to running a business?"

"It's been good. He likes the new challenge."

Silence dropped between them again. This conversation was like pulling teeth and Charlee really hated going to the dentist. She searched for something to get them talking. "I got the desk. The base looked really good. Thanks."

He just nodded, his intense blue-gray eyes not leaving hers.

"I, um, got it all sanded and scrubbed down. I'm just picking up some paint for tonight." She motioned towards the back of the store. Now Peter was shuffling his weight from foot to foot, his eyes dropped to the items in his hands. He was obviously just as uncomfortable as she was. Maybe the most humane thing to do would be to end the conversation. "Listen, it was good to see you. I'll let you get back to the office."

She stepped around him, grateful to end the awkward meeting even though it made her heart sink to see their relationship deteriorated like this.

She only made it a few steps when he blurted out, "Is this how it's going to be now?"

She reluctantly turned to face him again, afraid where the conversation might go, especially how it could end.

Peter's cheeks were flushed and his eyes intently watching her as he stepped closer and lowered his voice. "Is this the new us? Because honestly, Charlee, I don't want it to be."

A lump rose to her throat and she tried to speak past it, but couldn't.

"If this is the only conversation I get, you need to know the truth," Peter continued, his voice earnest. "I didn't know Dad changed the bids. When everything happened at your parents' house, I didn't know. Honest to God, Charlee, when I prepped the bids they were fair. I handed them over to Dad for a messenger, then spent the rest of the day with you. I heard Elliott Construction received both jobs the next day, but I was busy with the crews and didn't think anything about it." He took another half step closer, the warmth of his body invading her space. "I swear I would never—"

She looked down when his voice cracked, his words cut short. The lump in her throat thick and unwanted, accompanied by the sting of tears. She quickly swiped at them, then glanced up and into the jumble of emotions in Peter's eyes.

He took her arm and pulled her into a side aisle, down towards the end where Sylvester's prying eyes couldn't follow. Peter shoved the door hinges onto a shelf before he stepped close and cupped her face in his hands. His fingers weaved through her hair and his thumbs brushed the wetness from her cheeks.

"Please forgive me," he pleaded, pressing his forehead to hers. "Not just for that, but for being stupid about Hope. She wasn't anything other than a friend. I knew she was flirting, but I figured if I was firm, she'd back off." He paused, visibly trying to pull himself together to say his next words. "Then everything fell apart and you were gone. I love you, Charlee. Please don't give up on me."

She grabbed onto the front of his flannel shirt, breathed in the scent of Peter. Her heart beating, feeling like it would pound out of her chest. She swallowed past the thick tears that had clogged her throat, wanting desperately to get this next part right. "I'm so sorry. Forgive me."

He shook his head. "There was so much pulling at us, trying to pit us against each other. Can we let that be the past and move forward?"

"I'd like that oh so much," she said, wanting a fresh start, a new beginning for them both right here in Crystal Creek.

Peter dropped light kisses over her wet lashes, down her cheek, then pulled her in and wrapped her in a hug, one arm around her waist, the other cradling her head against his shoulder. Her arms slipped under his winter vest, over soft flannel and around his back, pressing him to her. Wishing she could block out everything else and just soak in all of Peter. The heaviness in her chest slowly eased as they stood there together.

"What are they doing, Mommy?"

Peter's body jerked in surprise, still holding her close. She opened her eyes and saw a mother shushing a young preschooler, then pulling him away from an aisle display of door knobs.

She eased back, feeling heat suffuse her cheeks. "Public displays of affection. Ew," she teased, trying to lighten the mood. "Maybe we could go eat dinner and talk some more?"

Peter sighed, his arms dropping from around her, but picked up her hand to play with her fingers. "I'm actually going back to the office. We have meetings tonight and all day tomorrow about the transition and new vision for Elliott Construction. I needed to escape for a few minutes and made up a lame excuse about needing to update some hinges. I pretty sure Cameron knew I just needed to be outside the office walls. I'll be done late, but how about I text you when I'm home and maybe we can talk?"

Peter's cell phone rang. He pulled it out, swiping to answer. "Hello, Cameron," he said, continuing to play with her fingers with his free hand, keeping her close while he listened to Cameron on the other end. "I'll be back in about ten minutes. Hold your horses." The call ended and Peter slid the phone into his back pocket. "I hate leaving when we've finally started to clear the air."

"I understand." She went up on her toes and lightly pressed her lips to his, lingering for a brief moment. Peter's grip on her hand tightened, pulling her hand up and pressing it on his chest where she could feel the fast beating of his heart before she broke the kiss. "Go, I'll talk to you tonight."

"Send me pics of the desk. I want to see how it's going." He grabbed the door hinges. At the end of the aisle, he turned and looked back at her, mouthing *I love you* before disappearing.

Taking a big chunk of her heart with him.

TARPS WERE SPREAD ACROSS the living room floor and the windows cracked open. Charlee shook the can of nickel-colored spray paint, then tested the spray stream. Satisfied it was good, she began painting the top half of the desk, sweeping her arm back and forth to get a good even coat on the inside of the metal desk. She checked the coating from different angles while shaking the can some more, then started on the sides. Before she could get to the legs, there was a knock on the front door.

She looked at the clock. It was after seven. Maybe Peter

finished his meetings and decided to come over rather than call. She quickly set the spray can down on a metal folding chair and made her way to the front door, looking down at her hands and the gray tips of her fingers. She never liked wearing gloves while spraying, preferring to just scrub her hands later. Hopefully Peter wouldn't mind the messiness.

She pulled open her front door, but instead of Peter, her mother stood on the front step. Charlee was surprised by the swell of anger just seeing her created. She took a deep breath, trying to calm the emotions boiling up. She wasn't ready for this talk. But then again, would she ever be?

"Can I come in?" Her mother fidgeted with the purse strap slung over her shoulder.

Charlee hesitantly opened the door wider and her mother stepped inside, stopping near the edge of the kitchen. It had been several months since the last time her mother visited. Charlee watched her glance around, most likely looking for changes.

"I see you're working on another project. Is it for the women's shelter?" her mother asked, trying to start the conversation on a safe subject.

Charlee folded her arms in front across her chest. "I haven't decided what I'm doing with it yet."

"Oh." Her mother was obviously fumbling, not sure what to say, which was new. She always had an opinion and never held back expressing it.

"Tyler said you wanted to talk to me," Charlee said, trying to give her an opening.

"About last Friday," she said, looking around, not meeting Charlee's eyes.

Seriously, what was the woman doing here? If she wanted to talk to her, then she needed to spit it out because Charlee certainly wasn't going to make it easier for her.

"I'm sorry if I behaved badly," her mother began.

If? Really? That was how she was going to start her apology? Charlee tried to hold back blurting anything out, to give her mom time to say whatever she wanted to say.

"I hope you know I wasn't choosing Peter over you. It was just that he's been a friend of the family for so long. I wanted to be clear that he was always welcome, even if you two broke up."

"Mmm hmm," Charlee murmured.

"And you are our daughter, so you know your dad and I love you. We just, you know, love Peter, too. You know, as Tyler's best friend and all."

"Mmm hmm." It all felt like it was just a repeat of Friday night. This wasn't an apology, it was a bunch of excuses for why she did what she did. And it made her even madder. "Anything else?"

Her mom shifted from foot to foot. "No, I just wanted to be sure you understood why things happened the way they did."

"I understand." Charlee laughed. "Oh, I understand that the only reason you're here is because Julie is mad and is withholding your grandchildren until you apologize. I understand that this," Charlee motioned between the two of them, "is nothing more than you reiterating what you said Friday night. The night when, I'll remind you in case you forgot, I found out my boyfriend's company sabotaged mine. And what did you do? You defended Peter."

Charlee sliced her arm through the air, cutting off her

mother when she tried to speak. "Let me tell you what you should have done. When you interrupted our fight, I turned to you and thought you were coming to hug me, to actually comfort me in the middle of a horrific moment. But instead you walked right past me to Peter. Can you even imagine how that tore me apart?" Her mother's face paled, but that didn't stop Charlee's rant. "I don't know why I hoped for an actual warm and fuzzy moment because you've never shared those sentiments with anyone other than your precious favorite daughter."

"That's not fair," her mother protested. "I tried but you were the one who didn't want my attention. You preferred to run with the boys, play in the mud and rip things apart. I didn't know what to do with a daughter like that, so I let you be."

"Yet you knew how to raise a son who was exactly the same, but the fact that I'm a girl meant you couldn't understand me? You chose to just leave me alone because I didn't want dolls and princess dresses and to be in your stupid girly pageants? You didn't even try."

Her mother pointed at her, her hand in a tight fist. "You pushed me away every time I tried!"

"Because every time you did, it was all about girly stuff you wanted to do, not stuff I was interested in," Charlee countered.

Her mother folded her arms. "You were stubborn, just like you're being right now."

"No, Mom," Charlee said, pressing her hand to her chest. "I was the child. You were the parent. It was your job to meet me on my level. The difference is now we're both adults and I don't have to live with your disapproval." Charlee marched to the front door, fed up with the conversation. "I think it's time for you to leave."

She opened the door, the cool air rushed into the room making the heated situation down right icy.

"You're being ridiculous. I'm your mother and you can't kick me out." She stood, her feet firmly planted in the foyer.

"Would you like me to call Tyler to find out what my rights are in my own home? After all, you made it very clear that your home followed your rules and was for the people you wanted to be there. Well, the same goes here and I want you to leave."

"Fine." Her mother walked past Charlee without looking at her, out the door and continued down the sidewalk without another word.

Charlee slammed the front door shut and growled in frustration. Why was her relationship with her mother such a mess? It was doomed. It would never be the warm relationship she thought it should be. Frustrated, she texted Tyler.

Mother came to see me. It was a complete disaster.

She clicked send. Then started typing again.

She was all excuses, excuses, excuses. There was no apology.

She clicked send and continued sending more short messages to her brother, only stopping when her phone rang. It was Tyler.

"Seriously, I can't text if you keep barraging my phone with messages."

"Then you need to learn to type faster," she said, still pent up with energy.

"Open the door. It's cold out here."

And there he was. Her idiot brother in uniform with his partner in tow.

"Geesh, just haul along an innocent bystander, why don't you," she said, inviting them inside.

"We're calling it a domestic intervention," Tyler said. At her astonished expression, he added, "I'm just kidding. We're on break. Ben Belliston, this is my sister, Charlee."

The tall officer took his police hat off and extended his hand. "Nice to meet you."

Looks like all the hot guys aren't just in California. She winced, then shook his hand. "Sorry you got dragged into this." She elbowed her brother. "What were you thinking?"

"You don't need to apologize," Ben said. "I've been raising my niece since her mom died of an overdose and her dad is in prison. Screwed up families aren't exclusive to yours."

Well, hot dog, if that didn't make her feel like a whiny brat. Some families had worse things going on than a mother who didn't understand her daughter.

"Point taken. Why don't you wait in the living room, Ben? We'll be a few minutes," Tyler said, ushering her into the kitchen. "What happened?"

She gave him the short version.

"It's true you both have never been on the best of terms." He held up his hand, holding off her comments. "I'm not taking either side. Just stating a fact." He leaned against the counter. "Listen, things aren't going to get better between the two of you overnight. You can't go from barely tolerating each other to a perfect mother daughter relationship that fast. And honestly, I don't think you'll ever have that kind of interaction."

Charlee's shoulders slumped, feeling unworthy and broken.

"I do think if you both could learn to talk to each other,

show interest in what you're each doing in your lives, then you could become friends."

"Sometimes I just wish she loved me, like she loves Julie." She sucked her bottom lip in and began to gnaw on it.

"She does love you," Tyler reassured her, leaning back against the counter. "She just doesn't show it the same way. Julie is a lot like Mom, so they spend more time together. Think of it this way. You're good friends with Victoria, Eden and Rachel, right?"

"Yeah," she said, nodding.

"But are you the same type of close with each of them? Is there one person you share more personal things with, someone you'd consider a closer friend or confidante?"

"Eden fills that role."

"Okay, think of you, Julie and Mom as friends. Except in this situation, Mom and Julie are the close friends and you're like Victoria or Rachel. Stop thinking of Mom as a parent and think of her as a friend. You can each learn to be nice to each other, to be friends, without needing to fill the best-friend role. Does that make sense?"

Huh. It actually did. It would be a challenge to figure out how she and her mother could accomplish it, but Tyler's advice changed her perspective. Instead of putting her mom on a pedestal and wanting her to fill an important role in her life, she needed to put her on even ground and build together from there.

"You know, this was the best girl talk. Just what I needed." She smiled at her brother.

"Shush," he said, grabbing her into a quick bear hug. "Psychology is part of being a cop. Now let me get back to work."

"Thanks," she mumbled into his starchy shirt.

"No prob, little sister." He ruffled her hair as he stepped back.

Officer Belliston stood when they came back into the living room.

"Thanks for spending your break here," Charlee said, still feeling bad the poor guy got stuck in the middle of their family drama.

"It was no problem. Not that Officer Jackson would have given me a choice," Ben teased, giving her a wink.

"Yeah, yeah," Tyler said, motioning for Officer Belliston. "Let's get moving while we still have time to grab something to eat."

Charlee let them out, then returned to her messy living room. She wondered what Officer Belliston thought of it all. The couch shoved back out of the way and the desk taking up most of the space.

She picked up the can of spray paint and shook it. She had a lot to think about. It was a good thing she had plenty to work on. Her brain mulled things over the best while she worked on a project. She pressed the spray tab and began coating the legs of the desk, contemplating everything Tyler suggested and weighing options for how to become her mother's friend.

Chapter Thirty-Two

BEFORE GOING TO WORK Friday morning, Charlee pulled out a yellow legal pad. She woke up with an idea about how to start over with her mother. Writing letters. No text messaging, no emails. Old fashioned letters written by hand, sealed in an envelope and stamped for the mail man to deliver.

It would give them each time to think, mull things over instead of feeling the need to immediately respond. Plus it might be nice to get something in the mailbox besides bill reminders, advertisements, and junk mail.

She put her pen to the paper and began.

Two crumpled drafts later, she wanted to bang her head against the table. Writing a letter shouldn't be this hard.

She pulled out her phone and texted Mari, who thankfully was up to date on everything that had occurred after their marathon texting last night.

I can't get the words right, Charlee messaged. It didn't take long before Mari replied.

They don't need to be perfect. Simplify. Pick two things you want to say, write it and send it off. Don't try to cram everything together at once.

You are one wise woman, Charlee messaged back.

She tapped her pen against the legal pad. Two things. What should she choose? Obviously, one should be to share the idea to start over and get to know each other through letters. The other should be something personal. Maybe that she's back together with Peter?

No, she didn't want her mother's approval or happiness to be based on a relationship she had with someone else. It needed to be something the two of them could discuss. Which also ruled out Transformations and business stuff.

Still not sure what to add for the personal part, she decided just to begin the letter.

Dear Mom

A wise person told me that sometimes it takes stepping back and starting over to mend a relationship. I've been thinking about that all night. This morning, I woke up with the idea that maybe we could exchange handwritten letters through the mail to get to know each other as adults and give ourselves the chance to become friends. I realize it's a little unconventional, but then again, so are we. I thought in each letter we could share something about ourselves that the other doesn't know, something funny that happened, or something we discovered.

Charlee paused, still not sure where to go from there. Instead of giving into frustration, she tore the letter off the pad, folded it and placed it in an envelope addressed to her mom. She slid the letter into her purse then went to the office.

Peter was waiting for Charlee when she arrived at

Transformations. He looked sexy all dressed up in a business suit complete with a tie. A tie she wanted to wrap around her hand to pull him close for a really good foot-popping kiss.

Instead she stopped next to where he was leaning against her desk chatting with Naomi and her daughter, Elise, who was playing with her My Little Ponies and munching on a donut.

"Who planned the party and didn't tell me about it?" Charlee greeted the group.

"Mr. Peter brought donuts and drinks for everyone," Elise said. It was a teacher in-service day and instead of taking time off, Naomi decided to try having her daughter in the office while she worked to see if it was doable or not.

"Donuts and drinks sounds like the perfect way to start a Friday morning." She accepted a cup of hot cocoa from Peter, but he held her donut just out of reach.

"You have to trade something sweet for your donut," he said, waggling his eyebrows.

"I didn't have to trade for my donut." Elise's eyebrows scrunched down, thinking hard. Then she popped up, grabbed something out of her backpack and gleefully presented it to Peter.

He looked down at the crayon scribbles covering the pony. "Wow, this is really good. Thank you."

"It's my favorite pony, Twilight Sparkle. She's gottest the biggest library!" She swung her arms wide to show just how big the library was.

While Peter was distracted, Charlee snagged her cream-filled donut out of Peter's hand and settled into her office chair. Peter simply winked and turned his attention back to Elise.

"And guess what?" The little girl lowered her voice and used her finger to motion Peter closer. "Twilight Sparkle has a pet dragon!"

"Now that makes her *my* favorite pony. Dragons are very cool," Peter said.

Elise giggled, ready to launch into even more Ponyville facts, but Naomi redirected her to her toys. Peter settled into the folding chair across from Charlee's desk.

"I thought I'd give you a head's up," he began. "There's going to be a news article coming out and some extra press about the changes at Elliott Construction."

Charlee nodded, swishing from side to side in her office chair. "That's to be expected. A local company changing leadership is big news."

"We're going to announce our new goals and focus. Part of that is pulling out of renovation work and focusing on hiring more architects to compete for more new commercial jobs. We'll be announcing some of our new architects with the press releases."

This made Charlee sit up straighter. "What about Indulgence Row?"

"I've already talked with Victoria about that. I made a commitment to help with the equipment-heavy renovations, like Sweet Confections. I gave her the name of some other crews I recommended, if she wanted to contact them for bids."

Charlee wondered how this would affect Transformations. If she received more bids, the company could expand faster. Hire on more crews, get them trained to Transformations expectations. At the same time, she worried about Transformations growing too fast. Besides, she reminded herself, Transformations still needed to prove they could get this next project done on time.

Peter cleared his throat, drawing her attention back to the present. "We've also withdrawn our contracts for the Bailey and Peterson projects. Their projects don't fit in with our future vision and since the work hasn't begun, we pulled out. I believe they'll be opening up for bids again next week."

"I hope you didn't do that because of me," she said.

Peter crossed his ankle over his knee and played with the shoelaces dangling from his dress shoes. "It was brought up by Cameron as he reviewed upcoming projects and how they aligned with our new focus. He proposed pulling out of those projects so we could concentrate on what we actually want to do."

"Well, just because you're pulling out doesn't mean Transformations is going to bid again. I'm not sure if I want to work with people like that." She was still peeved not just at George, but that the managers would agree to the scheme.

"I understand," Peter said. "I think things would have turned out very different if my dad had not personally put the pressure on."

"I'll think about it," she said, then took a bite out of her donut, hoping the sugar rush would give her brain the boost it needed to process all this new information. "You mentioned hiring new architects. Anyone in particular? Or do I need to wait for the press release?"

"I can tell you one of them is my sister." He chuckled at her surprised look. "Kimber went back to school a few years ago without telling Dad. Mom kept it a secret. She's been submitting designs under a pen name and actually sold a few of them. In fact, Baker's Classic Cars going in downtown is her design."

"Wow. I'm impressed." She saw the write up for the fun 50's design and build out in the Kansas City Star a few months ago. "Your dad's is going to be less-than-thrilled after he already told her she couldn't work there."

Peter shrugged and offered an honest-to-goodness smile. "I'm not worried about that. I'm looking at Elliott Construction's future. My sister and I should be there, working together, as well as any future Elliott generations. It shouldn't matter if they want to work on a crew or be a secretary. If they are trustworthy and hard workers, then they have a place at the company."

Charlee returned his smile, heartened to see the direction Peter was going with the family business. "Good for you."

They sat there for a moment, exchanging goofy grins, each thinking their own silent thoughts. Charlee's were circling around things she could do with that tie. If only there wasn't an audience.

Oh, Naomi and her daughter!

Charlee blinked and straightened in her chair. Peter caught onto her cue.

"I should get over to EC before Cameron starts calling." He stood and said goodbye to Naomi, Elise, and Charlee. "Enjoy the donuts."

"We will," she called before he disappeared down the hall. She heard his steps fade as he went downstairs, then the open and close of the front door. She sighed, missing his presence already.

"Back together again, I see," Naomi said, gathering some papers before taking the seat Peter had previously occupied.

"Don't bother denying it. Y'all look like lovesick puppies."

"Kissing is disgusting," her daughter chimed in. "Unless it's in Ponyville when someone gets married. Then it's okay. But other than that—" She made fake gagging noises.

Charlee's face flushed. There was nothing like being schooled by a kid. "Well, we weren't kissing."

"You were doing it with your eyes. Like when Rarity's eyes get all big and hearts float in the air." Elise shook her head. "Disgusting."

Naomi laughed at her daughter, but Charlee couldn't help but wonder if she really was looking at Peter like that, and if so, what she could do to control it. Maybe she should ask Naomi's daughter. She seemed like a gold mine of information on the subject, even if she proclaimed to dislike it. You know what they say, the more you protest you don't like someone or something, the more you probably do.

"Let's get back to work," Naomi said changing the subject. "I need you to review these bids for the upcoming Indulgence Row project. Let me know when you're done." She then returned to her desk, ready to work on checking things off her to-do list.

Charlee pulled out the letter for her mother and set it on her desk. She looked around the office space. She loved being in her grandmother's home. What would Grandma say? She had been a kind and service-oriented woman, but she had a kick of sass about her too. Charlee certainly hoped she had a lot of her Grandma in her. She smiled, remembering the trip to The Sock Hop diner with Peter and how it reminded her of a happy time with her family.

That was it! She grabbed the letter, opened it and started

to write.

One of the things I love about having my office on Indulgence Row is that it's located in Grandma's house. I think about her all the time when I'm sitting at my desk, looking through the doorways, down the halls, reminiscing about all sorts of things.

Do you remember the trips to that store with the soda bar Grandma liked to take us to? She always got a huge banana split to share, you got a vanilla Coke, Julie got a strawberry soda. I loved their chocolate malts. Tyler didn't care about the drinks. He just wanted quarters to go play music on the jukebox.

A few weeks ago, I discovered The Sock Hop Diner. It's this little tiny restaurant about twenty minutes from Crystal Creek. It reminded me so much of those trips with Grandma. I hope you can go explore and remember it, too. I don't know about their vanilla Cokes, but their chocolate malts were super delicious!

I hope you write soon.
Charlee

She folded the letter once again and replaced it in the envelope, but she didn't seal it. She looked over at Naomi and Elise. They needed a fun adventure, something just for the two of them to enjoy and make memories.

"Naomi, could I talk with you for a minute?"

"Of course." She joined Charlee, taking the seat across from her desk.

"Would you mind running an errand for me during lunch?

There's this old diner I want to get a gift certificate at, but just don't have the time to drive there. It's about twenty minutes away. I thought you and Elise might enjoy a little adventure together. Lunch would be on me since I'm the one sending you so far away."

Of course, Little Miss Elise heard the request and popped up and ran to her mother's side, bouncing with excitement. "Oh, please, Mom? Adventures are fun!"

Naomi smoothed her daughter's hair. "Yes, we can. Be sure to thank Miss Charlee though."

Elise continued bouncing, but adding clapping her hands to the mix. "Thank you, Miss Charlee!"

"Now, I have to get a lot of work done before we can go. So play and watch your show, okay?" Naomi smiled as Elise scampered back to her ponies and started chattering away, telling them about the upcoming adventure.

"You know she's going to think we'll go for lunch every time she comes now, don't you?"

Charlee just smiled. "Every girl needs a little spoiling. Working lunches sounds like a fun tradition to begin, especially if I get to join you in the future."

Naomi rolled her eyes, then went back to her desk. Charlee followed her example, a little smile lifting the corner of her lips.

CHARLEE PULLED OPEN the metal mailbox door, then slid the letter inside. She closed the door, then reopened it, checking that the letter to her mother was indeed deposited into the belly of the outgoing mail slot at the townhouse complex. She let out the breath she had been holding and hoped her mother would like the idea rather than think Charlee was a total idiot. She shrugged, then headed back to her townhouse. It would go one way or another. She didn't have any control over how her mother responded. Still, she hoped it would be favorable.

Back inside the warmth of her living room, Charlee turned on the stereo, chose a playlist on her iPod, then began to reassemble the desk. She screwed the newly painted metal bottom to the wooden top, then turned it right side up. She pulled out some bee's wax and rubbed it into the wood, nourishing it, giving it some much-needed moisture which also brought out the wood's natural shine. When everything was done, she stepped back and admired the desk.

It had transformed from something battered and forgotten into a beautiful item that would be enjoyed in someone's home. At least, someone with an old school or farmhouse decorating style. In fact, it would be a fun gift to give to the Wheeler's, kind of a thank-you-for-believing-in-me gift.

She grabbed a cream soda from the fridge, then settled into a bar chair, listening to Alan Jackson's rich voice sing about young love.

She realized she and Peter were a lot like the desk.

They started off new and shiny, like the desk was a long time ago, but they quickly hit a lot of bright construction signs warning them of big changes ahead. Tyler's reaction to the two of them together. Hope and the flare of jealousy and mistrust that brought out. All the George chaos. Not to mention her own relationship insecurities. All of it combined together left their relationship pretty battered like the desk they purchased at the auction.

But the interesting thing was what they learned and where their relationship was now. They weren't shiny and new, but they were working out the kinks and had a fresh outlook for their future.

She couldn't help but laugh at her very own relationship analogy. Peter would be so proud.

She wondered what their next step would be, and the one after that. Even though they had gone through a big rocky mess, she felt like they were on firmer ground now. Peter wasn't just a guy she was crushing on. He was the person she wanted to talk to first about anything and everything, to share the ups and downs of the day with.

She didn't just love Peter. She loved her best friend. What better love could there be than that?

A silly idea popped into her head, making her bubble with excitement. She set down her soda, then crossed the room to go through her woodworking supplies. She found what she needed, then began carving into the wooden desk top. She worked meticulously, shaping, chipping a little here, a little there. She smiled at the finished project. She quickly dusted off the top, rubbed some bee's wax into the carving, then put away her tools. She grabbed the legal notepad and once again wrote a short note, this time to Peter. She folded it up, all cute and fun like back in junior high, then used some tape to secure it to the desk.

Charlee quickly pulled a knit hat over her head, wound a scarf around her neck, then grabbed her truck keys and the desk. It was a short trip, just down a few blocks to Peter's house. She pulled over a few townhouses away and turned off the truck lights, hoping the evening darkness would conceal her little trip to drop off Peter's present. She hopped out of the truck, then pulled the desk out of the back. Thank goodness it was so light!

She tried hard not to laugh as she carefully made her way to Peter's front door. Then she quietly set the desk down, hoping Petunia wouldn't start barking. She double checked to make sure the note was still attached, then turned to flee the scene. Her cheeks hurt from the huge grin as she imagined Peter's expression when he discovered the surprise.

Chapter Thirty-Three

PETER ROUNDED THE CORNER on his way home from a walk with Petunia. Winter was the hardest time of the year with the dog park closing early because of the dark evening hours. Man oh man, these bitter winter walks were not on the list of things he enjoyed.

Petunia barked and pulled on the leash, drawing his attention from watching the sidewalks for ice and puddles to someone walking away from his front door. Someone who looked a lot like Charlee.

Afraid it might be her and he was going to miss a visit, he called out her name. She spun around, the surprised look on her face illuminated by the overhead street light. He let Petunia pull him into a jog until they met up where she stood, looking nervous. Petunia, though, didn't show any hesitation. She buried her head right between Charlee's leg and hand, urging Charlee to pet her.

"Hey," Charlee said to him, then dropped her attention to the dog. "What craziness are you up to on a cold night like this?"

"Just walking." He grabbed her hands and rubbed them

between his own gloved hands. "Talk about crazy. Where are your gloves? Your hands are all red."

She just shrugged. "I was just dropping something off. I wasn't planning to be out for long."

Peter looked over to his front door and saw the desk sitting next to it. "Wow, it looks great." He looked back at Charlee, confused. "You aren't donating it to the women's shelter?"

Her cheeks turned even redder. "Well, I just thought you'd like it and, um."

She looked away. He moved his body around, meeting her eyes, then smiled. "You're embarrassed! Charlee Jackson, what did you do?"

Her beautiful eyes went wide. "Nothing!"

He laughed, knowing she was fibbing. He grabbed the sleeve of her coat, not letting her escape from an opportunity to tease her. He really loved the deep blush that bloomed across her cheeks. "Sure you didn't. Let's go check out what you left for me."

She dug her feet in. "Oh no. I'll just go. I need to grab some dinner—"

"We can order Chinese. I haven't eaten yet either." He slowly pulled her along with him. Petunia thought it was a great game and jumped around them, barking and nudging Charlee along until they were in front of the desk.

"What's this?" Peter kept hold of Charlee with one hand and pulled off the note attached with the other, quite a feat with Petunia pulling on his arm at the same time.

Then he saw it.

Love Under Construction

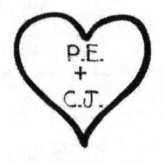

He traced his finger over the carving, his fingertips feeling the bumps and ridges beneath his glove. He imagined the time she took to carve it, sitting in her living room, and a warm glow spread across his chest. He glanced up at Charlee, who had her face buried in her hands, although not well enough that he couldn't tell her cheeks were still bright red.

"I wasn't supposed to be here when you found it. It was supposed to be a surprise," she mumbled from behind her hands. "I feel really stupid."

He tried to pull her into a hug, but she resisted.

"Did you read the note yet?" she asked.

"I'll do that now." He smiled when she groaned and dropped her chin, trying to hide her face.

"No laughing," she mumbled.

"Oh, I'm not." *Smiling, yes. Laughing, well, not yet.* He pulled the first little corner of the note out from where it was tucked and began the complicated task of opening it. He had not seen one of these in years. Did kids even know how to make notes like this anymore? Or was it all just texting? Finally, the paper was open and he could read the message.

Circle one.
Do you love me?   Yes or No
If yes, will you be my boyfriend?   Yes or No

Hoping for yes! Love, Charlee

CHARLEE PEEKED BETWEEN her fingers, watching Peter's reaction. She couldn't help but hide her face. She was mortified. This was worse than being back in high school, waiting to see if your crush returned your feelings.

His expression changed as he read the note. At first he smiled, but then it turned into a frown and he rubbed his forehead.

Her hands dropped away from her face, placing one on his arm. "Peter?"

He unzipped his jacket, pushing his hand into the inside pockets, searching for something. "I need a pen," he said, pulling one from an inside pocket of his jacket, then he shifted and leaned over the desk, blocking Charlee's view.

But she could definitely tell he wasn't just circling a few answers. He was writing. Now she was worried. Her silly idea spurred from a stupid song had backfired and she was right in the middle to witness it going up in flames. When Peter turned to face her again, she looked at his outstretched hand, where the refolded note was waiting.

She gulped.

Then reached for the yellow paper, trying to keep her hand from trembling. She flexed her cold, red hands, then began the process of opening each little fold, wondering what was inside.

Was this how he felt? It was nerve wracking being on the other side. The first question came into view.

Do you love me?

He circled yes!

She quickly glanced up at Peter, so excited and happy, only to be filled with apprehension when she saw the solemn look on his face. What could possibly be next that put such a serious expression on his face? She unfolded another section, then another to reveal the next question.

Will you be my boyfriend?

No.

Her heart plummeted.

But there was an arrow pointing down. She unfolded the note a few more times and found a question from Peter.

Will you marry me?

Her breath caught in her throat, her hand coming up to grasp the scarf at her neck.

The 'No' option was crossed out with another arrow pointing to the Yes and a little note above the arrow that said *Pick Me!*

She pulled on her scarf, needing some air to breathe. Peter stepped in close, his hands running up her arms, one coming to rest at the nape of her neck, the other pulling her hand away from the scarf and twining their fingers together. He tilted her head up so she could see his soft, serious eyes and the genuine love that emanated from them.

"There have been a lot of obstacles since we started dating. Nothing has been smooth, but I figure life is like that. The thing is, even with all that happened, the one thing I wanted was to be with you. I love you, Charlee Jackson."

The note fluttered to the ground as she brought her

fingertips to rest against his lips, wishing she could capture the words and keep them as tangible reminders. "This is insanity. You know that right?"

His thumb caressed her cheek. "It's crazy and spontaneous but I want us to think forward, to share the future together. Please say yes and give me the opportunity to show you how amazing and wonderful I know we are together."

His words were warm against her fingertips, his lips brushing against them in a whispery kiss. Her heart beat hard and her feet tingled, but didn't stop there. The tingles traveled through her, making her feel exposed, her heart laid out for him to capture. She loved this man and yes, it was crazy but she absolutely knew she wanted to share her forever with him.

"Yes," she barely got out before placing her lips over his and sealing the deal.

Falling Stars & Stolen Kisses

An Indulgence Row Novel
Book Three ✦ Coming Soon

Three years ago

MARI RESTED HER HEAD against the door jam and closed her eyes for just a minute, trying to will away the heaviness weighing her down. She could hear Xavier scampering around, crashing his toy cars against each other. The little guy was going to be two years old next week and was going through a growth spurt, which meant he was up most of the night with extra energy. She thought he'd have outgrown these up all night episodes by now, but parenthood continued to surprise her by not being at all how she imagined. She didn't understand how someone with so little sleep could have so much energy. He was like the Energizer Bunny disguised as a sweet toddler in 2T sized clothes.

So much for all those parenting books she devoured during her pregnancy.

"Mama," Xavier called from the living room. "Mama play cars."

As much as she loved her son, all Mari wanted was to take a nap, to give into the yearning her body craved for a pillow, blanket and the oblivion of heavy sleep. She laid her hand on the door of her husband's home office. Luis had been tucked away working on images from last week's photo shoot in Venice. She didn't like to interrupt when he was in editing mode, but if she didn't get some rest, the photographer for her shoot next week would have a hissy fit about the dark circles under her eyes. Not to mention she was a much nicer mother and wife when she wasn't sleep deprived. She knocked on the door, then turned the knob and slipped inside.

Luis was at his large mahogany desk, headphones over his ears probably listening to Vivaldi as he played with layers of light and texture on the images displayed on the big screen monitors. She smiled, or at least tried to, but the heaviness in her face overrode the effort. Their son looked so much like Luis and would one day be just as handsome with his father's Portuguese rich olive skin tone, soulful brown eyes and jet black hair. Thankfully, Xavier also inherited his mother's wavy hair.

She crossed the room and placed her hand on Luis' shoulder, briefly pulling his attention from the model on the screen. He lowered the headphones to rest around his neck, giving her part of his attention while he continued to work.

"Hey," he said, moving the mouse to click on an editing icon before making a selection on the screen. "Has Xavier finally conked out?"

She sighed, wishing that was the case. "No, he's still going strong."

Luis shook his head. "He's gotta drop at some point, right?"

"It doesn't seem to be happening in the near future." She scrubbed her hands over her face. "I have to take a nap. Could you please take Xavier to the park for an hour? Maybe that will wear him out."

Luis shook his head. "You know I'm in the middle of a project."

Her skin prickled and all sorts of retorts flew through her mind, like how parenting wasn't just the mom's job or how he had not even come out for lunch to give her a thirty minute break for a power nap. Nope. She's been doing it all on her own, all night and all day long. Oh how she wanted to let it all pour out, but instead she bit her inner-cheek to keep from picking a fight.

"Here's the deal," she said. "I can't do it. I'm a quarter inch away from turning into the Wicked Witch of the West and melting down in a very nasty way. I absolutely need to take a nap."

"Can't you just put a movie on and sleep while he watches it?"

She stomped her foot. Yes, it was juvenile, but the

alternative was she really wanted to break his computer and force him to look at her, pay attention to what she needed. "No, I can't. I won't be able to sleep knowing he'll probably leave the room and destroy the kitchen or something. It would be better if you could watch him. If you don't want to go to the park, go grab tickets to the new Disney movie. Just do something."

"Fine," he said, yanking his headphones from around his neck, tossing them onto the desk and shoving backwards, making her jump out of the way. "Go get his stuff ready and I'll take him out."

He brushed past her and disappeared upstairs. She knew he was mad. Heck, she was mad, but honestly, the only thing she cared about right at that moment was the promise of sleep in about ten minutes.

She rushed into the kitchen and grabbed Xavier's backpack. She threw in some snacks, his favorite water bottle with the flip top straw, and made sure there were diapers and wipes. "Xavier, come put your shoes on. Daddy's going to take you out for some fun."

"Daddy, Daddy, Daddy," Xavier said, running in on his chubby toddler legs. He went to the shoe bin and pulled out all the shoes in search of his sneakers.

Normally she made him clean them all back up, but she didn't care about the mess either. She knelt next to Xavier and helped him get his feet into the shoes, then allowing him to pull the Velcro strap across to secure them.

"Okay, buddy, let's go," Luis said, joining them in the kitchen. He slung the backpack over one shoulder, then took Xavier's hand to lead him into the garage.

Xavier turned to wave. "Bye-bye, Mama."

Luis was frustrated enough that he skipped their normal kiss goodbye and Mari let it slide. She'd make it up to him when she felt better. She blew a kiss to Xavier and as soon as the door closed behind them, she crossed the kitchen then headed for the main foyer. She heard the automatic garage doors raise, then close again.

Quiet. The house was blissfully quiet.

She gripped the railing and propelled herself up the stairs, kept her legs moving. Just a bit further, she thought. Finally, she crawled into her bed, burrowed under the down comforter to block out the mid-afternoon sun and sighed as much needed sleep took over.

Mari blinked, the dark room coming into focus. She rubbed her eyes and blinked until she could read the time on the bedside table clock. 5:27 pm. She was surprised Luis let her sleep that long. She stretched her arms high above her head, grateful to finally feel like her normal self.

She felt a pang of guilt for how cranky she had been, especially knowing how important Luis' deadlines were. They worked hard to keep work and family life balanced. If only they could plan for days like today. Luis was generally the laid back, fun one of the family and she was more structured and routine oriented.

Maybe once he was out with Xavier, his was able to shift out of work mode and into fun dad mode. She'd have to order dinner from his favorite Indian restaurant as a thank you for giving her the extra time to sleep. She sat up, then swung her legs over the bed, wondering what Luis and Xavier were up to. They were most likely vegging in front of the TV, watching the latest Pixar movie.

She padded down the stairs, turning on lights as she went through the house. If Luis was home, the lights would be on. He hated dark rooms. She'd have to call and find out where they were. Now where did she leave her cell? She did a quick run through of the time before her nap, then remembered putting it on the charger in the kitchen and wishing she could recharge her batteries as easily as the phone. She retrieved it and swiped to refresh the screen.

No missed calls.

She tapped on Luis' photo to call his cell, then listened as it rang and rang before going to voicemail. That was odd. She tried to think of what the two could be doing that Luis wouldn't hear his cell. Maybe they went to a movie and his phone was off? Or maybe Xavier talked him into hitting a restaurant with a play place, although they were high on Luis' list of places to avoid. But still, he was known to give in every once in a while. It was more likely they were driving through some yucky traffic and Luis didn't want to pick up the phone.

Falling Stars & Stolen Kisses

Thinking ahead, she went to the restaurants folder on her phone and tapped the icon to call The Bombay House. It was Luis' favorite, as well as a local spot. Since they discovered it, they had become great friends with the owner's family. If she placed the order now, it should be here not too long after Luis and Xavier returned.

"Bombay House. This is Rakesh."

Delighted that Rakesh was home for the weekend, Mari greeted him warmly. "Hi, Rakesh. This is Mari Diaz, how's college going?"

"Very good, Mrs. Diaz. I'm enjoying the challenge of the engineering classes, but not all the papers I have to write for my English Lit class."

Mari laughed. "If it were me, I'd be the absolute opposite."

Rakesh chuckled, too. "Will we see your family this weekend? I can make a reservation if you'd like?"

"Actually, the little guy is going through a rough growth spurt, so I think it's going to be a to-go order."

"No problem," Rakesh said. "Your normal order or are you brave enough to try the house special?"

The front doorbell rang before she could answer. "Um . . ." she said, distracted and making her way to the front door. "Give me just a sec. There's someone at the door."

She peeked through the window panel along the side of the door and saw two police officers on the door step. She quickly flipped the locks and opened the door.

The officers stepped forward, their faces grim.

The taller officer removed his cap. "Mrs. Diaz?"

The hand holding her cell phone dropped to her side. "Yes," her voice cracking over the word.

"Do you know a Luis Diaz?"

Everything slowed, making Mari hyper-aware of every little thing. The thud of her heart crashing against her chest. How her throat tightened, making it hard to breathe. Even the effort it took to bob her head up and down to respond to the officer's question. The officer with the deep gray eyes that reminded her of the ocean behind their house on a cloudy day. She couldn't look away from those gray pools, feeling as though if she focused on that one thing that somehow things would be all right.

Then his eyes watered and he blinked, breaking her focus. "I'm so sorry. There's been an accident."

The phone slipped from her hand, clanging onto the tile floor as the officer continued to speak.

A four car collision.

Ambulances. Hospital. They did all they could.

No survivors.

Her knees buckled. The officer's arms reached out to catch her as she sank to the hard cold tile floor.

The echo of Rakesh's tinny voice came from the cell phone. "Mrs. Diaz. Are you okay? Mrs. Diaz?"

All she wanted was blackness to devour her, to make the nightmare go away. It didn't come.

But the torture of reality did.

Present

Death
comes delivered
in stark white.
Satin pillows and hard wood.
Trapped.

One
tiny hand.
One perfect child.
A light snuffed out,
Gone.

Unimaginable
crushing emptiness.
Agony so bitter, crushing,
Crisp.

Memories
bitter-sweet moments
of fleeting life.
Yearning for one more
anything.

Danyelle Ferguson

*One
more touch.
One hour, day,
week, month or year.
More.*

*Time
halts as
that tiny coffin
creeps forward to rest
before you.*

*Pretty
cascading flowers.
Sickenly sweet perfection.
You want to rip,
shred.*

*Beg,
to scream,
make the nightmare
disappear, to go away.
Stop.*

*Instead
you suck
it all in.
Hidden behind a cracked
wall.*

Mari read through the poem that had haunted her for over a year. It started as an assignment from her therapist. The paper was crumpled and stained from being brought out over and over. Scribbles scratched out imperfect words and expressions. Every few months, she rewrote the poem onto fresh paper and tucked the older versions behind them. This one was almost due to be replaced, Mari noted. She clicked and unclicked her pen, contemplating the words welled up inside as she sat in on a private plane.

Her destination: Crystal Creek, Kansas.

Not Paris, Milan, New York or any of the other destinations she'd traveled to since her family's death three years ago. Each destination held a home they had shared. She renovated or redecorated each one as she tried desperately to find inner-peace. The trips ended with another step of closure by listing the house, villa or flat for sale. This time though, she wasn't retracing memories she made with her husband and son. No, she was returning to the one place she had avoided since her high school graduation.

Damn that Charlee Jackson. It was all her fault.

She shoved the thought aside and focused on the words that had been tumbling since the visit to Luis' and Xavier's graves that morning. She needed to get them out of her brain. She put her pen to the paper and began to compose.

Danyelle Ferguson

Time
is cruel.
Always moving forward.
Tick tock, tick tock.
Smash.

How
do you
hope?

Mari gripped the pen, searching for the next words.

What did she hope for? Relief from the torment still waging a war inside? That was a no-brainer. The ability to sleep without reliving the funeral would be nice. Heck, just to sleep for more than a couple hours would be miraculous. How was it that with all the therapy sessions and traveling around the world to study with experts in the fields of massage, yoga, essential oils, and meditation, peace still seemed a distant dream?

Her thoughts were interrupted by the flight attendant stopping beside her. Mari quickly flipped the poem upside down before turning her attention to Kara.

"Mrs. Diaz, Garrett informed me the descent is going to be pretty rough with the storm coming in. You'll need to stow your work in the side pocket or I can take it for you, if you prefer."

"I've got it," Mari assured her. "Thank you, Kara."

"You're welcome. Be sure to check your seat belt, too." Her smile was warm before Kara turned to take her seat at the back of the plane.

Mari tapped the papers on the lap desk's surface to straighten them out, then placed them in a black folder and clipped the pen to it before putting it all in the side storage pocket. She lifted the lap desk and slid it into its hideaway compartment. The business amenities were one of the many benefits of having a co-share on a private plane.

There were no fluffy white clouds or pretty blue sky when she lifted the window blind. Instead the plane was surrounded by thick ominous clouds that blocked the afternoon sunlight. The plane hit an air pocket, causing a hard drop before finding it's balance again. Mari pulled on her seat belt, checking that it was tight and secure, low on her hips like Kara recommended. Then she closed her eyes and practiced slow cleansing breaths from her yoga training, urging calm through her mind and body as the plane dipped from side to side fighting against the stormy winds.

That wasn't so bad, she thought when the wheels finally touched solid ground. At least until she opened her eyes and saw how tight she was clenching the arm rests. She slowly pried her fingers off it, then flexed her hands and rubbed them together, helping the slender fingers and muscles to relax once more.

"Well, that was adventurous, wasn't it?" Kara asked in a chipper voice.

"Are you and Garrett staying in Kansas City until the storm clears?" Mari asked, unbuckling the seat belt and gathering her folder while Kara opened the coat closet to retrieve Mari's purse and coat.

"I'm sure we will. The storm hit earlier than excepted. You'll need this," Kara said, handing Mari a large umbrella. "It's really coming down out there."

Mari pulled on the warm black coat she purchased especially for this trip. Spring in Kansas City meant lots of wind and rain, both of which were much colder than she was used to in sunny California. She took the umbrella from Kara, then followed the flight attendant to wait for the ground crew's signal before opening the door to exit the plane.

Garrett nodded to her, his pilot cap under his arm. "I need to secure the plane in the hangar for the night, then I'll bring the luggage to you. Be careful making your way to the terminal. It's pretty nasty out there."

"Nothing a Kansas girl can't handle," Mari replied.

When the door finally opened, she got her first glimpse of exactly what Garrett meant. She couldn't see the terminal entrance past the gray sheet of rain hitting the tarmac so hard, it sounded like the crashing roar of the ocean.

Well, it was time to put one foot in front of the other. Mari stepped out from the safety of the plane and made her way down the steps. The wind was so strong, she didn't bother trying to put up the umbrella. By the time she reached the tarmac, the bitter rain had drenched her and she could feel the cold soaking through her coat. She blinked, blinked, blinked as she scowled up at the stormy sky. Lightning flashed and thunder boomed, echoing across the small airport. The rain turned into a mixture accompanied by tiny hail pebbles.

Some would say it was a warning to hightail it out of there, but she wasn't afraid. At least not of a little storm.

The wail of tornado sirens rent the air. A frantic Kara grabbed Mari's arm, urging her towards the safety of the terminal's tornado shelter.

Mari just laughed. Good try, Kansas City, but not even an angry tornado could make her change her mind. Go ahead, bring it on. Nothing could be worse than what she had endured for the past three years. So either roll out the welcome mat or move on over.

Mari Diaz was here to stay.

Danyelle Ferguson

Praise for Best-Selling Author Danyelle Ferguson

"A delectable contemporary romance...with depth and heart. A must read!" - InD'Tale Magazine

"Ms. Ferguson's writing is solid, well-crafted, and spunky. If you like clean romances where you can get lost in the characters' world, then pick up a copy of Sweet Confections pronto. Not to mention there's a lot of dessert going on. Time to get in the kitchen and get your baking on!" - Romance author Lisa Swinton

"Oh yes, I just found my next favorite author! I can't wait for more!" - Andrea, Amazon reviewer

Other books by Danyelle Ferguson

Indulgence Row series
- Sweet Confections
- Love Under Construction
- Falling Stars & Stolen Kisses (Coming Soon)

A Christmas of Hope (A Holiday Short Story)

First Crush

IN THE GARDEN BOOK 2

HEATHER TULLIS

Now available!

One

"I'M THINKING PINK and blue for your colors. We could do a June wedding with pink roses and delphiniums for the flowers," Maddie said when she met Piper on the street outside of Dansie's Dental office, where Piper worked. She'd been thinking about this on and off for a couple of days. Piper was the first one of her close friends to get engaged and she knew Piper would feel overwhelmed. It was practically her duty to help plan the wedding, right?

"Pink and blue?" Skepticism hovered in Piper's blue eyes. She was bundled in a thick green coat that set off her red hair and peaches and cream complexion. "I don't think they have pink roses in a shade that will work with that dark blue delphinium."

"Delphiniums come in paler blue and even white," Maddie insisted. "And it would be perfect for an early summer wedding."

"Except that we're not getting married until September or maybe October. November isn't out of the question, either." They continued down the street toward the community garden. Or at least what would be the community garden when spring came around and they could plow and plant the space. Now the February cold blew across their faces and down the necks of their coats. The barren winter landscape didn't help the day feel warmer, but at least the snow had melted and they still had another hour or two of sunlight.

Maddie could hardly believe it was all coming together. When Piper had brought up the idea the previous fall, Maddie had known she wanted to be part of it. It hadn't been easy for Piper to acquire the land, even though it had been abandoned for years. Reece's company had owned the property, and he had jumped right in to help Piper get approval. Maddie suspected it had more to do with spending time with Piper than the garden, at least in the beginning. That was just as well, since it was doubtful they could have gotten to this point without his help.

Maddie pulled her coat tighter against the scarf she had wound around her neck before leaving the school across the street where she taught. It had been an unusually cold and snowy winter. The extended forecast said somewhat milder weather was on the way, though, and any minute a delivery truck would pull up with the greenhouse that had been financed by several generous donors in the community.

"I guess September is okay," she conceded after a moment, "but I know how much you like spring flowers."

"I like summer and fall ones too. I know I have exquisite taste, but I can't believe you're excited to wear a bridesmaid's dress." Piper grinned, as she always did when she talked about the forthcoming nuptials. It hadn't been easy for her and Reece to get past the bumps and bruises of their past, but they had made it.

"I do so love taffeta." Maddie had been very vocal with her friends about a puce gown in that fabric she'd worn for a cousin's wedding a couple of years earlier.

"Darn it, I was thinking no taffeta. What do you think of gingham check?" Piper's lips twitched.

Maddie's right cheek twitched at the thought. Gingham was on her never-wear list. She wasn't a pioneer and, so as far as she was concerned, there was no reason for her to have any contact with gingham. "You don't mind if I pick out the bridesmaid dresses for you, do you? Give me a color and theme. It's one part of the planning that I'm more than happy to take off your hands."

Piper laughed. "Don't worry, you and Adelyn will get plenty of say in the final choice. Just because it's my wedding doesn't mean you have to look terrible."

"You are an angel among bridezillas."

"I have a mother-of-the-groom-zilla, so one of us has to be reasonable," Piper muttered.

"I thought things were going well with her." They came to a stop on the sidewalk beside the empty lot. Maddie waved to Adelyn, their other best friend, who was walking in their direction from the city building. She cut right through the empty garden site on her way toward them.

"She's been nice, most of the time, but she has it in her head that we need a huge formal wedding with like a thousand of her closest friends attending. No doubt she'll want the bride's and groom's families seated separately. My family and friends will fill part of a row, and hers will fill the rest of the mausoleum of a church that she's trying to push on us for the ceremony."

"Do you and Reece have other places in mind? I'm sure Adelyn could make a few suggestions for smaller venues." Adelyn knew all of the appropriate spaces in town.

"If we don't get something reserved soon, it'll end up being held at city hall."

Adelyn chuckled a little as she joined them. "You must be talking about your wedding plans. I saw Reece's mom at the Women in Business meeting today. She had this idea of white on white with a horse and carriage to deliver you to the church, Cinderella style." When Maddie shot her a disbelieving look, Adelyn crossed her chest with her finger tip. "I'm not exaggerating."

"And you smiled and nodded, of course, because you never rock the boat," Piper said.

"No, I didn't smile and nod this time. I mentioned that I didn't think that was really your style, and that whatever you chose, it wouldn't fit the image she had in mind. Then I said that if she trusted you and Reece, she might be surprised by the tasteful, lovely wedding you plan. So *please* don't contradict me by coming to the city to have it performed. Seriously, your mother-in-law would never trust any of us again."

"So true. Don't worry, on my list of favorite places to be married, city hall is somewhat lower than the cathedral." Piper glanced up as a big rig pulled into the one empty spot by the sidewalk. Ben and Jason walked over from the opposite direction where they had parked in the city lot.

"Looks like most of us are here."

"No one said Ben was coming," Maddie muttered under her breath. Ben was her brother Jason's best friend—had been for as long as Maddie could remember. Sure, he had movie-star good looks, a face as chiseled as a young Brad Pitt and the most perfect honey-blond hair imaginable—that didn't mean she had to like him. At least that's what she told herself when seeing him like this made the breath catch in her throat. The fact that she'd had a totally unrequited crush on him since second grade didn't help her convince herself that she disliked him.

Adelyn shot her a knowing look, but said nothing, a forbearance that Maddie deeply appreciated.

Maddie didn't dislike Ben, she disliked the fact that she felt invisible when he was around. Even with as much time as they spent around each other, he'd never even glanced at her in a romantic way. Was she not good enough to draw a nice guy's attention? Her ex-boyfriend, Chaz, had twisted the knife a little more when he'd walked out, saying she was too boring to waste his time with. Her, boring? What he really meant was that he hadn't liked that her social life had been more than watching lame reruns with him every night after work. She had needed to get out and living a little.

Piper looked back at the street, which was getting busier now that rush hour was approaching. "You have to expect Ben to come if he's not at work and Jason is involved. When have they ever been separated? Where is Reece, anyway? He was

First Crush

supposed to be here by now."

Adelyn, as always, had the sensible answer. "He probably got caught up in a phone call. You know how the board of directors can be."

Piper frowned distractedly. "It's picking someone new for the board that's the issue. You wouldn't believe what a hassle it's been."

"I have a delivery," the freight driver said, getting out of his truck. "One of you Piper Daniels?"

"That's me. You've found the right place." Piper accepted the papers and looked at them, making sure they sent the correct item while the driver opened the back of his truck to unload the boxed greenhouse parts.

A car honked as it drove past and Maddie glanced over to see Reece pull into the alley between the future garden and Dequan's Chinese Restaurant next door. The wall beyond him had been painted the previous fall by the owners of the Chinese place, so it no longer had gang markers all over it, but Maddie didn't expect that to last for much longer. As soon as the temperatures rose above the teens during the day, the kids would be out in force again. Unless they could head off the graffiti before it started. She wasn't sure how to do that, though.

The guys all converged in time to help the delivery man unload the boxes of panels, poles, hinges, and whatever else made up a great greenhouse. Maddie's fingers itched to start putting it together. The parts were stacked in front of the empty apartment building next door, except for the bottom rails, which they would lay down first.

The weather warmed as they worked, attaching the base to

the bolts that had been cemented into the foundation. Ben had to drill a hole in one of the rails where the bolt's placement hadn't been as precise as they would have liked, but otherwise, everything fit perfectly. They were soon able to get to work on the walls. Maddie tried not to show how utterly freezing she was as they assembled pieces in the failing light. She reminded herself that her kids were excited about the greenhouse, and they were going to have a terrific spring quarter learning in it.

"I hear you have big plans for the greenhouse," Ben said to Maddie when she handed him a window panel.

"My class is already chomping at the bit to get out here and dig in the dirt." Maddie had been talking it up to her third-grade class since before Christmas as they discussed how the carbon cycle and photosynthesis worked. The seedlings they planted right after Christmas break were nearly ready for transplanting.

There were two other third-grade teachers who planned to use the greenhouse for classes as well. They had been working to put together discussions on nutrition, the scientific method, writing assignments, and myriad other topics to go with the greenhouse—some of which they would co-teach, but most they would teach independently.

"Sounds like fun, but what about the rest of your subjects?" Ben seemed skeptical.

"You'd be surprised how willing the kids are to learn when you combine gardening with it." The voice came from behind them and Maddie looked up to see Comfrey standing in what you could now tell would be the doorway. Her blond hair held streaks of blue and pink, her wool coat was hand-spun and crafted of multi-colored threads, and her warm, woolen scarf was rich and warm looking. Her gray eyes were so huge they

First Crush

seemed to fill the remaining space on her face.

A smooth grin slid onto Ben's perfect mouth. "I'm sure you're right. I don't think we've met, though I saw you on cleanup day." Ben extended a hand to Comfrey, who smiled and accepted the handshake.

Her lips quirked a little in admiration. "Call me Comfrey. You're Officer Belliston, right?" When he looked surprised, she explained, "I asked around."

Maddie tried not to let the flirting bother her even as her jaw clenched. She had absolutely no claim on the man, and she couldn't blame Comfrey for enjoying the sight of him.

"Call me Ben, at least when I'm here."

"Ben." The flirty lilt in Comfrey's smile dialed up a notch. "It's good to officially meet you."

Maddie turned away to pick up another window panel for Ben to slide into the metal wall studs. She would not be jealous. There was no reason for jealousy. They had never gone out, and it wasn't like she was in love with him or anything. It was just a crush. Still, she found herself feeling a little resentful that it was so easy for Comfrey, and that Ben practically forgot about Maddie's existence when the other woman appeared.

How stupid was she for even thinking about it?

Comfrey was a lot of help, and not at all afraid to get dirty. By the time the sun slid behind Dequan's Chinese Restaurant, they had finished installing the SIP walls and the roof joists, though there would still be a few hours of work to do the next day. The website said it would go together quickly, but she hadn't expected it to be so fast.

Maddie was pleased with their work, even if she was heartily sick of listening to Comfrey laugh at Ben's comments—as if he were the most interesting person around.

So what if his jokes were actually funny and the way he popped off in conversation often made her laugh. She didn't care that he'd put all of his attention on Comfrey. It hardly bothered her. Why would it?

"So, meet back here tomorrow morning?" Maddie asked when they had finished stowing the rest of the supplies in the abandoned apartment building next door. It was helpful that Reece knew practically everyone and was able to get permission.

"I'm in," Reece said as he put the key back in his pocket.

"Me too," Jason agreed.

"I have the day off, so count on me. I'll call dispatch now and have them send extra patrols past here tonight to keep an eye on everything to ward off vandalism," Ben said.

"That's a good idea. Half-finished buildings do draw a lot of curious people," Comfrey said. "This site will generate a lot of interest in the community. Wait and see."

"Thanks, I'd appreciate it," Maddie said to everyone. The garden was Piper's big dream and she'd been working most closely with Comfrey to set up the main plans, but the greenhouse was for the school, so it had been mostly up to Maddie and the other third-grade teachers. She'd conferred with the gardening board—which was basically everyone in attendance at the moment—on the location and made plans. She and the other teachers had applied for a grant and raised extra cash to cover the difference, and now it was coming together. "A couple of the teachers will join us tomorrow morning. It's supposed to be a little warmer, so hopefully we won't all freeze."

"Hot cocoa and coffee for those who want it at my house.

First Crush

I'll order in some pizza," Reece said.

There was a cheer of "Yes," and "Count me in" from the group.

"I have a class," Comfrey said wistfully.

Maddie tried not to feel pleasure at that but gave up after a few seconds.

I really need to get a life.

Acknowledgments

A huge thank you to all my amazing readers. Your messages on social media and through emails cheered me on through some very busy mommy months when writing was oh-so-difficult. Thank you, thank you, thank you!

This past year I've had lots of fun reader interaction and voting on my author Facebook page. Thank you to everyone who voted on covers, favorite quotes from Sweet Confections and helped with character names. Also a high-five to Eli Andrus for naming Charlee's renovation business, Transformations.

Every writer has a support group who helps throughout the process of creating and fine-tuning a novel. There's some chocolate lava sundae love in the futures of my two writing cohorts, Heather & Lisa. You're the best!

Great big hugs to my fabulous beta readers: Erin, Lisa, Cathryn, Beth, Emalee, and MJ. Thank you for being the fresh eyes Love Under Construction needed.

None of this would be possible without my family. Here's a shout out to my munchkins for working together and encouraging each other's goals. We made it through another book! Fist bump! I'm super grateful for my sweetheart, Mr. Ferguson. Thank you for being my very best friend and staying by my side as I work to achieve my dreams. I love you more!

About the Author

Danyelle Ferguson discovered her love for the written word in elementary school. Her first article was published when she was in 6th grade. Since then, she's won several awards and her work has been published world-wide in newspapers, magazines and books.

Danyelle grew up surrounded by Pennsylvania's beautiful Allegheny Mountains. Then she lived for ten years among the majestic Wasatch Mountains. She is currently experiencing mountain-withdrawal while living in Kansas with her husband and family. She enjoys reading, writing, dancing and singing in the kitchen, and the occasional long bubble bath to relax from the everyday stress of being "Mommy."

Website: www.danyelleferguson.com
Facebook: facebook.com/AuthorDanyelleFerguson
Twitter: twitter.com/DanyelleTweets

Made in the USA
Charleston, SC
03 April 2016